TEA ROSE ROMANCE....FROM JOVE BOOKS.
ENCHANTING NOVELS THAT CAPTURE
THE BEAUTY AND SPIRIT OF ENGLAND.

Dear Reader . . .

There's no place like England when it comes to romance. From the glorious cliffs of Dover and the lush green hills of country estates . . . to the grand courts of royal intrigue and foggy streets of London . . . England is a beautiful and timeless place that fires the imagination.

Tea Rose romance is a wonderful new line of novels that captures all the passion and glory of this splendid nation. We asked some of our favorite writers to share their most romantic dreams of England—and we were delighted with their enthusiastic responses! Whatever the period and style—adventurous, playful, intriguing, lusty, witty, or dramatically heartfelt—every *Tea Rose* romance is a unique love story with an English flavor and timeless spirit.

We hope you enjoy these special new novels. And please, accept the *Tea Rose* postcard as our gift to you, the reader, who makes all dreams possible.

Sincerely,
The Publishers

P.S.—Don't miss these *Tea Rose* romances, coming soon from Jove Books . . .

Sweet Iris

by Aileen Humphrey . . .

A playful romp through high society with a high-spirited girl who sparks scandal at every turn. Irrepressible Iris defies her family's romantic meddling—by forging an unlikely love of her own. *(Available in July 1994)*

Garden of Secrets

by Eileen Winwood . . .

A spicy tale of passion and royal intrigue. A clever beauty uses an herbal potion to kidnap England's most notorious spy—but then risks her life for his love. *(Available in September 1994)*

Tea Rose *romances from Jove*

EMBRACE THE NIGHT

ELDA MINGER

JOVE BOOKS, NEW YORK

EMBRACE THE NIGHT

A Jove Book / published by arrangement with
the author

PRINTING HISTORY
Jove edition / May 1994

ISBN: 0-515-11373-5

A JOVE BOOK®
Jove Books are published by The Berkley Publishing Group,
200 Madison Avenue, New York, New York 10016.
JOVE and the "J" design
are trademarks belonging to Jove Publications, Inc.

PRINTED IN THE UNITED STATES OF AMERICA

10 9 8 7 6 5 4 3 2 1

*To Beverly Ann Lyons,
scholar, mentor, and dear friend.
Some debts are beyond words.*

A writer never truly works alone.

To Alice Orr, agent extraordinaire.

To Leslie Gelbman, for liking something a little different.

To Gail Fortune, for a brilliant editing job which vastly improved this work while still allowing my vision to shine through.

To John Allen Baughman, for a most unselfish love. You continually give me both financial and emotional support as only another writer can.

And in memory of my grandmother, Avis Lorenson Minger, and to my great-aunt, Aline Virginia Monroe. Both of you taught me the value a garden has for the soul.

PROLOGUE

The fog had been thick and damp that night, the moon full. But all anyone in London talked of for weeks after the young woman's murder was that it had been on the same night that William Stedman, Duke of Grenville, had gone quite mad.

"I found her!"

The small group of men at the mouth of the narrow alley huddled closer together. Several held flickering torches, the flames casting shifting shadows on the damp street and sending thin plumes of black smoke into the frigid night air.

Another man, small and wiry, approached the group. He walked slowly out of the alley, his mouth grimly set in a tight line. The men tensed as he started to speak, then hooves clanging against cobblestones broke the silence.

William Stedman rode out of the fog at a full gallop like one of the four horsemen of the Apocalypse.

He took in the situation in a heartbeat as he sawed on the reins. The chestnut stallion reared up, then pranced nervously, his dark coat sheened with sweat.

William dismounted swiftly, his stallion blowing and snorting, his neck lathered. One of the men broke away from the group and tightly grasped the frightened animal's reins.

Afraid, William ran into the alley, but before he could see what awaited him there, one of the men grabbed his arm roughly, restraining him. He struggled against the firm grip as the others closed around him, blocking the alley from view.

1

"Your Grace, don't go in there—"

William looked into Charles Hailey's concerned face, and, suddenly terrified, fought his friend. But before he could break free, another man in the group came up behind him and held his shoulders.

"There's nothing you can do," Charles said, his voice rough. "She's already dead."

The terror mounted, began to spiral through him then, making his blood pound heavily in his ears. The cloying fog seemed to push against him, choking him.

Dead. My God, and I have caused it . . .

He had fought for control all his life and maintained it rigidly. Now he felt that same control violently shearing away as he thought of living the rest of his life without her.

"Let me *go!*" The words were more feral snarl than command. Charles stepped back, startled. William slipped from his grasp and lunged another few feet forward before he was caught again, held within the group.

"Steady, man, there was nothing you could've—"

He strained forward again, and finally saw her.

She was almost completely covered by a cloak, only a few tendrils of her flame-colored hair visible. But the cloak couldn't conceal the blood.

He could smell the warm, metallic, coppery scent, and his stomach rebelled. William thought of her then, her own scent; cool, dark, and sweet. His anguish mounted, unbearable.

Bloodstains darkened the fine woolen cloth and seeped between the cobbles. Bright moonlight turned her blood black.

The last of his control shattered. Painful, hot tears came swiftly to his eyes as he continued to struggle toward her, guilt and agony tearing at his soul.

Later it was said he'd thrown back his head like a great wolf and howled his anguish and rage to the cold, heartless moon.

And one man, hearing the story and expressing false concern in a most sincere manner, exulted.

CHAPTER
1

London, England
Once Upon a Time . . .

The pale spring sunshine provided little warmth, and Lucinda Townshend tightened her gray woolen shawl around her shoulders. She worked swiftly and silently as she knelt and added herbs from the small kitchen garden to her basket.

Cinda cut another sprig of rosemary, then took a deep breath of its resinous scent. It was impossible to work in this part of the garden and not think of her mother, who had designed the small walled area. She'd planted the herbs in open knots with great care, for both kitchen and medicinal purposes. Lavender, hyssop, rosemary, and thyme. Countless others had been added over the years.

Dwarf box hedges surrounded the plants. The entire design had been intended to bring the greatest pleasure when seen from the upper windows of the London townhouse.

She wondered what her mother would think if she knew that Cinda no longer lived within the walls of her father's house.

Toward the back of the property, the garden grew wilder with flowers of every color and scent. Aristocratic roses grew in the same garden with ordinary pinks. Her mother had loved flowers, and had planted a profusion of tulips and carnations, sweet william, daffodils, and double red peonies. The sweet peas were flowering again, their purple petals so dark, almost black.

The lilies would bloom very soon.

3

Cinda closed her eyes, willing the memories to pass.

It is pointless, after all.

Thoughts of her mother did not bring this sharp, stabbing emotion. She'd been dead many years now, and Cinda accepted that. No, the pain was caused by remembering all her mother had taught her about the various plants, flowers, and herbs she had so loved.

Rosemary is the emblem of fidelity for lovers.

She thought of William, and how much she still loved him.

Cinda slowly put the cutting into the basket and tried to concentrate on the task at hand. Cook wanted to roast a chicken, and rosemary sprinkled on the bird would quicken the appetite.

Yet try as she might, she couldn't put William out of her mind.

"It wasn't your fault. You've no cause to feel guilty, Cinda."

She recognized the familiar voice at once, and glanced up. Cook stood before her, another basket in her hand.

"I encouraged her," Cinda replied, her voice low, her back to the windows overlooking the garden. Nan, her stepmother, watched her servants constantly. Talking to Cook would be construed as a waste of time, and punishment would be swift.

"It wasn't your fault," Cook repeated, leaning over to take up the basketful of herbs and replacing it with the empty one. "He'll come for you, you'll see."

Tears came to Cinda's eyes, and she brushed them back with her hand. If Nan saw any weakness in her, the woman would use it to her advantage.

She smiled up at Cook. How the older woman knew her innermost thoughts had ceased to surprise her. Cook was the closest to a mother she had, and she loved the plump little woman with her sharp hazel eyes and short, iron-gray curls as fiercely as she'd loved her mother.

Once Cook left, Cinda forced her thoughts back to the present. She placed three generous cuttings of the rosemary bush in the basket, then moved to the far side of the herb garden, where the pennyroyal grew in the shade.

Adding cuttings of the mint to the large basket, she tried to avoid glancing toward the flower garden. She rarely had a leisure moment to spend there, unless she was preparing a vase of flowers for one of her stepmother's dinner parties.

Emotions flooded her whenever she worked among the colorful flowers, the roses and lilies. For it had been in that part of the garden, last summer, where she had first seen William.

Pointless.

Her moods had taken her prisoner these last few months. Cinda knew it was because of William, and what had happened between them. He'd come into her life last summer, loved her, and nothing had ever been the same. There were days when only instants separated the urge to laugh, then cry.

Scandalmongers had claimed he'd lost his mind the night Rosalind had died. There had been times she'd thought it would have been a blessing to have lost her own.

Just to stop feeling so much.

The earth was damp from the previous night's heavy rainfall. It clung tenaciously to the tiny roots as she thinned out the pennyroyal along the high stone wall. The strong peppermint scent was pleasing, and as her thoughts turned to what she was going to use this particular herb for, she almost laughed out loud at her own mischief.

Yet she stifled the sound. It wasn't wise to reveal any emotion in her father's house. One never knew who might be watching.

She resumed her work, her hands moving swiftly as she uprooted the tiny plants. Her stepmother continually threatened to take a hoe to the pennyroyal, as the mint had a tendency to spread. But Cinda wasn't worried. Nan was far too lazy to make good on her threat.

Once she'd harvested the pennyroyal, she stood up, stretched, and flexed her cramped, chilled fingers. Cinda started back to the warmth of the kitchen, taking great pleasure from the few small measures of retaliation she allowed herself.

The woman who stood in the window overlooking the garden was not attractive, and no amount of feminine primping could have made her so. Of average height, with dark blond, thinning hair and pale, almost colorless gray eyes, Nan Taunton, now Townshend, watched her stepdaughter from the slight opening in the heavy velvet drapes.

She had insisted on taking this second-story bedchamber for her own, even though she took no pleasure in looking down at the intricate garden below. Now, watching the girl at work, her eyes narrowed and her mouth tightened as she wondered what thoughts went through that clever little mind.

Deceitful girl. Trying to run away with him and all his money.

Cinda had almost fooled her, but not quite. A small, satisfied smile curved Nan's thin lips.

Rosalind, her youngest daughter, had found one of the letters William had written Cinda and discovered the man was deeply in love with her. The knowledge had charmed Rosalind's romantic little soul as much as it had enraged Nan's.

If wealthy William Stedman was going to marry anyone, it would be one of her own daughters.

Nan had found out about the elopement at the last minute, and devised a desperate plan. She'd ordered Rosalind to go to their arranged meeting place, while Nan herself would detain Cinda. Then, once Rosalind was thoroughly compromised, Nan would make sure William married her daughter.

Everything had gone horribly wrong.

Rosalind's body had been found late that night. Nan had been told that for the brief instant William believed Cinda had been murdered, he'd been bewitched by grief, lost all control over his baser emotions. Once the body had been properly identified, he had brought Rosalind back home.

Horace Townshend, full of rage and grief, had refused to let him speak to Cinda.

Nan's smile grew wider. She'd assisted her husband in making it impossible for the two lovers to meet again.

Her younger daughter's death had enraged her, not out of any sense of maternal affection, but simply because her plans had been thwarted. She wanted her daughters to marry well, to supply her with the money she needed in order to feel secure.

Nan had thought Horace had been wealthy when she'd married him. Disillusionment had set in as soon as she'd found out how little money he actually possessed, how much of his fortune he'd already squandered. And with Cinda still in the household, her three daughters would never catch any moneyed man's eye.

For the girl was beautiful. She resembled her mother, and that alone would have earned her Nan's enmity for all time.

Long, flame-colored hair, dark green eyes fringed with thick lashes. A face and form so fair, once William had looked out into the garden that midsummer evening, he'd been lost.

The solution, Nan decided that very morning, *is to find the girl a husband and marry her off. Get her out of the house.*

Banish her.

The heat in the large kitchen was overwhelming, even though the spring weather was still quite cool. Cinda set her basket down on the large oak table, then went swiftly to Cook's side. The older woman's face was red from the heat of the oven, and beads of sweat trickled down from her temples.

"Check the oven, that's a love."

Cinda reached for a small handful of flour from one of Cook's bowls, then carefully opened the oven and flung it inside. It burned brightly, with a blaze of sparks.

"Hot enough."

The two women had worked together for so long they had established a rhythm. Now, they swiftly filled the brick oven with the week's baking. That which took longest was placed farther back in the hot, cavernous mouth. Large loaves of bread first, then cakes and pies, then buns.

When they finished, Cinda turned to find Cook's face unnaturally flushed, her steady stance faltering. She was using the large wooden spade to help support herself.

"Sit." She took the peel out of the woman's hands, then helped ease her into a chair. "I'll prepare the bird."

"You do too much—"

"Sit," she whispered sharply. "We can't have Nan finding out! Where would you go? Put your head down on the table and rest."

"Perhaps your godmother will come and help you, Cinda," Cook said hopefully, breathing heavily. "And then—"

"No." Cinda knew, better than anyone, there was no one she could depend on but herself. As for Kathleen, her godmother, there was no help coming from that quarter. She'd always had a rather strained relationship with the woman, although she was hard-pressed to understand why.

No, for the time being, both women were trapped in Nan Taunton's household, and they knew it.

"Now, just rest. Please."

Cook's eyes were unnaturally bright, her expression a study of frustration. But she accepted Cinda's directions, and stayed seated, pulling the basket of herbs toward her.

"Cinda!"

She glanced up from preparing the chicken, then couldn't help smiling as she saw Cook pick up a small bunch of pennyroyal and wave it accusingly at her.

"A sin of omission," she replied softly, then bit her lip to keep from laughing.

"I'd catch the little things and put 'em in her bed myself if I didn't think I'd get caught!"

They both laughed, softly, carefully. There was little chance of Nan ever coming into the kitchen. She thought herself a great lady and considered the heat from both oven and fire something that made the servants hot and fretful.

But one could never be too careful.

Cinda used the pennyroyal to keep bedbugs out of her quarters. The tiny creatures ran rampant through London, and had no sense of class distinction, annoying rich and poor alike. Nan had a strong aversion to them, and Cinda received an intense, silent satisfaction in denying her a resting place free of vermin.

She had made Cook some of the sachets she slipped between her linen, and both of them enjoyed peaceful slumber.

"Collect 'em in a chamber pot, I would, and dump 'em in her clean linen!"

"I won't go that far, but I certainly won't share Mother's secrets with her. Now, rest while you can, I'll need your help in a minute."

She frowned as she concentrated on plucking and cleaning the fowl. Cook's condition worried her. The woman had been in service to her family since Cinda had been a little girl. When her mother died, Cook had chosen to stay on.

But when Nan Taunton had become mistress of the household, Cinda knew only the intense loyalty Cook felt for her kept her in service to the Townshends.

Now, older and in poor health from Nan's punishing work load, the woman had no alternative but to remain. Other households preferred to hire younger women, whom they could get at a cheaper salary and work much harder.

Cook was trapped and she knew it. Now it was only a matter of time.

Within the hour, the chicken was rubbed with butter, sprinkled with rosemary, and turning on the spit above the fire. The kitchen, while still hot, was filled with the smells of baking bread and roasting fowl.

Cinda fixed them a quick meal of bread, cheese, and small beer. For the moment, they had a short space of time in which to rest.

It had rained heavily the night before, and both women had put out every vessel they could find: pitchers and pails, buckets and bowls, even the kitchen pot. The collected rain-water would save Cinda numerous trips to the well.

Once again they were ahead of Nan and her endless demands.

Cook was boiling water for the family's morning tea when Victor, the French butler, came into the kitchen. He was a handsome man, with blond curly hair and bright blue eyes.

Nan had decided, in the last few months, that anything French was decidedly superior, and she knew her aristocratic female friends were impressed that she had a genuine French butler.

Victor could have taken advantage of the situation and simply lounged about, appearing only to impress guests with his accent or pop into the kitchen with various recipes from the Continent. But he was a good-tempered man, and a fair one. He did his share of the work.

Today, he had a resigned look on his face, and both women could guess the cause.

"She wants a dinner party prepared for tomorrow—"

None of them ever referred to Nan by her Christian name, simply as "she." And now "she" was asking for the impossible.

Cinda closed her eyes as Victor rattled off Nan's demands. The woman simply could not be pleased. Nothing was good enough for her. Compared to the slipshod work of other servants in London's aristocratic houses, she and Cook, Victor and Mary, the housemaid, ran the Townshend household superbly.

Nan seemed determined to work them harder and harder. And Cinda knew it was because she was angry with her. That had given her stepmother reason enough for this impromptu party.

Flowers. A clean tablecloth. Carpets turned. The dining-room floor scoured with sand, then sweetened with herbs. Nan's list of preparations would be endless.

Victor departed in a flurry to find Mary and give her the news of the added work load. Once the kitchen door swung shut behind him, Cinda simply stared at Cook, who shook her head grimly.

Maybe it's better this way. Maybe it gives me less time to think of him and what might have been—

"She won't be wanting to serve pie," Cook said, thinking out loud. "We'll have to heat the oven all over again, and I'll have to make one of my cakes—"

Cinda pressed her hand against her mouth as tears came to her eyes. She turned away, but not before Cook could see.

"He'll come to you, Cinda. Give him time. It was a horrible thing, what happened, but that man loves you and he'll be back for you. He'll come take you out of this place—"

She broke off as Cinda shook her head, then closed her eyes against the pain. She heard Cook come toward her, then she was wrapped in familiar, comforting arms.

"He'll come back," Cook crooned. "He's not forgotten you, you'll see."

And as Cinda began to cry, she wondered why she couldn't believe that anymore.

Will, why did you abandon me?

William Stedman, Duke of Grenville, rode one of his horses in the park every morning without fail. The exercise gave him a measure of peace, something that had been in short supply in his life of late.

This morning, he'd ridden quite early, and had just come home to his London townhouse. Looking for his uncle, he walked out the large French doors and onto the flagstone balcony overlooking the vast garden below.

John Stedman was sitting in a chair, several mastiff dogs at his feet. A knitted throw was carefully placed across his legs as he supervised the yearly clipping of the yew hedges.

"Have to watch the gardeners," he said briskly to William as he strode outside. "They'd destroy the poor things if I didn't care enough to supervise."

William nodded his head. His uncle had been a superb guardian, giving him a healthy balance of love and freedom. John Stedman was the father he'd never had a chance to know. Now, seeing his uncle sitting out on his balcony, his ruddy face turned toward the sunshine, the light catching his thick white hair and heavy beard, William sat down beside the older man and hid his fond smile as John watched the proceedings with a keen satisfaction.

Their relationship was remarkable, considering that John had been adopted into the Stedman family when he was seven. His father had been the groundskeeper, and William's grandfather had enjoyed the man and his extensive knowledge of ornamental plants.

John's father had been an honorable man. He'd worked hard to keep a roof over his only surviving child's head. When he'd passed on, William's grandfather had adopted the boy and raised him as his own, with William's father.

Though the majority of the Stedman fortune had been held in trust for young William, John had always been comfortably provided for. When William's parents died when he was nine, John had cared for him. And William had thought of John as his uncle ever since that time.

The older man had insisted on his having a rigorous program of study, including the arts and sciences. History, Greek, Latin, and art. Botany, anatomy, even astronomy. John had an insatiable appetite for knowledge, a desire to understand and clearly see his world. He had passed these traits on to William.

John's passions were, in order, his adopted nephew, designing gardens, and traveling. He didn't particularly care for London, except his nephew's small corner of it, and left the city as often as time and responsibilities allowed.

When William had been young, John had refused to leave him at school and taken him along. He'd wanted the boy to see other countries, experience other cultures. France and Germany, India and China. William had been familiar with foreign countries by the time he was twelve. The only real difference between the two men was that William loved London, and as a result stayed in the city.

William had also partially taken over John's pastime of designing gardens for his aristocratic friends. With an educated and instinctive blending of plants, strict composition, and design, William's trained eye had brought beauty to many a London estate.

But all gardeners, from time immemorial, have occasionally been seduced by some heartbreakingly beautiful, rare, and irresistible plant that was not originally in his design scheme.

He'd found her, fairer than any English rose, in her mother's garden.

As he did so often of late, William thought of Cinda. And remembered . . .

It was well known throughout London society that Nan Townshend wanted her daughters to make good matches. To this end, the woman entertained lavishly, and she had included William on her guest list for one of her infamous dinner parties.

He'd been bored with the idea from the start. Had it been left up to him, he wouldn't have even attended. But Henry gently prodded him into accepting the invitation, simply to show people he hadn't turned into an eccentric hermit.

"They love a good gossip, Your Grace," his trusted valet had said, dusting off his black velvet topcoat before helping him on with it. "And you know good and well that Mistress Townshend is among the worst of those women, her tongue the swiftest. If you attend this party and act the part of a man in possession of all his faculties, then no one can whisper any more unpleasantries about you."

Privately, William didn't give a fig what anyone thought of him. Was he so wrong, to live alone and enjoy his solitude? He hadn't grown up among a throng of brothers and sisters, puppies and ponies. He'd been the first and only child of his beloved parents before they both succumbed to fever.

John had taken him in and given him a great gift, that of being quite comfortable in his own company.

And that was seen as peculiar—and a threat—to all the mamas in London, clutching their marriageable daughters to their protective breasts like precious jeweled brooches and gossiping about how unfortunate it was for a man of his means not to have a bride.

"They'll always talk about me, Henry," he said as he shrugged into his jacket. "It's all the lovely money I've got.

They can't wait to get their greedy little paws on it."

Henry had merely sniffed, and given him "the look." He'd perfected it over endless years of service, and it conveyed equal measures of gentle reproof, disbelief, and quiet wisdom. For Henry knew him as few others did. There wasn't much William could hide from his valet.

"For argument's sake, sir, might I ask you something?"

William knew full well that Henry loved playing the devil's advocate to his many firm beliefs. It gave the man great pleasure to disagree with his master.

"Go on."

"What if you found a woman who was not interested in your fortune? What if she cared for you alone, and had not a whit of interest in wealth?"

"Does such a woman exist?" He'd had enough experience socializing in London that he had reason to believe otherwise.

"Most assuredly. Your mother never cared about your father's money, and both of them were happy to the end."

"My mother had a fortune of her own to bring to the marriage. She had no need of my father's money, therefore he could be assured that was not the reason she was interested in his company."

"Then you must find a woman with a fortune, sir."

"Unfortunately, Henry, most of the moneyed women I know are either decidedly plain or have no interest in being anything but a glorified broodmare."

"And what would you have a woman be, sir?"

William was silent for a moment, but Henry pressed on.

"Sir?"

William adjusted the lace on his cuffs as he studied himself in the mirror. He was not a vain man, but he took care with his appearance. Now, he feigned undue interest, trying to avoid his valet's intense scrutiny.

"I would have her be . . ." His voice trailed off as he thought about this. In truth, he hadn't given it much thought at all. For underneath his steadfast demeanor, William kept an emotional secret.

He wanted to fall in love.

From all his experience in the world, he still doubted the existence of such a dubious emotion. Yet he wanted to experience it. Somehow, he knew if something like love existed, he would be capable of recognizing it.

He glanced up at his valet, giving his cuffs a final, unnecessary adjustment.

"This is pure nonsense, Henry. I don't see the point of such a discussion."

His valet smiled, then turned away and began to pick up some of the formal clothing his master had tried on and discarded. "As you wish, sir."

Nan's dinner party had been predictably boring. He'd sat at the massive dinner table, feigning interest in one of her daughter's endless stories. And that same feeling of quiet despair had settled over him as he watched the various women sitting around the candlelit table, their faces glowing with avarice.

So it's always to be like this. Can't you accept it? Mayhap you should simply pick one, sire a few offspring, and keep the old man busy. He wants another generation of Stedmans to take care of, after all.

The thought gave him no joy. Yet he knew he had to give some serious consideration to his future. He was, after all, almost twenty-seven years of age.

As soon as it was politely possible, he excused himself from the table. He had no idea where he was going, but he just knew he couldn't bear to go back and listen to their inane chatter for another second.

Then he glanced out the French doors and saw the garden.

It intrigued him. The grounds outside were most carefully tended, yet he didn't think Nan had a gardener. And he couldn't picture any of the women sitting at the table finding any pleasure in getting their hands dirty.

It didn't look like a garden planted for show, to impress someone. The landscaping had a carefully tended look, as if someone had put quite a bit of love and care into the grounds.

Intrigued, he stepped outside. Though the early summer weather had been chilly of late, tonight the breeze was warm and filled with the scent of flowers. Feeling as if he had been freed, William shrugged out of his jacket and placed it on a small stone bench. Then he set out to explore.

The herb garden was most interesting, the beds laid out in carefully executed open knots. He knelt down a few times as he noticed a plant he was not completely familiar with. Whoever had planted this garden, and whoever tended it now, served his family well.

The light was hazy, with thin wisps of silver clouds scudding across the moon. Leaves rustled in the breeze, the tops of several fruit trees swayed, catching the silvery light. William sighed deeply, feeling more at home standing on this small plot of earth than he had inside.

His eyes adjusted more readily to the dark and he continued his exploration.

The garden reached far back, away from the townhouse. Here it became wilder, more lushly overgrown, and he could catch the scents of dusky roses, lilies, and the spicy scent of carnations.

Charming. The word popped into his head, and he realized he would never have thought Nan capable of such work as this. But the minute the thought flitted through his mind, he knew she wasn't.

Who, then, does this garden belong to?

The evening breezes picked up, and blew the cloud covering away from the crescent moon. The garden seemed like a silvery paradise, a nocturnal Eden illuminated by moonlight. The noises from the dining room had faded; he couldn't hear the softest murmur of conversation.

William stopped in front of a particularly beautiful rose. Intrigued, he knelt and inhaled its fragrance. Almost without conscious volition, he reached for it. Before he could pick it, a wickedly sharp thorn sank into the pad of his thumb and he cursed sharply, then stepped back.

At the same instant, he was suddenly aware he was no longer alone in the garden. Looking up, he saw her.

"Did you hurt yourself?"

She was coming briskly along the illuminated path, and the moment he saw her his heart started pounding slowly, heavily in his chest. Red-gold, glorious, unbound hair the color of flame fell to her waist. She reached up with a small hand and brushed it back from a face of such startling beauty it hurt him to look at it.

Then she took his hand, and all was lost.

"I've done it myself, forgetting. They're very beautiful, but the thorns can be quite nasty."

Her touch. Her scent. The sound of her voice. He couldn't stop looking at the top of her head as she bent over her task. And he wondered who she was, what she was doing in the garden, how loveliness such as this had managed to stay hidden away all of his life.

He also wondered if she was already spoken for, perhaps even wed, and the surge of jealous emotion that engulfed him was yet another shock.

"I'll get some salve—" She stepped away from him and was turning to go when he realized he couldn't let her.

"Don't."

She stopped, then turned slowly, looking up at him. Her face was obscured by the shadow of a tree branch, and he smiled, attempting not to frighten her.

"Come here."

CHAPTER

❧ 2 ❧

She stepped forward, cautiously, studying him with a new curiosity. The moonlight barely touched her; she stood at the edge of the shadows. And yet, looking at her face, he felt as if he were drowning in it. A full, soft mouth, a determined chin. Exquisitely defined cheekbones, a straight little nose. And eyes the color of green fire, intelligent eyes that looked directly at him with no fear whatsoever.

"Sir, if you are here for the horses, you surely cannot control them if your grip is painful. I won't be gone long, and your thumb will feel much better shortly."

He was careful to keep all expression from his face. Horses? What was she talking about? Then he realized how he must look, his hair ruffled by the breeze, his jacket off, and his shirt pulling out of his breeches.

She had mistaken him for a stableboy. The thought delighted him.

He stepped forward and took her hand, pulling her gently into the moonlight.

"Stay. Just a moment."

He recognized the exact instant she realized what this was about. Her gaze flitted quickly to his mouth, then to his eyes. Feminine knowledge warmed her own and she stepped back, cautious.

"I won't hurt you," he said, his voice low.

She stayed where she was, her hand still in his. But she watched him, eyes wary.

"Your name," he prompted gently.

"Cinda."

Just Cinda. Curious she should give him her Christian name and no surname. But he would let it be.

"Are you employed here?"

She hesitated, then said, "Yes."

"William Stedman," he replied, by way of introduction. Then he brought her hand to his lips and kissed it.

She tore it away, and he sensed at once she thought he was mocking her. As she whirled to run, he caught her around the waist and brought her up short against him. She struggled, but didn't make a sound, and he thought that unusual as he sought to quiet her fears.

"I'll let you go," he whispered against her ear, "but you must not run from me. Do you understand?"

She hesitated, then nodded her head. He set her down slowly, reluctant to break the intimate contact. She'd felt like thistledown in his arms, delicate and light, and he knew she was still frightened of him. He could easily overpower her, and both of them knew it.

Yet she kept her word, which intrigued him further. He'd been fully prepared for her to dart away.

"Why did you run?"

Her breathing was shallow, her hair tumbled around her shoulders and she pushed it back once again. The thought popped into his head that he'd like to buy her ribbons and ornaments for her hair; he'd delight in it.

Still, she was wary. He could see the heightened color in her cheeks, the frustration in her stance.

"Don't . . . don't trifle with me," she whispered. "Please."

He was incredulous. "Is that what you thought I was doing?"

"Weren't you?"

"No." And now he sensed deep pride in this woman, and silently vowed never to give her reason to believe he thought less of her.

She was quiet for a moment, and he wondered what she was thinking. William found himself intrigued by a sense of mystery, and wishing he had private access to her mind that he might know what she thought of him.

It occurred to him, suddenly, that this was what love's pain was about, that one could find oneself enamored of another, completely besotted, and find that the other had absolutely no affection for you.

I'll make her love me.

As soon as the thought came into his mind, he dismissed it. He'd been studying her eyes, the proud tilt of her chin, the wary stance of her body.

This woman would love no one by force, only by choice.

He decided to start over.

"You're waiting for a stableboy?"

She stared at him, and he recognized new knowledge coming to the fore. "You're not here for the horses?"

"No."

"Why are you here, then?"

He didn't even hesitate a heartbeat. "For you."

She looked at him for a long moment, then replied softly, "You're not making a mock of me?"

He shook his head.

"How did you get here?"

He nodded in the direction of the townhouse.

She stepped back and he caught her hand again.

"You know her? Mistress Townshend?"

"I accepted an invitation. Grudgingly."

She smiled. "You don't seem the sort of man who does what he doesn't want to do."

"Normally I'm not."

"Did your family insist?"

He smiled, anticipating her reaction. "My valet."

She was astonished. "And do you often do what your valet suggests?"

"Always. He's very wise."

She was relaxing with him now, he could sense it. A smile was forming on her lips, and he caught a teasing glint in her eyes.

"And were you enjoying yourself at dinner before you slipped out into my garden?"

"Your garden?"

He sensed she regretted the slip, but her reply came swiftly. "As I am the only one who tends to it, I sometimes forget my position in the household and consider it mine."

"An understandable slip. You take pride in your work, and you should."

There was a momentary lull in the conversation, and William jumped in to fill it.

"Is there a place where we could sit and converse? Farther away from the house. I should hate to have one of the ladies at dinner send out a search party. With any luck, they'll simply assume I went home."

She bit her lip, and he sensed she was restraining a laugh. And it surprised him how much he wanted to hear her laugh, make her happy.

"This way." She turned and walked ahead of him, and he paid no attention to where they were going, he simply enjoyed the sight of her slim hips, swaying slightly beneath her skirts, as she led him deeper into the garden.

When they emerged into a clearing, she indicated a small stone bench. It seemed they were now in the heart of the garden, within a riotous blooming of countless flowers. Scents blended, both floral and spicy. Vivid colors were muted by moonlight.

William watched as Cinda carefully settled her skirts and sat down. He joined her on the bench, being careful to leave a little space between them as was proper.

Above all, he didn't want to frighten her.

"I'd like to see this during the daylight."

"It's my favorite place."

"Do Nan and her daughters frequent it?"

"No. I believe they hardly know it is here."

"I would keep it that way, if I were you."

She sighed. "They have no real interest in the garden, unless they summon me to prepare flowers for the household. Even then, they have no curiosity beyond seeing the vases are kept filled." She glanced at him, took a breath, then said, "To them it is all for show, nothing more or less."

He appreciated the risk she took, offering him her opinion of her employer.

Another small silence ensued, then she said, "And what do you do with your time, William?"

"Before meeting you, I wasted it." He could see the blush rising in her face, and was glad he'd decided on a bold approach. He would try not to touch her, but he had to put what he felt into words.

"Pray, sir, do not say what you cannot mean. Do not trifle

with my heart, and what is mine alone to give."

She didn't look at him as she whispered the words, so he had no idea what she was thinking. But he had to try to convince her.

"Madam, I assure you, that will never happen." He paused, then took a deep breath. "I give you my word."

She glanced at him, and he wondered if she would ever feel even the tiniest bit of what he already felt for her.

"What is it you want from me?" she whispered.

"I hope, madam, that you are at present a single woman."

"Yes."

"And your affections are not engaged elsewhere?"

This time she looked directly at him. "I am promised to no one."

"Then may I come and call upon you?"

She was clearly astonished. "You cannot possibly mean this—"

"I do—"

"I have nothing, not much more than the clothes on my back, while if you possess a valet, then you must surely—"

"I have money, that is true. But that has nothing to do with what I wish—"

"You would be ashamed of me—"

"Never." He grasped her hand firmly, turning her to face him. And it came to him, with shattering clarity, that it was impossible for him to make her understand what had happened to him out in the garden this evening, when he'd first seen her. From the start, he'd *known*; he'd sensed he'd been waiting for her to enter his life and change it forever.

Now, staring down at her, he thought of trying to explain. Intense emotion, a powerful urge to possess, overcame any common sense. He wanted to make her his own.

Giving in, William lowered his mouth to hers.

She tried to evade him, but he raised a gentle hand to her chin and coaxed her to accept his kiss. William fought to keep it gentle. At first he merely touched her lips with his own, several small, soft kisses. She sighed, the tension beginning to leave her body, and where her hands had been curled into small fists by her sides, gradually he felt her palms slide up his arms, her fingers tentatively touch his hair.

Encouraged, he turned his head slightly, slanting his mouth

over hers, gently insisting she open to him. He heard the brief sound she made, mingled frustration and fear, then her lips parted and he truly tasted her. Such sweetness made his heart beat faster, and he cradled the back of her head in his hand, while his other arm went around her waist and pulled her closer.

It became impossible to think; he could only feel her full breasts pressed against his shirtfront, the touch of her fingers, now gripping his shoulders tightly as if she were afraid to let go. Her mouth was so sweet, so hot and dark, filled with feminine secrets and the most potent of persuasions.

It wasn't enough. Reason seemed to flee him as he bent her back and kissed her neck. He wanted more, and his hand moved as if of its own volition, up from her waist, to the soft, warm undercurve of her breast, then he was touching her through the bodice of her dress, cupping her soft flesh, feeling the taut nipple against the palm of his hand.

He took her mouth again, but this time all thoughts of gentleness left him. Now he was wooing, seducing, promising all sorts of mindless pleasures if she would simply yield to him, trust him to give her everything . . .

She tore herself out of his arms with a strength and suddenness that left him totally still. Shocked. As if he'd been doused with a bucket of icy water. He looked up, confused, and saw she was trembling, standing, just barely, her back turned toward him, rigid with rage.

He had to speak to her, tell her it wasn't what she thought at all . . .

But she whirled on him, and now he could see the fire in her green eyes, the trembling, full lower lip, her breasts rising and falling as she took shallow breaths, trying to calm herself. Her hands were wrapped tightly around her, beneath her bosom, as if she could by sheer force of will stop the violent reaction he had clearly engendered within her.

"No." Just one word, but such a wealth of meaning in it. Her tone was low, vibrant with anger. This woman did not consider herself to be any man's plaything.

He was about to reassure her that this sort of conduct was the furthest thing from his mind; he opened his mouth to apologize for his lack of control. Then he saw the look in her eyes. And understood.

Fear. Of the unknown.

A virgin.

He'd assumed otherwise. Most serving wenches this comely did not retain their maidenheads long. Even though Nan's household was largely female, the woman was notorious for entertaining marriageable men, and William had wrongly assumed one of them had put an end to this woman's innocence.

She was staring at him, her breathing now under control, but the expression in her eyes broke his heart. He sensed she was a woman who didn't hope for much anymore, who was afraid to even entertain such an emotion for long.

"No." This time it sounded like a sob, and William watched as she turned away from him, lifted her skirts in her hands, and slipped out of the moonlit clearing. He considered pursuing her, stood, then thought better of it.

Leave her be. For now.

The sound of her slippered footsteps faded away, and he was left alone among the flowers.

And though William was a man who had never feared being alone, he found himself sitting on the bench once again, staring down at his clasped hands, more lonely than he'd ever been in his life.

The man's shout startled him, brought him back to the present, and William resolutely pushed his memories aside. As much as he longed to see Cinda, he couldn't. Not if his suspicions had any substance.

Both he and his Uncle John raised their heads when they heard the shout once again.

"Damnable fool," John muttered. "He's lost again." But the humor in his expression belied his words.

William smiled, laugh lines forming in his weathered skin. At the back of the garden was an intricate maze, the yew hedges exactly eight feet tall. The rich, dark green foliage had a beauty all its own. Full of deceptions and puzzles, blind alleys, twists and turns, the maze was the culmination of John's talent.

"I'll help him," William volunteered, and before his uncle had a chance to reply, he started for the bottom of the lush garden.

He'd played in the maze since he was a small boy, and the tall hedges held no fear for him. The densely textured, glossy leaves were quite beautiful in his eyes.

John had taught him well, both in and out of the classroom. Many times during his childhood, his uncle had conferred with his tutor, postponing classes and taking him out into the world. They'd spent entire days roaming the streets of London; others, they'd spent in the garden.

John Stedman had never been afraid of dirtying his hands, and William had loved those long days outside, planting and learning.

"Speak up, man!"

"Over here!"

Carefully following the sound of the worker's voice, he came upon the man in one of the blind alleys within the large maze.

"Sorry," he said, and it seemed to William he was ashamed of having been lost.

"It can be confusing," he replied. "I'll guide you back out."

They approached the other workmen in silence, and as William walked he remembered something John had once taught him about the maze.

It's a symbol, William. Remember that. A symbol of the soul in pursuit of the elusive goal of perfection. Paradise.

John would be horrified if he knew the thoughts that had consumed his nephew's soul the last six months. Ever since Rosalind's murder.

It had been deliberate, of that he was sure. Not the sort of accident done by a frightened, desperate man. The girl's murder had been quite calculated.

And there was a pattern.

All his life, with his uncle's keen help, he'd worked with patterns. Whether learning Latin and Greek, memorizing the bones of the human body, or laying out a garden's design, it had simply been a matter of pattern upon pattern upon pattern. He was quite good at spotting them.

This one was truly horrific.

Once the workman had rejoined the group of gardeners, William stepped back, then turned and entered the maze again. He walked swiftly to the heart of it, a small pagoda John had designed himself. The perfect spot for some solitary contemplation.

Someone getting their throat slit was common enough. What Rosalind had been doing out alone in London that night was something he would never begin to understand. The girl had seemed younger than her years; she should have been sheltered and protected. If sent out into the heart of the city, someone should have warned her of the dangers she faced.

Sitting down inside the delicate oriental structure, William took a deep, calming breath. He could never think of that night with any semblance of control. Remembering how he'd felt when he'd believed Cinda had been murdered, he closed his eyes and waited for the fear to leave him.

Once he'd reached the still body and pulled back the cloak, he'd been shocked once again. For it had been Rosalind, not Cinda, who had been murdered.

He'd carried her body back to the Townshend house, where Horace had made it clear he was never welcome again.

William opened his eyes, staring blindly at the lush greenery around him. He'd had night terrors after the murder, and his dreams had given him answers. William had seen Rosalind's face. The dark purple bruising on her throat. The damaged jaw. The vulnerable bald spots on her scalp where her fiery hair had been pulled out by the roots.

In the early hours of dawn, sitting in a chair next to a blazing fire yet still shivering with the cold, William had reconstructed the murder.

The killer had been strong. And tall, considering the angle of the blow. Swift, practiced, and deadly. He'd probably grabbed Rosalind by the hair, forced her head up and back, then taken the butt of his dagger and smashed her trachea, splintering the hyoid bone.

At that moment, knowing what the girl had gone through, William had desperately wished his uncle had not been so insistent he include a thorough study of the human body in his education.

A slit throat was generally quick. You drowned in your own blood. A smashed hyoid bone would make for a slow suffocation, with plenty of time for the victim to realize she was going to die.

Afterward, the murderer had slit her throat with the blade.

A simple distraction, really. It hadn't been a neat cut, but an enraged slash.

He closed his eyes against the grisly image of the girl's face, knowing it would haunt him for the rest of his life.

Three nights after the murder, the same night he'd dreamed and seen the dead girl's face, William knew he had to find the killer and stop him.

Because it wasn't just Rosalind. It didn't end there. Patterns rarely did, if they were truly intricate.

His mistress, Anne McConahay, had died eight months before he'd met Cinda. William had never thought of himself as a particularly passionate man, but he'd caught sight of the blond beauty at the theater and used his influence to meet her. It had been only a matter of time before he'd set her up in rooms of her own.

He hadn't loved her, but he'd cared for her, and caring had seemed all he was capable of at the time. He'd treated her with kindness, and been faithful to her.

They'd found her in her small parlor, and William had been notified. It had been several days after the actual murder, thus the bruises at her throat hadn't been as vivid as Rosalind's.

He'd cared for Anne, and had been devastated by her death. He hadn't been sure the murder had been connected to him that first time. The second time, there had been no doubt. He'd lived with intense guilt over both women's deaths for months.

He couldn't tell anyone, for they would surely think him mad. Even locked in his townhouse, away from London society, he'd been well aware of what was being said about him. William had thought his silence would work to quell the ugly rumors, but it had the opposite effect.

He couldn't share his thoughts, not even with John. All he had in his favor was instinct. That and the strange similarities in the two murders. They'd been cruel and calculated, designed to make the victim suffer, not the quick work of a thief desperate for a few coins.

Someone was stalking him.

He was sure of it.

And that someone believed he'd killed the woman William had almost married.

*   *   *

Cinda gently pushed open the double doors to her step-mother's bedchamber. The heavy velvet drapes were shut against the bright spring sunshine, and it took her eyes a moment to adjust to the room's darkness.

"Come in. Don't dawdle."

She moved swiftly toward her stepmother's large curtained bed, setting down the breakfast tray. Not wanting to stay any longer than she had to, she turned to leave. But her stepmother's voice stopped her.

"Don't go. We have something to talk about, you and I."

She stilled the slight trembling in her stomach by sheer force of will, then met her stepmother's gaze.

Nan gave nothing away. She was a master of the game. Long ago Cinda had come to the conclusion that her father was a weak, ineffectual man. He'd fallen into Nan's hands like an overripe plum, and she had wreaked havoc on the Townshend household ever since.

Cinda remained silent, knowing her stepmother would tell her what she had on her mind in her own good time.

Nan carefully added some sugar to her tea, then slowly broke open one of the hot muffins and spread it with butter. Her motions were precise. Calculated.

"How old are you, Lucinda?"

The tone of her voice sounded kind, but Cinda knew better. The only thing she could do was endure this woman's company, answer her questions, and leave as soon as it was politely possible to do so.

"Seventeen."

"I thought you were older."

"I'll be eighteen in September."

"I see."

Nan took a bite of the buttered muffin as she lay reclining in her huge bed, propped up on the fine lace pillows. In France, from what Victor had told them, it was quite common for people to eat their meals in their bedrooms. Nan had apparently decided it was appropriate for her to do the same.

"That William fellow. What was his name?"

Cinda willed herself not to show any emotion whatsoever. She wouldn't answer this time, would not rise to her step-mother's cruel baiting.

Silence.

Nan took a sip of her tea, and Cinda could feel her appraising glance.

"Stedman, I believe," Nan said softly. "William Stedman, Duke of Grenville. The only son of an only son."

Cinda simply continued to look at Nan, her expression completely emotionless. Her stepmother might be a master at this sick gamesmanship, but she had watched and learned, and determined long ago never to give the woman the pleasure of knowing what she was thinking or feeling. Nan would have to beat a response out of her.

"Primogeniture. Quite a lovely word, wouldn't you agree?"

She wondered where this conversation was leading. Surely her stepmother hadn't detained her in her bedroom to discuss the right of the eldest male son to inherit the estate of his parents.

"All that lovely money. You were much more clever than I gave you credit for."

Cinda fought against the sharp impulse to tell her that William's money and her lack of it had ceased to be an issue between them. She would have run away with him even if he'd been a penniless stablehand.

"You've heard, of course, that he's . . . not the same man you knew before."

The savage barb hit home, but Cinda kept her face impassive. She'd heard. Heard that William had gone back to his townhouse and locked the door, rarely going out into polite society anymore.

She hadn't believed the ugly rumors that he'd lost his mind. He'd lost heart, lost hope, been shattered by what had happened to Rosalind.

But not madness. William had a strong, sure mind. He possessed a fighting spirit. The only thing that could possibly defeat him were his own dark moods.

"So quiet today," her stepmother mused. "Pray, why is that, Lucinda?"

Instinct told her to answer the question and bring this conversation to its inevitable end.

"There's much to be done in order to be ready for tomorrow."

"Ah yes, the dinner party. Don't you ever miss attending parties, Lucinda? Wearing pretty gowns and gloves and jewels?"

When Cinda remained silent, Nan took another delicate bite out of her muffin, then continued.

"Talking with handsome men and flirting behind your fan? Are you truly content?"

Bitch, you dare to ask this when you made certain to put me where I am.

Cinda fought to control her temper, having learned from painful experience that once she showed any sign of emotion, Nan had a weapon she could use against her. Painful effort had been spent acquiring the cool control she now called forth effortlessly, almost without thinking.

"Madam, I am."

"But you would perhaps . . . welcome another change?"

The woman was playing with her. They both knew it. Still, Cinda did nothing to reveal her growing unease. She'd have to endure Nan's little cat and mouse maneuvers, simply wait it out until she revealed the nature of this conversation.

"Your father and I were talking the other day, and as we have both always tried to consider what is best for your well-being . . ." She paused, then took another sip of tea, another bite of muffin.

My well-being. You've never been concerned with anyone's well-being but your own.

"When I brought it to Horace's attention that I thought you were getting rather—long in the tooth, he agreed with me."

This was dangerous ground.

"He agreed that the sensible thing to do was to find you a husband as quickly as possible."

She heard nothing else her stepmother said for the next few minutes as the import of the casually spoken words fully hit her emotions.

To belong to anyone but William was unthinkable. And what man would have her, once he found she was no longer a virgin?

"The wedding will be held at the church in Bedfordshire, near his country estate. I believe the date we decided on was near the end of June." Nan tilted her head in a playful manner, but Cinda sensed she was watching her carefully.

"I can't remember the exact date, but it should give us plenty of time to"—Nan paused, then wrinkled her nose prettily—"find you a suitable bridal gown."

June. Little more than three months away.

She swiftly composed herself, praying her voice wouldn't break.

"And this is what you wished to discuss with me?"

"Yes. I trust you will allow Horace and I to decide what is best for you."

Play along with her, until you can think of something . . . anything . . .

"Of course."

Cinda could have sworn Nan's expression was faintly disappointed, as if she had been anticipating a royal row. She felt a brief flash of triumph at the thought of denying her stepmother something she wanted.

"You may return to the kitchen." Now Nan sounded vaguely angry, and Cinda turned and left the bedroom before the woman she despised could say anything more.

CHAPTER
❧ 3 ❧

Late that same night, in her quarters above the stable, Cinda sat in her window and looked out over the stableyard.

It was a small and shabby bedchamber, but it was her own. For the moment she didn't have to worry about Nan's ever watchful eyes. The woman was simply too lazy to mount the steep stairs leading to the small chamber.

Cinda turned her face up toward the sky. Still clad in her servant's garb, she was wrapped in her knitted shawl against the chill night air. The moon was new and shone brightly, surrounded by stars.

She wondered if William ever looked at that same moon, and if he thought of her.

She'd tried to put him out of her mind, but the conversation with her stepmother made that impossible.

Marriage.

She'd given the matter little thought, one way or the other. Seeing the direction her mother's marriage had taken, Cinda had never thought that highly of the entire arrangement.

Until she'd met William.

Then, the first few weeks after they'd met, marriage had been the furthest thing from her mind. She'd wanted to be close to him, lived for the sound of his voice, the look in his eyes, the touch of his hand. Everything about him had enchanted her, made her feel as if she no longer knew who she was or what she'd ever wanted.

She thought of going out into the night, finding William, telling him everything. But London could be dangerous, especially at night.

Roads were filled with ruts and potholes for the unwary rider or unfortunate coach. Watchmen took bribes from burglars rather than do their proper jobs. Drunkenness, aided by the ever-present flow of gin, accounted for the almost constant violence and disorder.

The streets were dark at night; a traveler was at the mercy of the moonlight. Crevices in cobblestones were filled with filth; the shadows in alleys concealed toughs and thieves. Killers.

Even on the eve of her elopement, Cook's son Robbie would have accompanied her. Cinda had never had any desire to go out alone into the London night. Until tonight.

The direction of her life had changed once again. If William knew her stepmother had found the perfect way to be rid of her, marrying her off to some man in the country, and he still didn't want her—

Then it won't really matter what you do with the rest of your life, will it?

What she was contemplating was dangerous, and a desperate move. A woman alone in London at night—it had cost Rosalind her life.

But if I can see him, tell him, if he still loves me—

That he might have stopped loving her was the most frightening thought of all. Fighting back her fears, Cinda studied the star-studded sky and thought of all that had been taken away from her. Yet she'd managed to survive. Nothing Nan had done had defeated her.

Until now. This marriage was a total impossibility. Because she was no longer innocent. And William had taken more than her innocence, he'd captured her heart.

She closed her eyes and leaned her head back against the rough, cold stone of her makeshift bedchamber. How frightened she'd been of him that first night in the garden, then how angry. He'd kissed her, and she'd sensed the restless, restrained passion within him.

So much had been taken away from her, and she'd been determined that this man, this stranger, wouldn't take even more.

But though he'd frightened her, he'd also fascinated her. William had been unlike any man she'd ever known. What she'd come to value, above all his other qualities, was that he always kept his word.

He'd promised not to trifle with her feelings, but that night she hadn't known whether to believe him. There was so little she had the luxury of believing in anymore.

Thus she'd merely raced to her room, then stood very quietly by the window, her heart thundering in her breast, her pulse beating a wild, savage rhythm in her throat and wrists.

She'd watched him leave her garden that first night, part of her glad to see him go. But another side of her, a darker side, had wanted to call him back and find out what it was that so fascinated her. Then anger came, the intense feeling engulfing her.

She knew, staring blindly out into the night, that he would be back. Whether his intentions were honorable or not was still unclear, but she knew he would be back.

Cinda took a deep breath, trying to slow the racing of her heart. Just the thought of seeing William again, of going to him, brought painful emotions to the surface. She couldn't think of him without feeling so much. And she couldn't let him go, not yet.

The thought of marriage to a man she'd never want as much as William filled her with anguish. She loved him. She needed him. Thus, she couldn't resign herself to the fate her stepmother had mapped out for her.

I want more.

The sense of yearning that filled her was painful. She'd never stopped loving William, even when she hadn't understood his actions toward her. How could he have come into her life, opened her heart, then left her? Why had he done it, when all her instincts told her he was an honorable man?

Oh William, you should have never come into my garden and let me know there was more.

Cinda looked back up at the moon, realizing her decision was made. She had to find out how William felt. If he'd truly lost all capacity to love her, then she would leave him alone. Gathering her courage, her fingers clenched in the wool of her shawl, she closed her eyes and tried to conjure up his image in her mind.

I can't let him go. Not just yet. Not before I see him, face-to-face . . .

"Out of my way!"

Cinda grasped her basket tightly against her and dodged the gang of street boys who pressed closer. Pickpockets. She wasn't having any part of it, not in the mood she was in.

"Come on, lads, run along!"

She glanced up at a newspaper vendor, and he gave her a wink. Grateful, she tossed him an orange from the overflowing basket.

"Thank you!" She was sure he couldn't hear her, could only see her lips moving over the noise in the street.

"Thank *you*, love!" he called out. "It's quite a nice view from here!"

She blushed, then pulled her gaze away from his.

The day of Nan's dinner party and market day had dawned one and the same. A lucky coincidence. That she would be allowed out longer than usual in the city was very well timed, indeed.

Cinda hurried along the crowded street, the large basket bulging with her purchases. Nan wanted a difficult French menu, in order to impress her friends. She and Victor had drawn up the recipes last night.

Now, the basket crammed with pullets, fillets, beef steaks, pigeons for pie, ham and quail, fresh peas and artichokes, oranges and grapes, she had one last stop, for cheese.

The marketplace was crowded, the streets congested. Milk girls, orange sellers, water carriers, knife grinders, and chair menders cried out raucously. Some of the vendors blew on tin trumpets and rang strings of bells. On the cobblestone street, the clatter of iron wheels and horses' hooves added to the din.

Even if she could have afforded a hackney coach or sedan-chair, Cinda knew she would make swifter progress on foot. The streets were continually congested with vehicles of all description.

She kept her eyes open for the distinctive Grenville family crest, quickly glancing at each richly appointed carriage as she passed it. Cinda didn't truly expect to see William out and about, but if she happened to meet him while shopping, it would certainly be a safer means of speaking to him than the plan she was devising.

Within fifteen minutes, she was trying to find space in the huge basket for her last purchase. It wasn't working. She'd have to set the basket down in an out of the way spot and rearrange its contents.

She suddenly had the strangest feeling someone was watching her. As she glanced up, Cinda noticed the woman.

She was standing on the outskirts of the crowd, dressed in ragged clothing. As Cinda studied her more carefully, she noticed the small baby, wrapped in another rag, in the woman's thin arms.

As Cinda set the heavy basket down, she wondered at all the rich food Nan would waste tonight. Would the selfish woman even notice if a little was missing?

Her mind made up, she started toward the stranger.

As Cinda approached her, the woman's face tightened with fear. She reminded Cinda of a deer, ready to bolt.

"Wait! Please!"

She hesitated, and Cinda saw the fear in her pale eyes. She'd been pretty once, but lack of proper food and the harsh London winters had taken their toll.

"I'm not going to hurt you."

Up close, she was even more damaged, and her child was heartbreaking. The infant, small and silent, had a pale, waxy cast to its flesh. The spring morning was brisk, and the child was barely protected, wrapped in a thin, faded piece of material that had once been part of a petticoat.

Her mind made up, Cinda set down the basket, balanced the cheese on top of it, then started to take off her soft gray woolen shawl.

The woman watched her with pale, unblinking eyes.

"Give me the child."

As if not used to resisting orders, the woman handed her baby to Cinda.

She swiftly unwrapped the infant from the grimy, threadbare cloth, then began to swaddle it in the thick shawl, wrapping it tightly to keep out the chill morning air.

"Oh, no, miss, I couldn't—"

"Take it." Cinda had seen enough children like this one. Her chances for survival weren't good, but if she could be comfortable and warm for the rest of her short life, where was the harm? The shawl was her own, knitted over several evenings while she sat by the kitchen fire.

Once the babe was tightly wrapped and back in her mother's arms, Cinda quickly glanced around.

"Come this way," she said, and when the woman didn't respond, she took her elbow and, struggling with the basket, led her to the mouth of a side street. Cinda made certain they were standing just inside the narrow street, out of sight.

"Don't let anyone see, or they'll take it from you." She worked swiftly as she made up a small packet. A bunch of grapes. An orange. One of the smallest beef steaks, and a sweet, sticky bun.

"I wish I had money to give you for milk," she said, rearranging the food in the basket and stowing the cheese next to the fruit. "But my mistress keeps a sharp eye on every penny spent."

The woman met her gaze, her hollow eyes so full of pain Cinda almost looked away.

"Thank you. The shawl. I—thank you."

"Would that I could do more. Keep your little girl warm."

"I'll try to repay you," the stranger said.

Pride. How well she knew its sting. How many arguments she'd had with William, stubbornly insisting they do things her way. She recognized the same emotion in this woman, buried under layers of despair.

"You'll do something for me someday." She said it more for reassurance than anything else.

"I will," the woman replied softly. She stared after Cinda long after she turned the corner and was out of sight.

The carriage jolted over deep ruts in the road. Its lone occupant, a silver-haired woman dressed in a dark blue traveling gown, braced herself in her seat. Kathleen Stanhope lifted the leather flap and took in the city she'd hoped never to return to.

London was more crowded than ever.

I'm far too old for all this. She gently eased the flap into place and settled herself back against the seat.

The crowds of people seemed less mannerly and far more ruthless than the last time she'd visited. She'd never enjoyed

London, and far preferred hiding out in the country.

She would have never come back at all, except for Cinda.

Lucinda Kathleen Marie Townshend. Her godchild. Her niece's only child. When Cinda had been baptized, Eleanor had named Kathleen godmother.

And what a splendid job you've made of it.

It galled her to think of Horace Townshend living in her family home with—that woman. Nan had probably taken great care to destroy Ellie's garden, as well as her daughter.

Kathleen had been afraid, and until now had done nothing.

No, not afraid. You cannot bear to look upon her.

She could be truthful with herself in the privacy of her own thoughts. Cinda looked like her mother, reminded Kathleen so much of her dead niece. She'd loved Eleanor enough to fight for her life, try to tell her the truth, challenge her niece's opinion of what constituted happiness.

But Ellie had been stubborn. She'd rushed, blind with passion, into the arms of the man who had destroyed her. Even after the marriage, Kathleen had argued with her niece until she'd been emotionally exhausted.

In the end, she simply hadn't had the courage to stay and see events unfold. So she had retreated north, to stay with friends, far away from Horace Townshend's evil influence.

Now she could no longer look away, for the man and his whore had gone too far.

It didn't matter that Cinda had the same temperament as her mother, and had fallen in love with a man Kathleen considered as destructive to her as Horace had been to Ellie. Kathleen felt as helpless in the face of her godchild as she had with her beloved niece.

She had to do something, no matter how ineffectual.

As Cinda's great-aunt and godmother, and as a mere woman—and older at that!—she knew her influence was limited. But she had her weapons.

Never having mastered the trait of feminine modesty, she knew she possessed a strong constitution and a clever mind. And she was quite aware of where all the bodies were buried, had made it a point to find out about numerous skeletons in closets. Her family, like most, had its share of devious and greedy individuals, intent on fighting with the others for the last scraps.

And in the end, her plan was to outlast them all.

Kathleen knew who her enemies were, and until now had been content to leave them alone. She also had many close friends in London who managed to relay gossip back to her. Thus, she knew exactly what Nan Taunton planned to do.

Working the girl in the kitchen like a common servant. Giving Cinda's ball gowns and jewels to her daughters, making sure she is dressed in rags and was absolutely no competition for them.

And now, attempting to marry her off to a feebleminded fool so his younger brother can wrest control of his fortune. Oh, Nan, you are too greedy by far.

How her brother-in-law could have given Eleanor to a man like Horace was beyond her comprehension. That was when all the trouble had started.

Kathleen had chosen never to marry, because of the accident. She'd fallen from her favorite horse at the age of fifteen, and had walked with a pronounced limp ever since.

When she remembered.

She'd deliberately exaggerated the injury, and brilliantly mangled the one London season she'd had. Her father had been enraged, but she had defied him. For Kathleen had never wanted to marry.

She was quite afraid of men.

Horrible creatures. Nothing but trouble. Look what happened to Ellie, how that bastard betrayed her, and all the time she still thought he loved her . . .

Kathleen had never aspired to the roles of wife and mother, but she had been deeply honored when her niece had chosen her to be godmother. Eleanor had loved her daughter with all her heart, and Kathleen had taken the promise she had made to her niece quite seriously.

She'd been deeply shamed at what a coward she'd been thus far, and had determined to return to London and face people she feared in order to try to set things right. Now she hoped she wasn't too late to undo some of the damage.

She had a special debt to settle with Horace, for he had not only squandered Eleanor's fortune, but Cinda's as well. The man had an insatiable appetite for the gaming table, and from what Kathleen had heard, Nan was quite fond of cards herself. Both of them were money-hungry creatures, self-centered, with never a thought beyond their own well-being.

Certainly never of Rosalind's.

Kathleen sighed, not enjoying the memories. Several days in this carriage had left her exhausted. Yet she was beginning to feel a sort of edgy restlessness, as she thought of putting her plan into effect.

It was dangerous, but Cinda was capable of it. The girl would have to deceive her stepmother. Kathleen had disliked Nan Taunton from childhood, and knew she had a crude temper when riled.

Cinda would have to be cautious and clever. But once the girl found a good man who would champion her, take care of her, get her out of that house . . .

Kathleen thought of William Stedman and closed her eyes. The one thing that might cast all her planning awry was Cinda's headstrong sensuality. Her great-niece had written her a letter, telling Kathleen about the love she had found with this man.

Kathleen had read it, then crumpled the missive into a ball and tossed in into the fireplace. It had seemed, while reading Cinda's carefully chosen words, that Ellie was talking to her again, that same hopeful note in her voice.

I won't let it happen again.

The love Cinda felt for William was of the worst sort, a dark, violent, headstrong passion that could not turn out well. Still, Kathleen realized she didn't know the entire story of what had happened that night. Cinda was keeping something from her, she was certain. Shame engulfed her as she thought of how ineffectual she'd been up until now.

Why should she take you into her confidence? You haven't been around much of late.

The coach hit a pothole and lurched. Kathleen's eyes flew open and she struggled to keep her balance. The vehicle slowly righted itself, and she sat back in her seat and closed her eyes, willing herself to remain calm.

She was tired, her eyes felt gritty. Once she reached Julia's house, she could rest. Unpack. Her widowed friend would fix her a cup of tea. Then they would sit and have a nice long chat, and she would tell Julia exactly what it was she planned to do.

* * *

The dinner party had been over hours ago, and now the only evidence that it had even occurred were the piles of dirty dishes on the large kitchen table.

Cook slept in her chair by the fire, while Cinda had sorted out more wool and was casting stitches on her knitting needles. Both of them should have been attending to the dishes, but by unspoken agreement they'd decided to leave them for the morrow.

The door squeaked softly as it opened, and Cinda turned in her chair with a start. She relaxed when she saw Mary come in with another tray of dirty dishes.

"Shhh. Don't wake her." Cinda pointed toward the sleeping woman.

Mary nodded, then set down the tray of dishes. Little more than a girl, very slender with silvery-blond hair, she was a gentle wraith who flitted around upstairs. But though her looks were fragile, her strength was not.

"Sit down, I'll make you a cup of tea."

Mary raised her pale brows at this, and Cinda laughed softly.

"Don't ask me how I acquired it, just enjoy it."

Within a short time, both women were sitting in front of the fire, tea in hand. Cinda had also found five cherry tarts left over from the party.

"Can't stay long," Mary whispered before she took a bite of the rich pastry.

"Why not?" Surely by now Nan was asleep and her demands at rest for the night.

"I'm packing for her and the daughters. They'll be leaving at daybreak."

Cinda's hand, which had been reaching for a tart, stilled.

"Where is she going?"

"To that friend in the country. She's having an immense party, and Nan wants to try her luck at cards."

"How long will they be gone?"

"Almost two weeks."

Mary talked on about the party while Cinda thought of what Nan's departure meant.

You want to see him, face-to-face.

She wanted to go to William. Now, if Nan was to truly leave for even this short period of time, Cinda knew she could find a way to slip out of the house. It would have to be at night, she couldn't risk anyone coming to harm because of what she was determined to do.

She couldn't let Victor or Mary know of her plans. Nan routinely questioned her servants whenever she returned from a journey, even if it was only a matter of days. Cook would have to be told. The older woman could practically see inside her head. And Cook was a consummate liar, as Cinda herself was.

She'd long ago come to terms with it, and decided surely a merciful God wouldn't bar her entry to heaven because of tales she'd told in order to survive. Nan's cruelty knew no bounds, otherwise Cinda would have tried to reason with the woman.

It had something to do with her mother, and the fact that Cinda resembled Eleanor. Nan had an animosity toward her that went beyond the bounds of what was natural. Cinda frowned, keeping her gaze on the fire. Planning.

Yes, Cook would have to be told. She'd know anyway, with that sixth sense of hers. And also for her own protection, in case something were to go wrong. Robbie, Cook's son and the Townshends' stablehand, could be trusted. He rarely came into contact with either Nan or her daughters.

None of her duties would have to be neglected if she were only gone for a short time.

Just to see him, speak with him . . .

Mary continued talking about the party, while Cinda nodded and made appropriate murmurs of response. And all the while, she plotted.

She knew, from talking to Robbie, that William was expecting the delivery of two blood bay mares tomorrow night.

Perfect.

Terrifying, but perfect.

If she could travel the distance from her dwelling to his on the back of a horse—

There were countless things that could go wrong, but she didn't have the luxury of time, she couldn't wait for a safer opportunity. Nan had given her notice of her future, and Cinda refused to accept it.

Now I have to know why he didn't come back for me.

She didn't want to sit meekly in her father's house and accept the fate that Nan had decided was hers.

But getting back . . .

Cinda forced her doubts out of her mind. Once she was with William, she trusted him to find her a safe way back. Even if he no longer cared for her, she knew he would see to a woman's safety.

It just might work.

She started as she felt a gentle hand upon her shoulder.

"I'm going back upstairs," Mary whispered. "Thanks for pinching the sweets."

"Good night, Mary."

Mary closed the kitchen door quietly behind her, and Cook slumbered on. Cinda sat staring into the fire, too restless, too excited to continue with her knitting.

Her sphere of kitchen, garden, and stable, with occasional forays to market, was all she'd known since her mother's death. It was a familiar world, all she'd had for years. And there was a part of her that feared leaving it.

"And what might you be up to, pet?"

She started, then turned and looked at Cook. The woman had just woken up; her face was still flushed with sleep.

No one knew her better than Cook; she'd helped care for her since she was a baby. Now, contemplating this dangerous night ride, Cinda knew she had to tell the woman the truth. What if she never made it back? Cook didn't deserve lies.

Keeping her voice low and her eye on the door, Cinda told her the plan.

To Cook's credit, she didn't immediately try to discourage her. She sat silent after Cinda finished, staring into the fire with a somber look on her face.

"He has to have a good reason for not coming to you. I'd like to hear it m'self."

"I just want to know, I have to know—"

"You're a lucky woman. Your mum, God rest her, would be happy if she could see you now, for not many women ever have what you had with him."

Cinda didn't have to ask what Cook meant because she knew. She'd been to several weddings before her mother's death, and sensed the bride's fear and displeasure. For a long time she'd thought of following her Great-aunt Kathleen's example and never marrying.

Not for her that fear of the marital bed.

She hadn't counted on love transforming fear into desire, reluctance into passion. Though she'd been truly frightened of losing her virginity, and had known the importance of the step she'd taken, once she'd met William it had been as if the choice had been taken out of her hands.

She'd wanted to give that part of herself to him. By the time she was in his arms, lying with him secretly in her narrow bed above the stable, she hadn't been afraid.

And he had made it wonderful.

"You'll need a disguise," Cook said quietly. "I'll snitch some clothing out of the wash. A stableboy, perhaps."

"I have boots, and a hat."

"Pin up your hair," Cook said softly, thinking out loud. "And hold on tightly, because if you fall off—"

Neither had to elaborate, both knew the fate of a woman alone in London at night.

"Try to come back during the day."

"I should be back by afternoon at the latest, and I'll stay up all night and catch up the work—"

"Don't think of it, just keep your wits about you long enough to get back safely. I'll be saying a special prayer for you tonight, and asking God to guide your steps."

Her throat closed with tears. Cook was the closest she'd had to a mother since her own had died, and she loved the old woman fiercely.

"Thank you for not . . . trying to stop me."

"What, you think I can't remember what it was like?" Now Cook reached for the last tart, then left her chair and settled back comfortably on her pallet by the fire.

"I'm not all *that* old."

The knee-length, fitted breeches were too loose, but she found a piece of rope and hitched them tightly around her waist. The ruffled linen shirt was torn in front, but the dark waistcoat concealed it. The coat was split in back to high hip level, and decorated with bound buttonholes.

All I need now is a lace cravat and I'll look the complete dandy.

But the clothing was dark and well worn, and she knew it wasn't unusual for stableboys to wear castoffs. It was crucial she do nothing to call attention to herself.

Her hair had been pulled back, then tightly braided and pinned into a knot high on her head. The three-cornered hat would cover it, and it wouldn't come off because she'd sewn pale pink ribbon she'd stolen from her stepsister's dress on each side. With the ends tied securely beneath her chin and the collar of the coat turned up, her face could hardly be seen.

Wool stockings and her riding boots completed the outfit. She wanted to look as much as possible like a young male servant delivering fine bloodstock.

That morning Cook had talked to her son Robbie and found out more details. Several bottles of confiscated port had changed hands in exchange for the promise that the blood bay mares would make a short detour before reaching William's stables.

In moments, she would be leaving everything familiar and safe for whatever lay beyond the high stone walls.

Almost time.

She heard the clang of hooves on cobblestones, the shrill neigh of one of the mares. Her heart picked up speed, as she descended the long flight of stairs and ran swiftly and silently to the edge of the stable.

She stayed concealed in shadow, just as planned.

Robbie was handing over one final bottle of port, then the two men beside him laughed heartily, slapped the young man on the back, and disappeared into the night.

Cinda watched as Robbie ran his hands over the mares, quieting them. She counted slowly to ten before she came out of the shadows and joined him.

"Last chance to change your mind," he said as he caught sight of her. "Jamie can always help me deliver 'em."

She shook her head, not trusting herself to speak.

"Here. Give her this piece of apple, like I told you."

She offered the horse the piece of fruit, and felt the mare's soft lips graze the flat of her palm.

"They're good girls. Steady, but with a bit of fire. You're sure you can ride one?"

She hadn't been on a horse since she was a child, and hoped it would all come back to her. Cinda hadn't dared tell Cook there was no saddle, that she'd be riding bareback. Robbie certainly wouldn't squeal; he had no desire to bring his mother's anger down on his head.

During her childhood, Cinda had spent many a summer day with her skirt tucked up under her legs and her pony's hooves flying beneath her. But a horse was certainly different from a pony.

Even if she stayed on the mare's back, Cinda knew riding the mare would be the least of their problems this night.

"You're sure?" Robbie was studying her closely, a doubtful look in his eyes.

She nodded her head.

"Good. Get on up, then." He made a stirrup out of his entwined fingers and gave her a leg up.

The mare seemed taller once she was up on her back. Cinda steadied herself as the horse shifted restlessly beneath her.

She senses my fear.

Robbie handed her the reins, his expression serious. He was usually quite a jokester, but he knew the importance of this outing.

Cinda took them from him, then gathered them firmly in one hand. With the other, she stroked the satiny neck.

"You'll do fine," Robbie said quietly.

She nodded. The mare didn't frighten her as much as what was beyond the garden wall.

"Take this." He handed her a pistol. "It's readied. If we come up against any trouble, we'll try to outrun it. Otherwise, aim it up into the air and fire."

Sheer force of will kept her hand from shaking as she took the pistol from him and tucked it into the waistband of her breeches. It was an uncomfortable reminder of what awaited them outside.

Robbie swung up onto the second mare, then gently nudged the animal with his heels.

"We're off."

CHAPTER
4

The night was quiet, the only sounds the striking of hooves on cobblestones. They passed several houses, all of them dark. Only the very rich could afford candles and fires in every room. But soon the houses gave way to the town.

The various shops were closed and deserted, their signs creaking and swaying in the wind. Feeble tavern lights winked through small windows, but other than an occasional link boy leading a party with his flaming torch, the great city was dark.

As they continued, more people, on horseback and in carriages, joined them on the street. Cinda had feared thieves and footpads, but she soon came to realize they had more to fear from the carriages in the narrow cobblestone streets.

"Watch your way, man!" Robbie shouted angrily to a particularly reckless driver. Glancing back over his shoulder, he motioned to her with a flick of his wrist.

"Come on!"

He urged his mare faster, the reins held in one hand, the other flicking their leather tips against the mare's broad rump. Following Robbie's expert example, Cinda did the same.

For one frightening instant she bounced jerkily on the mare's hard backbone, then Cinda fell into the rhythm as the animal broke into a smooth canter. She narrowed her eyes against the chill night air, but her vision blurred with tears.

She blinked them away, kept a firm grip on the reins, and followed the mare in front of her. There was confusion and noise all around her, but the only thing Cinda concentrated on was Robbie's back. If she lost him, she wasn't sure she could find William's townhouse on her own.

They cantered in silence for a distance, then Robbie pulled hard on the reins, causing the mare to turn sharply. This new road was narrower, more deserted. Cinda followed, and as Robbie slowed their pace, she brought her mount's head up flush with his.

"We're almost there," he said, raising his voice above the blowing and snorting of the horses. "We'll walk them the rest of the way. Cool them off."

She nodded. They'd agreed beforehand it was wisest if she spoke as little as possible. Even trying to make her voice sound gruff and masculine, she still sounded too much like a woman.

"Hand me the pistol," Robbie said quietly. "I don't think we'll be needing it now."

Relieved, she did as he requested. Glad to be rid of the firearm, she turned her attention to her surroundings.

The townhouses were more elegant, the grounds larger and more imposing. A few of the windows sparkled with candle-light, and Cinda thought suddenly how strange it would be to live surrounded with light whenever she wanted it.

And to finally see how William lived.

What if he'd never taken her to his home because she had been a mere diversion? An amusement? What if, when he saw her, he had no desire to speak to her? What if—

"We're here. Follow me closely." Robbie urged his mare forward with gentle pressure from his knees, and the animal broke into an eager trot, her ears flicked forward. She smelled the other horses.

"They know they're in time for their dinner," he joked. Cinda kept her posture ramrod-straight and masculine, but her knees trembled. Though she was deeply relieved they'd made it without mishap, the events that were to test her courage were far from over.

Now, the greatest danger lay inside.

"The horses are here, Your Grace."

William looked up from his desk at his valet, Henry Graves. A portly man, with snowy white hair, Henry had served William's father until the day of his death, then calmly taken over most of the practical aspects of William's life. A loyal and trusted servant, William considered him more a member of the family than his personal valet.

That was what came of being merely a child when fate had brought Henry into his life. At nine years of age, he hadn't particularly wanted a valet, but Henry had been adamant.

"Have both mares rubbed down and fed. I'll see them in the morning."

Henry cleared his throat, making a disapproving sound. "I don't think that will do, sir. The boy is quite insistent. Claims he has to talk to you about one of them. Her right hind leg, he said."

William set down his pen and pushed his chair back. It wouldn't hurt to talk to the lad. It wasn't as if he were truly accomplishing anything tonight.

He left the library, his stride purposeful, Henry dogging his heels. As William came down the curved double staircase and headed toward the immense kitchen at the back of the townhouse, he wondered at a stableboy admitting a horse he delivered had something wrong with her.

An honest lad. Something very unusual in that.

He lit a rushlight in the kitchen from the fire, then walked out toward the cobblestone stableyard. The two mares had already been settled in their stalls, and the lad stood by the back door, his hands in the pockets of his coat.

William's heartbeat quickened as he recognized the young man. Robbie. Had Cinda asked the lad to deliver a message? But he remained aloof and polite, for there was no telling who was watching.

"The mare?" William prompted.

"Both in the barn, feeding. And fine horses they are, Your Grace, if I do say so."

He was a cocky lad, with ginger-colored hair and dark, laughing eyes. William glanced at Henry, who scowled down at the boy.

"About that hind leg, young man—"

"Can we talk, m'lord?" The boy addressed his question to William, glancing pointedly at Henry. "Privy like?"

Henry bristled with barely suppressed outrage, and William couldn't help the hint of a smile. How hurt his valet would be if he weren't included in everything that went on in the great house.

"He can be trusted."

"Sir, if you would rather I go back inside—"

"No, Henry. I'd rather you remained here."

"Very well."

The boy had been watching the entire exchange, and seemed satisfied. "I'd like you to come back to the stable with me, if you would, sir."

"Lead on, then."

The three men silently crossed the immense yard, then entered the stable. The boy led them to one of the large stalls in back, and at the sound of their footsteps, the two mares poked their heads over the stall door.

"They are beauties, aren't they, Henry?" William moved slowly and spoke soothingly as he stroked first one satiny nose, then the other. Then he turned to the boy.

"Which one was injured?"

The stableboy took a deep breath, then spoke quickly. "It's not really the mares I'm talking about, sir, but a different sort of filly altogether. She asked me to assist her in coming here, and I wanted to make sure she was safe before I left her in your company."

He knew, before the final words were out of Robbie's mouth, who he was talking about.

"Cinda?" His voice was quiet. Hushed.

He heard the sound of soft, booted footsteps behind him, and turned in time to see her come out from behind several large bales of hay. As she walked closer, the faint illumination revealed her face.

A face he'd never thought to see for a long, long time.

She'd taken off her hat. It dangled in her fingers as she played with the ribbon ties, and he realized she was nervous.

He felt every kind of cad for how he had to look in her eyes, but he'd had no choice. Though his first instinct was to gather her into his arms, he was not a man given to displays of emotion in front of others. Having absolutely no idea how he was going to explain his actions to her, or if she even wished to hear an explanation, William stared at her for almost a minute.

Her expression was guarded. Tense. Those green eyes revealed nothing. It saddened him that because of what he'd felt he had to do to ensure her safety, they had started to keep secrets from each other.

Finally, William chose to look away, fully realizing what she probably thought of him. Knowing Cinda as he did, and being familiar with her spirit, he guessed she'd come to his home tonight to tell him she wanted nothing more to do with him.

He couldn't blame her if she did exactly that.

It wasn't something he looked forward to, but they couldn't stand out in the stable all night. He turned to his valet. Henry's face was impassive, revealing nothing. But his bright blue eyes were sharp and alert, and William knew the jig was up, as far as his valet was concerned.

"There are two pallets made up in the kitchen, but obviously one of them is now totally unsuitable. Henry, I'd like you to go ahead and make up the blue guest room. The lady will sleep there."

Henry had barely left the stable when William directed his next question to Robbie.

"Do you have any idea whether you were followed or not?"

"No, sir. We were quite alone on the road for the last stretch of the journey."

"Good. We'd best be getting inside."

And with that, he extinguished the small flame and the three of them made a strained and silent procession to the main house.

I shouldn't have come.

He wasn't pleased, she sensed it from the first moment he'd seen her. But it had been worth all her fears, no matter what the outcome, to be able to gaze upon his face one last time.

Black Irish, her mother would have said, even though William claimed no Irish blood in his ancestry. Dark hair, almost black. Deep blue eyes and sun-darkened skin. A strong nose, straight as a blade, and slashing cheekbones. His jawline was square, with the tiniest cleft. She'd run her finger over it many a time.

Knowing the expression in her eyes was undoubtedly giving away her thoughts, Cinda glanced down at her booted feet and wondered what he was going to do with her.

He'd already shown Robbie to his pallet by the fire, and arranged a meal for him. Now, as she followed him up the long flight of stairs to the upper floor, she had no idea what was to come.

William was a private man, she knew that. She hadn't expected him to take her into his arms in front of Robbie and his valet. But as she'd looked in his eyes, she'd tried very hard to see the faintest of welcomes in their expression.

It had been difficult, trying to read his mood in the faint glow of the rushlight, but she was sure she hadn't detected any welcome at all.

Now he entered what appeared to be an immense library, with shelves of leatherbound books stretching from floor to ceiling. A blazing fire crackled in the grate, and two chairs were pulled up close to it, facing each other.

She walked into the room, crossing in front of him as he held the door open for her. Then he closed it, and they were finally alone.

He didn't say anything, simply stared at her. She averted her eyes, and directed her attention downward, to the oriental rug. The red and gold pattern began to blur before her eyes.

"I'm sorry," she whispered.

"Don't be."

"I shouldn't have come. But I had to—"

"I know." He reached for her hand then, his fingers laced securely through hers. And at his touch, the tension and fear she'd been holding at bay for hours finally broke. She put her free hand up to her eyes, as if to shield them from his gaze, and started to cry.

She hated herself then, knowing how uncomfortable William was with feminine tears. But she couldn't hold back the strong surge of emotion. He stepped forward, then pulled her the rest of the way into his arms and held her tightly. He smelled the same, familiar, safe and dear, and she cried even harder.

"Don't. Darling, you'll make yourself sick."

She felt his arm slide beneath her knees, the other around her shoulders, then he picked her up and carried her toward one of the chairs by the fire. He sat down, settled her in his lap, and let her bury her face in his shirtfront as she desperately tried to compose herself.

When she could finally speak, she cleared her throat and said softly, "I had imagined it all a different way."

"So did I."

The question stuck in her throat, made her tremble with fear, but she had to ask it.

"Why did you leave me, Will?"

He sighed then. His chin rested on top of her head; she couldn't see his face. She wasn't sure, at that moment, she wanted to.

"I didn't want to. I just—thought it would be for the best."

"Did you—were you ever going to see me again?"

"Yes!" The word was out of his mouth in a rush, and he shifted position so their faces were mere inches apart. She saw the depth of feeling in his eyes, in the way his hands held her, the tension in his face.

Fresh tears rushed to her eyes, for this was the man she had fallen in love with. For several terrifying minutes out in the stableyard she had thought him a stranger. Now, behind this closed door, she had the man she loved beside her, and felt suffused with joy.

The soft knock on the door distracted them from each other.

"Come."

Henry opened the door carefully, stepped inside, then closed it behind him.

"I just wanted to inquire, sir, if you need me for anything else tonight."

William glanced at her, and she could see him making swift decisions.

"I'll have supper sent to my bedroom, enough for both of us. I should like you to bring it up, Henry, as I don't want any of the other servants to know she is here. Also, I'd like a bath prepared. When all is in readiness, come and let me know."

"Very good, sir." Henry paused, just a heartbeat. "And the guest room?"

William looked at her again, and her heart leapt as she realized he was leaving the decision up to her, letting her set the pace at which they would become intimate. Her head advised playing coy, making it more of a challenge for him. Her heart urged her to forgive, to understand, to be close to him.

To love him.

She shook her head, the slight movement almost imperceptible, and was warmed by the light that came to his eyes.

"It won't be necessary, Henry."

"As you wish, sir."

Then the door closed behind them, and they were alone.

"You're far too thin," he said, watching her as she reached for another slice of beef.

"I shouldn't eat as much in front of you, you'll think me a pig." She wrinkled her nose at him and cut into one of her potatoes.

"Never."

There were so many things he wanted to tell her, share with her. It had been easy to banish her from his mind, but never his heart. Now, watching her in this bedroom, wrapped in one of his silk dressing gowns, he marveled at how perfect his elegant townhouse was as a setting for her.

He wanted to keep her with him forever.

There are so many things you want to tell her, except the most crucial . . .

She was a living dream, the embodiment of everything he'd ever wanted in a woman. Beauty, certainly that. He loved beauty in countless forms, but a woman's beauty was something he'd always thought most highly of. A sense of fun, a lively wit that was a gift in itself, capable of bringing him out of his darkest moods.

And tenderness. He remembered his mother faintly, as she'd died when he was a boy. Brought up in a largely masculine household, he'd been fascinated by the fairer sex, but had never felt this . . . *passion*, for lack of a better word. Only for her.

He'd first seen her in the garden on a moonlit summer night, and she'd appeared to him as something ethereal, a spirit, loveliness too delicate and transitory to touch.

Her earthiness had delighted him, a total contradiction of how she appeared. Cinda possessed a lusty spirit that fought and laughed and loved with a courage that left him breathless.

"Will?"

"Hmm."

"What are you thinking?"

He smiled then, and looked away from her. She had the most infuriatingly wonderful way of sensing his moods.

"That I'm probably going to rush you."

Her green eyes darkened; he could see deep emotion in their depths. He couldn't stop looking at her; this time he didn't look away.

The dark blue of his dressing gown heightened the paleness of her skin, flowed over the curves of her body. He'd left the room for a short time while she'd changed out of her masculine attire, not trusting himself to let them get through dinner without ending up in bed.

"I don't think you will." Her eyes never left his as she took a sip of the Bordeaux Henry had so thoughtfully provided. The old man had a romantic soul, and William silently blessed him for it.

"I might surprise you," she said softly.

"You always surprise me. And delight me."

He saw the delicate color in her cheeks, and was suddenly, fiercely glad what he'd said had pleased her. He wanted to touch her, but he didn't reach for her hand, couldn't feel the softness of her skin, couldn't trust himself.

"What would you like to do after supper?" he asked her quietly.

He knew what he wanted to do, but he would treat her with kindness and let the decision be hers. She hadn't been part of many decisions since the night of the murder, and he intended to make that up to her. He'd spend the rest of his life making the last few months up to her, if only he could think of some way to keep her from harm.

"Will?"

He brought his attention back to her, saw the questioning expression in her eyes.

"What were you thinking, just then?"

He couldn't tell her a falsehood, but he couldn't tell her the truth.

"Nothing."

"Nothing." She set down her fork, then leaned back against one of the chairs. They were both sitting on the floor in front of the fire. "Is it something you'll tell me eventually?"

He sensed her worry, and hated being the cause of it.

"Not tonight." He took her hand, brought the callused palm up to his lips, and kissed it. "Tonight, I don't want to think about anything but you."

She smiled, slowly, and he could see the devilment in her eyes. "Didn't you request that Henry prepare a bath? And if it was for me, I should tell you you're a thoughtful man. A gentleman. Or perhaps it's because I smell of horse."

"You," he said, putting his forefinger beneath her chin and raising her gaze to his, "would be shocked at how indiscriminate most gentlemen are."

She blushed again, and he ran his finger slowly down her neck, toward the deep vee of the robe. She caught his hand, tensing, then looked up at him.

"Nothing has happened as I thought it would, Will. I've thought of seeing you for so long, imagined how it would be. And now—I can't conceal what it is I feel for you, or act the part a clever woman would—"

"And I'm thankful for that."

"But—" She paused, then took a deep breath and said swiftly, "I'm not coming to your bed before bathing."

"I wouldn't think to change your mind, knowing how stubborn you can be."

"Then you don't mind waiting?" He saw the mischievous twinkle in her eyes. "I know how impatient you can be."

"Madam," he said, pulling her to her feet and sweeping her up into his arms, "your wish is my command."

The man inside the lone carriage didn't shiver from the cold, despite the brisk night air. He barely moved at all, his attention riveted on the elegant townhouse across the lane in front of him.

Another wasted night, damn him.

William had lived the life of a monk since the night of the murder. The killer smiled at that, pleased to have brought him such pain that being with a woman was something he still had no desire to do.

The man kept his attention focused on the estate. Nothing of any import had transpired tonight. Two horses had been delivered, but he'd known about the sale. He made it a point to know everything about William. But he wasn't at all interested in two stableboys, it was news of a special woman that he wanted.

He can't stay celibate much longer.

It infuriated him that William no longer attended any of the endless rounds of parties and dinners the aristocracy was so famed for. His enemy had become a hermit, an eccentric recluse. Now, with the London season and several lavish masquerades approaching, he wanted William Stedman to be back in the thick of it all.

And he wanted him to care for yet another woman.

For how else, William, can I know how to hurt you?

With a swift, decisive movement, he rapped on the ceiling of the coach with his walking stick. He heard the driver start upright, then slap the reins smartly on the horse's rumps. The carriage creaked, then hooves and wheels clanged over cobblestones as he began the short journey home.

"A room just for bathing?" Cinda was incredulous.

"Blame my uncle. It was an idea he picked up during one of his trips. He described it to me, and I thought it sounded quite reasonable."

The small room, formerly one of the bedrooms on the upper floor, had been transformed into a luxurious setting. The fireplace was lit and blazing merrily, and an enormous copper tub sat in front of the fire, steam coming up off the water. An oriental carpet covered the floor, and thick towels, totally unlike the linen strips she was used to drying with, were piled on a plush chair next to the tub.

She walked over to the tub and trailed a finger in the steaming water.

"It must have taken countless buckets to fill this."

He nodded. "I don't use it often. Only when I have company."

A few seconds passed before she understood his words.

"You're bathing with me?"

"Only if you want me to."

"I do, but . . ." She found it so very difficult to say the words, knowing instinctively he would see any refusal on her part as a lack of love. She'd known from the start he was not a man who voiced his emotions easily. He was much more comfortable showing her how deeply his emotions ran.

I just need time . . .

She hadn't been able to undress in front of him before, and now she felt just as vulnerable. But she wasn't sure how to tell him.

"Cinda, look at me."

She met his gaze, sure he could see the confusion inside her.

"I want this night to be perfect for you. Tell me what to do. Anything or nothing. I leave it in your hands."

That he should trust her so overwhelmed her that she instinctively sought to give back to him.

"Tell me what you want," she said softly.

"Take down your hair."

That much she could do. She watched him as he removed the towels from the chair by the tub and sat down on it, facing her. She'd left her hair up in its tight bun, and now her fingers felt suddenly stiff and clumsy.

She slowly unwound the braid until it hung almost to her waist, then untied the thin piece of pink ribbon at the end and began to loosen it. Catching his eye, she looked away.

And all the time, he watched her.

She had no idea what this was doing to him.

Waves of flame-colored hair tumbled unconfined, fanning down her silk-clad back. When the last tendril had come loose and the vibrant mane of hair was totally freed, she looked back up at him.

Waiting.

He let her wait, let anticipation and even the tiniest edge of fear come to the fore.

"Will?"

"Come here."

She walked toward him, the silk whispering against her as she moved, her hair shimmering in the firelight. She'd been cool and mysterious in the garden, he thought suddenly. But tonight she would be fire, pure sensual heat.

He was selfish enough to be fiercely glad he'd been her first lover, and determined enough to know he'd be the only man she'd ever know.

She stopped in front of him, one hand cupped in the other, her gaze steady as she looked at him.

"Closer."

She obeyed him, and didn't flinch when his hand closed over the knot in the dressing gown's sash. Words were unnecessary, for he could see she knew what he wanted. His fingers worked the knot free; the sash slipped over her hips and fell to the floor. Then, with both his hands, he drew the heavy silk material apart.

Beautiful.

He took her naked form in slowly, so slowly, starting at her feet, curled against the carpet, and moving up until their eyes met. Hers were bright, her color high.

Reaching out, he touched her cheek, then took a lock of her vibrant hair in his fingers and rubbed it softly between them.

"Will," she whispered, then surprised him by slipping the dressing gown off her shoulders and going into his arms.

She was everything he'd remembered. The feel of her, the heat, the warm, feminine smell of her hair. He closed his eyes, his arms tightened around her. And strangely enough, he understood. Her own nakedness was far less threatening than his.

She shivered, and he held her closer against him.

"Cold?"

"No." The word was a whisper, muffled against his shirtfront. He held her just a little longer, then eased her to her feet and stood up.

"Into the tub." He had to get her away from him, or he wouldn't be able to give her the time he'd promised.

She balanced herself on his arm as she stepped into the deep tub, then sighed with pleasure as the warm water closed around her legs. And he thought of what she'd risked, coming to him, and determined to let her set the pace.

"Shall I tie back your hair?"

She nodded, and he found the pink ribbon and helped her bind her hair up on top of her head, more loosely this time. Then she sank into the water, resting the back of her neck on the rolled rim, until she was immersed from the neck down.

Her eyes were closed, her mouth open, and as he watched her he marveled at his good fortune in falling in love with such a totally sensual creature.

He wasn't sure how much time passed before she opened her eyes, looked directly at him, and held out her hand. His shirt was up over his head in an instant. He'd kicked off his shoes and stockings at dinner, and now merely had to unfasten his breeches and strip them off.

She averted her head when his fingers went to the fastening, and this surprising bit of modesty charmed him.

He lowered himself into the water across from her, and the level rose, forcing her to open her eyes and push herself slightly higher. She started as she felt his hands encircle her foot, then bit her lip as his fingers dug into her calf and began to rub her leg.

"Sore?" he asked.

She nodded, then closed her eyes and sighed with pure pleasure as his skilled fingers gently soothed the tension out of her limb. This was another skill he'd acquired during his travels, this incredible knowledge of the human body and what felt precisely right.

He finished the one leg and started with the other.

"Why did you come to me tonight?"

"I missed you."

She said it so simply, so artlessly, that it touched him. Yet he saw something, a new knowledge behind her eyes, and he wondered if that was the only reason.

Already we're keeping secrets from each other.

He didn't want it. At that exact moment, he realized how incomplete his life had been without her, both before he'd met her and after the murder.

It was no good this way. He'd been privy to enough disgusted male outbursts, always along the line of not understanding what the devil women wanted. He couldn't say he was any closer than any of his friends to discovering the truth about the fairer sex.

But he wanted to know all about this particular woman.

He let go of her other leg, then reached for her hand.

"Cinda, there are things we have to talk about."

She seemed frightened for an instant, then slowly nodded her head. He knew what direction her mind was racing.

"Nothing like that." He curled his fingers tighter around hers. "I don't want any other woman but you."

He could see her visibly relax, then she tried to smile, and her courage in the face of his blundering broke his heart, just a little.

He reached for the scented soap on the table with his free hand, then pulled her closer.

He washed her with great tenderness, keeping his touch caring and not sensual. And as he did so, he thought of the fact that probably no one in her life had pampered her or seen to her needs for a long time. And William was surprised at how strongly he wanted to be the one.

The water was cooling as he helped her out of the tub, wrapped her in several of the thick towels, then sat with her in front of the fire. He took both her hands in his own, then leaned forward and spoke.

"If I tell you why I didn't come for you after Rosalind died, will you promise me you'll do exactly as I ask of you?"

He could tell she felt a sense of foreboding as she looked up into his tense face. And he remembered the first time he'd seen her, how innocent she had been.

And you took that innocence, and it has cost her.

He'd taken her virginity, and now he was taking her innocence again. Destroying it. For he knew, from bitter experience, that once you had knowledge of how dark and evil the world could be, your life was never the same.

"Will?" She touched his cheek. "Don't be afraid. You can confide in me."

William thought of himself as a fair man. But he knew where Cinda was concerned, he was selfish. He would risk her losing an even more precious sort of innocence rather than have her not remain a part of his life.

But I cannot risk her life.

He captured her fingers, then kissed them.

"I didn't want to believe you would leave me," she whispered. "I knew there had to be a reason."

He relaxed, and for an instant let himself believe they would escape the nightmare. He could survive anything as long as nothing happened to her.

"I wouldn't have left you without one."

Relief flooded her features, and she started to speak, then hesitated.

"Go on," he urged.

"I don't know if I can promise you anything until I know the truth. About what happened."

"You must, for I cannot tell you until I know I have your word."

She hesitated again. "Tell me," she whispered.

"Promise me," he replied.

He knew she was considering arguing with him, and decided to forestall her.

"I have my reasons, Cinda, and you must respect them. Now, promise me."

Slowly, almost reluctantly, she nodded her head. He helped her up, then assisted her into his dressing gown. She stood silently, watching him while he briskly rubbed himself dry and donned his breeches and shirt.

Then, lighting a beeswax candle from the fire, he slid his free arm around her waist and led her out the door.

CHAPTER

5

"Murder?"

Cinda couldn't look away from William, from the anguish in his eyes as he quietly finished telling her all he knew. She sensed instinctively he'd spared her the more brutal parts, and wondered if that had been wise. For her imagination, left unchecked, ran rampant with thoughts of what had been done to her youngest stepsister.

He'd brought her back to his bedroom and sat her down in one of the chairs in front of the fire. During the course of the story, she had desperately needed the comfort of his touch, and now she sat on his lap, staring unseeing into the flames. Their warmth barely touched her; she felt ice-cold inside. Numb. Shadows danced across the ceiling, and where moments before the room had seemed safe and comforting, Cinda knew she would not sleep easily this night, nor many after.

Murder.

Rosalind was murdered.

And Will believes the killer meant to kill me. To make sure we could never be together.

She felt violated, as if this unseen, unknown man had come into the relative safety of her life and torn it wide open.

Chance. Fate. Words whose meanings she'd never really pondered before. Now she couldn't stop thinking about them. She glanced away from William, guilt washing over her.

If Rosalind hadn't been so in love with the idea of love, if she hadn't gone out that night, if she hadn't looked so much like her, if the girl had arrived at their arranged meeting place moments later, if the killer had managed to find her instead . . .

If, if, if . . . It was enough to drive a person mad. She looked back up at William, wondering how he'd managed to live with the knowledge so long, wondering at the rumors that had swept the city.

Lost his mind, he did. Poor bloke, when he found her dead, he threw back his head and howled like a wolf.

Lost his mind. She wouldn't have blamed him if he had.

She was not a stranger to cruelty in the world, and had long since ceased thinking like a wealthy man's pampered, sheltered daughter, a luxury she could no longer afford. Nan's intrusion into the Townshend household had caused her to adapt quickly to the various roles forced upon her.

Where once she would have never left her father's house without a chaperon, now she was sent out into the streets whenever Nan's whims needed to be satisfied. Before she'd never given a thought to spending coin, but now she bought nothing and her meager sum of money stayed securely hidden. Her hands, once smooth, soft, and ladylike, were an angry red and severely chapped.

She had been taught all manner of attending to a household, in preparation for the day she would marry and see to her husband's. Now she did backbreaking servant's work from sunup to far past sundown.

None of this had broken her. She'd become used to Nan's endlessly petty manipulations, but even her stepmother had her limits. She might want to marry her off, get her away from her daughters, but Cinda was sure she would never want to see her murdered.

She closed her eyes tightly as an image of Rosalind's slightly scared, pale little face filled her mind. Try as she might, Cinda couldn't help wondering what last thoughts had gone through the girl's mind, or if she had even been conscious of her killer.

Her throat felt unbearably tight, but she forced the whispered words out. She had to know.

"Did she—did she know? At the end, I mean? Did she suffer, Will?"

"No."

She sensed he was still protecting her from the worst of it. Tears burned behind her eyelids as she thought of how scared Rosalind must have been.

Poor, sweet, gentle Rosalind. She'd been no match for her mother. The few times Cinda had been witness to their arguments, Nan had been cruel and abrupt with the younger girl, interrupting her and mocking her, making her feel small and insignificant.

And Cinda knew, from the few swiftly whispered discussions she'd had with Rosalind in the garden, that the girl had wanted to get away from her mother.

Was she trying to escape with us the night of our elopement? And did I encourage those dreams?

So lacking in love from her own family, the girl had spun fairy dreams of being taken away from her mother's house by a knight on a white stallion. Rosalind had thought of nothing but love, and had been truly delighted when she'd discovered the love letter William had written.

If she hadn't found it, if he'd never written it, if you'd never met him, *if, if, if*—

Cinda covered her face with her hands as guilt and pain overwhelmed her. If not for her actions, Rosalind might still be alive . . .

William embraced her, his arms completely encircling her within their warmth. She was curled in his lap, as if by making herself smaller she could somehow get away from all he'd told her. Now, her head down, her hair covering her face, she couldn't stop the tears.

Tears for a dreamstruck girl, who had committed no sin worthy of the ending she'd found. Whose only error had been to be in the wrong place at the wrong time.

Oh, Rosalind, you took the violence meant for me . . . And if not for me . . .

She started to shake violently, and felt Will's arm around her, warm and steady.

"Cinda?"

She had to look at him, to answer the concern she heard in his voice. Though she would have far preferred to have stayed hidden away forever, the one thing she'd learned in the past few years was that life, however painful, had to be faced.

He'd poured her a glass of brandy and now offered it to her. The amber liquid glowed softly. The crystal glass sparkled, catching the light from the fire, but Cinda felt no warmth from its flames. She shook her head, then put a hand over her mouth, as if she could somehow contain all she felt with the simple gesture.

"Take it," he said, his voice gentle.

Cinda tried to reach for the small crystal glass, but it was as if her hand belonged to someone else. It started to shake. She barely heard him set the glass down. He tightened his arms around her and rose from the chair, his movements effortless. Twining her arms tightly around his neck, she buried her face in his shirtfront and closed her eyes.

William tucked her into his bed, then went back toward the fire, picked up the glass of brandy, and brought it to her. She thought of refusing it, but recognized the implacable expression in his dark eyes.

"Drink it, darling. You'll never sleep otherwise."

It felt so strange to have someone taking care of her. She was so used to doing for others, then falling into her uncomfortable bed at night completely exhausted. Now, with William, she realized how much she'd missed being cared for.

She took his hand in hers, then brought it up to her lips and kissed the back of it. Her tears flowed freely, as both emotion and exhaustion overtook her.

"Drink, darling. Then you'll sleep." His voice roughened. "I won't leave you alone. I'll be here beside you when you wake."

She smiled up at him tremulously, and he brushed her cheekbone lightly with his knuckle.

"I love you," she said, her voice soft and trembling with anguish. For a moment she thought she saw pain in his eyes, but then he was calmly offering her the glass. She downed the spirits in one fiery swallow, then eased her head down on the pillow as he turned back and tucked the bedclothes securely around her.

William lay down beside her, carefully, outside the covers. Cinda turned her face toward him, feeling the coolness of the pillow against her cheek. He was staring up at the canopy. She knew he hadn't wanted to tell her about Rosalind. He'd wanted to spare her that knowledge.

The thought of her impending nuptials seemed so inconsequential compared to murder, and she resolved not to tell him as yet. Her problems could wait.

"Will?"

He glanced toward her, his expression unreadable.

"Thank you for telling me." She reached out above the covers and took his hand in her own.

He shifted to his side, facing her, but still keeping a certain amount of distance between them.

"All I've managed to do is bring pain into your life, and now danger—"

"No! No, Will, don't you understand? We can face anything, as long as we face it together." She turned her head slowly, feeling the effects of the brandy. His arm came around her then, and she snuggled closer, determined to make him understand.

"Anything," she whispered, suddenly so very tired.

She sensed he was displeased, yet before she could ponder his mood, the brandy began to affect her and she couldn't find the strength to answer him. Cinda rarely drank spirits, and the spirits were clouding her thoughts with cobwebs. Her eyelids were so terribly heavy, her body felt so warm . . .

Cinda closed her eyes, and darkness finally claimed her.

Her words hovered in his mind. *As long as we face it together.*

Never.

William lay in bed, Cinda sleeping quietly beside him. Her breathing was deep and gentle, and as he watched her face in repose he knew he could not go on living should something happen to her.

It was selfish, thinking only of his needs, what he wanted, how he desired things to be done. He couldn't help it. This mere slip of a girl had managed to rip his heart wide open, laying bare his emotions for all to see.

He loved her passionately, yet a part of him resented her just as much. For exposing his deepest needs to himself, making him feel more than he ever had in his life.

She couldn't possibly understand how it felt to believe yourself incapable of such ordinary feelings. And then realizing that love made you just that—an ordinary, vulnerable man.

He couldn't be vulnerable now. There was too much at stake. What he wanted, more than anything, was to tuck Cinda away in a safe place, track down this madman, and put an end to his sick game. Then he would marry Cinda, bring her to his home, and take care of her.

But he could not put her in danger. Though he would never have admitted his weaknesses to anyone, he could not lie to himself.

You couldn't go on if something happened to her.

Still, he continued the silent argument with his soul.

So is it for your sake or hers that you want her out of it? Are you acting out of love or simply insisting you have your way once again?

He didn't want to examine his thoughts too closely. The night was always a dangerous time for him, alone with his thoughts. And his conscience.

The dream was always the same. He was running through darkness, at night, alone, his heart pounding, terrified, hearing Cinda's screams and knowing he was helpless to save her.

He turned his head and looked at her, almost as if to reassure himself she was still near. The light from the fire touched her delicate profile and highlighted the gentle rise and fall of her breasts.

She was safe. She was here. And she was his.

He moved gently across the large bed, wanting to be closer to her, wanting to breathe in the soft scent that was hers alone. Still outside the heavy covers, he lay closely curled around her, his cheek against her hair, and finally closed his eyes.

He could sleep now, with her by his side, safe in his arms.

Not far from William's townhouse in the same fashionable district, dim candlelight illuminated a small room on the third floor of another townhouse. All around, dwellings were dark and quiet, save for this small, shimmering light.

Inside the room, a woman sat at a writing desk, her quill poised above a piece of parchment, her face tense.

She would have been attractive had she not been so obviously ill. Hair, once a rich chestnut-brown, was now sparse and dull, pulled back neatly in a girlish braid. Her complexion was pale, save for a few freckles. Even the rich, sapphire-blue velvet dressing gown could not disguise the thinness or frailty of her limbs.

She was a woman who had once had considerable beauty, but time and despair seemed to have etched its lessons firmly upon her countenance.

The hand above the parchment wavered, as if in consideration of what she was about to do. She rested her arm against the desk, every movement an effort. Then, with renewed determination in her gentle blue eyes, the woman began to write.

Slowly, with great effort, the words appeared in a fine, spidery script. *To William Stedman, the only man who will truly understand this story. I pray you, William, be merciful, if only in memory of me and what we might have shared had I not been so very frightened of my brother.*

She paused, considering what she had just written. Then, determination clear in her expression, the woman continued writing.

The only sounds in the bedroom were the snap and hiss of the fire and the scratch of quill against parchment. She wrote slowly at first, then began to pick up speed as her thoughts tumbled out.

The woman wrote feverishly, not stopping until she set the quill down hours later, exhausted. The sun was just barely coming up over the horizon when she pushed herself away from the desk. Slowly, painfully, she stood. Carefully bracing herself against various pieces of furniture, she limped to her bed and lay down, and within minutes fell into an exhausted slumber.

A small smile touched her lips, and her hand, resting on the pillow against her cheek, was clenched, as if still in possession of the quill.

William slept peacefully, and dreamed of the first time he'd seen Cinda, in her mother's garden.

He'd come home that evening, and even Henry had noticed the difference.

"Good evening, Your Grace. I trust it was a pleasant one."

"Indeed it was, Henry."

William had smiled as he'd mounted the stairs and headed toward his study. Henry had barely been able to contain his curiosity, and he wondered how long the older man would wait before he would ask a carefully worded question. For Henry wanted nothing more than for him to marry and be happy.

A thought that had never appealed to William—until tonight.

He remained silent as his valet brought him his usual glass of brandy, then waited expectantly by his side. Henry was not to be budged until he'd been reassured his instincts were correct. William sighed, lifted the glass to his lips, took a sip, then set it down.

"All right. Damn it all, I've met a woman—"

"Splendid, sir!"

It touched him, seeing Henry so happy for him. For a moment he wondered what it would be like, living a life in service to someone else. And he thought of Cinda, of the countless ways he wanted to please and protect her. In that instant, William had a small inkling of what Henry had always felt for his family.

"And"—Henry was treading carefully now, not wanting to upset him—"you'll be seeing this woman again?"

"Most certainly."

"That is good news of the best sort. I take it she is not the sort of woman—" Henry paused, searching for words, and William was astounded to see a bright red flush slowly creep up over the collar of his starched shirt.

Henry, embarrassed? The night was full of surprises.

"Go on," he said, his voice gentle. He and his valet had an odd relationship, rather more like father and son than either cared to admit. Now William suddenly found that it was important to him to find out what Henry was thinking.

"I was just about to say that it seems as if you've found a woman with a fortune." His sharp blue eyes twinkled, and William smiled slowly as he remembered their earlier conversation.

"I've found a woman *worth* a fortune, Henry."

"Splendid, sir. This is simply splendid."

William finished the brandy; Henry took up the empty glass and walked silently toward the study door. When he reached it, he glanced back at his charge and said, "I'm quite happy for you, sir, as I'm sure the entire staff will be."

"Don't say anything to them yet."

"Sir?" Now Henry looked rather uncertain, and William regretted his impulsive words.

"It's simply that—" He glanced down at his hands, tightly folded together on top of the desk. It was a foreign thing, this talking of feelings, and it didn't feel comfortable at all.

He could sense Henry's unease, and was just about to dismiss the man when his valet took a deep breath and spoke.

"You're not sure if she has the requisite feelings for you."

He nodded his head. It wasn't often that William found himself in a quandary about anything, and he didn't like it.

"Might I offer a suggestion, sir?"

"Certainly."

"It has always been my impression that women are rather fond of romance. In fact, I'd go so far as to say there are not many who are capable of resisting it."

"Romance?"

"You must know what I mean, sir."

"No, I do not. Enlighten me, Henry."

Again, William saw traces of a blush flow up the portly man's neck. "Long walks in the park. Bonbons. Ribbons and lace and all that sort of frippery. Love poems. Flowers." He paused, his face a bright pink. "Surely you must understand what I mean."

It was a most extraordinary conversation, and William was deeply touched by the lengths Henry was willing to go to ensure another generation of Stedmans.

"I believe I do." He got up from behind the desk and walked over to the fire blazing brightly in the fireplace. Sitting down in one of the large chairs by the hearth, he looked up at his trusted valet and grinned.

"You'll like her, Henry."

"I'm sure I would like anyone you chose." Henry cleared his throat and once again became the perfectly discreet servant. "Is there anything else I might do for you this evening before you retire?"

"No, thank you. You've done more than enough."

His servant was almost to the door when William spoke, so softly he wasn't sure if his valet heard the words.

"Thank you, Henry."

Alone, William gazed into the dancing flames and thought of Cinda.

Romance.

Henry was right, of course. His own approach, reaching for Cinda and kissing her in the garden, had gotten him nowhere. She'd been frightened of him, and he couldn't have that. He would have to woo her, court her, gentle her fears. But first he had to convince her he was a man to be trusted. How to do that?

Slowly, and with great enjoyment, William went over every detail of the evening in his mind. He took great care to try to remember everything about Cinda, what she'd liked and disliked, what would win her favor.

The thought slipped into his mind so easily. What better present for a gardener than flowers? And flowers that would speak the language of love, and reassure her most eloquently his intentions were honorable.

He smiled, and closed his eyes. Happiness was new to him, this light, buoyant feeling that chased out the darkness.

Just before he fell asleep in the comfortable chair in front of the fire, William resolved he would win her, claim her as his, marry her. And in his heart of hearts, he found he was happy, for he had finally, unequivocally, fallen deeply and completely in love.

Cinda came awake slowly, as if traveling back from a great distance. For the briefest of moments, she didn't remember where she was, then before she even opened her eyes she smelled William's scent on her pillow.

Within seconds she remembered it all; where she was, why she was here, and what had happened mere hours ago.

How was it possible that within minutes William had shattered her world all over again? The first time he'd done so, they'd met in the garden. Now he had caught her up in a dark and dangerous threat to her very survival.

Yet I cannot find it in my heart to blame him.

The thought came to her instantly, and she slowly opened her eyes, still reluctant to return to a world where such horrible things existed.

Her gaze fell on William, sitting by the fire and staring into the flames. She could imagine his thoughts, for she knew he was an honorable man. Guilt. Even shame. Certainly sorrow. He hadn't known Rosalind well, only from what she had chosen to tell him. But he would have recognized her, even bruised and battered.

She didn't move, not wanting to call attention to herself. Her body ached with tiredness, and she wondered at the shock she had sustained. Nothing in her entire existence had prepared her for the fact that there was a man loose in London who, if he knew of her identity, would want to take her life.

Fear started to close in around her, and she kept her eyes open, determined not to succumb to its grasp. Cinda concentrated on the fire, on its light and warmth, on William's averted face. Just the fact he was here, that he hadn't been angry with her and still loved her, was enough for now.

As much as she loved him, she didn't want to intrude upon his private thoughts. Her eyes closed despite her attempts to stay awake, and Cinda knew sleep would soon claim her. Not wanting to return to those dark thoughts where images of a killer dwelt, Cinda drifted toward sleep remembering. Dreaming of a happier, safer time . . .

She was working in the kitchen. Cook was saying something to her, and she couldn't hear her because of the sudden confusion outside. Then Robbie was racing down the stairs, his ginger-colored hair windblown and a wide smile on his freckled face.

"You'd best check your bedchamber, love."

"And why should I trouble myself to climb those stairs when I don't have to?" Cinda answered.

She enjoyed teasing Robbie. Everyone in the household did the same because he gave as good as he got. Cook had borne eleven children, and she'd always told Cinda, "Robbie was the one who made me laugh." He'd stayed on, in service to the Townshends, in order to look after his mother. And she loved him for it. Cinda considered him the brother she'd never had.

"Your gentleman friend has been up to some mischief."

That remark caught Cinda's attention. She swung around, staring up at Robbie, whose lips were twitching, threatening a smile. Cook was clearly incredulous, and miffed at the fact that she had no idea what this was about. Now she looked to Cinda for a full explanation.

"I'm on m' way," Robbie remarked, giving the sash of Cinda's apron a tweak. "Don't even try to make up a story for her. Mum's tough, she'll have the truth ferreted out within the minute."

He sauntered out the door, and Cinda was left alone to face Cook. The woman crossed her arms over her ample bosom and eyed Cinda sharply.

"And who is this *gentleman*?"

Cinda toyed with a scrap of piecrust on the table, not daring to meet the older woman's gaze. Cook was like a fiercely protective mother hen to those she loved, and Cinda knew she would not be pleased.

"I met him last night."

"The dinner party?"

She nodded her head, praying she could somehow hide the intense reaction she'd felt toward William. She didn't understand it herself. Her feelings were still too new.

"And what were you doing, miss, anywhere near one of *her* parties?"

"I wasn't anywhere near. He was in the garden."

She was aware of her mistake the moment Cook's silence stretched just a heartbeat too long. Horrified, she glanced up and met the woman's disapproving gaze.

"You were *alone* with him?"

She hesitated a moment, then nodded her head.

Cook threw up her flour-covered hands and shook her head. Turning her back on Cinda, she stomped over to the oven and, using her apron to protect her hands, opened it. Reaching for the peel, she checked the currant buns inside, then began to take them out.

Cinda couldn't stand the silence. Cook was her dearest friend in the world, as well as the last link she had to her mother. The thought of the woman being displeased with her was more than she could bear.

"He wasn't—he's not like—"

"They're all alike, every one of 'em!"

"No, he was a gentleman, he—"

"Hmph. Scalawags, all of 'em. Did he try anything?"

She could feel hot color flooding her face, see Cook's calculating assessment.

"Did he touch you?"

Silence.

"*Did* he?"

"A . . . kiss."

"And?"

"I ran away."

At this, the woman smiled. "Now you're showing some sense."

"I didn't know what else to do."

"You? With that smart little tongue of yours?"

"I didn't know—"

"Yes you did, and that's why you ran and that's why you showed some sense. He's a gentleman, you say?"

She nodded her head.

Cook turned away from her and stared into the fire, her gaze intent on the dancing flames. Cinda sensed some of the fight leaving the woman from the way the tense set of her shoulders slowly relaxed.

When Cook finally turned to face her, she paused. The woman seemed reluctant to voice her thoughts, and Cinda knew the words would be difficult for her friend to utter.

"It can only end one way, you know that." Cook's tone was softer now.

Cinda nodded her head again, this time blinking back tears, surprised by how badly she wished it could be different.

"She won't let you keep a baby, you know that." Cook glanced at the door leading to the dining room, parlor, and the rest of the townhouse. Her expression betrayed how little she thought of her mistress.

"I know."

"She'd force you to rid yourself of it, and that would tear your heart out."

Cinda nodded her head, then furtively swiped at her cheek with her fingers. She was tired, that was the reason for her easy tears. She turned her head away as Cook set down the peel, wiped her hands on her apron, and came swiftly to her side, putting a comforting arm around her.

"I'm overstepping my bounds, of that I'm sure. But I'm only telling you what your mum, God rest her, would have told you, what she would want me to tell you. You can barely survive, let alone with a little one tugging at your skirts—"

They were interrupted as Robbie stuck his head in the door.

"God's blood, Mum, let her go up and see what he's brought! Why are the two of you standing there sniveling when Cinda has a surprise upstairs? Go on with you!" He darted in the door and took his mother's hand, then turned toward Cinda.

"I'll just keep her here so's you'll have a chance to go see—"

Cinda wiped her face with her hands and cleared her throat. "No, I'd like her to come with me."

Robbie looked down at his mother, affection clear in his expression. "I warrant you've never seen the like."

Cook let go of his hand and smoothed the front of her apron, then ran her fingers through her close-cropped, gray curls. "Have a care, my man. Your mum used to cut quite a figure."

"Oh, ho, got your dander up, have I?" He started to laugh, but before the sound was out, Cook clamped a warning hand over his mouth.

"Where have your wits fled to? If she hears us—"

Robbie deftly eluded her restraint. "She's gone to one of her friends for tea. I saw the carriage leave almost an hour ago."

"The three of them, as well?"

"Aye, the daughters went with her. The sow and her piglets are out a' the pen."

"Well, then," Cook said. "I'm curious as to what your gentleman thinks is a proper present."

"And how do you know it's not the gentleman himself?" Robbie asked, then ducked out of reach of a disapproving pinch.

"Robert, if you were to let Cinda—"

"Mum, it's a jest, to be sure! I wouldn't leave her alone with him!"

"I should hope not!" Cook muttered. Taking one last glance around the kitchen, she offered Cinda her arm and the three of them swept out of the kitchen toward the stable.

"This had . . . better be . . . worth the climb," Cook muttered to her son, five steps from the top of the steep stairway. She was huffing and blowing, and they had taken the stairs slowly for her sake.

"I wouldn't let you come all this way if it wasn't," he assured her.

His mother continued her muttering. "Probably a tiny bunch of flowers he picked in the park. Or perhaps a pretty ribbon his last mistress had no liking for. Men can be devious creatures, Cinda! I don't want you going all soft for him over a few posies."

"I won't."

"Now chocolates, that's another story. If he's brought you a box of bonbons—"

"Here you go, Mum." Robbie practically carried his mother up the final step, and the three of them stood on the narrow landing before Cinda's closed bedroom door.

Cook panted slightly, then waved a hand at Cinda. "Go on in. I'll . . . catch up with you."

Cinda stayed at her side, worried at the way she was breathing, but Robbie indicated the door with a quick jerk of his head.

"Go on, Mum'll be awright."

She hesitated outside, wondering what William had decided to bring her. Whatever it was, it would reveal how he felt toward her, and that gave her pause.

What was it gentlemen usually brought to women they cared for? She didn't know, having never received a gift from a gentleman in her life.

Her heart in her mouth, she opened the door.

Immediately after, she grabbed the latch as her knees started to tremble and her hand flew up to her mouth.

The flowers were everywhere, hundreds of them, covering her bed, the trunk, the chair, placed in the windowsill, even on the floor. Lilies, white and delicately fragranced, with deep pink inner petals and rich green foliage. The sweet scent filled the small bedchamber, and Cinda bit her finger hard to keep from crying.

She knew what he was telling her before she picked up the first bloom. Madonna lilies. Only a gardener would know their significance.

For they symbolized virginity.

She held a fragile bloom to her face, feeling the softness of its petals, inhaling its scent. Turning, Cinda saw Cook standing in the doorway, Robbie still supporting her. The woman was speechless.

"Just some posies he picked up in the park, eh, Mum?" Robbie said softly. Then he led her over to one of the chairs, swept off the blooms covering the seat, and settled his mother upon it. Turning, he started down the stairs, the sound of his boots echoing back up to them.

Cinda stared out the window overlooking the stables. Her throat was unbearably tight with emotion; she couldn't look at Cook without betraying herself completely. She brought the bloom back up to her face, trying to control her trembling fingers.

"Ah, you've feelings for the man, don't you?" Cook's voice was flat, as if she recognized the futility of arguing with her.

Cinda nodded her head.

"And he does for you."

She heard the woman rise slowly, painfully, out of the chair. Cinda turned toward her, took a few steps, and grasped her arm, steadying her.

"I didn't mean for it to happen."

"Hush, it's nothing you can control." Cook smiled at her, but her mouth trembled. "We'll just have to make certain he treats you well."

Cinda put her arm around the woman, pulling her close. She glanced back around the room, taking in the enormity of what William had done. For just an instant she was frightened, sensing something had been set in motion that night she might not be strong enough to be a part of.

She glanced back down at Cook.

"I don't want things to change."

The woman's face was tired. In the pale afternoon sunlight slanting in the window she looked suddenly older.

"It's too late, my darling girl. They already have."

Battle plans were discussed around the fireplace.

"Don't make it too easy for him," Cook advised, sitting back in her favorite chair and toasting her stockinged feet.

"I'll try not to."

"He gets you wild, does he? Those men are the best kind of the lot, so long as you don't expect much more from them."

"I'll be careful."

"Make it hard for him." An amused smile lit the older woman's face. "Strictly a manner of speaking, of course."

Cinda laughed, immediately smothering the sound with her hand. Nan had been in quite a temper when she'd returned from her tea, and now she'd barely retired for the night.

"I won't have you going into it ignorant, if that's your choice. But make him wait, Cinda, because then you'll be able to tell if he truly cares for you. If he'll stay once he has what he wants."

Cinda leaned toward the fire, warming her hands. "And what is it that men truly want? Besides *that*."

"If I knew that, love, I'd be the richest woman in London." She reached across the small space separating their chairs and took hold of one of Cinda's hands.

"Have a care, my precious."

"I won't be foolish."

Cook narrowed her hazel eyes as she gazed thoughtfully into the fire.

"It's not you I'm worried about."

CHAPTER
ᣔᣗ 6 ᣗᣔ

Thus began, in Cinda's estimation, what was probably the strangest courtship William Stedman could ever imagine.

Cook helped her ascertain when Nan and her loathsome daughters were out of the house. Rosalind, the youngest of the three, spent most of her time with her head in a book in the library. Robbie ran messages back and forth between the two dwellings. And William was the perfect soul of discretion.

But he didn't take kindly to having Robbie as a chaperon.

"It was Mum's idea, not mine," Robbie said carefully. Cinda could tell he was not entirely at ease with William, which she could understand perfectly.

Neither was she.

William was eyeing Robbie as if he wanted to pick him up and throw him out of the garden, and Cinda could feel the coiled tension inside him. She knew he was angry at Robbie's assumption that he meant to do her harm.

Their first few meetings took place on the same stone bench where he'd kissed her. Conversation was stilted and awkward, with Robbie looking as miserable as both of them felt.

And Cinda was astonished, for William not only endured these strange meetings, but continued to call on her, bringing her small presents. A ribbon the same shade of green as her eyes. A sweetly scented pomander. Flowers, or a plant for her garden. French lace for her petticoat.

Cook retaliated by insisting on making refreshments. Strawberry tarts, cherry pies, and assorted tea breads. She confiscated minute amounts of coffee, tea, and sugar from Nan's pantry, and had Robbie leave Cinda's side just long enough to fetch the various foodstuffs she made.

The weeks that followed were full of revelations for Cinda. She discovered primarily that William was a patient man. He had a sense of humor, a gentle way of being with her that captivated her heart even further.

Each time he left her, they shared a chaste kiss, under Robbie's watchful eye. And she thought of that first kiss in the garden, and wondered what he thought when he kissed her now.

But eventually, after almost three months, he took a stand.

"I won't have him with us anymore," he announced one evening. She knew from his low, quiet tone of voice that this was one discussion she was not going to win.

She took Robbie aside, and they walked a short distance down the path, until they were out of earshot.

"Tonight, why don't you sit on the bench by the willow. That way he can't see you, but you're still close enough in case I need you."

"Mum will have m' *hide* if she finds out. She doesn't want you alone with him."

"I'm beginning to trust him."

He hesitated, then said, "He's a good man, Cinda. I like him. But I still won't see you taken advantage of."

"He won't hurt me."

"How do you know that?"

"He won't." She gave him a kiss on the cheek. "And your mum won't find out. Just give me a little more time."

She approached the clearing to find William staring in the direction she and Robbie had taken.

A short silence ensued, then he walked over to the stone bench and sat down.

"Come here."

She thought of disobeying, but temptation proved a stronger incentive. Slowly, watching him carefully, she went to his side. Positioning herself a certain distance from him, she sat down, taking an inordinate amount of time to arrange the skirt of her gray woolen dress.

Badly frayed and patched, the dress was still clean, the material warm against the early autumn chill. It was also too small, and she knew he had a clear silhouette of the upper half of her body. But she'd added a ruffle to the skirt, so at least her ankles were covered. And she'd styled her hair in a most becoming fashion, and threaded her prized green ribbon through the curls.

"Are you still frightened of me?" The way William asked the question, it seemed to her he'd pondered asking it for some time.

"Yes." Then she saw the look on his face, the quick flash of frustration and hurt in his eyes, and she hurried to make him understand.

"Not of you. Of the . . . the way that I feel when I'm around you."

She could tell the exact moment when frustration left him and his familiar fighting spirit was rekindled.

"Then you do—feel differently around me. Tell me what it is you feel."

She frowned, and was concentrating so very hard it was with a sudden jump of awareness that she realized he was holding one of her hands. And sliding closer.

"As if I cannot take in a complete breath when you look at me that way."

"What way is that?"

"You know."

"Do I?" He seemed to sense her own frustration with the situation, and slowly brought her hand up to his lips. But this time, instead of kissing the back of her hand, he turned it and pressed an entirely different sort of kiss into her palm.

Her free hand tightened on the cold stone bench, needing to feel the rough texture against her palm, needing that slight anchor against the feelings that were flooding her senses. And she thought of being alone with William, in her bed, and what it would feel like to have those lips touching other places on her body.

With a muffled cry, she snatched her hand away, then brought both of them up to her face. She felt confused, overwhelmed by all he had introduced her to.

And there is so much more . . .

It seemed her body was not her own when he was near; it was as if it craved some sort of final completion her mind still remained unaware of.

Cinda was achingly aware of him, sitting on the bench beside her. With all her heart, she hoped he would understand her feelings if she tried to put them into words, and she prayed he wouldn't laugh at her.

His fingers felt hot against the skin of her neck. Her hands left her face and she almost jerked away again until she realized he was merely smoothing a curl back over her shoulder.

"Tell me." His voice was low and soothing. The clearing was bathed in dusky light, and Cinda knew Robbie couldn't watch over her much longer. The horses had to be fed, and Cook would be needing her help.

"You frighten me. The feelings frighten me. It's as if—I'm not myself when I'm around you. You make me want to—you make me imagine things I'm certain no decent woman thinks of."

"I'm certain they do."

She turned to face him on the bench, nervously pulling on a strand of her hair. "It's no mystery to you, I'm sure of that. Don't you understand, Will, you know what's going to happen, and even after that happens between us, you know what the outcome will be. You *decide* it."

She ignored the sudden change in his expression, the sense of knowledge that was now in his dark blue eyes, and stumbled on, desperate to make him understand, staring down at her hands, now folded in her lap.

"I know that men don't put as much importance in the same things women do. I—I don't think I'm as strong as you are, Will, and if you love me as you want to and then leave me, I'll die."

He was very quiet, and she chanced a glimpse at him, peeking up from beneath her lashes. He'd gone very still, yet continued to stare at her, his expression intense.

"Tell me what you think is going to happen between us," he said, his voice very soft.

"I think," she began slowly, feeling utterly miserable, "that this particular story has been played out many times."

"And pray tell, how does that story go?"

"I will surrender to you," she said, her voice barely above a whisper, "and you will enjoy me for a time and then find a much more suitable woman to take my place. You might even be kind enough to set me up in a house of my own, but

I would refuse that, and then you would certainly tire of me. I think things would reach a point where I would be too difficult. Too much trouble to you."

She chanced another glimpse at him, and he was looking out over the garden, a rather bleak expression on his face. A tiny muscle in his jaw jumped, tightly, and she was fascinated by the control she sensed he was exerting.

"I would ask of you that when the time comes when you cease to regard me, pray don't use me ill, nor treat me cold-ly—"

The look on his face stopped her in midsentence.

"Too much trouble," he replied, his voice so low she barely heard it. "Too much trouble. You find me in this garden with a thorn in my thumb, and from that moment on I have been in constant pain. I've given in to your every whim, yielded to your every desire, endured a chaperon the likes of which I have never seen before and hope never to see again—" William took a deep breath, his eyes on her all the while. "And restrained myself from touching you, kissing you, taking you right here in this garden."

He was angry now, yet she wasn't afraid for she knew he would not hurt her. Cinda listened carefully, knowing there was much yet to understand about this man.

"And you think you would be difficult? Madam, you *are* difficult."

He attempted to take her hand, but she pulled away from him, rigid with pain.

"I'm sorry—"

"Don't be. For you value yourself and don't wish to be involved in an arrangement such as the one you just described. But how you could *ever* think I would hold you in such low esteem is what enrages me."

She locked gazes with him, shocked.

"You *are* an innocent. Had I wanted you in the manner you think I do, I would have taken you out of this garden the night I met you. By force, if necessary. I wouldn't have *asked* you if you wanted to be set up in a house, I would have simply *put* you there."

She tried to pull away, confused, but he caught her wrist in a tighter grip.

"Don't you understand what it is that I want from you?"

"Let me *go*!" Cinda struggled furiously now, ashamed at what she had revealed, and how foolish he thought her to be. She'd exposed what had been hidden in her heart and hurt him terribly. Now she didn't want to face him.

"Stop." His hands came up and cradled her face.

"Please, Will, let me go—"

"I can't. Stop, darling, you'll hurt yourself."

She was starting to cry and hating herself for it all at the same time. Desperately in need of some sort of comfort, she lay in his arms, her cheek against his waistcoat.

"What is it you want from me? I know I must seem abysmally ignorant, but I don't know what it is you want. Will, please tell me and then we can go back to the way we were before—"

"We can never do that."

"Please," she whispered. "Please don't leave me because of what I said."

His arms came around her, solid and strong. She felt the warmth of his hand, gently stroking the top of her head. When he finally answered, his voice was low and filled with emotion.

"We can't go back to the way we were before because I want to marry you."

She went perfectly still, then slowly moved away from him until she could look up into his face, touch his cheek with her fingers.

"Marry you?" She could barely force the words out.

"Is it so terrible a thought?" He was making an attempt at being lighthearted, but she could see the wealth of emotion behind the carefully chosen words.

"Marry you." The implications of his words were finally beginning to penetrate her consciousness. To live with William for the rest of his life, be the mother of his children. To know that he loved her enough to want her with him every day of his life. To finally have a home where she belonged, and to know he would always be there.

"Oh, Will!" She threw her arms around him and burst into tears.

"What's this? What have you done to 'er?" Robbie had come into the clearing, and now looked worried.

"It's nothing to worry about," William said, his voice soothing as he held her against him.

"Cinda?"

"I'm fine, Robbie," she replied, her voice muffled. Cinda raised her tear-stained face and smiled at him over William's shoulder. "Don't worry. Go and feed the horses, I'll be out shortly."

"Don't be long."

Robbie left, still looking rather doubtful of the outcome. Cinda felt William's arms loosen, and she leaned back in them so she could look up at his face.

"You need a handkerchief," he observed.

She couldn't stop smiling, even when she took the small scrap of cloth from him and wiped her eyes, then blew her nose.

"Feel better?" he asked.

"Much."

"I have a ring for you. It belonged to my mother. I don't have it with me, as I hadn't intended to ask you in quite this way—"

She put her fingers to his lips, and when he looked down at her questioningly, she said, "I love you. I don't know when it happened, or how, but I do. I can't bring anything to this marriage—"

He grasped her hand swiftly. "You have no idea how much you give me—"

"—but I'll give you my heart, for the rest of my life. I'll love you so much, you'll never regret—"

"—I don't regret anything now, you have to understand that. I'm not asking you to marry me out of pity, Cinda. You may not believe this." And here, to her delight, his voice roughened with emotion. "But all of my life I've been waiting to love someone, to feel something for a woman beyond anything I've ever known. I thought I knew what it was, I guessed at it. But the night I first saw you in this garden, I knew I'd had no idea what it would really be like."

"You loved me even then?" She felt incredulous.

"I knew. The minute I saw you, I knew we belonged together. My God, why do you think I've endured week after week of being close to you but not being allowed to touch you? Why do you think I race over here any chance I can? I never thought to make you my mistress; I only thought of you gracing my home and possessing the only part of my heart I've ever wanted to give to a woman."

Tears came to her eyes again as she thought of how deeply her words must have wounded him. "I'm sorry. For what I said—"

"No, it was my fault. I thought you needed more time before I told you what my intentions were. I didn't . . . I didn't want you to be scared of me."

"I'm not. Scared of you. But I'm still scared of that."

He laughed softly, and she knew his confidence had returned in full. "You won't be."

"What if I disappoint you?"

"Never."

"What if—"

"Kiss me."

His hand was at the back of her neck, his face close to hers. She closed her eyes an instant before their lips met, and felt again the same sensations she'd experienced so long ago, that first night in the garden. He urged her lips apart and she felt his tongue inside her mouth as the kiss swiftly grew shockingly, thrillingly intimate.

Desire kindled within her. When she felt his fingers slip inside the neckline of her bodice, she didn't deny him what he wanted.

The touch of his fingers against her bare breast caused her to cry out, the sound muffled against his lips. His hand caressed her, cupping the soft flesh, then gently teasing the nipple.

Sensation, brilliant and overwhelming, made its presence known between her thighs, and Cinda pulled away from him, then glanced cautiously up at his face. She was breathing deeply, almost shaking in the aftermath of what he'd caused.

His hand was still inside her bodice, his other arm firmly around her waist. Without saying a word, she took his hand, kissed it, then held it in her own. She couldn't look at him, the sensations he'd engendered were overwhelming.

How disconcerting to find out your body could betray you.

He broke away, got up and walked the length of the clearing, then stood with his back turned toward her. Cinda's fingers shook as she adjusted her bodice. Her breasts ached, but the feeling was not unpleasant. She thought of when she would eventually come to his bed, and what he would do to her when that time came.

After a short interval, he walked back to the bench and

offered her his hand. She took it and he helped her to rise. Fingers entwined, they started back toward the townhouse.

"Sometimes I forget how innocent you are," he said.

She didn't reply, not trusting herself to speak.

"Still scared?"

She nodded her head, then blurted out her fear.

"What if I don't like it." She couldn't even face him. This was certainly not a fit topic of conversation, even for a betrothed couple.

"You will." She could hear the smile in his voice, and for just a moment desperately wished she possessed a small amount of his confidence.

They were almost to the edge of the garden when she tugged at his hand, pulling him back into the shadows.

"I have but one favor to ask of you. If I tell you what it is, will you promise to grant it?"

He studied her face, clearly puzzled, then said, "As long as you don't believe in a celibate married life, your favor is as good as granted."

"Would you come back tonight? To my bedchamber?"

She had shocked him again, she was certain of it.

"Why do you wish me to do this?"

"I don't want to spend the next few weeks dreading what is to come. I don't want to remain in fear for that long a time. Will, I want to know what it's like to be with you, and I want to make sure I please you."

His grip on her fingers tightened. "You please me now."

"But what if—"

"Madam, have you so little faith in me that you think I shall abandon you yet again if you don't fulfill my carnal inclinations?"

"Will!"

"If that was all I wanted, I could find it in any street in London for a pint of wine and a shilling."

"Haven't you ever been frightened of something, and wanted to face it so you knew exactly what it was you were frightened of? You've never felt that way?"

He released her then, and stalked back toward the heart of the garden, then stopped when he was several feet away. He turned to look at her, the expression in his eyes so fierce she backed slightly away from him.

"As you wish, madam." He came toward her, then cupped her face in his large hands so she couldn't look away from him.

"I want this to happen, more than you will ever know. I'll come back, and we'll lie in your bed and put an end to your fears tonight, for I cannot endure the thought of you being frightened of me."

"Thank you, Will."

"I'll meet you at the hour of ten, in the garden."

She nodded her head, not trusting herself to speak. And had the strangest sensation, of setting something in motion that couldn't be stopped, saying words she couldn't call back.

"Ten o'clock," he said again, letting her go.

She watched him until he rounded the corner of the house, then picked up her skirts and raced toward the kitchen.

Cinda stood by her bedchamber window overlooking the stableyard, and wished it were morning. By dawn, her fears would be gone, her knowledge complete. She would know what marriage to William involved, and not possess this feeling of dread that now consumed her.

Yet there was a small, secret part of her emotions that stubbornly remained excited. Full of anticipation. How could something that began with such sweetness be so very horrible? Why was she so frightened by an act that was ideally only consummated out of deepest love?

The only thing that kept her from renouncing her promise was the knowledge that William would never willingly hurt her.

That she had ever come to trust him was a fantastic event in itself. It was a fragile feeling, born out of the weeks he'd courted her. He'd shown her what kind of man he was, and what she'd seen had pleased her greatly. What had touched her most was his endless patience with the entire unorthodox arrangement. Hope, an emotion she'd not allowed herself to feel of late, had begun to bloom.

Now, facing the night and what it would bring, Cinda shivered and reached for her woolen shawl. She hoped William would bring a generous amount of his endless patience to her bed this evening.

He didn't even press you to do this. You were the one who didn't want to wait any longer.

She sat in the window and shifted her gaze so she was looking at the far end of the garden. It would be different tonight, knowing she wasn't going to stop him. Knowing that by the time she finally went to sleep, every mystery would be revealed to her.

She knew what happened, well enough. It was impossible to live in a large household and serve a family without hearing about it, for it seemed most people were obsessed with the entire business. Especially men.

As a servant, she was considered by her stepsisters to be someone they could talk in front of or around, never expecting an answer. They treated her as if she were deaf and dumb, the times they did not mock her. Many an afternoon she'd worked upstairs with Mary, pressing a ball gown, fixing a ruffle, stitching a torn seam, and all the while listening to her stepsister's love of gossip.

They talked quite frankly concerning their female friends' various escapades with the opposite sex, so Cinda had no illusions about what was going to happen. It seemed an awkward, embarrassing, even messy business at best, but something men never seemed to get enough of.

They must derive some pleasure from it, otherwise they would never take the chances they do in order to obtain it.

She was sure she could endure it. The kissing wasn't something she found repugnant; William had made that part quite pleasant. More than pleasant. Cinda brought her attention around to the great townhouse. Candlelight glowed in two of the upstairs bedrooms, and she knew her stepmother and stepsisters were still up, engrossed in the details of their own worlds. And she wistfully remembered what it was like to light a candle whenever one felt like it, as opposed to living in darkness.

Her thoughts skittered back to William, to the way his kisses made her feel. She knew what he wanted, on a purely physical level. But she was sure he would be faintly disgusted if he knew how he made her feel. If he even suspected that all thoughts of control flew from her mind when he merely glanced at her.

His kisses revealed a part of her temperament she was sure no real lady ever felt. Or if she felt such things, she never revealed the fact, and surely not to her betrothed.

And Cinda quietly despaired, knowing she would be hard-pressed to win this battle over her own passionate feelings.

How I wish I could be cool and aloof, mysterious and gracious, instead of feeling this—desire.

A dog barked somewhere in the distance. One of the horses in the stable neighed sharply; she heard the stomping of hooves and the swishing of tails. The scent of damp earth and green leaves drifted up from the garden. Flowers still bloomed, but all seemed poised in readiness for the winter ahead. Soon the garden would be blanketed in snow, all dazzling white and crusted in ice. She and Cook would spend long, dark evenings around the kitchen fire, trying to keep warm.

She wondered if she would still be in residence in this house, or if William would have taken her away by then. She would have to convince him to let her take Cook with her. Once both of them were ensconced in the Stedman household, Cinda would make sure Cook did as little work as possible. Perhaps William would let the older woman live with her as a companion of sorts. Cook's poor health was a constant worry to Cinda; it was only a matter of time before Nan turned the woman out into the streets.

Cinda took a deep, steadying breath.

Her garden would calm her. She would sit on the stone bench and wait for him. She would think of her mother, and try not to miss her on this night her comfort and reassurance were so desperately missed.

She was aware of him the moment he stepped into the clearing.

The night was surprisingly mild, the air soft and still. It was quiet in the garden, with no errant breeze to rustle the leaves or play havoc with her hair.

Cinda stared at him for a long moment from her position on the bench, then slowly rose and walked toward him. She wasn't sure what she wanted to see in his expression, but what she found was not what she'd expected.

She sensed he was nervous, feeling much the same as she did. The knowledge was strangely comforting; it seemed to form an unspoken bond between them.

He took her hand, clasped it between both of his, and looked down at her.

"I will certainly give you the privilege of changing your mind." His tone was soft. Gentle.

She felt a fierce burst of love for him, knowing he placed her needs above his own. That he was still thinking of what was best for her, beyond his own masculine pleasures, made her trust him all the more.

She shook her head, still looking up at him.

"Frightened?"

He was looking at her with so much love in his eyes she couldn't deny him the truth.

"Yes."

He placed her hand on his chest, then covered it with his own. She could feel the slow, steady beating of his heart. Then, to her surprise, the rhythm increased.

"Do you see how you make me feel?"

She found her voice with an effort of will, feeling the need to talk with him, just a bit, before they retired to the small room above the stable.

"Certainly not frightened."

"No. Hesitant in a different way." He paused, then gently squeezed her hand. "You mustn't feel you need follow through with tonight simply to please me—"

"Don't." She pulled her hand from his and backed away, needing to put some distance between them. She'd dreaded this evening from the moment she'd suggested it, and the thought of sending him back to his home and then having to anticipate it all over again was more than she could bear.

She glanced back up at him, and saw that he was watching her carefully.

"Cinda?"

"I should like us to retire to my room now."

She thought he was about to say something further on the matter, then he simply nodded his head.

Neither spoke until they reached the stableyard. All was quiet and dark, save for the small amount of light coming from the kitchen. Cook was probably sitting by the fireplace, dozing. For just a moment, Cinda wished she could turn and run from William, and never leave the warmth and safety of that fire again.

He surprised her then, by sweeping her up into his arms and entering the stable, then mounting the steps with a sure, steady stride. And she knew, once he set her down outside the door to her bedchamber, that there was no turning back.

Once inside, she had a moment of agonized embarrassment when she saw the small, plain room through his eyes. She knew he'd seen it before, when he'd brought her the lilies. Still, it looked so unbearably shabby; the scarred bedstead and side table seemed cheap and tawdry.

A small trunk stood at the foot of the bed, filled with worn clothing. A miniature of her mother sat on the scarred bedside table. Her favorite childhood companion, a faded but dearly loved china doll, rested on a three-legged chair.

It seemed a sad little place to consummate something she hoped would be beautiful.

She walked over to the bed and sat down, then nervously rose and approached the window, letting another blanket she used as a curtain fall over the opening. At least the room offered them a certain measure of privacy, she was confident of that. No one disturbed her here.

The darkness in the room was soothing. As her eyes adjusted to the dim light, she could see William standing by the doorway.

"If you'd prefer, we could go back to my residence."

"No, I—this is fine." She didn't have the courage to face his great house, or his servants. Just for a little longer, before she had to, she wanted to keep him all to herself.

"Very well. I'll light a candle—"

"It's not necessary."

The silence stretched between them, and Cinda wondered how she could have felt so very close to him mere hours ago in the garden. Now, he seemed a stranger standing in her bedchamber, and she didn't know what to do with him.

"You don't want any candlelight?"

"No."

"Do you feel safer in the dark, Cinda?"

She felt utterly naked with him, even though she was still fully clothed.

"Yes. I do. But if it would please you to have candle-light—"

"No. As you wish."

She didn't know what to do, and his unbroken scrutiny of her was unnerving. Slowly, supposing it was the correct manner to proceed, she began to unwind the woolen shawl from around her shoulders, then stopped.

"I must go down and see Cook, just for a moment."

"As you wish."

Cinda raced swiftly down the stairs. Her request had not been made out of fear, but from necessity.

Cook would see Robbie tomorrow early at morning prayers, and Cinda wanted her to ask her son to tap lightly on her chamber door afterward. She had to make sure William was safely away from the house before Nan or one of her daughters had a chance to set eyes on him.

She entered the kitchen slowly, and saw Cook in her favorite chair by the fire. Thinking the old woman asleep, she tiptoed slowly toward her, then stopped when she heard the low voice.

"She won't be sleeping much this night, poor little thing. Ah, Thomas, I remember me own bridal bed. Thoughts I 'ad afore 'e came to me, 'tis a wonder the marriage lasted through the night."

Cinda smiled. From the slightly slurred tone of voice and the slips into common speech, it was clear the woman had pinched a few nips of Nan's rum. Now Cook was lost in her own hazy thoughts, and talking to the husky tomcat she'd befriended years ago. He spent many a night, purring in her lap. The contented sound was loud in the warm kitchen.

"Though now I think of it, me'aps they won't be doing much a'tall. 'Ow anyone could have the strength to perform 'is manly duties after totin' 'er up that 'ellish stairway is somethin' I can't fathom, can you, Thom?"

Cinda put a hand over her mouth to quell silent laughter. She'd simply return to her room, and try to wake a little earlier than she usually did. On impulse, she tiptoed to the pantry, easing the door open so it didn't squeak. Reaching inside, she found the two rushlights she searched for, then, thinking better of such boldness, only took one.

It would burn for merely half the hour, and surely whatever William had in mind for her couldn't take longer than that.

When she returned to her room, William was lying on the bed, his arms behind his head. For a moment she thought he might have fallen asleep, until he spoke.

"Did you speak to Cook?"

"No. We'll have to be careful and wake early. I don't want Nan to know you've been here."

"I'll take care of that. I don't want you to worry."

She hadn't been able to light the taper from the kitchen fire without disturbing Cook, so now she searched for tinder and flint. Finding them, she sat down on the bed, by William's feet.

Her hands trembled so badly she couldn't create the necessary spark.

"Let me."

Within minutes the room was suffused in a soft glow. Facing William on her bed, Cinda knew the time had come. Feeling like one of Nan's chickens being readied for Sunday supper, she started to unfasten her bodice.

"Don't you think I'd like to do that?" His voice was soft, almost lazy.

She started. Did men derive great pleasure in assisting women in disrobing? How could she have thought otherwise?

"I'm sorry."

He moved then with such grace and speed she didn't have time to be frightened. Grasping both her hands, he pulled her down beside him on the straw mattress.

"This is not going to work," he said quietly.

"No, it will. I won't presume anything, nor be as bold. You may undress me now, Will." And she closed her eyes, resolute.

She heard his sigh, and when he made no move to unfasten her dress, she chanced a glance up at him. He had the strangest expression on his face, a mixture of tenderness and frustration.

"What is it you fear?"

When she said nothing, he pressed on.

"I cannot decide what's best for both of us if you don't help me. Tell me what makes you so frightened."

She tried to put her feelings into words, but couldn't. Instead, she put her arms around his neck and rested her cheek on his chest.

"You can tell me," he said, and she could hear his voice rumbling in his chest.

"I'm scared I'll do something wrong."

"The chances of that are highly unlikely."

"I'm afraid I won't please you."

"As I've said before, you already do."

"In this way."

"You will. I'm sure of it."

She closed her eyes at the thought of bringing up her next fear, then resolutely pushed on. With no mother to confide in, she had no one else to turn to.

"I've been told . . . Will, does it hurt?"

He paused just a fraction too long. "Yes."

"Horribly?"

"Having never been a woman, I don't know." His attempt at humor made her laugh, but she quickly stifled the sound. Giving oneself to a man was a crucial step; she was sure William would not appreciate her regarding the event with levity.

"I'm sorry. I shouldn't have laughed."

"It doesn't have to be a totally serious business, you know. Do whatever you feel like doing. The only secret is, Cinda, that I want to make you happy. I can't do that if you're frightened."

"I know," she whispered.

"I would assume the experience is different for each woman." He slid slightly down the bed, until he could face her, then smiled and touched her cheek with his fingertip. "I'm your servant on this night, here only to please you in any way I can."

Embarrassment flooded her and she lowered her eyes.

"Look at me, Cinda." He waited until she did so, then continued in the same soft, soothing tone of voice. "I want you to trust me to do what is best for you."

"I want to be able to do that, Will."

"Should you feel discomfort or embarrassment, you can ask me to stop at any time."

"Truly?"

"I promise."

"But won't that cause you discomfort?"

"And how much comfort could I derive from knowing you were frightened or unwilling?"

She hadn't considered that. William thought in ways no other man did—for all she knew of other men.

"Please," she whispered. "Tell me what to do."

He sat up, bracing his back against the scarred headboard. "I would enjoy it enormously if you would undress for me. Would that cause you too much embarrassment, with the light?"

Cinda glanced at the swiftly burning rushlight, then back at William. "I've been wasting time, and we only have another twenty minutes at best. Does it take much longer than that?"

He couldn't seem to help the grin that came to his lips. "I sincerely hope so."

She moved slightly away from him, so she was still sitting, but at the foot of the bed. Forcing her fingers not to tremble, she swiftly unfastened the bodice of her dress, then shrugged it off her shoulders. She couldn't look at him as she pulled the coarse wool dress over her head. Draping the garment over the foot of the bed, she sat clad in only her ragged chemise, single petticoat, and old woolen stockings, extremely conscious that her legs were totally exposed to his gaze.

"Is this pleasing to you?" she whispered.

"More than you will ever know. Take off your stockings."

That proved a bit harder, as the thought of letting him see her bare legs was daunting. But she did, leaving both stockings and garters on the wooden floor where they fell. Then she discarded her threadbare petticoat.

Now she didn't dare look up, for she knew what he wanted her to remove next.

"Into bed," he said calmly, getting up and pulling back the covers.

"You don't want me to—"

"I think it might prove difficult for you."

"Thank you," she whispered as she slipped beneath the covers, hugging them to her chin. She averted her eyes as he shed his clothing, then joined her in the small bed. The coarse straw mattress was rather lumpy, and their combined weight caused it to dip slightly in the middle. As she fell toward him, Cinda grasped his shoulders to steady herself.

His skin was rough, his body muscular and so very warm. It almost seemed he gave off heat, like a fire. She twisted slightly, in an attempt to regain her own side of the bed, but all that movement accomplished was to pull her chemise up above her hips. As she slid against him again, she felt his hair-roughened chest, the hard muscles of his thighs, the taut flatness of his stomach, and the fullness and strength of his erection.

"Don't pull away," he said, his breath close to her ear. She went quite still then, and he curled his body around hers. His arms came around her, and she felt great strength in them.

They lay like that for a short time, and it seemed his warmth was being transferred to her body, relaxing her, soothing her. Her cheek rested against his chest, and she could feel the strong, steady beating of his heart.

"We'll start with the familiar and go slowly. You won't have a chance to be frightened."

CHAPTER
❧ 7 ❧

She turned her face up to his, and it seemed her entire world had narrowed to this small bedchamber. The man she'd known in the garden was now unfamiliar, his naked body so different from her own.

He took her chin in his hand and she couldn't meet his eyes. She closed her own, then felt his lips cover hers in a kiss that, for all their intimacy and the ways their bodies were touching, was as chaste as if they were beneath Robbie's watchful eye.

He goes slowly, so as not to frighten me.

She wished with all her heart she were more knowledgeable. He broke the soft kiss, and she whispered, "Is it far more pleasurable when you're with a woman of some experience?"

"It's different."

She opened her eyes then, needing to see his face. "How?"

"You," he said softly, "don't wish to do this. I'd best leave."

She reached for his shoulder, stilling his move to the side of the small bed. "No, I want you to stay."

"There's something else that frightens you. Tell me what it is."

She lowered her lashes and wondered what he would think of her if she told him. It was something a man would never understand.

If I confessed I was afraid of being thought a complete wanton, of losing control over my most base emotions, of letting you see me in a most vulnerable state . . .

98

She couldn't confide in him. Her plan had come to naught, for had this lumpy straw bed been the softest of feather mattresses in William's great townhouse, she still would have felt the same.

Cinda slid out of bed and reached for her woolen dress.

"Would you let me leave once more? For one moment?"

He was lying back in her bed now, beneath the covers, his hands behind his head as he watched her every movement.

"Do you wish me to be here when you return?"

She leaned over and gave him a quick kiss. "Don't go. I just need a little more time."

"As you wish."

She raced down the stairs again, intent on talking to Cook. Surely the woman could confide some little trick to her, a method for making what was to come slightly less intimidating.

She found Cook where she'd left her, in front of the fireplace with the drowsy cat purring in her lap.

"Cook? Cook?" Cinda whispered her name softly as she shook the woman gently by her shoulder. She had no desire to raise the entire household.

"Hmmm." The older woman slowly opened one eye, then the other. For a moment she gazed at Cinda as if she wasn't quite sure how she'd gotten into the kitchen. Then she straightened slightly and shook her head.

"I knew 'e wouldn't be able, after th' climb. 'Tis some liniment you'll be needin', isn't it?" She nodded her head sleepily, as if she approved.

"No, not that. I need—" Cinda glanced around the kitchen as if the walls had ears, then lowered her voice further and put her lips to Cook's ear. "I'm scared, and I need you to tell me of a trick to help me through it."

"'E's a patient man, 'e is. Not many would endure your hoppin' up and down those stairs like a frightened 'are."

"I know. I want to please him and I'm so scared I don't think I will."

"'Ere." With a completely confident air, Cook picked up the bottle of rum near her feet, almost causing her cat to fall out of her ample lap. "A sip o' this, and 'e'll never know you're scared. Ye must be bold, my precious, and take what's yours."

She handed Cinda the bottle, and she eyed it for just a moment, then took a small sip.

"Just a wee bit more, pet. Not enough to make you sleep, just enough to quiet your fears."

She took another sip, then set the bottle down. "Thank you." Cinda squeezed Cook's shoulder, then started toward the door.

"Not yet!" Cook whispered.

She glanced back at the woman, who indicated the basket full of herbs on the long kitchen table.

"'Ave a care not to let 'im know. Men, they're a funny lot. 'Urt 'is pride, you will."

"What? What are you talking about?" Now Cinda was intent on rejoining William and finishing this night.

"Parsley."

Realization stung Cinda as she thought of how William would feel should he realize she needed Dutch courage in order to join him in bed. She couldn't hurt him that way.

"There's a lamb. In the basket. You picked it this morning." Cook settled back into her chair and closed her eyes.

Cinda plucked a sprig of parsley from the basket and chewed it, then took another. She glanced at Cook, but the woman was already asleep.

Bless you.

And without another word, she silently let herself out the door.

Later, much later, William would tell her what had gone through his mind that night when he'd swept aside the blanket covering the window and watched her flight to the kitchen.

She's scared. Well, we're even then, for what I feel for her frightens me.

He wanted the evening to go well, but so far felt he'd made a total botch of it. He'd thought of nothing else since she'd issued her invitation, and had been confident of her passionate nature making the transition from girl to woman successful.

She's terrified.

It was something he knew he couldn't understand. The sensual side of his nature had been something he'd wanted to explore from the time he was a boy. He'd lost his virginity with an equally eager serving girl, and that night remained a treasured memory. But he'd never been afraid. Until tonight.

It was an emotion he couldn't confide to anyone, for he was shamed by it. Yet he would not deny his emotions to himself. He knew fear for what it was.

Strange, how in loving a woman, it gave her such power over you. He knew Cinda had no idea the influence she wielded over his emotions, and he wasn't sure he ever wanted her to know.

Nervous, he let the curtain fall and walked back to the bed. He'd left his clothing on a nearby chair, and now he reached for his cloak, and a specific pocket.

The silver flask fit his palm perfectly, and he swiftly unstopped it and downed several swallows of the fine Jamaican rum. Warmth spread through his body within seconds, and he replaced the small flask within the folds of the heavy cloak.

The room was chilly, and the liquor helped warm him. He climbed back into the bed, and within minutes heard her footsteps at the door, then the scratch of the latch.

Cinda quickly shed her clothing, then slipped into the bed and shifted close to William. She felt more relaxed, perhaps even a little more sure of herself. William's arm came warmly around her as he pulled her close to him.

Be brave. Make him proud to share your bed.

"Kiss me," she whispered.

He did, and to her dismay and despite the two sprigs of parsley she'd chewed, she tasted the rich, full flavor of the rum.

"It didn't work," she whispered sadly when he broke the kiss.

"It didn't?" Dismay was evident in his voice.

"No."

"You didn't feel anything?" he asked.

"The parsley." She had to confess now, for surely he had tasted the rum on her breath as well.

"Parsley." There was a note to his voice that clearly indicated he had no idea what she was talking about.

She rolled onto her back, an arm behind her head, and stared up at the sloped ceiling.

"I took a few sips of rum in the kitchen . . . to quiet my apprehensions. I thought the parsley I chewed masked the spirit's flavor. But I could taste it when we kissed."

"Oh." She could hear laughter in his voice.

Relieved that his pride hadn't been bruised, she couldn't resist the humor of it all. Cinda turned and buried her face in her pillow as the laughter burst out of her. When she finally turned her head to look at William, she found his face close to hers on the pillow.

"Madam, you are surely difficult."

She smiled, more confident. "I feel less poorly now. We can continue, if you still want to."

"I've been wanting to since you first issued your invitation. Now, no more trips downstairs?"

"No."

"Would you like one more sip before we commence?"

He laughed at the puzzled look on her face, mere seconds before the rushlight burned out.

"God's blood, what else can happen this night?"

Cinda smiled in the darkness. Though William was clearly frustrated, he wasn't angry with her, and the thought warmed her almost more than the rum.

"What was this about one more sip?" Now she felt daring, even a bit the coquette.

Her eyes had adjusted to the darkness, and she saw him search through the pile of clothing on the chair. When he sat back down on the bed, she saw the flask.

"You—"

"Yes."

"For courage?" she asked softly.

"For warmth. It's bloody freezing up here. Now, another sip?"

She nodded her head, and he passed the flask to her. His rum tasted smoother than Nan's, and she took a large swallow, then passed it back. William drank from it, then capped it and set it on the table by her bed.

"We need light," he said. Again, he searched through his clothing and she watched as he lit another candle. But this one was nothing like the meager rushlight. It was a beeswax candle, and Cinda knew from using them in Nan's household that the light would burn for hours, and much more brightly.

"I thought you might not have a candle, and I do want to see you tonight."

"I can't think of anything else we need," she whispered, her throat tight at the thought of him looking at her.

He cupped her breast and she drew her breath in quickly. The spirits she'd consumed seemed to intensify the sensation, and she felt her nipple harden until it was almost painful. Without thinking, she reached out and attempted to remove his fingers from her aching breast.

"No," he breathed softly. "Don't stop me." He tightened his grip, ever so slightly, and at the same time lowered his head and caught her lips with his.

She could feel him pressing her back against the bed, felt the warmth and heaviness of his body as he moved, swiftly pinning her beneath a muscular leg.

When he broke the kiss, she murmured his name, then made a soft sound of protest.

"You want this or you don't, Cinda. I'm only a man, but I have a man's needs and can't remain in this bed with you much longer and not take you. Now, tell me what you want."

Her breathing was erratic; his hand still fondled her breasts while the other rubbed the small of her back, easing her tighter against him. She couldn't think while he touched her thus.

"Tell me." He shifted his weight slightly so they were both lying on their sides.

"I don't want to be bad." She whispered the words into his ear, then hid her face against his shoulder.

His hand abruptly stilled its exploration, then he whispered, "You're afraid you'll enjoy this too much?"

"I don't want to be bad." She had to see his face, know what he thought of her whispered confession.

He was smiling, and she relaxed, then reached out and gently touched his hair.

"Madam," he whispered. "Dear heart, you can be as bad as you want in my bed. But only for me."

"You won't think less of me?"

"Never. I promise."

"Can I touch you?"

He kissed her brow, softly, sweetly. "It would give me great pleasure."

She explored his body with her hands, and as what had seemed so frightening became familiar, she relaxed. His shoulders and chest, his back, his thighs. Roughened with hair, firmly muscled, so different from her own.

Then, finally, that part of him she was most curious about.

"It's like a little man," she said softly. "With a will of its own."

"It does have a Will of its own."

She laughed at the silly pun.

"You make it less frightening." Her caress was featherlight, tentative, and unsure.

"Don't be afraid to really touch," he whispered.

"I might hurt you."

"You won't." He put his hand over hers, clasping tightly, and showed her what he wanted. He kissed her, much less gently this time. Cinda reached up with her free hand and curled her fingers into his hair, grasping tightly.

The rum seemed to have pooled deep in her belly, spreading warmth and heat, a slow, steady fire burning within her. Wanting more, she moved into the kiss, moved closer to his hardness and heat and strength, and found she wasn't afraid.

He kissed her for a long time, until she felt hot and dizzy, open and pliant beneath his touch. His mouth moved over hers, alternately teasing and playful, then dominant and demanding.

He broke one of the kisses, leaving her weak and trembling. Before she had a chance to gather her riotous emotions, he kissed her neck, then gently bit the taut flesh. She cried out and grasped his shoulders, then arched beneath him as his hand found her breast again. This time he teased her, pinching first one nipple, then the other, rubbing the flat of his palm against the sensitive peaks.

She moaned, but before she could do more than move beneath his touch, he lowered his head and claimed the full, aching flesh.

If his kisses had brought her to the edge of losing control, then this newest assault threatened to drive her over the brink. His mouth was warm and hot, incredibly supple around her. Cinda cried out as he suckled strongly, and for a brief moment felt the intense sensation might abate, but he seemed to know how to bring her up to a certain height, then let her drift down before she had a chance to find relief.

His lovemaking never ceased, even for the briefest of seconds. She arched her head back into the pillow, and it seemed she was divided within herself. Part of her wanted to push him away and give herself a chance to catch her breath and regain control, and the other part wanted him to continue to dominate her and drive everything from her mind but his taste, his touch, his scent.

He was slowly conquering her, with the feel of his lips on her breasts, his fingers tangled in her hair holding her still, the warm press of his belly on her fevered skin. And always, the feel of his arousal, fully erect, rigid with the need for release, hotly pressed against her.

She tensed when she felt his hand on her inner thigh.

"Open for me, Cinda," he whispered.

This was what she'd feared most, yet she couldn't find the strength to deny him. She spread her legs slightly. He urged them farther apart as he settled himself between them.

She couldn't think, could only feel. His lips on her breasts, his hand between her legs, touching her, rubbing her, making that aching warmth pool between her thighs. Making her push herself against him, searching for a consummation, an ending to the blinding ache within her body.

His finger gently slipped inside, and it was as if he'd burned her, the feeling was so sharp. Her hips bucked upward, his finger slipped deeper, then he was moving it slowly, deeper each time, soothing and arousing her.

Though she'd never imagined it before, Cinda felt strangely empty where he touched her. Her thighs trembled, she bit down on her lip hard to keep from crying out, and wondered wildly how she was to see to his needs when everything he did brought these frenzied bursts of sensation.

She could feel her control slipping, shearing away, and she wanted to make him feel the same way. She wanted him as desperately out of control as she was; there was nothing she desired more than to see what wildness she could bring out in him.

Cinda shifted until she could touch his erection, and this time grasped him strongly. His low groan seemed to come from a long distance, but she ignored it, determined to bring him ultimate pleasure.

He took her hand away, then grasped both her wrists in one hand and pulled them up above her head. She felt his weight on top of her now, and she breathed deeply, knowing what she feared was about to happen.

He kissed her, then she felt him settling between her legs. Reflexively she tried to close her thighs against this primitive invasion, but his hips, settled strongly between them, prevented her from doing so.

She made an unintelligible sound as he gently sought and found her, then thrust. Pain shot through her, and she tore her mouth away from his and cried out. Before she closed her eyes she saw the tension in his face, then she felt him thrust again. Still, her body resisted his.

The tears came then; she felt one slide down her cheek and into her ear. Cinda squinted her eyes shut tightly as she felt William thrust strongly one more time.

Then they opened in astonishment, for the barrier was finally breached and she felt him fill her body with his own, felt the power and strength of him sheathed inside her. He let go of her wrists, and she grasped handfuls of the faded blanket.

Holding him within her body was uncomfortable, and she shifted her hips, then caught her breath and, panting, looked up at him.

He gazed down at her, resting his weight on his elbows. When their eyes met, he kissed the tip of her nose, then her mouth. It was a sweet kiss, full of regret at hurting her, and she felt emotion well up inside her as he kissed the path the tear had taken down her cheek.

"I'm sorry," he said, his voice low and taut with emotion.

She said nothing, simply turned her head away.

"Cinda, talk to me."

She took a deep, shuddering breath. "There's parts of it I like, but I'll never like this."

"Your maidenhead put up quite a battle." He kissed her lips again. "But I promise you, it won't ever be as painful again."

"It won't because we're never going to do this again." She could feel the tenderness between her thighs, and didn't even want to consider how sore she would be the following morning, what with him stretching her so.

"Does this hurt?" he asked. He carefully eased out of her, then gently pushed back inside.

"A little."

"As much as at first?"

"No." The one word was grudging.

His eyes never left hers. "You're angry."

"You tricked me."

"I told you about the pain."

"Not pain like that!"

"I couldn't know it would be like that for you."

"Oh, finish it then and get off me!"

He studied her for what seemed like a long time. Finally, she couldn't meet the fierceness of his gaze and had to look away.

"I'm sorry, Will. I knew I wouldn't be any good at it. That's why I suggested—this."

He didn't reply, and she grew nervous.

"Of course, I won't hold you to the marriage."

"Hurt me," he whispered.

She simply stared up at him, wondering if he'd lost his mind.

"What?"

"Hurt me. There's no need for you to be shy with me any longer, for I've seen and felt you in ways no other man has. But unless you let loose some of that temper of yours, you'll resent me for this and I won't have it."

"I told you, you don't have to—"

"Don't you want to?"

The temptation was overwhelming. She was angry with him, angry at the fact that he would have nothing but intense pleasure from this evening's sport, whereas she would be sore for hours afterward. But she was also deeply frightened that he should have the power to affect her so, and that made her even angrier.

She shifted her hips, and was rewarded by the low, abrupt sound he made.

"Does that hurt you?" she asked, smiling up at him. In truth, she wasn't as uncomfortable with him deep inside her as she had been only moments before. It seemed her body, in its infinite wisdom, was accommodating itself to his possession. But the way she felt now, her emotions raging out of control, she would die rather than tell him that.

"In a different way."

They were both silent for almost a minute, then William spoke. "Hurt me, then, Cinda, and even the score. For I won't have this evening coming between us."

"You won't have this, you won't have that—"

"Watch your tongue or I'll finish this and then give you a good spanking for your impertinence."

She stared up at him, completely motionless, knowing he was perfectly capable of doing as he said.

"Then I may hurt you," she said softly, feeling her dignity was in shreds.

"In whatever way you wish."

"What if I decide not to, and therefore am the better person for restraining myself."

"How utterly boring that would be. You disappoint me, Cinda." There was just a hint of humor in his voice, and she squelched the urge to laugh. In the midst of her temper, this infuriating man could still make her laugh.

"How shall I do it?"

"However you wish."

"I'll bite you, then. I'll mark you the way you've marked me." Swiftly, before she lost her nerve, she linked her hands behind his head, pulled him down against her, and sharply sunk her teeth into the side of his neck.

She felt him stiffen, and when she fell back onto the pillow, he was looking down at her in amazement.

"You're a bloodthirsty little wench. I hurt you that much?"

She nodded.

"Then you had a right to be angry with me."

Suddenly she felt ashamed of herself, needing such a petty form of revenge to feel better. But William had been right, she did feel better.

"You're bleeding," she said softly.

"Take care of it."

She kissed his neck where she'd marked him as her own, and felt an overwhelming tenderness toward this man. Reaching up, she twined her fingers into his hair and brought his lips down to hers. The kiss was hungry, fierce, a mixture of anger, fear, and love. He started to move then, and she made a small sound against his mouth but didn't stop him.

He took his time, his thrusts strong and slow, building tension until she was shaking with sensation all over again. When he reached his release, she clung to him, full of wonder at the power and beauty of this man.

Afterward, he rolled onto his back and pulled her into his arms.

"I can see why men want it," she whispered. "It must be beautiful, to feel that much."

He looked at her, his chest rising and falling as he breathed deeply.

"It wasn't as bad as I thought, after that—horrible part." She paused, her finger tracing a pattern on his chest through the thick, dark hair. "I won't mind this part of marriage, Will, and I'll serve you well."

He started to laugh then, deep tremors that shook his body. He slid his forearm over his eyes but she could see the smile curving his lips and it infuriated her all over again.

"Will, how can you—" She jumped as he reached over and grabbed her arm, then brought her up so they were both in a sitting position on the bed.

"A wager, madam. Just a small one. If I can show you what it is you'll find in my bed, then will you be content to let me have the last word?"

"I've found everything I need to know. What else is there?"

"This." Before she knew what he was about, William had her pinned to the bed again, but this time he swiftly dropped a kiss on one of her breasts before slowly kissing his way down her stomach.

She could feel the taut skin quivering at the touch of his lips. "Will, what are you doing?" she whispered. "I'm not going through it again, not the same night. Oh!"

He was kissing the very heart of her, his strong hands holding her thighs apart, and she brought her hands down and gave his hair a sharp pull.

He glanced up at her and grinned, then rested his chin on her belly. "So you're going to deny our wager?"

"I didn't know this was what you intended to do!"

"I thought you said you'd found everything you needed to know about it."

She struggled up, leaning back on her elbows. "Obviously I haven't!"

"You're bleeding," he said softly.

"Will!" Her voice was mortified.

"Then I'll take care of it," he said, and she knew from the tone of his voice that he would permit her no leeway in this matter.

She lay back down on the pillow, covering her flushed face with her hands. And this time, when he entered her, there was no pain, only a frenzied coupling, a reaching for sensation, and an overwhelming brilliance of feeling and emotion that made her his own.

Afterward, she lay contentedly in his arms, totally exhausted.

"You had a decided advantage," she reminded him, then yawned. "You know all too much about women's bodies."

"As long as you allow me the last word, our bet is fulfilled." They had long ago snuffed out the candle, but she could hear the smile in his voice.

"I'm going to torment you," she said, feeling herself drift off to sleep.

"I'm sure you will." His arm tightened around her.

"I'm going to make a study of you, and find out as much as I can about a man's desires, and then I'll pay you back in kind."

"Go to sleep." They were curled up like spoons in a cutlery drawer, the warmth from his large body filling the bed. Cinda found she liked sleeping with him; she felt safe and warm and protected.

She sighed as William kissed the back of her neck.

"I will," she whispered, almost asleep.

He laughed softly, his breath tickling her neck. "Then I surely won our wager after all."

Cinda came slowly awake from her dreams of the past, as if traveling a long distance. William was not in his bedchamber, and the fire had gone out hours ago. Still, it wasn't terribly cold, even though most of the heavy velvet drapes were drawn and the great bedroom seemed to slumber in shadows. She got out of his bed slowly, fastening the sash of his silk dressing gown around her waist.

The sun streaming in the one undraped window suggested morning was long gone, and she wondered if Robbie was still here or if he'd already ridden home.

She was about to leave William's bedroom when Henry came silently in the door, bearing a silver tray loaded down with various foodstuffs.

"Good day, miss," he said.

"Good day," she replied, watching him carefully as he set the tray down on one of the small tables by the fireplace, then attended to the fire itself. Within minutes, the flames were crackling, spreading their warmth throughout the cool, shadowed room.

She wondered how much he knew about her relationship with William. The man's tone of voice had been quiet and respectful; he'd given nothing away during the quick exchange. He seemed terribly protective of his master.

"Your breakfast, miss," he said, indicating the tray.

"Could you tell me where William is?"

"He had to attend to something for his uncle, but he should be returning shortly. In the meantime, you are to remain here and rest."

"And Robbie?"

"He left early this morning."

The valet paused for an instant at the door leading out into the hallway, as if waiting for some further request. When none came, he exited, shutting the door silently behind him.

Cinda felt frustrated, standing by the great bed and not quite knowing what her fate for the day was to be. Apparently Robbie and William had already discussed what was to happen, and decided things accordingly.

A pity they hadn't thought to consult her.

There was nothing she could do for the moment but sit in front of the fire and eat her breakfast. She walked slowly over to the table and studied the silver tray. Breads of all descriptions, muffins and scones and crumpets, were piled on a china plate. The various condiments were lavish: sweet butter, jams and jellies, honey and marmalade. And a small silver pot of tea.

In another mood, at another time, she might have been charmed. How odd, to have someone wait on her when she was the one who was used to doing the serving. She couldn't remember the last time someone had brought her breakfast, and she sat down, determined to enjoy it.

She was halfway through her second scone when William walked into the bedchamber.

"Did you sleep well?" he asked, striding toward the fire. He kissed her quickly. She noticed his hair was windblown, his color high. It had to be cold out, for after stripping his gloves off, he warmed his hands by the fire.

"Very well. And you?"

"Well enough."

"Would you like any of this? There's enough for an army."

"I breakfasted with Robbie. He assured me you could be spared from household duties for a few days, so that we might have some time together. He asked if he might come fetch you two days hence, for washday."

Cinda nodded her head, her mouth full. How good of Cook to let her have this time.

"What would you like to do today?"

"I'd like to open the curtains and let in the sunlight."

He did as she asked, and the huge room was flooded with light.

"Anything else?"

She thought for a moment, then said, "I should like to finish breakfast, then talk with you of your plans to apprehend this man."

She could tell he wasn't pleased by her request. Cinda took a deep breath and hurried on before he could refuse her.

"I understand you don't wish me to have any part of it, and I promised I wouldn't. But I need to know what it is you plan to do." He didn't answer, so she rushed on. "Will, I need to know you'll be safe."

He considered this, then approached the chair across from her and sat down.

"Your request is fair. You gave me your word you would yield to me on this matter, but I can see no reason why you shouldn't know my plans. And after that?"

"Then I should like to return to bed."

"To sleep?" A slow smile curved his lips as memories darkened his eyes.

"For a while."

She poured herself another cup of tea as he watched her, but his gaze didn't make her nervous anymore.

The small room on the third floor of the tumbledown house in St. Giles was beneath a sloped roof, and far too cramped for the three occupants who normally resided there. Now, even in the midst of day, little light nor air penetrated the filthy windows. The pervasive scent of dampness lingered throughout the rotting building, and an appalling stench rose from the narrow courts and alleyways far below.

There was hardly any furniture inside the small room, an old pallet in one corner and a table with two rickety chairs in another. Though the dwelling possessed no washing or sanitary facilities, it seemed someone had made an effort to keep the living area clean.

A single candle burned brightly on the table, illuminating the man who dipped his quill into the inkwell and began scratching out sentences on the piece of parchment before him.

Bess huddled in one corner, her baby Annie drowsing on the pallet alongside her eight-year-old son, Ned. It was far safer if her children slept during the day, for at night they needed to be awake and on their guard. The district came alive with thieves and toughs, men who would just as soon slit your throat as ask your name.

She tucked the soft gray woolen shawl more securely around Annie, and the infant stirred in her sleep. Her cheeks flushed with the tiniest stain of color, and Bess was fiercely glad she'd traded in most of the food that girl had given her for milk for her daughter. She and Ned were strong; they'd both survived for years now. It was Annie she worried about, every single day. She'd almost lost hope before receiving that unexpected gift at the marketplace.

And, as always, she wondered why the girl had done it. No one did anything for anyone out of the goodness of their hearts, she was sure of that. In her struggle to simply stay alive and provide some sort of sustenance for her children, she'd seen the worst of human nature. Not much surprised her anymore.

Ned stirred in his sleep, and she smoothed her hand over his brow, ruffling the sandy-colored curls. Bess glanced up anxiously at the man. He was still staring at the piece of parchment as if it were something alive.

Above all, she didn't want to call his attention to either her or her children.

He was a strange man. He made her uneasy, for she hadn't been able to figure him out as easily as she did her other customers. He refused to give her his Christian name, claiming he preferred anonymity. This hadn't bothered her—at first.

He dressed in rather fine clothing, and clearly possessed the manners of a gentleman. Yet he seemed quite at home in this dark part of the city, among the whores and pickpockets, the thieves and toughs.

She had to admit he'd been good to them, in his own way. She'd persuaded him to pay for this room, in exchange for her being available to him all hours of the day. He bought them a minimal amount of food, just enough to keep them alive, but far more than she'd had out in the streets.

It wasn't as if she expected much more. Men couldn't be trusted, not for long. Her brother had brought her to London when she was thirteen years of age on a seeming whim, to show her the city after their parents died. She'd lived in the country all her life, and the great city had been both exciting and terribly frightening. Too late, she'd learned her brother had promised her to a brothel, in exchange for a few coins.

His betrayal had cut her deeply, an emotional wound she'd never recovered from.

She'd lost her virginity in one of the small, dingy rooms, then been worked and abused like an animal until the Madam discovered she was pregnant and threw her out into the street. Bess had been fifteen then, and all alone.

Frightened, she'd despaired at being pregnant, had even tried to rid herself of the child growing within her. Yet now she realized God had intended for something else to happen.

When Ned had been born, it seemed to Bess a miracle occurred. The babe hadn't demanded anything from her; he had simply wanted to be close to her. There was absolutely no trace of deception or malice in that trusting little face, and she knew this child would never hurt her.

Slowly, she grew to love her son. The bitterness she'd harbored in her heart melted away, to be replaced by a tough resolve to survive at any cost.

And she had. Bess survived by trusting no one, by caring for no one except her two children, both of whom she loved with a fierce devotion. Not for either of them the loss of love and bitter betrayal that had marked her early years. Not for them the blinding realization that they would have to live their lives out among this filth and squalor.

If she died in the attempt, she would see them leave this place. Above all else Bess wanted her children to be safe. Thus everything she did, she did for Ned and Annie.

Now she watched the big man as he painstakingly scratched out the letter, and wondered at the hatred that seemed to fuel his actions. Sometimes it was turned against her, and more than once she'd felt the force of his fists against her body. But he kept a roof over their heads, he offered Ned and

Annie a chance of surviving, and for that chance she would have endured anything.

And as she watched the man, she thought of the girl at the marketplace. Why had she given her the shawl? Why had she risked her position in her household by giving her some of the mistress's food? Simple acts of kindness were beyond her comprehension, so Bess merely watched the man and waited, trying to make sense of the puzzle that was her life.

Nan Townshend stood in the doorway of one of the upstairs bedrooms at her friend's country estate and watched her two daughters as they slept.

She considered both children to be a burden to her, slovenly and ignorant. Neither had inherited her cleverness, nor her desire for the finer things in life.

They weren't making the slightest bit of effort in their search for wealthy husbands. They loved to lie abed and rise early in the afternoon, then call on their equally lazy friends and gossip into the late hours.

They attended dinners, balls, and even a few of the more proper masquerades, but nothing had come of it. Neither Helena nor Miranda made any effort with the opposite sex.

Nan's mouth tightened as she gazed down at her sleeping children, and for a moment she was tempted to see if she could snuff the life out of them with a feather pillow. How much easier her own existence would be if she were rid of these worthless chits. They gave her nothing, simply took and took, spending money rightfully hers, wiling away their days in idleness and endless chatter.

She'd come to their bedroom this evening to awaken them for the party. Her friend had some lively and most amusing entertainment planned. Everyone from all the neighboring towns had been invited. Surely there had to be an eligible— and wealthy—bachelor among the lot.

Her mouth hardened further as she continued to peruse her offspring. Helena and Miranda. She'd named them after two of the characters in Shakespeare's plays, hoping such elegant names would contribute to their fortune in life.

But Helena—short, plump, and squint-eyed—and Miranda— tall, heavy-boned, and clumsy—could not have been considered elegant if their lives depended upon it. Grooming them and finding suitable apparel to hide their various figure flaws was a chore in and of itself, and one she was wearying of as the months progressed.

Rosalind had been the changeling, left by fairies. The girl, while not possessing anything close to an intellect, had a sweet countenance and a gentle manner. But she'd been frightened of men, and preferred her quiet world in the library, sitting in one of the comfortable chairs by the fire. Dreaming.

The little fool. Dreams get you nowhere in this life. Proper action and clever plans are the only way to ensure success.

Nan tore her attention away from her daughters and crossed silently to the door. She'd let them sleep. The carriage ride had certainly been taxing enough, jarring and jouncing the three of them, knocking them about until they were black and blue. The roads had been abominable, muddy and full of deep ruts. They'd been lucky the carriage hadn't overturned or lost a wheel.

She'd rather have a tooth pulled before she came to the country again.

Nan narrowed her eyes as she studied her sleeping offspring. Helena and Miranda would wake eventually and find their way downstairs, for the rich refreshments and idle chatter if nothing else.

Greedy little pigs.

What she wanted them to find, each of them, was a rich husband. After all, it was far easier to marry a peer than obtain a peerage. Would the stupid little chits ever understand the importance of her plans?

Nan paused, her hand on the doorknob, and looked back at her slumbering children. Repulsed by what she saw, she silently opened the door and slipped into the hallway.

He woke late at night, to find her standing by one of the large windows, gazing out into the night sky. Silently, so as not to frighten her, William slid out of bed and padded toward her, his bare feet soundless on the thick carpets.

He stopped behind her, then carefully placed his hands on her shoulders and drew her back against the warmth of his body. She'd wrapped herself in one of his dressing gowns, and now looked out into the sky, at the faint rumblings of thunder and flashes of lightning.

She reached for his hand, covered it with her own. The small gesture was the only move she made that let him know she realized he was behind her.

"There's a storm coming, Will."

He heard the thoughts behind the words.

"I know."

He felt the light tension that gripped her slender form.

"And we will survive it?" she whispered.

He kissed the side of her neck gently, so gently.

"I give you my word."

They stood silently, watching the play of the thunderstorm until tiny droplets began to hit the panes of glass.

"Do you believe in absolute evil?" she asked.

"Yes."

"Have you ever seen it?"

"Yes."

"Have you ever had it directed at yourself in such a manner—as this man does?"

"No."

He could feel her fear, feel the pause before the next question.

"Will? Are you afraid?"

"Yes."

Her hands were cold. Like ice. He rubbed them, absently. One thing he'd learned about Cinda was that it did no good to try to rush her.

"I keep thinking. About Rosalind."

"I know."

"Do you think the same thoughts I do?" she whispered, and he could hear the tightness in her throat.

"I've had—nightmares." Only her need for absolute truth could have wrenched that admission from him.

"They made me—" She drew a deep breath. "She made me dress the body. For burial."

He closed his eyes as pain tore through him. He hadn't known that, hadn't realized either Horace or Nan would be capable of such cruelty.

"Cook tried to make me leave the room, but I had to—I had to see her."

He knew where she was, what tortuous paths she was walking within her mind, because he'd been there. And he knew sometimes the only cure for it was talking to someone who would listen.

"I whispered a prayer, and asked for God's mercy." She took a deep breath. "Will, she didn't have time to prepare or repent, she didn't even know she was going to die."

He tightened his grip on her, slipping his arms around her waist.

"Now she's all alone. She should be lying with a lover and she's lying with worms. And . . . I cannot help but think that . . . if not for me—"

He swept her up into his arms and carried her to the bed. The fire had burned low; the room was cooler than it had been. Tucking her beneath the covers, he took her hand and pressed the palm against his cheek.

"There's nothing you can do to change what's been done," he said, speaking softly. Firmly. He had to reach beyond the pain and make her understand. "But I swear to you, Cinda, I'll find the man who murdered her and make sure he does no further harm."

"He'll take you away."

Already some of the anguish was leaving her eyes, to be replaced with exhaustion. She would sleep tonight, he knew from experience, the sleep of one who was truly emotionally exhausted. Heartsick. And he wished her gentle respite from the nightmare, wished her good dreams and not the dark imaginings that had been tormenting him of late.

"I'm not going to leave you. Ever."

"No," she said softly, then her eyes drifted closed and the death grip on his other hand lessened. He waited until her breathing was slow, deep, and even, then got up and replenished the fire. He could have called one of the servants, but he didn't want anyone disturbing Cinda.

William went back to the window and gazed out at the night sky. The rain had abated, to be replaced by masses of clouds scudding across the sky and obscuring the moon.

There's a storm coming, Will.

His world had been thrown into utter chaos the night Rosalind had died. From the moment he'd awoken from the nightmare, he'd known he could not live with himself until he stopped the killings. The night Rosalind had died had also shown him he couldn't go on should anything happen to Cinda.

He'd keep her out of it, while tracking down this man and putting an end to it. Then, if things went the way he hoped they would, and if it was God's will, perhaps he and Cinda would have a chance at a life together.

And happiness.

CHAPTER
8

"Why the masquerade?" Cinda asked.

She was walking with William in his extensive garden on their second day together. He'd decided no one would question his decision to examine the horses with one of the stableboys who had delivered them. From the back of the stable, it had been a simple task to slip out into the garden.

This unexpected leisure time was a blessing, made all the sweeter by being in William's company. Now Cinda determined to know as much as possible about what William planned to do. If she could not help him herself, then she could at least understand what was to happen and pray for a good outcome.

"I tend to believe people will speak more freely behind their masks. The events I plan to attend are huge, with most of the aristocracy involved. Their love of gossip should provide me with ample information.

"Perhaps this man will even approach me himself, in disguise. He is certainly not a fellow of rational thoughts, and it seems he likes this peculiar cat and mouse quality in our relationship."

"Do you think he's wellborn?"

"I hesitate to say what he is. I'm not quite sure. Perhaps." William's voice was low, and Cinda had to remain close to his side to hear his replies to her questions.

"Whoever he is, he's not hiring out the murders. I placed many people on the streets, offering a handsome reward for anyone who could tell me about this man. Had the murderer been a hired tough, he would have taken the chance to obtain a large sum of money and escape without punishment. This man does his own killing, of that I'm sure."

"And you have no known enemies?"

"None capable of murder."

"He concentrates on women you love. Is there anyone in your past whom you thwarted in love, perhaps? Someone who desired a certain woman who preferred your company?"

"No one I'm aware of."

Cinda continued to turn the various possibilities over in her mind as they walked down the graveled path.

"Do you gamble, Will?"

"Not to excess. Only for sport, then occasionally."

"Thus there is no one who would kill you because of a debt?"

"No."

Cinda paused, admiring a particularly beautiful rose. "I'm sorry if I tire you with my questions. Certainly you've thought of the same things in trying to find out who this man might be."

"I have, but it's prudent to go over the same ground again and again. Some new memory or incident might come to light."

"You have no intuition as to who it might be? An uneasy feeling toward one of your friends, perhaps? Or an old servant who might be capable of slipping in and out of the house?"

"No. My own investigation into this matter has given me no further insights. Thus, the masquerades."

"I have heard they are wonderful," Cinda confessed. "I must admit, they intrigue me."

"Perhaps when this killer is safely caught and no danger to you, and once we're properly married, we might attend one of the less risqué affairs."

A brief flare of resentment welled up inside her. It was a hard task to sit back and see William enter the world of the masquerade in search of the killer. A part of her wished she might be right at his side, attending the masquerades, as active in the search as he was.

But she had promised him she wouldn't, and she was not a woman to take such a promise lightly.

Cinda was surprised how much it scared her, thinking of marriage to William. When he'd first proposed, she'd been ecstatic at the thought of being his wife, creating a home for both of them to enjoy. She'd wanted nothing more than to make him happy, and ensure his complete contentment.

The months after Rosalind's murder had changed her.

As much as she had loved William, and still loved him, she had finally, sadly, resigned herself to a life without him. Thus, the smallest seeds of independent thought had been planted within her, to grow strong roots, and finally flower and bloom.

This change frightened her, because it was a part of her nature William was not familiar with. She sensed he believed he knew her completely, but he did not know the woman whose character had been shaped by months of waiting.

Now, with her new knowledge and feelings about herself, Cinda saw a pattern emerging. William would be the one who would set the course their ship would sail, whereas she would sit quietly at the rail and watch what happened.

It was not a future she looked forward to. Not now.

Oh, to be like so many other women and simply be thankful he cares enough to keep me out of it. He doesn't want to risk my life in this quest; he thinks only of my comfort.

She wrinkled her forehead, deep in thought, as she knelt to examine another rose.

Then why can't I stop thinking about it? And as much as I still love him, why do I resent him equally as much for the restraints he places upon me? For the promise he exacted? Now I must keep my word, for to do otherwise would be wrong, and would make him extremely angry.

She didn't want to be angry with him during this short time they were allowed to be together. Yet there was a tightness in her throat as she swallowed back her feelings and followed him down the garden path.

She thought about the lilies he'd given her, so long ago. A symbol of innocence. A quality he'd found attractive, but one which she no longer possessed.

And Cinda knew, as she stared blindly at the lush flower-beds, that William would not be particularly fond of the woman she had become.

The only question that remained was whether she would choose to let him see that woman.

They walked through the extensive garden in silence. Cinda chose not to converse with William while her thoughts were so turbulent. She didn't particularly pay heed to where they were going until they headed into the mouth of the maze at the far end of the grounds.

She hesitated, then looked up at him.

"We won't get lost?" she said, touching his arm.

"I know the way."

"Could he . . . could the murderer be watching us, even as we speak? Could he have found a way onto your property, perhaps to spy on you?"

"I doubt he even knows I'm here. Several mastiffs are always on the grounds. My uncle asked me to attend to their care while he's traveling the Continent." He grinned suddenly, and she was amazed to see how much younger he appeared when he let himself smile.

They took another few turns in the maze, and now she could no longer see where it had begun. The carefully shaped hedges were above her head, and they were completely enclosed within the greenery.

"Tell me about the dogs," she said, needing to concentrate on something besides the fact that they were walking deeper and deeper into the maze.

"Juno and Jocasta, the two females, refuse to let strangers onto the property. They wouldn't even let you walk in the garden were you not with me."

"Are they vicious animals?"

"Not to those they love. Juno is especially protective, as she is expecting pups."

She hadn't seen the mastiffs since her arrival, but if William said they were here, they most certainly were.

As if reading her mind, he said, "I couldn't have them frightening the new mares, so they were shut inside the house. I've given the dogs a room of their own."

"Like the room for bathing," she murmured. "You're certainly an original thinker."

"An eccentric, some say."

She remained silent, not wanting to answer this particular line of thought.

"I know what is said about me by those in town," he said quietly. "Both good and bad."

"And it doesn't bother you?"

"Not if I know the truth."

"You're never lonely?"

He was silent for a time before he replied.

"I've been by myself for a long time and, with my uncle's help, have learned to enjoy my own company. No, I've not been lonely. And especially not since meeting you."

She took his hand, certain they were not being watched. No one could see beyond the dense foliage.

"It's rather frightening," she murmured, brushing the free palm of her other hand against the glossy yew leaves. "Could we get lost?"

"I've played among these hedges since I was a child, there isn't a corner of the maze I'm not familiar with." He led her farther in. "I won't let anything happen to you, Cinda."

She clasped his hand tightly as they continued their walk, glad to have his comforting presence at her side, yet frustrated at the thought of being denied so very much.

It would be the same with any man.

She knew this to be true, having listened carefully to frustrated female conversation at her stepmother's various dinner parties. There were men who considered women to be not much more than upper servants, and treated them as such.

But somehow, she'd rather fancied William might transcend the restraints of his sex, and realize she could be a valuable partner in his search for the killer.

Cinda wanted to help, in whatever small way. She knew the action would help cleanse her of the guilt she'd felt since learning of Rosalind's fate. It was maddening to sit and do nothing, to be told to wait until everything was put back to rights, until order was restored from chaos. Yet she'd made William a promise.

He tricked you, after all, she thought, then immediately tried to banish the thought from her head.

He's concerned for my well-being, that is all.

But what if your well-being depends on helping bring Rosalind's murderer to justice? What if that action were the most healing endeavor you could make?

They reached the middle of the maze, after an intricate set of twists and turns. And she was enchanted by the pagoda that resided at its heart.

"It's beautiful!"

"My grandfather spent considerable time in the Orient. He brought back the design with the express intent of someday using it within his garden."

"I would have thought it would have looked out of place, but it doesn't. It looks as if—as if it has been here for the longest of times."

"Exactly the effect he was striving for."

They entered the shelter of the small pagoda, surrounded by lush green grass and the high walls of the hedges. From any point inside the small structure, it was difficult to see the various entrances back into the maze, thus creating the illusion of a tiny dwelling completely closed off, sufficient unto itself.

"How old were you when you first saw this?" she asked him. Their fingers were still entwined as she explored the small structure.

"Two or three. I thought it was magical. My mother used to take me inside the maze. We'd bring food and a good book, and spend the afternoon out on the grass, in the shade of the pagoda. She read to me, and told me other stories as well. Adventures, mostly. Pirates and such. Highwaymen."

Cinda held her breath, willing him to go on. William had never spoken much about his family. She knew his mother and father had died within months of each other, both victims of fever. She knew he had only been nine years old at the time. He never talked of such things, and she realized he knew far more about her than she knew about him.

He was a lonely man, in many ways, despite what he said. A loner. Her instincts told her this. Perhaps because of his upbringing, which she knew had been unusual. William had learned to take care of himself. He had friends in London, to be sure, but none of them close.

They walked back outside and stood in the shadow of the pagoda.

"It's going to rain again," she said, glancing up at the sky.

The air had changed while they'd been walking within the maze, the sky growing darker and filling with clouds. The sunlight had been weak at best, almost watery, but now was obscured. She felt the wind at her back, and put her hand over her hat, not wanting to lose it.

He was staring up at the sky, studying it with an intent expression on his face. And she realized, at that moment, that they both loved the wildness within nature, the flashing lightning and thundering skies, the windswept rain, the feel in the air just before the storm broke.

"We could try to outrun it," he murmured, and she tightened her fingers around his.

"I'd like to watch it," she replied, tilting her face up toward the sky.

The first few raindrops began to fall, and he pulled her beneath the overhanging roof and into the shelter of his arms.

"You're a wild thing," he murmured against her ear, and she smiled.

"And you like it," she replied, looking up at him, knowing he was going to kiss her.

He took her mouth with care, and she slid her hands beneath his coat. He hadn't bothered with a waistcoat, and his linen shirt was warm from the heat of his body.

"You're quite appealing in that stableboy's outfit," he whispered after breaking the kiss, placing his hands on her buttocks, and pulling her more tightly against him. "I can see the outline of your legs quite clearly."

Cinda could feel his excitement in each muscle of his tall frame, could see it in his dark blue eyes. Their proximity to each other was as clearly charged as the air before the storm.

She couldn't resist teasing him. "I trust I won't hear of you attending any of the fancy dress balls at the molly houses."

He smacked her buttocks sharply, then whispered, "And how do you hear of such things?"

She laughed, and pulled slightly away from him. "I'm not the complete innocent you believe me to be, Will." She paused, fighting the tightening in her throat as she approached a truth she desperately wanted to share with him. "I never was."

He sighed, then pulled her back into his arms. "You don't know how many times I regret taking your innocence."

Her words were muffled against his shirtfront. "You certainly didn't act like it."

"I thought I knew our future, that I was doing what was best for both of us. You believe me, don't you, Cinda?"

She knew him for what he was. An honorable man.

"Yes."

"Had I known what was in store, I would have never put you in the position I subsequently did."

"I know."

The rain started to come down in earnest, lashing the dark green hedges and pounding down on the pagoda roof.

"I mean to finish this, then put it behind us. But in the meantime, I need to know that you're safe."

She nodded her head, understanding his feelings and knowing they were completely contradictory to her own desires.

"I've always felt safe with you, Will." The words were whispered as she glanced back up at him. "I've never felt as safe as I do when I'm with you."

The ground beneath their feet was starting to become muddy, so they retraced their steps back into the pagoda and sat down on one of the benches inside. The small structure had been outfitted as authentically as possible, and Will lit one of the lanterns, causing a soft light to bloom within the small, paneled room.

"So we shall wait out the storm here," she said.

"I think it would be best."

He seemed so serious, she found she wanted to lighten their mood. Will had a somber nature, and she liked helping him play, making him laugh, doing anything at all to bring a little brightness into his life.

"My coat seems to have gotten rather damp," she said, shrugging out of the garment. He took it from her, folded it, then lay it across the bench on which they sat.

She waited a moment longer, then unfastened one of the buttons on her waistcoat, then another.

The movement did not go unnoticed.

"Madam, what are you playing at?" But his stern tone was belied by the slight smile and the light in his eyes.

"My waistcoat seems tight." She cast it off swiftly, then pulled her shirt out of the tight breeches. "And this shirt is made of rather coarse stuff, and irritates my skin." Before he could reply, she caught the hem of it in her hands and swiftly pulled it over her head.

"Those breeches do seem rather indecent," he said, a smile in his voice as he reached for their fastenings. She trembled slightly at the touch of his fingers against her bare skin, then he was stripping them down off her legs, along with her stockings and boots.

She stood naked before him, totally unselfconscious, enjoying the feel of the cool, moisture-laden air against her heated skin.

"People in the Far East satisfy their most sensual urges in most creative ways, do they not?" she asked, taking his hands in her own and urging him to his feet.

"I believe there's a private area beyond that sliding panel." He'd already discarded his shirt and boots, and was now stripping off his breeches. "You'd best get to it," he said softly, nodding his head toward the panel.

She found it, opened it, and saw a pair of sofas piled high with soft, jewel-colored pillows. A thick oriental carpet covered the floor.

Will followed her, lantern in hand, then set it on a low table. The velvet sofa was cool when she sat on it, then William joined her and the warmth of his body made her forget all else.

She leaned up and blew out the lantern, then lay back on the silken pillows. The rain still pounded on the roof, the wind still blew, but they were snug within the walls of the small room, and totally alone.

"Darkness suits you this time, then?" he whispered.

"*You* suit me." Feeling bold and wanton and very free, she twined her arms around his neck and barely touched her mouth to his.

Passion bloomed between them yet again, effortlessly. Magically. She teased him, kissed his cheek, his temple, his chin, then slid her fingers into his hair and met his lips with her own.

He took command, establishing his sensual dominance easily as he sat up, then moved over her, covered her, never breaking the kiss. He kneed her thighs apart. She opened for him, ready for his possession, feeling her flesh quiver and warm at his touch. Feeling the blunt, masculine insistence of his invasion, the satisfying stretching, then filling.

She'd missed him so, and been afraid she might never see him again. Now, in his arms, that desperation lessened and a new, more urgent emotion took its place.

His hands cupped her buttocks as he positioned her for their mutual pleasure. She complied, a more than willing captive, settling her legs around his waist, her heels against his back.

He was silent as he moved, long, powerful strokes that gave such intense pleasure she couldn't contain it. The sound of rain pounding on the roof mingled with their deep breathing. Both pleasured and agonized moans filled the dark room.

They reached completion quickly, for it seemed he was just as desperate as she. Afterward, William found a heavy coverlet and they nestled beneath it, their bodies touching, their limbs tightly entwined.

"I rushed you—"

"No," she said, then sighed deeply, her face against his muscled chest, her cheek tickled by the sprinkling of hair. She breathed in his scent, and it calmed her. "No, I was as eager as you."

The rain had abated, as had the wind, and the heavy coverlet kept the chill air at bay.

"Can we sleep, Will?" she asked, already starting to dream.

"Sleep, darling. As long as you want."

The card party was not going at all the way Nan had envisioned it.

She sat at one of the tables in the brightly candlelit room, hiding her immense frustration behind a falsely calm facade. A vast amount of coin had slipped through her fingers this evening, and, whether at faro, whist, or loo, quinze or vingt-et-un, luck had deserted her tonight.

Glancing around the tables at the other gamblers, Nan bit her lip until she tasted blood. The one thing a gambler could never afford to do was inform the world they knew when they were losing.

It was becoming harder and harder to keep up with her rich friends. She'd thought this particular party would have helped, it was certainly lavish enough.

Two card rooms had been set up, blazing brilliantly from the numerous candles on both tables and chandeliers. The country house was exquisite, the walls of this particular room a pale yellow silk damask.

The foods displayed in the dining room were plentiful, a veritable wealth of epicurean delights, designed to stimulate and amuse the most jaded of palates. As for expense, nothing had been spared.

Several of the guests were conversing in the drawing room, but most had congregated within the card rooms. But what was for them a mere evening's divertissement was something much more for her.

What Nan longed for more than anything else was to be able to associate with them all and have not a care for finances. To have so much money she need never worry again. And if she relied on her worthless husband to help her achieve such an aim, they'd all end up in a workhouse.

One of several waiters approached the table, refilling wineglasses, offering various other spirits, and proffering a steady supply of snuff. Nan simply placed her hand over her glass. It never was wise to drink and gamble at the same time. If her wits were addled, it would make losing all the easier.

She couldn't afford to lose. The stakes were simply too high.

They had taken a break from their cards. The portly gentleman with the stained waistcoat who sat next to her had retired to the dining room. Thus she was surprised when the seat was suddenly occupied. Glancing over, she came face-to-face with Jeffrey Templeton, second Viscount Hoareton.

They were alike, the two of them. Cut from the same piece of cloth. Aspiring to enter the charmed circle of the aristocracy, and each firmly on the fringes.

But they could help each other, and they both knew it.

"Lord Templeton," she murmured, glancing round to see who was within listening distance.

"Nancy," he said softly, bringing her gloved hand to his lips. "You must call me Jeffrey. After all, within weeks we shall be related, in a manner of speaking."

Nan smiled. Jeffrey's oldest brother, Colin Templeton, was Cinda's prospective bridegroom. Heir to the entire Templeton family fortune, he was a man who had more than enough money to finance anything either she or Jeffrey desired.

Colin was also quite mad.

The family kept him locked up at home at their country estate. While Jeffrey's three sisters had all married quite well and started families of their own, and his two other brothers had emigrated to the Colonies, Jeffrey had remained at home, determined to find a way to cheat Colin out of his inheritance.

It was certainly simpler than finding honest work.

Not many knew the extent of Colin's deterioration. The family chose to veil his madness from outside eyes. They considered Colin's madness an abomination. Jeffrey had professed great love for his eldest sibling, and made the sacrifice of staying on at the Templeton estate and caring for Colin.

Not for Colin the public lunatic asylums, or even the private madhouses. No, Jeffrey treated his brother at home, and ensured the child-man never saw the light of day.

Colin was rarely let out of his rooms. Jeffrey's treatment of his brother was brutal, relying on beatings, cold-water baths, and regular bleeding and purging in order to divert the morbid humors from his head.

Now, Colin needed an heir. A male child.

And once that heir was produced, Jeffrey would have no trouble at all convincing his family that control of the estates should be passed on to the boy. Then it was only a matter of keeping the child within the sphere of his considerable influence.

He needed a woman who would consent to being bedded by a madman. At least once. Just enough to ensure that gossiping servants and prying eyes believed the child to be Colin's.

"Is she a virgin?" Jeffrey whispered as he signaled a waiter. "Will I have the pleasure of her maidenhead?"

"I have watched the girl since I came to her father's house. She is most certainly pure." Nan had her doubts, but would never voice them to this man.

Jeffrey smiled sweetly at the waiter as he poured him a glass of expensive claret. The viscount had the most angelic of faces, as innocent as a child's. To the people who thought they knew him, he had sacrificed all to care for his brother. But behind the facade, Nan knew him to be utterly ruthless, quietly determined. And fiendishly clever.

She admired that cleverness.

His pale blond hair was powdered and arranged just so, his clothing immaculate and expensive. Jeffrey received a generous allowance from his brother's estate, which his brothers and sisters were more than willing for him to have. None of them wanted to care for Colin.

"How do your daughters fare this evening?" he asked.

Nan was sure the question had been asked more out of politeness than interest. For how could any man in his right mind be interested in gangly Miranda or oafish Helena? She'd caught sight of her daughters in the drawing room, laughing hysterically at the sight of a gentleman shaking the bugs out of his wig in front of the ladies.

Even Rosalind, as weak and childlike as she had been, would have been an improvement over those two.

Now, the only winning card she had to play in this particular game was that of Cinda. She would marry Colin, be bedded by Jeffrey, and, one way or another, produce an heir. And both she and Jeffrey would profit from it. She was already making plans for ridding herself of Horace. Her offspring would be on their own once she had the money she desired.

"More interested in the delicacies in the dining room than any prospective husband," she whispered.

Jeffrey laughed, and she was struck once again by how charming he appeared. One had to look carefully to find the signs of debauchery, but they were there. The expression in his eyes when he thought he wasn't being watched. The slight softening of the skin around his face, the result of too much drink and indulgent behavior.

"Have you need of a loan?" he whispered, glancing around the card room. Nan swiftly brought her thoughts back to the present.

"Why do you ask?" she countered, suddenly afraid of him.

He smiled lazily, his blue eyes amused. "I have been where you are, Nancy, and have no wish to see you suffer needlessly."

Liar. She didn't trust him, and, once she had what she wanted from him, would cut him out of her life as swiftly as she had the others.

Her instincts told her not to take the loan, as the interest due might be more than she would want to give.

"Then I shall suffer no longer," she replied, forcing a note of gaiety into her voice. "Come, Jeffrey, be a gentleman and escort me into the dining room. I wish to see what is being served that has enthralled my daughters so."

He laughed, then they both stood and he took her arm.

"The girl is willing, then?" Jeffrey asked, and Nan thought how deftly he changed the subject to something they could agree upon.

"One way or another, she will be."

They laughed then, their thoughts in perfect accord.

Cinda stood in the library of Will's townhouse, studying the two invitations on the massive desk.

What she was considering would be a flagrant disregard of everything she'd promised Will. It was not in her nature to be willfully defiant, but both instinct and emotion called out and drove her to action.

She picked up one of the invitations and studied it. She could have easily memorized the address and time, even written it down. From what she'd heard, it was easy to slip into a masquerade, as long as one had a costume. This one promised to be so huge, she could conspire a way to be lost in the vast crowd.

Yet she could not deceive William in that particular way. If she took the invitation, he would know she was attending. He would look for her.

They could search for Rosalind's killer together.

The two invitations rested beneath a silver snuffbox. Whoever had given them to William had assumed he would want to attend the event with a member of the fairer sex. She certainly wasn't worried about his inviting anyone else, for she knew he walked alone while hunting this madman.

Why do I always want what I cannot have?

But it was within her grasp, on this desk.

William would be furious with her. Yet she knew the action she contemplated was the right one.

She would be leaving the townhouse within the hour. William had gone to see to the horses, leaving her to finish dressing, donning her stableboy disguise in case they should be watched. He would see her safely back to her stepmother's house, where she would be expected to watch, wait, and pray.

She closed her eyes, trying one last time to battle the desires that raged within her. And as she did, her fingers touched the invitations, picked one up.

You cannot . . .

She closed her hand around it.

I cannot wait and do nothing. I cannot.

And if it should cost you William?

The thought was too horrible to contemplate.

Yet Rosalind died in my place . . .

She heard his booted feet in the hallway, heard his approach toward the library. Within seconds, when he entered the room, she would have no choice.

Slipping the one invitation farther beneath the snuffbox, she slid the other into her waistcoat pocket.

CHAPTER
❧ 9 ❧

The moon rode high in the sky, surrounded by twinkling stars, the night was foggy and cold. Rain beat against the townhouse walls, dripping off the three-story building's eaves, running into the cobbled street below to form vast, dirty puddles. The fog muffled all sounds, and hoofbeats and voices seemed farther away, lost in the night. Signs swung over closed shops, taverns, and chophouses, their creaking mingling with the sighing of the wind.

Inside, Cinda and Cook remained huddled by the vast kitchen fire, warming their toes and toasting slices of bread.

Cinda had decided, during the ride home, to tell Cook everything, for she needed the older woman's opinion and good faith concerning the risk she was contemplating.

"You've no cause to feel guilty," Cook said as she spread butter on the toasted bread, then glanced round for the strawberry jam.

"But I do."

Cook frowned. "Part of the story is still not clear to me. Rosalind was a dreamer, that much is true. But she had enough sense to know the risk she took, going out after dark. And alone." The older woman shook her head. "Something is out of place, here. A piece of the puzzle is missing."

Cinda had changed into her servant's garb, hiding her boyish disguise in her room above the stable. She'd had time for a quick wash to remove the smell of horse, then immediately started in on the various chores she'd neglected.

Now, late at night, with both Victor and Mary sound asleep and Nan and her daughters still in the country, she felt safe confiding all in her friend.

"She was in love with love," she said now.

Cook cocked her head, and Cinda knew the older woman had heard the slight cynicism in her voice. And was waiting for an explanation.

"When I was first with Will, it was as if I could do no wrong," she began.

Cook nodded her head, silent, encouraging her to continue.

"But now—it's as if he wishes to put me up on a shelf, to take down and dust and play with when he finds the time."

Cook, a bite of toast in her mouth, had started to laugh. She swallowed, her generous shoulders still shaking.

"No, my precious, I'm not laughing at you. It's just that they're so alike, these men of ours. When the first flush of excitement has passed, they like to get on with their lives, and they wish to see us as simply waiting for them to make our lives complete."

Cinda grinned. Cook understood.

"My husband, God rest his soul, couldn't understand why everything didn't simply come to a stop when he left the room." She laughed again, then wiped amused tears from her hazel eyes with the back of her hand.

"We were eating at a chophouse once, and I introduced him to a woman I had met. He looked at me as if to say, 'When did this happen?' I loved the man, and I respected him, but that isn't to say he didn't have his little peculiarities." She took a quick sip of tea. "And they all do, but we love them just the same, because it's part of God's plan."

Cinda pierced another piece of bread with a long fork and held it carefully over the fire. She had to find the right words to convince Cook to help her. If she thought there was great danger involved, she might become as overprotective as Will.

"So, my girl, what's the plan?"

Cinda averted her face so Cook wouldn't see the mutinous tightening of her jaw. How well this old woman knew her. And had from the day she was born.

Without a word, she reached into her apron pocket, then handed her friend the invitation.

Cook studied it for almost a minute, and Cinda could feel

her agile mind working, jumping ahead. There would be very little she would have to explain, she was sure of that.

"He doesn't want you to go."

"He cannot do this alone."

"You're probably right."

Cinda, expecting an argument, felt as if all the wind had been taken out of her sails.

"I am?"

"It's too much for any one person. Your poor William's up against the devil himself this time. He needs your help."

"No one *knows* me, not since Nan shut me away in this house," Cinda began, trying to keep her voice from shaking. This meant so much to her. "I could slip in and out of crowds, find out things a man never could."

Cook nodded her head. "Men are certainly stronger, but there is a certain cleverness that belongs to a woman. How do you propose to fool *her*?"

"I won't go out until she and her daughters have left, and then I shall return before they do."

"And the night of this masquerade?" Cook asked, tapping the invitation in her hand.

"She goes to a dinner with Miranda and Helena. I—stole a look at the invitations in her desk—"

"Don't trouble yourself over the deceit, it was necessary—"

"And there will be cards afterward, and you know she never returns until the early hours of the morning."

"And William?"

"I'll make him bend to my will."

"You're a confident one."

"I can't afford not to be. He needs me!"

"And he doesn't want to. No man wants to have what he thinks of as a shortcoming brought to his attention."

Cinda was silent. Frustrated.

"He'll know you're there," Cook continued, "the minute he realizes the second invitation is missing."

"I never meant to deceive him."

Cook sighed. "He'll be angry. And rightly so. Should this madman know who you are, you would be his next prey."

"He won't find out."

"Feeling lucky, are you?"

She set down the toasting fork and grasped her friend's

hand. "I have to do this. It doesn't matter why or how Rosalind went out that night, all that matters is that she is dead because of me."

"'Tis no fault of yours—or William's."

"Why do I feel it is?"

"That's something you must search your soul to answer."

They were silent for a time, staring into the flames.

"Are you being completely truthful with yourself?" Cook said at last.

Cinda shook her head, marveling at how the older woman cut to the heart of the problem so effortlessly.

"It's no shame to simply want to go to the masquerade."

The tears filled Cinda's eyes before she could stop them.

"There's no shame in that being a part of it." And Cook patted her cheek. "She's taken so much away from you. I know. And you'd like to believe that before you marry William, you have a chance to go to the ball."

Cinda nodded, feeling unspeakably selfish.

"But it eats at your heart that she died in your place."

She put her hands over her face and began to sob.

"I know," Cook murmured comfortingly as she moved her chair closer and enfolded Cinda in her arms. "I know."

She let her cry, and Cinda was grateful. She cried until the tears no longer came, then sat back and wiped her eyes with the hem of her apron.

"When I was small, I didn't know I was being protected," she began, then blew her nose on a handkerchief. "All that I wanted in the world was within this house and garden. When my mother died, I felt as if I'd been torn into pieces."

Cook nodded her head, tears standing out in her eyes, and Cinda remembered how much the older woman had loved her mother.

"Before I could recover, she moved herself in and shut me away from the world."

"I know."

"Now Will tries to do the same, and he—*disappoints* me so very much."

"He's trying to protect you. Cinda, you might defy him, but you cannot blame him for acting like a man."

"Why can't I simply obey him? Why is it that I always want more than is good for me—"

"No. You have a different temperament than most. And it is this spirit that he loves, as much as he might attempt to change it. But you cannot blame a man for being true to his nature."

Cinda got up and poured them each a little more tea, warming their cups. Then she picked up the long fork and resumed toasting her bread.

"So if you were in my place?" she whispered, her throat tight in anticipation of her friend's answer.

Cook's eyes were dancing as she leaned back in her chair.

"I should be planning my costume."

Kathleen set the ivory silk ball gown aside, then stood up and stretched her arms, trying to relieve the tightness in her back. She flexed her cramped fingers against the chill, then pulled her shawl tighter around her shoulders.

The single candle had burned low. She reminded herself to buy another tomorrow, and not deplete her friend's larder.

Even plying her needle round the clock, it was going to be a struggle to have Cinda's first dress ready by the time of the masqued dinner party.

Julia had been more than generous. Immediately upon learning of her friend's dilemma, Julia had insisted she come upstairs and look through the ball gowns her daughters had left. They'd been clean and pressed, quite carefully preserved. Now, the only job left was to cleverly adapt them to the current styles, so Cinda would not look hopelessly out of fashion.

More than anything, Kathleen wished some of her family's fortune might have been left. Then she would have taken Cinda to the finest French seamstress and had a gown designed that would offset her godchild's fiery hair and brilliant green eyes. And gloves, fine shoes, and the most cunning of fans . . .

She glanced down at the dress she'd placed on the chair.

Be thankful for what has been given to you.

The ivory silk was a good color, and would set off Cinda's complexion. But all the jewelry had been sold a long time ago, and it had taken a goodly amount of her savings to have gloves made to match the gown, along with a length of fine Brussels lace to adorn it.

At least Eleanor thought to provide the shoes. Though not in the exact way she envisioned.

Kathleen opened her bedroom door onto the dark hallway. A candle in hand, she descended the stairs toward the kitchen. Careful not to make a sound, she prepared herself a cup of tea from the small amount she had brought with her, not wanting to trouble the sleeping servant.

She'd made a promise to herself she would not cause any upset in Julia's home. Fortune had been kind enough in that her friend let her stay on, when she had no home in London of her own.

Taking the cup of tea back to her quiet bedroom, she enjoyed the brief repast, then set to work with her needle again.

The bedroom was icy, the fire had died down long ago, but she refused to use any more coal than necessary. Kathleen would do nothing to cause Julia more expense. Her bare fingers were cramped and chilled, but still she worked the needle through the fine cloth.

By the light of a single candle, as the rain fell against the walls and the fog obscured the light of the moon, Kathleen worked far into the night.

William feigned interest in his cards, all the time considering the other men at his table.

They'd had supper together at the club, and planned to play cards all night. Though not a gambler by nature, William knew it was the most efficient way of finding the man he sought.

Charles Hailey.

Philip Fleming.

Ashley Blessington.

He'd thought he knew his three friends quite well, as well as anyone could be known. But since the night he'd come to understand he was being stalked, William had realized he had to assume he knew nothing.

He'd made it his business, since Rosalind's death, to quietly find out as much as possible about all who knew him, starting with the men with whom he played cards, enjoyed the hunt, and shared meals.

Their closeness was deceptive, as none of them were truly intimate with their emotions and feelings. They simply enjoyed one another's company, joked and laughed and engaged in friendly masculine competition.

Thus William played cards, his attention half on the hand in his possession, half on the men who shared the table.

Each had a secret, of that he was sure.

Charles Hailey, tall and dark-haired with pleasing features, gambled to excess. Thus, William had deliberately kept tonight's wager low. He'd made it his business to find out how deeply Charles was in debt, and discovered his friend was in serious trouble. He'd even attempted to speak with Charles's father. That had caused no amount of animosity between himself and his friend, for Charles believed he might yet wager himself out of financial tragedy.

Philip Fleming, a strongly built man with blond hair and gray eyes, was illegitimate, but his father had loved him all the same and recognized his claim to the family fortune. His mother had been quite a beautiful actress. When she'd drowned, Philip's father had taken the little boy into his home and raised him as his own, claiming he was a distant cousin.

None of the aristocracy knew of Philip's secret, as the family had chosen to keep it quiet. But older servants had a way of knowing things, and William had made discreet inquiries. Money had exchanged hands, silence had been promised, and the information had been tucked away, to be mulled over and considered.

Ashley Blessington had the most damning secret of all.

The eldest son of an eldest son, he was expected to pro-duce an heir to continue his family's illustrious line. But this feat would be all but impossible, considering Ashley's sexual proclivities. William knew he frequented private clubs that catered to his taste for young men, and he was also fairly sure Ashley's family was aware of his predilections. They simply chose to look the other way.

William had not enjoyed delving into their private lives. He'd felt the voyeur. What had interested him was that each man possessed considerable anger concerning his situation. And William wondered, as he calmly played cards, if that anger was enough to motivate one of them to kill.

Cinda had retired for the night, falling asleep on a pallet in front of the kitchen fire. Cook remained sitting by the warming flames.

Though the windows and doors were shut tightly against

drafts of cold, wet air, the single candle she had lit suddenly flickered. Her scarred old tom raised his head, disturbed out of his dreaming sleep in her lap.

Cook smiled, running her callused fingers through the rough gray fur. *He feels her presence, too.*

"Nora?" she called softly to her friend.

The candle flame flickered again, as if in answer, though Cook felt no draft of air.

Cook glanced at Cinda, sleeping by the fire.

"I've done my best for her, but I don't know that either of us can protect her now."

This time the flame burned steadily, but it didn't matter. Cook could feel the dead woman's presence strongly. Eleanor had come to her before, had whispered to her in her dreams. Cook knew Cinda's mother could not move on. Not yet. Like most ghosts, she'd chosen to return to right wrongs, to warn the living about a threat.

Eleanor hadn't been able to leave her home. Though she hadn't appeared in front of the servants, walking the house at night and causing them to shriek with fright, she had a habit of moving objects, making noises, and leaving just a hint of her scent.

More than once, Cook knew Nan had been unnerved.

It pleased her that Eleanor should choose to stay close, but worried her at the same time.

She continued the slow, rhythmic petting of the old cat, running her fingers over his scarred head. He settled back, closed his eyes, and kneaded her lap with his claws.

"You'll have to move on, sooner or later," she whispered.

The candle's flame flickered. *Angrily*, Cook thought.

"And how am I to stop her when her temperament's a reflection of yours?" Cook replied, gently amused. "You couldn't stop her from going to him if you stood in this kitchen a flesh and blood woman."

The flame glowed brighter, then subsided.

"We'll have to work together, else we'll be no help to her at all."

Cook felt Eleanor's acceptance, and smiled.

"Can we trust Kathleen?" she asked the silent room. "Once for yes, twice for no."

The soft tap came once, and Cook nodded.

"She's back in London. Her friend's footman left her card for Cinda, I forgot to tell her. But I will first thing in the morning, and send my Robbie to accompany her when she visits her godmother."

Silence.

"I'm sure Kathleen is trying as hard as she can."

Silence.

Nora, talk to me.

Cook watched, completely unafraid, as a piece of bread on the table slowly rose into the air, then just as slowly was set back down on the wooden surface.

Tears filled her eyes.

"Don't you think I remember, Nora?" Her voice broke.

The candle's flame flickered.

"Don't you think I know exactly what cruelty that woman is capable of?"

Cook had caught a fever one winter, and spent several days in bed. At the same time, Nan had decided Cinda deserved to be punished for a perceived insolence. When Cook had finally taken control of her kitchen back, the girl had been locked in her stable room for three days and given nothing but stale bread and drippings to eat.

There had been mice dirts in the drippings.

And Cinda had been nine years old.

"Aye, she's had it hard," Cook whispered. "We all have, since that woman came. But don't you see? She's found a way out! With him!"

The word floated into her mind.

Killer.

"So you heard? And what would you suggest I do to stop her? She's only doing what you would do."

Help her.

"With my life, Nora. With my life."

The presence was fading, and Cook wondered if it taxed Eleanor's strength to appear in such a way. She couldn't have explained it to a living soul, even to Cinda, but she knew the exact moment her friend and mistress was no longer in the room.

She glanced over at the pallet by the fire, and the sleeping girl. Cinda was exhausted, and Cook knew what it had cost her to steal that invitation.

"Ah, Thomas," she whispered. "Would that I were young and strong and could really help, instead of old and worthless like I am."

The tom meowed softly, and she laughed.

"And you a kitten, playing with a ball of wool."

He looked up at her, his eyes mere slits, and purred.

"Some cream, perhaps?" Cook smiled down at her cat. "At our age, Thomas, we take our pleasures where we can find them."

William slid into bed, thankful Henry had thought to put a warming pan between the sheets, insuring they would not be icy and unwelcoming.

He hadn't stayed at the club much past four in the morning. As he'd left, he'd seen Charles join another table, where the wagers were much higher. He'd said nothing to his friend, knowing what his interference had cost him the last time.

Philip had decided to leave at the same time, and Ashley had slipped out, off to one of his private clubs, no doubt.

William's bare leg jostled one of the small sachets Cinda had given him. In the past, she'd supplied him with others at regular intervals, and he'd marveled at the way the bedbugs had promptly removed themselves. Always, she thought of his comfort.

He missed her. Each time he realized how completely she'd wound herself around his emotions, he marveled at the power she had over him.

It terrified him.

She'd made his life complete, yet they could not be together. She made him want to get up in the morning, made his life so much happier, yet the darkest thoughts he'd ever entertained centered around what he would do should he ever find himself without her.

He sighed deeply, alone in the dark room and remembering what it had been like to have her in his bed. Erotic, certainly. She had as much spirit in bed as out of it, and pleased him greatly. But it was more than that, for physical comfort could be found in any brothel.

She gave him a sense of peace he hadn't had since his mother had died. He marveled at her gentler qualities, and how he'd missed that feminine influence over the years.

A noise by the door caught his attention, and he turned his head, then raised himself up on one elbow.

"Henry?" he called softly.

Juno's head appeared around the door, her dark eyes beseeching. She was a sensitive animal, and missed her master. Missing the one you loved was an emotion William could understand.

"Come, Juno," he called, patting the side of the curtained bed.

The massive dog entered the room, then curled up on the floor at the foot of the bed, by the warmth of the fire. She gave a great sigh before she tucked her head down onto her paws and closed her eyes.

And William, wishing he could find sleep as easily, stared at the firelight and thought of Cinda.

Kathleen had fallen asleep in her chair, the ivory ball gown slipping out of her fingers and falling to the carpeted floor. The rain had stopped, but the fog was still thick in the night sky.

The single candle had long since burned itself out, and the only sound in the upstairs bedroom was her gentle breathing.

She woke suddenly, feeling a chill in the room. Shivering, Kathleen took off her spectacles and placed them on the small bedside table. Then she stood, went to her bed, pulled down the bedspread, took off her wool wrapper, and slipped beneath the thick blankets. Her eyes closed, and she drifted off to sleep, exhausted.

Within minutes the fog cleared and the bedroom was bathed in silvery moonlight. Kathleen, sleeping deeply, didn't see the ivory ball gown slowly drift up the chair and take shape over an invisible lap, nor the silver needle that began to flash in and out of the silk as the thread joined the lavish lace trim to the bodice.

"She's here in London?" Cinda asked the next morning. She and Cook were taking a much-needed rest from the weekly baking, and were sitting around the old oak table.

"The footman said as much. I forgot to tell you of the note."

Cinda waved this aside as she took the small card from Cook's hand. "I couldn't have done anything last night, I was too tired."

"Robbie could run a message to her."

"When will Nan return?"

"None of us is sure."

Nan liked to keep her help on their toes by never letting them be too sure of what she was up to.

"We could stop by Sunday, after church," Cook suggested. "That way, Nan wouldn't have to know."

Cinda nodded her head, then stood up.

"I'll fetch paper and a quill."

Her message was written posthaste, the ink was dried, and the note sealed and given to Robbie. He saddled a gray gelding, then left with Cinda's missive.

"The masquerade is less than a week away," Cinda said, rolling out piecrusts as she spoke. They had resumed their work, knowing Nan would not be pleased to come back and find they had fallen behind.

"I'll see what materials I can find in the wash."

"It would be too risky to steal a ball gown," Cinda mused. "Or even parts of one."

"They'd know," Cook replied. "They've had Mary mending and pressing all their gowns, even the older ones."

"She's running out of money, then," Cinda said. "She'd have bought new ones by now if she thought she could afford them."

Both women knew of Horace Townshend's gambling, and his continual drunkenness. Nan had long ago stopped viewing his habits with indulgence. He was rarely home anymore, preferring to live at his club.

No one, including Nan, knew what kind of debts he'd run up. It was only a matter of time before the house was given to his creditors.

"We can do this," Cook said quietly, her hand firm as it covered Cinda's on the old, scarred tabletop. "You'll get to that masquerade if I have to sacrifice my last good petticoat."

Cinda threw her arms around the woman who was as close to her as her mother had been. Though upset that William didn't understand what drove her, for now it was enough to know Cook did.

CHAPTER
❧ 10 ❧

Even Nan didn't dare keep her servants away from God.

If she could have found a way around the biblical injunction that stated no work was to be done on Sunday, she would have. But Cook ruled the spiritual side of her kitchen with a sure and steady hand, and part of that responsibility entailed ensuring the servants kept up with their religious instruction. This included prayers twice daily, and church on Sunday.

Thus, Cinda found herself in church with Cook, as usual. Robbie, Mary, and Victor also attended. They all sat in one of the back pews and listened to the service, but Cinda found her mind wandering.

Perhaps because it was a glorious spring day. She never felt closer to God than when she was in her mother's garden. Now she thought of that favorite plot of earth, what she needed to do to maintain the beds of vegetables and flowers, the various plants she still wanted to incorporate into the design, the questions she wanted to ask William.

Resolutely, she turned her mind away from introspection, and tried to listen to the service. It concerned the afterlife, and the preparations that had to be made in the present.

For life is an endless circle, which soon joins the grave with the cradle . . .

She closed her eyes and thought of Rosalind, and wondered what had become of the girl. Her breathing became more shallow, and her heartbeat picked up speed.

Preparation for Death is the whole work of life . . .

She felt Cook's hand cover hers and squeeze gently. It was as if the woman could see within her mind and sense her great agitation. Had her stepsister suffered? Was she suffering now?

The eyes will close and turn into sunken cavities, the hand will instantly freeze at Death's touch . . .

She thought of the small grave where her stepsister's body now resided. To dwell on the frightened, shy girl resting in that cold, damp earth was painful, and her heart pounded heavily as her agitation increased.

Surely God had been merciful. Had Rosalind passed through the gates of heaven?

Her thoughts unbearable now, Cinda bowed her head, closed her eyes, and thought of the flowers beginning to bloom in her garden. She did this often, flew away from her present circumstances with the power of her imagination. It was as if her soul took flight, and she allowed it to go where it might, knowing it had to seek a better place than the pain in the present.

She thought of the masquerade . . .

They walked the short distance to where her godmother was staying. Victor and Mary went on to a cookshop to pick up several meat pies for dinner, and Robbie and Cook accompanied Cinda to see Kathleen.

Cinda knew of Julia, as did Cook. The widow had been a good friend to Kathleen for many years. Now, soon to see her godmother again, Cinda tried to understand why her godmother had never come for her. And with those thoughts came old and bitterly familiar feelings.

"I want you to consider forgiveness," Cook said, seeming to see inside her mind once again.

Cinda bit her lip, as hot, angry words sprang to mind. They'd had this particular discussion before.

"I will be civil."

"You'll be more than civil," Cook replied softly, and Cinda knew when she'd been beaten. She nodded her head.

"Your anger will poison you," Cook said, putting a reassuring arm around Cinda's shoulders.

"I know. I'll try. But for you, not for her." It was a childish outburst, but it made her feel better for saying it.

Cook merely smiled.

*　　*　　*

Kathleen's hands were like ice as she rearranged the delicate tea cakes on the silver serving platter. Julia had insisted that her housemaid attend her today, and Kathleen had not been able to refuse her friend's request. Still, she was nervous. She hadn't seen her godchild in a number of years, and she wanted this first meeting to be free of the usual tension.

She knew she'd failed her niece, Eleanor, and she didn't need to see the reproach in Cinda's green eyes to be aware of that fact.

The brisk knock on the door stilled her nervous movements, and she listened as the butler came to the door and admitted her guests.

Cinda entered the parlor, and Kathleen recognized Eleanor's cook and her youngest son standing behind her. They both looked uneasy at being there, but Cinda merely seemed quietly resigned.

Kathleen stood, willing her legs not to shake.

"Come in." She smiled, feeling the tentativeness of the gesture as she did it. Her godchild paused for a moment in the doorway, then entered the room and took the seat farthest from her.

What did you expect? You haven't really been a part of the girl's life.

But she was no longer a girl. Kathleen looked at her godchild and saw her beloved niece all over again. Quick, emotional tears sprang to her eyes before she could restrain herself.

"She looks like Eleanor, doesn't she?" Cook said, and Kathleen merely nodded, grateful for the woman's kindness and understanding. Cinda might be unreceptive to her overtures, but the cook wasn't. Kathleen was grateful for any tentative emotional bridges.

She swallowed down the intense emotion that filled her throat. "Yes. She does."

"Thank you." This was from Cinda. "I remember my mother as being quite beautiful, and will take what you said as a compliment."

Her tone was cool, but at least she hadn't refused to see her. Kathleen's smile faded, but she determined to try to build something of a relationship with her only living relative.

The housemaid entered with a silver tea service. Though Kathleen used her own tea leaves several times before she disposed of them, Julia had wanted this particular tea party to be special. The tea was fragrant and strong, the coffee brewed perfectly. And Kathleen wondered if her godchild would go away believing she'd always lived with such luxury.

There had been times she'd lived out of her carriage. Many winters had been brutally cold, and only the kindness of various friends and the warmth of their houses had kept her alive. It was not a pleasant fate, to be so dependent on others, but she'd survived thus far.

Living with Julia for a time had strengthened her. Julia's husband had loved her and their three daughters dearly. When he'd died, he'd left them well provided for.

There were times Kathleen envied her, but she kept her thoughts to herself. Now, she concentrated on her godchild.

"What would you like in your tea?" she asked, directing her question at Cinda.

"I prefer coffee."

Kathleen didn't miss the look that was exchanged between Cinda and the cook. Her son simply seemed uncomfortably resigned to spending the afternoon.

She knew how out of place most men felt at women's gatherings, and took pity on him. Kathleen glanced at the cook.

"Is it—Robert?"

The woman smiled and leaned forward, her broad hands clasped tightly together. "How good of you to remember. Robbie was born two years before Cinda, and they've grown up together." She cleared her throat. "You gave me a christening shawl, and I never forgot your kindness toward us."

Kathleen knew an ally when she saw one.

"I remember." She turned her attention to the young man. "Robert, there's a warm fire in the kitchen, and several comfortable chairs. I'm sure you'd be bored with what women discuss, and I believe a piece of pie and a tankard of ale would please you much more than tea."

He was already on his feet, his eye on the pretty, dark-haired housemaid. "Thank you, Mistress Stanhope."

She was touched by the fact that he remembered her name,

when she'd barely recalled his own.

Once he left, she turned her attention to the matter at hand. She handed Cinda her coffee, then fixed the cook a cup of tea. The silver serving platters were piled high with scones, pastries, tarts, and several varieties of tea breads.

Kathleen picked up one of the small china dishes.

"Cinda? What would you like?"

"Just the coffee, thank you."

She was too thin. The gossip around London was that Nan worked her mercilessly and fed her inadequately. Still, the girl was strong, to have survived. And Kathleen realized she possessed the same harsh pride Eleanor had displayed, and grudgingly admired it.

I would probably do the same, were I in her position.

The cook requested one of the tarts, then broke off a piece and chewed it slowly, her expression thoughtful. And Kathleen, knowing full well this might be the last chance to establish any sort of connection with her godchild, took a deep breath and plunged ahead.

"You have every right to be angry with me, Cinda."

Kathleen watched as her godchild carefully set down her china cup and gazed at her with brilliant green eyes.

"I don't even know you. How could I possibly be angry?"

The barb hit home, and wounded her deeply. Still, Kathleen continued.

"I would like to use this time in London to get better acquainted with you."

"As you wish." Her reply was cool, and Kathleen didn't miss the way the cook was looking at her godchild, and the quite pointed way Cinda was ignoring her.

"Does Nan—does she allow you to attend any social functions?"

Cinda smiled at this, but it didn't reach her eyes.

"No."

The cook swallowed another piece of tart. "Whatever you have planned will have to be done without her having any knowledge of it."

"I thought as much—"

"Don't discuss me as if I weren't here."

"Cinda, I—"

"What is it exactly that you have in mind?"

Kathleen stood, her hands in front of her, her fingers spread in a gesture of appeal. She didn't know what to do with the girl. She obviously didn't want to be here.

"Would you both come upstairs with me, just for a moment?" Defeat tasted as bitter as bile in the back of her throat, and she conceded to herself that she might never have another chance with her godchild. She met Cinda's gaze with her own.

"If after I've shown you what I intend and—explain my plan, if you still want to leave, I—I won't stand in your way."

This surprised Cinda, she could sense it. Her godchild seemed to hesitate, and Kathleen let her breath out slowly as the cook walked over to the girl and placed a hand on her arm.

"As you wish," Cinda said.

The ball gown was glorious.

Cinda tried to hide her surprise, and failed miserably. The dress had been spread out across the bed, the ivory silk shimmering in the afternoon light. Kathleen quietly explained that it had been one of Julia's daughter's castoffs, but she'd redesigned it. A bit of lace here, a dart there, and a whole new gown had been created.

The gloves were new, as were the ribbons for her hair. But the jeweled slippers were what made Cinda cry.

"They were your mother's," Kathleen began awkwardly. "She asked me to give them to you. They were to be worn on your wedding day, on the day you left your father's house. But I'm sure Eleanor wouldn't begrudge us using them now, for such a good cause."

She placed the slippers in Cinda's hands, then curled her fingers around them. And Cinda, holding a tangible link to her mother, began to cry, hating to reveal her feelings in front of her godmother.

That gilded leather and paste jewels could bring up such painful memories astounded her, but knowing her mother had wanted her to have these slippers caused her emotions to rush to the surface.

She couldn't control herself, and Cook enfolded her in her strong arms as she sobbed.

Kathleen simply stood by the bed, two of the ribbons crushed tightly in her hands.

•

She thanked her godmother, promised to come back on the night of the dinner party, and left with Cook and Robbie.

"I know what you're thinking," Cook began as Robbie walked on ahead.

"It's the same night as Will's masquerade. I can go to Julia's house, get dressed, and attend the masqued ball!"

"Kathleen must never know you didn't attend the dinner."

"She won't. I doubt she'll even check with the hostess. I'll simply tell her some sort of story—"

"She loves you, Cinda. In her own way."

They walked along in silence for a few minutes, then Cinda said, "I remember those slippers. Mother wore them to a ball one night. I remember the way they sparkled on her feet."

"They must have looked lovely when she danced."

"Why do you think she's doing all this for me now?"

"Maybe she's able to give to you at this time." When Cinda didn't answer, Cook said, "Maybe she wanted to give to you from the beginning, but until now couldn't afford to."

"She left me."

"Your father would have never let her take you away. You know that."

Horace's actions hadn't been dictated by any paternal affection. He'd simply wanted her there to help care for him. Even as a child, Cinda had been far more the adult than her irresponsible father.

"She could have taken me away."

"Sometimes," Cook said, "you ask too much of people."

"Perhaps I do."

"Let us think on it this way. Perhaps God heard our prayers, and listened to Kathleen's as well. And He let us all meet in the middle."

"Do you ever stop looking for the good in people?" Cinda asked her friend.

Cook merely tugged on her braid, and they continued on their way home.

•

William came upon Ashley Blessington while riding in St. James's Park Monday morning. His friend was riding an exceptional mount, a dappled gray stallion with a fiery spirit and excellent gait. As William was himself an admirer of horseflesh, he cantered his black stallion toward his friend and the two men began to converse.

Finding out about Ashley's sexual preference had not changed the way he felt about their friendship. If anything, he felt a kind of sorrow for the man, keeping so much of himself so carefully guarded. The subject had never even been hinted at between the two men, and William doubted it ever would.

Ashley would be horrified if he suspected William knew as much as he did.

Though William had originally thought Ashley's family was aware of his friend's tastes, now he wasn't as sure. The Blessingtons were an extremely close-knit group, and defended members of their family to the death. If anyone knew about Ashley, no one was saying a word.

The information had come to William by chance. None of the aristocracy was unaware that certain of their members had such preferences. Most simply chose to accept the fact and look the other way. There were private clubs and molly houses catering to such leanings, the same way flagellants' clubs took care of that particular masculine vice.

William had been at a masquerade with his mistress, Anne, almost two years ago. As he and Ashley were built along the same lines and even shared the same coloring, he'd been surprised when a young man he'd been talking to had become increasingly familiar with him. When the fellow had realized his mistake, he'd turned quite red and melted back into the costumed crowd.

William had never mentioned the incident to a soul. Had not the man called him by Ashley's name and seemed to have known his friend quite intimately, William would have never thought a thing about it.

For Ashley was not an effeminate man in any sense of the word. He was both big-boned and well muscled, with all the strength necessary to murder two women.

William had wondered, late at night alone in his townhouse, if the young man had recognized him or mentioned his mistake to Ashley. And if the incident could engender such hatred and be worth killing for.

Today, Ashley looked as if he'd spent a sleepless night, but not one of pleasure. He had circles beneath his eyes. Though his posture was rigidly correct and his seat on the stallion superb, it seemed his friend was exhausted.

They talked of inconsequential things, the weather, their horses, mutual acquaintances. Then Ashley surprised William by bringing up something far more personal.

"Why is Charles angry with you?" he inquired.

In a rare moment of absolutely clear insight, William realized Ashley was in love with Charles Hailey.

He said nothing for a moment as he pondered this fact.

"If I've offended you by asking, you needn't answer."

"No. Certainly not. I've been worried about the amounts he's been losing at cards."

"As have I." Ashley grinned ruefully, his handsome, mobile mouth lifting at the corners. "You were kind the other night, to keep our wager low."

"He has enough debt."

"He won't talk to me about it."

William considered this. He was positive Charles had absolutely no idea of the depth of Ashley's feelings.

"He's not discussing his problems with anyone," William said.

"That's ridiculous. It does no good to keep things bottled up and hidden away."

How well you know that.

"No, it doesn't."

Once Ashley's secret had been revealed to William, he remembered the man rarely joined in the spirited debates over certain women, nor went out with his friends in their search for passionate female society of the most degrading sort.

How little we really know one another, after all.

"If I tell you something, it must remain in complete confidence," he said, glancing around the park. They were on one of the riding trails, and the leaves from the trees made a green canopy over their heads.

"You have my word, William."

"I talked with his father, and the man was not at all pleased."

"The Haileys are a strange sort."

"I could not understand a father being unconcerned when his son is clearly headed for disaster."

"He's a cold man. I've met him before."

"Have you any thoughts as to what we could do for Charles? Or rather, what you could do. He's not terribly pleased with me."

"Only because you were brave enough to show that you cared about him. I admire that quality in you, William."

"Would he listen to you?"

"He might. That explains his deep anger toward you."

"Enlighten me, Ashley."

"Ever since I have known him, Charles has desperately sought his father's approval. And though he treated you coldly when you brought his son's problem to his attention, James Hailey is an admirer of yours."

This last piece of information took William totally by surprise.

"He thought so highly of your father," Ashley continued, "and believes you are a brilliant reflection on the man and his ideals."

"I had no idea—"

"It's no secret within the Hailey family." Ashley grinned again and glanced across at Will. Their eyes met. "Had I been in competition with you all of my life, I might not feel as kindly disposed toward you."

"How could I have been unaware?"

"Charles is certainly loath to discuss it."

William thought furiously, his heart picking up speed. Charles had been there the night Rosalind had been murdered. He'd expressed his compassion as he'd tried to keep him away from the bloody body.

Charles Hailey.

He rolled the idea around in his mind. Certainly an anger and frustration that had been fueled since childhood, then sharpened by disastrous gambling losses, couldn't result in murder, could it?

William felt he'd been silent too long, and rushed to fill it.

"Thank you, Ashley. You've made Charles's actions of late much more understandable."

They rode on in silence. Though William usually wasn't a man who jumped to conclusions, he decided that spring morning that Ashley Blessington was most certainly not a murderer.

But perhaps Charles was.

*   *   *

Dear William,

I don't feel pain anymore, and perhaps that is why I can finally write about what happened and face it at last. I know there is little chance of your actually reading this account, but perhaps I do it more for myself than for you. You will understand, as you read, why I am already in mourning for my brother, for he will never come back to me. It is far too late. But I have to tell you, William, that he was not always like this. I have to tell you from the beginning, and try to make sense of what happened. Then, I may find a measure of peace.

I will not trouble you with the details of our childhood, except to say it was a living nightmare. Our father was a monster, a man given to brutality and cruelty. I know not what was wrong with him, only that after our mother died, he was uncontrollable in his rages.

He took them out on both my brother and myself, though I want you to know, you must know, that Daniel took the brunt of it. He protected me, in his own way, and even though he has turned into another sort of monster, I cannot discount these memories. There is a part of me that loves him still.

As children, we were reduced to nothing. Shame was our daily companion, as was terror. I distanced myself from my world. It was all I could do to survive.

Daniel could not.

I hesitate to write what comes next, even though I must. You have no idea, William, what can go on in the mind of a child. What Daniel felt he had to do brought the Furies down upon our heads, to drive both of us mad. But in different ways.

For Daniel committed the greatest sin, and killed our father one night. The memory is vivid, as if it occurred mere hours ago instead of years. He murdered our father in order to save me from his killing rage, but that action destroyed him.

Oh, William, I knew his mind as I did my own. He was never the same. He had taken the first steps in a harrowing journey, and could never return.

We survived in the streets of London, until Daniel

managed to place me in service to an elderly woman who lived with two female relatives. He had no wish to see me in the company of men, perhaps remembering our father.

I spent several quiet years there, but suffered in my own way. I tried to deny what had happened, but the nightmares would not leave me. They came in groups, each more violent than the last. Daniel beating on my father's back, tearing at his face, his hair. Daniel reaching for the knife.

I could not escape the trap that was in my mind. The nightmares would vary, each dream coming to me in a different way, wearing a different mask each time.

I could not cry. I felt frozen. I felt nothing. I wanted to see my brother again, missed him terribly despite what he'd done. And felt shame and guilt gnawing at my insides, knowing it had all been done for me. Because of me.

I moved throughout my days in this frozen state, and spent the next six years in service. My mistress was good to me. A religious woman, she taught me to read the Bible and to write with a fine hand. Though a few of my days were happy, I still felt as if I was waiting. Waiting until Daniel returned.

I never doubted he would come for me. What I did not understand was how he had amassed such a fortune so quickly. And that, William, is the story you must understand, for Daniel's fate is inextricably entwined with yours.

I grow tired now, the quill feels heavy in my hand for I am not a well woman. I will write more very soon, as I am determined to finish this tale once and for all.

I pray for you daily, as his hatred is so strong. I pray for you, and anyone you love. And I wish, with all my heart, that fate might have been different . . .

"*Mo-ther!* The green silk simply will *not* do!"

"I can't find the sash to my pink ball gown! Where did Mary put it?"

"Did you call Cinda yet, and is she ready to dress my hair?"

"Get out of the *way*, you hairy little brute!"

Cinda heard the commotion clearly from down the long hallway, and she quickened her pace.

Miranda and Helena were always impossible before any event that required them to show themselves to their best advantage. As their mother was never satisfied, so they had observed her through the years, and were now hideous little replicas of their parent.

"Well, here she is at last!" Miranda cried as Cinda entered the room. "Get over here and see what you can do about my hair. The way it is now, my face looks far too thin."

"Did you see my pink sash?" Helena inquired from her vantage point on the bed. Plump to the point of obesity, she was lying down as if this entire exercise were too much for her. But it still didn't stop her from nibbling from the tray of rich confections on her bedside table.

"Girls, girls, girls," Nan said, her voice low and soothing as she glided into the room. Cinda had never cared for the way the woman slunk around the house. Nan enjoyed coming upon a person unaware. Upsetting them.

"She's here now, Miranda, and will dress your hair to best advantage. Helena, that sash is on the floor at the foot of the bed, where you left it. Mary can press it again. And *what* is that cur doing in the bedroom?"

The cur in question was an eight-month-old spaniel pup.

Nan had commissioned a portrait of her daughters, and wanted a dog included in the picture. A friend had given her the pup, and the animal had looked quite fetching as it lolled in Helena's arms. Now that it had grown older and had been given absolutely nothing in the way of either training or affection, the animal was considered nothing but a nuisance.

"Oh, Mother, can't you just get rid of the little beast? All it does is leave mud and hair all over!"

"As Mary and Lucinda take care of the upstairs house-keeping, that's really none of your concern, Miranda." Nan smiled at Cinda, a look designed to make her aware of her place within the Townshend household.

"I could take her to the kitchen for you, and Cook could keep her locked in the pantry. At least until you leave for dinner this evening." Cinda made the offer with the utmost skill, attempting to make herself sound totally unconcerned with the outcome, whichever way it went.

"Oh, Mother, *do* let her take that horrid little dog away! The animal makes me nervous, what with its snuffing and running all around!"

"A generous offer, Lucinda," Nan mused, and Cinda could see she was thinking it through. Nan delighted in causing as much trouble for her as was humanly possible, no matter how petty. Now she'd picked up a hand-painted fan that had been thrown on one of the beds and was tapping it against her wrist.

"Take the animal, then. Secure it in the kitchen. But I wish you to return swiftly, as you must take both time and care with my daughter's coiffure."

"Yes, mistress," Cinda murmured, keeping her gaze on the bedroom carpet. She couldn't bear to see an animal mistreated, and the spaniel pup had known nothing but abuse once she had outgrown her ornamental purpose.

She'd make sure the poor thing never returned.

She knelt on the floor and snapped her fingers at the pup, huddled beneath one of the beds.

"Come—" She glanced up at her two stepsisters. "What is her name?"

"Did you name it?" Helena said, glancing over at her sibling.

"Certainly not!"

"Come along, pup," Cinda called, and when the dog, afraid, scrabbled farther back under the bed, she crawled beneath it.

The little dog made no great resistance as she cornered her, then eased her out from below the bed. Keeping the puppy in her arms, Cinda stood, then turned and headed toward the kitchen.

Robbie was sitting at the table close to the fire, finishing his dinner when she rushed in the door.

"Take her to William as soon as you can. If he's not home, give her to Henry. Ask them to keep her for me until I should think of what to do."

"Stealing their dog, are you now?" Cook remarked as she cleared the remains of dinner from the table. "They won't even be aware the poor little thing's gone."

"I have to go back upstairs. Just make sure she's out of this house for good." She placed the pup in Robbie's arms, and he ruffled her fur affectionately. Cinda was heartbroken to see the animal make a desperate play for affection as the small pink tongue lashed Robbie's fingers.

"Just take her away," Cinda whispered, then headed back toward the stairs.

Miranda was fussier than usual about her hair, until even her mother snapped they would certainly be late if she took more time.

Cinda had a talent for dressing hair, and as much as she would have loved to send her stepsisters out with ridiculous styles adorning their heads, she did the best work she was capable of. What she hated the most was dressing Nan's hair.

The woman left her wig on almost constantly, as her own dark blond hair was sparse and rather limp. She took great pride in her wig, powdering it constantly and adding as many false curls as she could.

But she rarely cleaned it.

Many a morning Cinda took Nan breakfast and found she'd even slept in it. She'd set her stepmother's breakfast tray in front of her and avert her eyes as the woman inserted a long ivory stick with a tiny ivory claw attached to its end into her wig and scratched her scalp with it.

Thankfully, Mary had to dress Nan's hair this evening, as Cinda concentrated on the whining Miranda.

And finally, the three women were descending the stairs, Nan in yellow silk with a beautifully embroidered petticoat, Miranda in royal-blue, and Helena in the palest pink, complete with sash.

The door barely closed behind them before Cinda dashed to the kitchen. Cook glanced up from the preparation of one of her herbal concoctions.

"They're gone?"

"Just out the door."

"Wait till the carriage clears the drive."

Both women raced up the back steps and hid behind the bushes as they watched the carriage roll down the drive and ease its way into the crowded street.

"Robbie's already back from dropping the dog off," Cook said, wheezing slightly as she followed Cinda back into the kitchen. "Were you daft? Sending him out on such an errand when he has to escort you to your godmother?"

"I couldn't stand to see that dog mistreated a minute more."

Cook sighed, then a conspirator's grin lit her face. "I'll simply say I left the door open on my way to the kitchen garden tomorrow morning, and the little thing raced off after my Thom."

"That's as good a story as any."

"She's gone," Robbie announced as he stomped down the stairs and in the back door. "I've readied a coach."

"You're coming with me?" Cinda asked Cook.

"Do you think I'd miss this? Now, I've already prompted Mary concerning what to say in case something should go wrong. My cousin is ill, you understand, and I'm taking her this herbal syrup for her cough . . ."

William sat in one of the back bedrooms, deep in thought.

A map of London covered the wall behind him. He'd also made a list of the various suspects, and written down as much as he could remember about each man and both murders.

He'd marked the sites of the murders, and now sat with his hands behind his head, studying the map.

"Your soup, sir."

"What?" He hadn't seen Henry come in, and now the valet set a tray down on the desk in front of him and lifted the lid off a steaming bowl of broth.

"You must eat something before you go out tonight, Your Grace."

"Of course." He doubted he'd remember to eat at all unless Henry reminded him at times. This investigation was becoming an obsession.

"I've a nice chop prepared for you, along with vegetables from the garden. And damson pie for dessert."

"I won't be eating dessert; there will be plenty of food at the masquerade," William told his valet between absent sips of soup.

"Might I suggest, sir, that you take your meal without worrying about other concerns? Strictly for the benefit of your digestion, of course."

Realizing that Henry would insist on standing silently over him until he completed his meal unless he did otherwise,

William pushed the mass of papers to the side and paid full attention to the soup.

Seemingly satisfied, Henry left the room.

William finished his dinner, and Henry assisted him into his costume. He was almost to the door when Henry called after him.

"Might I inquire, sir, as to whether or not you have your invitation?"

He couldn't have functioned without his valet, of that he was certain. Henry went back to the library while he adjusted his cloak and gloves. He'd chosen the part of a pirate for tonight's festivities, and the ragged black knee breeches and billowing red silk shirt weren't far removed from clothing he wore in his everyday life.

"There you are, sir," Henry said, placing the invitation in his hand.

"You may throw the other in the fire, Henry."

"The other, sir?"

"The other invitation."

"You must be mistaken, sir. There was only the one."

"It must have fallen on the carpet," William replied, already starting for the library.

"I don't believe so, sir, as I cleaned there this morning and would have noticed such a thing—"

Henry dogged his heels as he swept into the library and scattered some of the papers off the large desk. He checked beneath the snuffbox as a horrible certainty grew stronger within him.

Cinda.

How she could have flagrantly disregarded her promise to him was the flint that gave spark to his temper. It burned bright and hot as he thought of what she was risking by attending Madam Avice's masquerade.

Certainly it was no place for a lady. The woman who was providing tonight's entertainment for the jaded members of London's aristocracy was well known indeed, considering the debauchery she provided.

For Madam Avice's masquerade was an orgy.

CHAPTER
❧ 11 ❧

She literally didn't recognize herself.

Cinda couldn't stop staring at her reflection in the looking glass. Someone else was standing there.

The ivory ball gown's lustrous silk reflected the light, the skirt belled out around her ankles, the material given form from the gentle shaping of the hoops. The front of her skirt was open, allowing a view of the elaborately quilted petticoat beneath, the delicate handiwork executed with a different shade of ivory silk thread.

She was laced tightly into the bodice, and the sleeves of the gown ended just below the elbow. The bodice itself was deeply décolleté, but kept its modesty with the elaborate lace trim that had been carefully hand-sewn all around the neckline and sleeves.

Cinda knew Kathleen had borrowed a substantial sum from Julia in order to outfit her with such exquisite underclothing: corset, chemise, petticoats, white silk stockings, and garters. The fine material felt strange against her skin, she was so used to coarser stuff.

Her hair had been coaxed into an elaborate style, partly pulled up on top of her head, but some left to brush her shoulders in elaborate curls. She hadn't wanted any powder, and her godmother had agreed, saying she hated to spoil the contrast between the ivory ball gown and her titian hair.

As she had to have a costume, she'd chosen a simple one she knew would be fairly easy to execute. Aurora, goddess of the dawn, was usually portrayed with a yellow gown, but the ivory had seemed close enough. The goddess visited the countryside every morning with her basket of flowers, thus she and Cook had picked various blooms from the garden this evening to support her costume. Now, several were entwined in her hair, and more spilled from the small basket she carried in her gloved hands.

It was also a terribly convenient costume considering she had no jewelry to grace herself with. Aurora was a goddess of nature, and would wear the jewels of the forest, the loveliest flowers.

The guests at any masqued ball, familiar with gods, goddesses, and all sorts of mythological creatures of the classical era, would recognize who she portrayed instantly.

Cook had touched her emotions, rummaging within the deep pockets of her cloak and producing both a pot of rouge and a tiny scrap of black velvet to make a face patch. Cinda had chosen to highlight her mouth with a tiny star at the corner of her lip.

But the final touch, and most lovely in her estimation, had been when she'd slipped into her mother's shoes. The paste jewels had peeped out from beneath her skirts, winking merrily in the candlelight as if they had a life of their own.

Having never seen herself in such finery, Cinda kept staring in the mirror. Her silk skirts rustling, her golden shoes sparkling, she finally believed she was going to attend a grand ball after all.

"You must leave before midnight, before your stepmother returns," her godmother admonished her as she reached for her evening wrap and draped it around her shoulders.

"Robbie will see her there, and be waiting by the carriage to take her home," Cook reminded Kathleen.

The woman's eyes filled with tears as she looked at her godchild, and Cinda reached out a tentative hand and touched her arm.

"I cannot thank you enough—"

"It's not that, my child." Cinda watched as her godmother swallowed, then dabbed at her tired eyes with a lace handkerchief. "It's simply that this should have been your birthright, not wearing rags and scrubbing floors."

Cinda smiled then, and gently kissed her godmother's wrinkled cheek. How wise Cook had been when she'd spoken of forgiveness. Even if Cinda found no clue concerning the killer tonight, something was changing within her, seeing herself in these clothes.

Thinking of herself in a different way.

"I hope I shall make you proud of me," she whispered to her relative.

"Oh, my dear, you already do."

Julia's footman assisted Cinda into the carriage, then Robbie climbed in after her.

"Now, wait here, Mum, don't go running home."

"I won't move an inch until you come for me," Cook replied, and Cinda caught her friend's eye. Cook gently pulled her earlobe, and Cinda smiled. They'd developed certain coded gestures for when they had to endure Nan's company, and the one Cook had just employed meant good luck, Godspeed, and much love to you.

She waved to both women, her fingers feeling strange inside such fine gloves, then reached up and touched her earlobe, looking at Cook while she did so.

"Have a care, my precious," the older woman called out, and Cinda knew what she was really saying. All of them were aware of the danger she was putting herself in, but only Cook knew the real reason she had to go out this night.

"Remember everything, that you might tell us about it," Kathleen called. Cook took her arm as she stepped back into the doorway, and Cinda found herself glad the two women were going to be keeping each other company.

Then reins were slapped down on the horse's sleek flanks, the carriage creaked, wheels turned, and Cinda found herself on her way to her very first masquerade.

William arrived at Madam Avice's in a fine rage. He spoke with no one, simply searched the room for any woman who might resemble Cinda.

He'd recognize her, he was sure of that. There would be no possible means of hiding that glorious hair, or the graceful way she had of comporting herself. He would find her, and when he did, he'd let her know what he thought of defiant, willful women who chose not to keep their word.

* * *

She was so excited she thought she might be sick.

Cinda remembered Cook's words as the carriage rattled over the cobblestones, harnesses jingling, the horses puffing and blowing.

It's no shame to simply want to go to the masquerade.

How could William possibly understand what drove her? He hadn't been forced to deny his birthright from the time he was a child. Though Horace Townshend had not been as wealthy as William's parents, her mother Eleanor had come from just as fine a family.

Cinda could remember, as a small child, watching her mother descend the stairs in exquisite gowns. The whisper of gossamer silks, the way she'd smelled, the faint perfume that was always a part of her.

Her mother had been a woman much sought after, and had taken her place in London society as effortlessly as she'd done anything else. But shortly after Cinda's fifth birthday, she'd become ill. After taking to her bed the first time, she'd never completely recovered her health.

Cinda had loved the nights her mother had gone out, and always watched her apply rouge and attend to the maid's dressing of her hair. Elaborate jewels had winked at her ears, throat, and fingers, and it had seemed to Cinda that her mother was a fairy princess, too ethereal for this world. Dressing for the ball tonight had brought back so many memories.

The carriage hit a deep rut in the road, and she was jolted back to the circumstances at hand. *The masquerade.*

There wasn't much to remember. Her godmother had told her what to expect as she'd helped her dress.

"The unmasking, should they wish it to occur, will happen late at night before supper. Until that time, you must act the part you choose to wear, you must support your costume. For the fun of the masqued party, Cinda, is that no one suspects who you are until the mask is removed."

She'd acted the part of a humble serving wench as long as she could remember. The thought of being a goddess was most delightful.

They'd barely gone a mile when Robbie rapped the ceiling of the carriage sharply with his fist. The driver slowed the horses, and the carriage came to a complete halt.

Cinda handed Robbie her invitation, then listened as he conversed with the driver. She and Cook had agreed that Robbie had to accompany her, in order to make the driver change his mind and take Cinda to the other masquerade—and to make sure she returned home safely. The coachman never would have taken orders from a woman, but Robbie could charm the birds out of their branches.

He swung back inside the carriage as it started to move again, giving her a smile and a nod.

"You're on your way, Cinda, to meet your William." He laughed then, and chucked her under her chin. "Such a fine lady you've turned out to be! Now, my girl, put on your mask before you forget!"

She picked up the mask, a confection of ivory silk trimmed with glittering glass beads. And as she fastened it, she thought of how deliciously fun it would be to become someone else for a night.

She entered the great house with absolutely no expectations of what was to happen, and found every dream she'd ever envisioned brought to life.

Hundreds of candles created a false day in the midst of night. Their brilliant light was reflected in the enormous looking glasses that ran the length of the walls. As she stepped down into the huge ballroom, the crush of costumed people almost overwhelmed her.

A man dressed in the frightening costume of an Indian from the Colonies had greeted her at the door, his face bright with war paint, his long black hair entwined with brilliant feathers. He'd insisted on seeing her invitation. She gave it to him, then almost stumbled and fell as a short, spry chimney sweep, covered in soot and broom in hand, attempted to rush the door.

The Indian grabbed him by the scruff of the neck and threw him back down the stairs.

"*You* now, *get* out of the way! Only the Quality have tickets for this one! On with you, before I take my knife and scalp you!"

Now, as she entered the main room of the party, she wondered what sort of information she could have found for

William. There was barely room to move, let alone observe other people.

She started as she heard the sweetest-looking shepherdess let loose a string of obscenities. Her partner, a pregnant nun, bent over double with laughter.

A dancing bear swept by on the arm of a feathered man, and Cinda recognized John Bull, Mad Tom, and Falstaff engaged in a heated debate.

It was too much to take in at once, through the eyes of her mask. But she found herself totally enthralled and, lifting her skirts, started for the center of the huge ballroom.

A dairy maid kissed an Arabian sultana; two orange girls squealed with laughter over something a Spanish caballero whispered to them. The lights from the candles were dazzling, and Cinda felt as if she'd been swept into the eye of a storm.

The noise was deafening, but not one voice seemed recognizable as belonging to a human. Everyone seemed to be making the greatest of effort to disguise themselves completely, including their voices. Thus, words came out higher and lower then usual, both infant and bestial, with a great many hoots, peeps, catcalls, and squeals.

Realizing this event was quite different from any supper party her godmother would have been privy to, Cinda decided to listen and learn. The conversations around her were enlightening.

"*I know you.*"

"*Do you know me? No, but you don't, I am sure you don't.*"

"*Yes, but I do, and will be better acquainted with you.*"

She couldn't simply stand there and observe, drawing attention of a different sort. Remembering what her godmother had told her about supporting her costume, Cinda reached for a handful of flowers and cast them toward an old man dressed as Merlin.

"'Tis Aurora, queen of the dawn!" he cried out in a high, squeaky voice. He raised long, thin arms out of the folds of his dark blue robe, and gestured toward the candles in both chandeliers and wall sconces. "And you rule here, for by my eye, 'tis bright as sunrise!"

She couldn't stop the smile that broke over her features. It had been so long since she'd had any fun, outside of the various ways she and Cook found to amuse themselves. No matter what happened tonight, she wanted to remember it well, and feel as if she were alive for a short time instead of merely existing.

For she didn't feel like Lucinda Townshend tonight. She felt as free as the air, as light as the flower petals in her basket. Tonight was a time of magic, revelry, and beauty, for all too soon the clock would strike midnight and she would have to return to the life she normally led.

"Give me one of your finest flowers, dear goddess, and kiss an old man who has seen better days."

She plucked a white rose out of her basket and gave it to him, but when she went to kiss his weathered cheek, he moved suddenly and she found herself kissing his lips.

It was a kiss more quick than familiar, and she found she could not be mad at the mischievous man, his blue eyes twinkling behind his mask. Laughter broke out behind them, along with several ribald comments as to what the old man really wanted.

And a sense of joy filled her, along with a newfound discovery of power. It would be all right, she could do this. She would enjoy the masquerade to the fullest, and all the while look for William and see if she could uncover any clues.

William recognized her the instant she entered the ballroom.

The crush of people prevented him from reaching her sooner. He made his way through the throng with a quiet determination, not paying any attention to the various women who plucked at the billowing sleeves of his pirate's shirt and vied for his undivided attention.

Aurora might herald the dawn, but this particular goddess had no idea that, like Prometheus, she was playing with fire.

Merlin had barely stepped away when a man dressed as a monkey took his place.

"Giving away flowers, are you, Aurora? And might I have one?"

She thought quickly, as a crowd was now pressed 'round to observe their exchange.

Cleverness was the rule at the masquerade.

"If I give away all, then I shall have no more for the dawn."

A slender young man dressed as Mary, Queen of Scots, laughed and laughed, a high-pitched, unnatural giggle. The crowd made approving sounds.

"Then is there anything else I might have?" the monkey inquired in his deep voice, and Cinda knew quite clearly what he was referring to.

"A goddess consort with a monkey?" she teased, trying to soften her refusal. He was a large, muscular man, and she was no physical match for his strength.

"Didn't Zeus tumble a cow?" someone shouted, and the crowd roared with laughter.

She could tell the monkey man didn't like being trifled with.

"I won't take a flower, but I insist on a kiss," he said, and she recognized the determination in his voice. He was almost upon her to take her into his arms and claim his request when a strong hand on his shoulder stayed his action.

"I shall plunder this beauty's flowers myself."

She turned toward that confident voice, saw a pirate, and recognized William instantly. He was dressed in ragged knee breeches and a brilliant red silk shirt with billowy sleeves. His shoulder-length dark hair was drawn back in a queue and tied with a length of leather, and his mask was black.

"Shall I kidnap the dawn?" William called out to the crowd. He was taller than most people present, and therefore had a better vantage point from which to voice his question. "Shall I kidnap Aurora and ensure that we might have endless night in which to continue this festival of misrule?"

The crowd roared, giving him their blessing, and Cinda barely saw the monkey skulk away, she was so caught up by the expression in Will's eyes behind his mask.

He was angry. A quiet, cold, deadly anger.

His emotions fueled hers, and she lifted her chin in a most defiant manner, totally befitting a goddess.

"Do I know you?" she asked him, not bothering to disguise her voice.

"Madam, I have *known* you a great many times." William also made no effort to disguise his deep voice, and his words carried clearly to the crowd surrounding them.

Cinda heard gasps and laughter as the throng pressed closer, instinctively surmising they were to observe a battle of wills.

"But, sir, I am sure you *don't* know me," she replied, truly angry now. She might have broken her promise to him, but however angry he was, William had no right to make their personal relationship public, and in a most mocking way.

"Then are you virgin, like the dawn?" he asked, tilting her chin farther up with one of his fingers.

"Truly, sir, I am." She smiled sweetly as she looked into his eyes. "Many times over."

The crowd roared, and Cinda grabbed her chance, losing what was left of her inhibitions from behind the safety of her mask.

"For does not the dawn come back each morning, fresh and pure? And is not each sunrise as new and untried as any virtuous maid?"

The crowd roared their approval once again, and William reacted by pulling her into his arms, crushing her basket of flowers between them. The onlookers quieted instantly, not wanting to miss what was to happen next.

"Might I have one, then?" he asked quietly.

"Might you have one what?"

"Are you determined to be *difficult*, madam?" he asked, and she remembered the moment in her mother's garden, before Will had proposed. The memory almost made her soften her resolve, but she could still see anger in his eyes.

Now was not the time to weaken. She had to stand up to his disapproval of what she'd done, or she might never find what she sought.

"Difficult, sir? The dawn is never difficult," she said, stepping slightly away from him and tossing a peony to a surprised bishop. "But then, no two men look at Aurora's sunrises in the same way."

"Might I have one of your *flowers*, madam?"

She swallowed down her fear and took her courage in both hands. "But you already took the fairest flower I possessed, *kind* sir, and do not seem to value it in the least."

The crowd grew silent, sensing something more than entertainment here.

Cinda knew Will had heard her, for a tiny muscle jumped in his jaw and his blue eyes were hard.

"Come with me, Aurora, and show me the heavens above." He gestured toward the upper floors of the great house, and several of the men surrounding them began to laugh. "Share your golden warmth and natural instincts with a rascal like myself." Though his words were teasing, his expression was not.

"And should I choose not to?" she said quietly, feeling his heartbeat pick up speed. They were so close together she could feel the primitive, masculine rage vibrating throughout his muscular body.

"You have no choice." He lowered his voice for her ears alone. "You had no choice from the moment I saw you and decided to make you mine."

"But, Will," she whispered. "The clues—"

"I don't want you here, damn you!"

And with that, he picked her up in his arms and slung her over his shoulder, crushing the hoops and delicate silk of her skirts. William started toward the darkened stairway, acting the part of a pirate perfectly as the great masqued crowd roared its approval.

The dreamscape became different as they left the lighted ballroom and journeyed upstairs. The hallways were darker, illuminated only by single candles placed farther apart.

"Will," she whispered, beginning to feel afraid.

"Don't," he replied curtly.

"Will, I—"

He silenced her with a hand over her mouth. She didn't struggle, not wanting to make matters even worse. Cinda realized she couldn't have behaved more badly than she had, but she couldn't find it within herself to feel repentant for what she had done.

Now, she simply waited to see what William would do.

He carried her up two long flights of darkened stairs, the small candles flickering in their wall sconces offering scant illumination. On the last few steps, her small basket, still clutched precariously in her hands, tilted crazily. A shower of flowers and their petals covered the oriental carpet runner.

William didn't slow his pace.

He finally set her down at the far end of the hallway and stared down at her, his expression fierce, looking for all the world like he really was a completely uncivilized pirate.

"What in the name of heaven did you hope to accomplish by attending this gathering tonight?"

"You would not listen when I offered my help—"

"I do not *want* your help in this endeavor!"

"I cannot sit and do nothing!"

"That is exactly what you'll do, if I have to—"

A door opened, and William stopped speaking instantly. He positioned himself so he was standing in front of her, shielding her from view. Cinda peered over his shoulder at the disheveled couple that left the room across from them.

As soon as the couple was but a short distance down the darkened hallway, William put a hand to her shoulder.

"Madam, we need a private place to discuss such matters."

She did not dare disobey him now, and stayed by his side until they were in the room and the door locked.

Only they were not alone.

"Have you come to join us?" a feminine voice whispered.

Cinda turned toward the large canopied bed, and her eyes widened as she beheld its occupants. Three women, in various stages of undress, were draped across the sumptuous bed-spread.

In the middle was a drunken young man, completely naked, with a glass of wine in his hand. Even in the dim light, with the fire almost burned out, Cinda could see him clearly. His body was firm and muscled, and his erect phallus rose heavy and thick from its nest of dark blond hair.

Two of the women were naked to the waist, one completely so. Their nipples were hard and flushed with excited color. One was unfastening the ties on her petticoats.

Cinda felt Will's hand catch hers and squeeze it, and she knew enough through her shock to remain silent and let him handle this peculiar situation. It wasn't their nakedness that disturbed her as much as the unbridled sexuality that seemed to emanate from the bed.

The young man eyed them and smiled.

"A pirate and a lady. Why don't you join us in our private masquerade?"

The naked woman laughed, then fastened her black, feathered mask over her face. Watching William the entire time, she lay down upon the bed and spread her thighs wide. The young man glanced down at her, then put his hand between her legs and began to stroke the sensitive flesh.

She closed her eyes when he touched her, arching her back and touching her breasts. Her low, excited moan sounded loud in the stillness of the room.

Cinda felt William's arm come around her, strong and sure, as he caught her to his side. "Mayhap we'll join you later," he said to no one in particular.

"Godspeed," called the young man, then he gave a drunken laugh. Another woman was now completely naked, and she pressed her generous breasts to his back, then rose up on her knees. He tilted his blond head back and took one of her nipples in his mouth.

Cinda turned away, and allowed William to escort her out of the darkened bedroom.

They spied another open door, and William briefly checked its interior before motioning her to follow him inside.

Once the door was locked behind them, he indicated she should come sit by the fire. The bedroom seemed cast in shadows, and Cinda could not keep from thinking about what was transpiring in that other room down the hall.

"What am I going to do with you?" he finally asked. Though his voice was low, it seemed loud in the stillness of the room. The only other sound was the ticking of a clock on the fireplace mantel.

"All I would ask is that you listen."

"I cannot condone what you wish to do."

"Will, I—"

"You put yourself in great danger."

"I am aware of the risk—"

"It cost Rosalind her life."

They were silent as the clock ticked, each remembering the young girl who had met such an untimely end.

Each remembering the part they had played in her demise.

She broke the silence by moving slightly away from him, then standing by the fire and staring into the flames.

"You've been to masquerades like this before." She made it sound a statement, not a question.

"I have."

"And have you consorted with several women at a time?"

His silence was her answer.

"Did you find it—pleasurable?"

He closed the space between them within a heartbeat, grabbing her arm and turning her to face him.

"Is that what this is about then, Cinda? Would you have me escort you back to that room to complete your education?"

She didn't answer, simply turned away from him, the rustling of her silk skirts loud in the silence.

"Is that what you came here for?"

The question was so outrageous she had to face him. And just as suddenly, she decided to call his bluff.

"Would you take me to them?"

The silence was thick with tension, then William reached for her and pulled her against the length of his body.

"If he touched you, I'd kill him," he whispered. Their faces came closer together, their lips almost touching. He averted his, still angry. She reached out with her hand and gently stroked his cheekbone with one gloved fingertip.

"I know you, William, for a fair man. And you cannot believe this is fair—"

"Damn you!" he whispered.

"I didn't know what transpired upstairs; I couldn't have known from the invitation."

He remained silent, but she could feel his tension.

She continued stroking his cheekbone with her finger, then his cheek with her hand. He turned his head toward her, and she leaned up on tiptoe and brushed his lips with hers.

"Madam, what are you playing at?" he whispered.

"It was a most extraordinary sight, was it not?"

He was looking at her as if he'd never truly seen her before in his life.

She kissed his lips again. "And I thank you for protecting me." She swallowed, knowing the next words were going to prove difficult. "But I do not wish you to protect me from too much, for I've already been denied too great a taste of life."

She watched his expression carefully, and could see the knowledge in his dark blue eyes. He understood, if only a little.

She kissed his neck, then brushed her lips against his ear and whispered, "I never dreamed such things were possible."

"Are you saying," he said slowly, carefully, "that you would welcome company into our bed?"

She shook her head, then whispered, "I'm saying that I wish you'd stop treating me as if I were a china doll you found in a shop, and treat me like a woman."

His hands moved to her shoulders as he pushed her gently away from him so as to study her face.

"And what would that entail?"

She licked her dry lips, and swallowed once more against the tightness of her throat.

"What would you have done if you'd met me here tonight?"

He smiled, and this time it reached his eyes. The anger was gone, replaced by a desire so potent it stole her breath away.

"The outcome would have been the same. I would have wished to be alone with you and brought you upstairs."

She moved into his embrace and rested her cheek against his shirtfront.

"What is the hour, Will?"

"Half past eight."

"I must leave before midnight."

"And what is it you're asking for?"

She caught his hand, brought his fingers to her lips, and kissed them. "Make me feel alive, Will. Just for tonight. Let me see some of the wildness I know you're capable of."

His eyes darkened.

"Show me what I might have found here, were my fate not already bound to yours."

The clock's ticking sounded loud in the silent room.

"Turn around," he said softly.

She obeyed him.

"Lift up your hair."

She did as he requested.

And she felt him begin to expertly unlace her bodice.

CHAPTER
❧ 12 ❧

The group of costumed men were trading gibes, each having eaten and drunk their fill from the long table piled high with refreshments. Now, having guessed each other's identities and realizing they were among friends, none needed to remove a mask to know who they were conversing with.

"'Twas good to see William out and about again," said one, a soldier. "He's been by himself far too long."

"'Twas doubly good to see him sparring with that fetching goddess," remarked the second, dressed as Merry Andrew.

The third, costumed as Harlequin, had arrived at the masquerade much later than the other two. Now, he frowned.

"A goddess?" he said.

"You didn't see them?" questioned the soldier. "She was lovely. That ivory gown displayed her ample charms. A quite simple costume, merely a basket of flowers and ribbons in her hair."

"Aurora?" said the harlequin. "Of course. Goddess of the dawn."

"William's been holding out on us, clever fellow," mused Merry Andrew. "And here we thought he was all alone, nursing a broken heart over that fiancée of his who came to such a bad end. But that's our William, nothing can keep him down for long."

The men all laughed, and gave one another knowing looks.

"Beautiful hair on the girl, wasn't it?" said Merry Andrew,

resuming the conversation. "The color of fire. No wonder he wanted her so badly."

"But he was in a fine temper," remarked the soldier, "tearing his way through the crowd to be by her side. Then he slung her over his shoulder in a truly piratical fashion and carried her off. I daresay they're still having at it upstairs."

"Aurora, show me the heavens above," said Merry Andrew, and laughed out loud. The soldier, having taken a mouthful of punch, promptly choked, and a small amount spewed out his nose.

"Blast it, Ashley, look what you've done!"

The harlequin remained silent.

The soldier wiped his nose with a handkerchief, then dabbed at the front of his uniform.

"It did not do much damage," the harlequin remarked, his eyes on the staircase across the vast ballroom.

"No," said Merry Andrew. "I say, did you see that orange girl over by the refreshments? She was quite a fetching sight."

"I think I shall refresh my cups and join you gentlemen later, at the club," remarked the harlequin. Before either Merry Andrew or the soldier could offer any opinion on this, he slipped into the crowd to position himself at the foot of the stairs. He'd been patient, and could wait this little while longer. Tonight he meant to catch a glimpse of the girl, and see for himself how much she meant to William.

He undressed her with a passionate haste that stole her breath away.

"No, leave the gloves. And the stockings." He was lying in bed, clad only in his breeches, and she had been unfastening a garter and about to unroll one of the white silk stockings.

They'd both discarded their masks.

"Come to me," he said softly, extending a hand. She refastened her stocking and joined him on the bed, feeling wild and alive and dangerously free. Something had changed for her tonight at the masquerade, and she knew as much as she loved Will, no one could ever take away that precious moment of absolute freedom she'd experienced on first entering the lavish ballroom.

She came to him, but only because she wished it so.

He kissed her, nothing tentative in the gesture, his lips and tongue claiming hers with practiced ease. For an instant, she thought of all the other women he must have bedded to possess such a level of skill.

Then nothing mattered, for when he kissed her she could think of nothing else.

He eased her down on the bed, moving so they were lying side by side. Then he broke the kiss, and studied her face. It seemed he was trying to see inside her, to the changes she'd felt occur this very night.

"Very pretty," he finally whispered, touching the beauty mark at the corner of her mouth.

"Do you like it?"

He kissed the small piece of black velvet.

"Very much."

"Does it make me somewhat different?"

He grinned, then shifted their position so she was lying on top of him. "Madam, tell me your intent, for I have no idea what you are about."

"Does it excite you, my being different?"

"*You* excite me. I daresay it will take me a lifetime to know you."

The word brought back memories.

"You hurt me, Will. What you said."

"You did not keep your word."

Passion turned to frustration in a heartbeat. She couldn't meet his eyes, for indeed, she had not kept her promise, and she kept great store by such things.

Slowly, carefully, she forced herself to meet his gaze.

"There is a wildness inside me, Will, that has been kept at bay for too long a time."

He was perfectly still, listening intently, and she knew this moment might be one of her only chances to make him understand.

"There is part of me, no matter how much I love you, that cannot be yours."

His blue eyes darkened, and she felt his body harden even further beneath hers. How like a man, to see such a truth as a challenge.

He kissed her again, his fingers tangling in her long hair. She felt her body softening, melting, warming to his touch like a beeswax candle melting before an insistent flame, while his own became harder and stronger.

"Yet this is mine," he whispered between kisses as his hand slid down the side of her body and came to rest with unerring boldness between her thighs.

She shifted her legs and moved against his touch. "Yes," she whispered back, her breath coming out on a fevered sigh.

"No one else shall ever have this," he whispered, tightening his hold just enough to make her gasp. She kissed the side of his neck, then raised her head and looked down at him. There was absolute masculine determination in his expression, and she suddenly smiled.

"No one," she whispered back. "And you've stolen my heart as well. But this," she said, touching her brow, "is my own, and it's where we shall always be in conflict."

He caressed her while their eyes met, and hers started to drift shut. Then both his hands came up, to cradle her face. His fingers spread, and he held her head gently.

"You know I'll spend the rest of my life trying to lay claim to it."

"I'll give you what I can."

He laughed then, cupping her buttocks and pulling her hard against his rigid erection.

"You please me more than any woman ever has." He couldn't keep the delighted smile from his mouth.

She kissed his nose, and tried to mask the importance of her words with a lightness of tone. "I don't ever want to be locked away again, Will."

He sobered instantly. "I know." His hand came up to tangle in her hair as he pulled her face down to his. Their lips met, touched, kissed. "But I couldn't bear it if something were to happen to you," he whispered roughly. His confession touched her deeply, and she suddenly understood part of what drove him in his quest to keep her from harm.

She sat up, straddling him, looking down at him lying on the bed. He put both his hands behind his head and gazed up at her. She felt his self-consciousness at what he'd revealed.

"I've heard you've quite a reputation," she teased, trying to lighten the moment.

"And who told you this?"

"All those women on the ballroom floor, grabbing at your sleeves."

He smiled. "But you're the only wench I consented to remove my shirt for. I'm a very modest man, you know."

She laughed at that, for she didn't think she could meet a man more comfortable with his own nakedness. There was something of the savage in William; he was not like other men.

"Then I shall not set too rapid a pace, my poor pirate king, for fear of frightening you."

His mouth twitched. "Do as you will, gentle Aurora."

"Sit up, then, and let me kiss you."

He did as she asked, and she sat in his lap, facing him, kissing him. Their caresses grew more fevered, he cupped her breasts and she arched her back, pressing them against his hands. Her hands went to the fastening of his breeches, and she shifted slightly that she might free his engorged, aroused length.

She touched the hot, hard flesh, and he caught her cheek with his hand and kissed her roughly. She kissed the palm of his hand, and his thumb slipped into her mouth.

"Then that's what you want," she whispered, smiling at him.

He touched the beauty mark at the side of her mouth, then whispered, "Show me what this lovely mouth can do."

His words excited her. She gently pushed him back on the bed, then took her time getting to where he wanted her, kissing his chest, licking his nipples, nuzzling the flat, hard muscles of his chest. Circling the evidence of his desire with her fingertips, but not touching it. Letting anticipation build as she removed his breeches, then nipped at his inner thigh.

"I told you once I was going to torment you," she said softly, remembering the night he'd taken her virginity in her room above the stable.

"Madam, you surely do," he whispered, his voice strained.

She smiled at that, then touched him with her gloved hand. His groan sounded loud in the quiet room. She didn't prolong his torment, but still moved slowly, delicately, as she lowered her head and kissed the hard, hot, fully aroused shaft.

It seemed all his breath left him in a rush. Out of the corner of her eye, she saw his fingers clench the bedsheets as his hips thrust upward, gently.

She kissed him again, then took him into her mouth. And again she felt powerful, but it was power of a different sort.

She wanted to please him, wanted to give him even half the pleasure he'd shown her.

She felt his hand on the back of her head, gently stroking her hair as she caressed him with lips and tongue. She took time, as if they had all the time in the world and not simply a few stolen hours in a stranger's bedroom.

His entire body felt so very alive, especially that part which proclaimed his virility. She cherished it, pleasured it, and brought him to the point of imminent release before she raised her head and slid up his body.

"Might I take my pleasure now?" she whispered, feeling for all the world as if they had just met that night.

Without forming a reply, he grasped her hips and positioned her over him. Slowly, ever so slowly, she sank down upon his strong erection, taking it into her body, prolonging the exquisitely sensual moment.

Holding him just on the brink of fulfillment.

Making him wait for his pleasure.

Once fully seated, she stilled all movement. Their eyes met, and she delicately stroked him by clenching her muscles. His hips surged upward, but she put a restraining hand on his muscled chest.

"Don't," she whispered. "I wish to prolong it for us both."

"Then give me respite, else our evening will be over shortly."

She laughed gently as he held her still, his fingers biting into her hips. Then she rocked on him, the movement slow and steady, until he stilled her again with a touch. His hand slipped between their bodies until he found that which he sought.

"What a little beauty," he whispered.

She'd thought she was beyond blushing, but hot color flooded her face.

"What, still shy after all we've done together?" He pressed his finger against her, stroking and rubbing, arousing. His other hand came up and grasped her hair, holding her still so she could not look away from him.

"It is a beauty, a rose-tipped beauty, and my most precious possession." He watched her reaction carefully as he touched her. "And what a powerful little erection it sports."

She closed her eyes and he laughed softly.

"A jewel above price," he whispered, and she felt the first

tremors take her, then she cried out as she reached fulfillment.

"Do you want more?"

She couldn't speak.

"Look how hard your nipples are," he whispered, touching her aching breasts.

She moaned softly, and he laughed. She sensed her response delighted him, and realized he'd taught her well.

"Who torments who? I wonder," he whispered.

She was incapable of a rational thought or reply.

"I'll give you more."

She didn't resist as he began to move, thrusting up. She felt unbearably sensitive to his touch, and reached for his broad shoulders to steady herself. Her eyes opened reflexively as she peaked again, and she saw his face below hers, darkly intense.

He pressed a hand to the small of her back and brought her face closer for a kiss. His other hand caressed her breasts, and this time when she climaxed, he met her with his own, his thrusts hard and powerful.

Her legs trembling, a fine sheen of sweat covering her body, she simply fell forward on his chest. His strong arms enfolded her protectively, as if he never wished to let go.

Her body spent, her eyes closed, she buried her face in his neck. Safe in his arms in the darkened bedroom, she slept.

The candle's flame flickered wildly, and Cinda opened her eyes, gradually coming awake. Despite the briskly snapping fire warming the bedroom, she felt a sudden icy draft. The cold air had awakened her from a deep sleep, but the flickering light had ensured she reached full consciousness.

William lay next to her, his arms around her. She sat up slowly. He came awake as she moved. And the clock on the mantelpiece softly chimed the hour.

Midnight.

"Will, I must leave!" She glanced 'round the room, at the rumpled sheets and their scattered clothing. Swinging her legs over the side of the bed, she reached for her lace-trimmed petticoat, then the delicate chemise.

"I must return before my stepmother finds me gone."

"I understand."

They dressed quickly. He laced her with lightning speed.

Not bothering to do anything with her tousled hair, Cinda grabbed her mask and fastened it back over her face.

William did the same, then grasped her by the upper arms and stilled her nervous movements.

"We must use care in departing this place."

She nodded, still nervous. How could she have done something as foolish as falling asleep?

"Let me check outside the door."

He did as he said, then motioned for her to follow him. Cinda picked up her basket, grabbed her gloves, and followed him out of the room.

"There's a back staircase," he whispered against her ear, then took her hand. With the greatest of stealth, they ran soundlessly down the hall and disappeared into darkness.

The harlequin stopped halfway up the second flight of stairs and gazed down at the showering of flower petals on the carpet. Kneeling, he picked up a single red rose, then brought it to his lips and inhaled its fragrant scent.

He smiled, then tucked the flower into his pocket.

He continued his ascent, then walked slowly down the hallway, contemplating what he should do next.

The single open door captured his attention.

He entered the room, and a smile slowly spread over his face as he saw the few flower petals on the carpet and at the foot of the large bed. Walking back the way he had come, he shut the door, then began a methodical search of the bedroom.

Within minutes, he'd found what he needed. Two thin ivory ribbons. He slipped these into his pants pockets, along with a few more flower petals. Then he checked the bed.

It smelled of sex, and the bedsheets sported a telltale dampness. The harlequin smiled, but his expression would have chilled any who saw it. His eyes were cold and totally without feeling behind the black and white mask.

William, you consorted with your beloved on this very bed, of that I am sure.

He'd found a trail at last. Patience and cleverness had won out. Now it was simply a matter of starting the hunt and running this young woman to ground.

He sat at the foot of the bed they'd shared in carnal delight, his senses filled with triumph, and thought of the note he would compose to mark the occasion.

> *A goddess in ivory, dressed so fair,*
> *With blushing cheek and titian hair . . .*

He laughed out loud at his cleverness. William was a passionate man, and passion caused a man to become careless. He had no need of finding them this evening; they had already flown from this room and most probably from this evening's entertainment.

But now he had a clue. Because William had stepped back into society and made himself vulnerable, he now had a chance to destroy him all over again.

This time, he'd finish him for good.

Oh, William, what sport I shall have with you . . .

Fingering the two ribbons in his pocket, the harlequin glanced around the deserted bedchamber, then threw back his masked head and laughed.

She was back in the kitchen dressed in her servant's garb, the flowers picked out of her hair, its long length brushed out, braided, and coiled beneath the white cap, a mere forty minutes before Nan and her daughters arrived home.

And the mistress of the house was in a foul temper.

Mary rushed into the warm kitchen as if the hounds of hell were nipping at her heels.

"She's wanting one of those herbal brews you make—"

"For when she has overindulged," Cook finished. She put a small amount of water on to heat, as Cinda went back to one of the far walls of the kitchen. There, herbs had been picked, cleansed, tied, and hung from the ceiling, drying for the cold months ahead. Some had been picked mere hours ago, and would provide the necessary oils to soothe Nan's system.

The two women worked together efficiently as they prepared the tisane. Mary had already rushed back upstairs to assist Nan and her daughters as they undressed.

"Will they even miss that little dog?" Cook muttered. "I'll wager they won't."

Cinda laughed softly as she prepared the herbs for steeping. Peppermint, caraway, pennyroyal, catnip, melilot, and marjoram slipped through her fingers as she separated leaf from stem. The small pile grew in front of her until she was satisfied with the amount.

Mary came back, clearly exhausted. Her request startled them.

"She wants Cinda to take it to her. Says she has something to tell her."

Cinda glanced at Cook, who merely shook her head. There was no predicting Nan's capricious moods. The woman was utterly impossible.

Cinda placed the delicate china cup on a tray, then picked it up and headed toward the stairs. Once outside Nan's bedroom door, she knocked softly and was admitted inside.

The room was shrouded in darkness, and Cinda was reminded of the opulent bedchambers at the masquerade.

"Put the tray on the table," Nan whispered, and Cinda took a quick glance at her stepmother as she did what the woman bade her.

Nan was not looking well at all. Her skin was pasty and pale, devoid of all color. Her eyes seemed dull, and Cinda wondered what she might have eaten or drunk that hadn't agreed with her.

Usually, her stepmother's face was carefully made-up, with both powder and rouge. Tonight, the cosmetics seemed to have worn off, and Cinda could clearly see the smallpox scars on her chin and cheeks. There was but one candle, by Nan's bed, and Cinda stepped away from the faint circle of light.

It was safer to wait in shadow.

"Thank you, child. You are valuable to me, in your way. I have yet to come across anyone with your knowledge of herbs." She coughed into a lace handkerchief. "Your mother taught you well."

Something was very wrong, for the woman to compliment her. When Nan chose to converse with her, the words were either laced with ugly sarcasm or lashed her with stinging criticism. More often than not, she chose to remind her of her station in life, and how far she'd fallen.

Something was very wrong.

"Do you miss her?" Nan asked suddenly, her voice small and frightened, like a child's.

The question was an abomination. Cinda had no more desire

to discuss her most intimate feelings toward her mother with this woman than she would have wished to have opened the bedroom window and leapt to the hard ground below.

Nan was not only sick, but very drunk.

Cinda wondered what could have occurred at the dinner tonight to put her stepmother in such a mood. She'd already forgotten the question, and was sipping the tisane, her eyes closed. This near to her, and without the illusion of her face paint, Cinda could see that Nan was quite a hideous woman. She thought fleetingly of the church sermon, of the corpse with sunken eye and freezing hand.

It was almost as if the woman were already dead.

She closed her eyes to clear her mind of the strange thought, and when she opened them, found her stepmother staring at her. The cup was empty, and Cinda gracefully gathered the china dishes on the tray in preparation for leaving.

"What has changed about you? I wonder," Nan murmured.

Cinda didn't answer, hoping the woman would not remember any of this strange conversation come morning. Though the large windows were tightly closed against the night air, the candleflame flickered wildly, seeming to come to sudden, vibrant life.

"What is different about you?" Nan whispered.

Cinda swallowed hard, willing her voice not to tremble.

"Nothing, I'd warrant." She didn't dare ask permission to leave, for as soon as Nan had divined her intent, she would surely insist on the opposite.

"Something about you . . ." Nan yawned then, not bothering to cover her mouth with her hand, and Cinda saw spaces where the tooth-drawer had been hard at work.

"Madam, will you be needing anything further this evening?"

"Go." Nan made a weary motion with her hand. "Go on, get out."

As Cinda gathered up the tray and made for the door, she heard the woman's whispered words follow her.

"For I cannot stand the sight of you . . ."

"She's ill," Cinda said as she returned to the kitchen.

"Drunk, you mean."

"No. Something's wrong."

Cook, who had been clearing the great oaken table, stilled all action. Disease was never taken lightly, as fevers or small-pox could ravage a household and brutally claim its occupants.

"What did you see?"

"She's very pale, and coughing—"

"A deep, tight cough?"

"No, just enough to clear her throat. But when she spoke, her words made no sense."

"Fever, perhaps," Cook mused. "Did she feel hot?"

"I couldn't bring myself to touch her."

Cook glanced toward the stairs, and Cinda knew her friend would not choose to make a trip upstairs unless it was absolutely necessary. But while she despised Nan, she surely did not wish her to die.

"I'll wake Mary and send her."

"I'll put more water to boil," Cinda replied, knowing they were in for a long night.

"Gather me coltsfoot and mullein, and we'll start with seeing what we can do about that cough."

William arrived home in a better mood than when he'd left, and was taking off his black cloak in the front hallway when Juno and Jocasta came galloping in to greet him.

The mastiffs, dark brindle with black muzzles, leapt up and placed their massive paws against his chest. William laughed, then patted their heads as they barked.

"Welcome home, Your Grace." Henry stood in the doorway, and William recognized the look his valet gave him, assessing what sort of mood he was in.

"Thank you, Henry. It was a splendid event, but I believe I'll retire early. I'll be going riding in the morning, and I'd like to get an early start."

"I'd advise taking these two for a run at the same time."

"They aren't usually in such a state—"

A small, black and white bundle of fur came skidding around the corner, then stopped upon spying him. The spaniel pup backed up, and would have turned and fled had not Henry knelt down and restrained her with a gentle hand.

"Henry?"

"You see, sir," his valet replied, choosing his words careful-ly, "that stableboy came by earlier in the evening and said it was at your lady's request that you keep this little one." Henry stood, the spaniel in his arms. The small dog was wriggling against the older man and trying to swipe at his lined face with her pink tongue.

"Just for a few days, sir, you understand, until the lady can figure out a way to find her a proper home—"

"I see. She certainly seems taken with you."

"There was a bit of leftover beef from the joint roasted yesterday, and she looked so very thin."

"She's a frightened little thing."

Henry petted the silky black and white head. He eyed the dog fondly, and William knew the spaniel had found herself a champion.

"Sir?"

"We'll keep her." William could barely keep the amusement out of his voice. He had no doubt where the pup had come from, nor who she'd belonged to. He'd had occasion to see the rather unattractive portrait of Cinda's stepsisters hanging in Nan's drawing room at her last dinner party.

How like Cinda to simply make off with the little dog.

"They don't mind her?" he asked, indicating the mastiffs.

"Not in the least, sir. Why, I'd even go so far as to say they mother her whenever they can."

Judging by the nervous expression in the spaniel's eyes, William decided she could do with a little affection.

"Well then, Henry," he said, smiling down at his valet as he gathered his gloves and cape, "you may keep her."

Nan did indeed have a fever, and it worsened during the night. Both Cinda and Cook remained in her bedroom, neither waking her daughters, who would have only been a nuisance.

The woman tossed and turned on the bed, and Cook bathed her face and arms with cool water. During the brief moments Nan was lucid, Cook made her drink various herbal remedies, designed to both purify her blood and help drive the unbalanced humors from her body.

"If she's not better by morning, her daughters will demand a physician," Cinda remarked. She did all the running up and down stairs, as she didn't want to further tax Cook's health.

"He'll use those blasted leeches and bleed her. That will take even more of her strength," Cook muttered, wiping the mumbling woman's hot brow. "Could you distract those two and let me have the morning with her?"

"If Mary doesn't wake them, they'll sleep well past noon."

"Then let me tend to her."

Between errands, Cinda remained at Cook's side.

"—rid of her," Nan muttered, her brow furrowed as she twisted beneath the blankets. The herbs were doing their work, for she was beginning to sweat profusely.

Neither Cinda nor Cook responded.

"A monster!" the sick woman cried, then fell into a fit of silent laughing. "She'll marry a monster . . ."

The room grew suddenly colder, and Cinda shivered.

"Be a good lass, and run and get me my blue shawl," Cook said quietly, her eye on Nan.

Cinda nodded, and was off.

The room grew even colder, and one of Nan's embroidered slippers rose into the air, to be thrown violently across the room, hitting the wall.

"Calm down, Nora," Cook said softly, her eye on Nan.

Marry a monster!

"Not while there is breath in my body. You know that."

Helpless . . .

"I know. There are times I feel the same way."

Let her die?

"Nora." Cook's tone was reproving.

Do nothing, let her die . . .

"I can't. Would that I could, but I can't."

So cruel . . . I know her mind . . .

"'Tis not for us to decide. She'll have many things to settle at her end, but we'll let Him decide when that time should be."

She could feel the sorrow and frustration in the room, along with the chill. Then Cinda swept in with her shawl, and Cook felt Nora's presence lessen, the chill slowly fade away.

"I brought Mother's herbals as well," Cinda said, placing copies of *The English Physician* and *A Curious Herbal* on the chair next to Cook's. "I thought we might look and see if her notes yield a better tincture."

Cook knew the books were part of a legacy Cinda cherished. Her mother had been as active a gardener as Cinda now was, and both herbals were riddled with notes, stuffed with receipts for sachets, medicinal tinctures, scented waters, tisanes and the like.

Each woman picked up a book, and they read in silence, the only sound Nan's raspy breathing.

"Oh, look!" Cinda breathed, and Cook watched as she slipped a small piece of paper out of the herbal. She handed it to her, and Cook smiled as she recognized the familiar drawing.

"Quite a fairy princess, wouldn't you say?" she teased Cinda, all the while remembering that day in the garden Eleanor had sketched the picture of a fairy for her small, excited daughter.

"Wood sorrel, thyme, and foxglove," Cinda whispered.

"The foxglove for the wee folk's clothes. I remember, I told my own Robbie that story after I heard her tell it to you."

"They had hazelnuts for carriages, and their hair was dodder," Cinda said, smiling as she looked at the rough sketch.

"And fairy steeds of ragwort seed," Cook finished for her.

Both women laughed, then Cinda studied the picture in her hand. "I'm going to take this to my room to keep, if you don't mind."

"She drew it for you, darling girl. Mayhap someday you'll tell the same to a daughter of your own." Cook smiled as she leaned back in her chair. "You must tell me of your evening, once we've finished with this," Cook whispered, her eye on the unconscious Nan.

Cinda grasped Cook's hand, then moved her own chair closer.

"It was like a dream brought to life. So full of beauty, but frightening, too."

"And was he angry?"

"Terribly."

"But you thought of a way to calm him."

She laughed beneath her breath as she saw the blush that ran up Cinda's neck, into her cheeks.

"'Tis worked for hundreds of years, and no doubt will be effective hundreds more. 'Tis glad I am you found each other."

She caught the quick sheen of tears in the girl's eyes.

"What now? Tell me."

"I wish—oh, how I wish she'd been able to see me tonight! And in such a dress! I wish she'd had a chance to meet Will, and come to love him as I do."

Out of the corner of her eye, Cook saw the rouge pot on Nan's dressing table move, barely an inch. She smiled at Nora's mischief, then squeezed Cinda's hand tightly in her own.

"She saw you. Of that, I'm sure."

William woke the following morning feeling better than he had in months.

He felt as if perhaps the greatest danger was behind them. Perhaps he'd overreacted and seen a pattern that wasn't truly there. Perhaps Anne's death had nothing to do with Rosalind's. If someone had been trying to harm Cinda, wouldn't they have been approached at the masquerade?

The thought that he and Cinda might have a safe future in front of them was a tantalizing one. And it was a future he wanted to begin as soon as possible.

The spaniel pup trotted in, and William smiled at the silly little dog. Henry was right behind her, his breakfast and some letters on a silver tray.

"Good morning, Your Grace."

"Good morning, Henry. I'm thinking it's time I got married."

His valet looked at him as if he'd gone quite mad, then his face broke into the widest of smiles as he set down the breakfast tray and headed toward the curtained windows.

"Now, *that* is a splendid idea, sir," he said as he opened the heavy drapes. Brilliant sunlight streamed into the bedroom, filling it with light. "Why don't you eat your breakfast, take a look at your correspondence, and I'll lay out your riding apparel."

William took a sip of his coffee, then tore into the stack of envelopes Henry had brought up. The first three were invitations to various parties throughout London, the fourth a note from Ashley expressing how much he'd enjoyed their ride in the park.

The fifth almost made what little breakfast he'd consumed come right back up.

When he opened the envelope, two ivory ribbons and several faded rose petals fell out. He went perfectly still, then slowly pulled out the card. The handwriting was precise and delicate, the words horrifying.

A goddess in ivory, fashioned so fair,
With blushing rose cheeks and soft titian hair,
But her lover will cause her a brutal demise,
She'll have dirt for her bower and worms for her eyes.

CHAPTER

❧ 13 ❧

William rode in St. James's Park that same morning, both Juno and Jocasta loping behind. He'd decided, after receiving the note, that the pattern of his life had to appear normal. He couldn't afford to let any hidden enemy know his entire world had just been rocked off its foundation.

He'd sat in bed like someone turned to stone, staring at the damning little poem. Henry had to ask him three times which of his riding jackets he wished to wear before he came to his senses and answered.

It was one of the few times in his life when he'd wished with all his heart he'd been wrong. Instinct had told him someone was stalking him, killing any woman he cared for. He'd wanted the pattern to end, wanted to have something of a normal life with Cinda, but now that was an impossibility.

He kept his senses finely tuned, and it seemed to him that every tall, strong man within the confines of the park became a suspect. About the only one he was sure had nothing to do with this was Ashley.

He'd compared the two handwritings, and Ashley's was heavy and masculine, the ink slashed across the paper with quiet confidence. The horrid poem had been written with a delicate hand, and for the first time William pondered the fact that the madman might indeed be a madwoman.

Yet that theory made no sense. No woman, no matter how largely proportioned or emotionally enraged, could have done such damage with a dagger.

He wondered if the killer had a woman writing his notes. That made a certain sort of sense. But what kind of woman would deliberately choose to become mixed up with such a man? And how could she write such lines, knowing another of her sex was to suffer so horribly?

Perhaps the one who wanted to harm him was a woman, one who thought he'd wronged her. Could she be paying a strong man to do her horrible deeds?

That theory still didn't seem logical to William, for he had put word of a princely sum of money out on London's meanest streets as a reward. No hired killer could have resisted such an amount.

He'd locked the note away in the top drawer of the desk in his library. Once again, he had to attempt to find some sort of pattern. For time was running out.

Cinda couldn't be contained. Her actions frustrated him, but he would not play the hypocrite and say he didn't enjoy her temperament. Yet that same temperament put her in danger each time she set foot out her stepmother's door, masked or not.

If only she hadn't been shut away for much of her life, worked like a servant and treated far worse. If she'd had anything resembling a normal life, she might have been content to patiently wait until he could flush out this madman and finish his sick game once and for all.

She'd been forced to fend for herself far too long. That fate had changed her. Toughened her. She thought for herself, in ways most women did not.

He knew she would not change. He knew this, deep in his heart.

The only alternative left to him was to find the man who wished to kill her. And in order to have time to do so and ensure Cinda remained alive, he had to figure out a way to lead this brutal hunter off the scent of the woman he loved.

"Let me attend to that," Cook said from her pallet by the fire.

"You stay where you are," Cinda answered, preparing a dinner tray for Nan. "Up all night tending to her, and now you want to exhaust yourself with more of her chores. She won't know if you rest for a few hours."

Mary came bustling in, a torn ball gown in her hands.

"They want you, Cinda. Miranda's complaining again. Says it's something to do with Rosalind."

"The tray's for Nan. I'm on my way."

She hurried for the stairs, wondering what either stepsister had to say to her. Neither had cared for their younger sister. They'd continually made fun of her love of reading, her endless daydreaming. Knowing how shy she was, they'd found sport in teasing her mercilessly.

Cinda had been fond of the girl. She'd even tried to toughen her up a bit. When that had proved impossible, she'd simply shown Rosalind several places she could hide in the garden, taking a good book with her.

She reached the stepsisters' bedroom, and knocked.

"Get in here!"

Helena was sitting at a small table by the window, gorging on cream-filled pastries. The rose-colored silk dressing gown barely covered her tublike form.

Miranda had been cutting a wide and ruthless swath through her various ball gowns, judging by the utter mess she'd created. Dresses were draped all over both bed and chairs, and several of the delicate gowns had slipped to the floor.

"Mother put this in my closet, and I want you to dispose of it." She indicated a large basket, and Cinda bent to pick it up.

She'd learned from experience never to question what her stepsisters wanted. They'd boxed her ears and cuffed and slapped her in exchange for too many supposed insolences for her to give either of them a chance to do further damage.

Feigning subservience, she picked up the basket and started for the stairs.

"Send Mary back up, I've found another gown that needs mending, and one to be pressed."

Cinda merely nodded her head and walked away. Once in the kitchen, she set the basket down on the table, relayed Miranda's message to an exhausted Mary, and pulled up a chair next to Cook.

"I could fix you a bowl of broth," she suggested.

Cook was lying still, her eyes closed, but Cinda had known the older woman wasn't asleep.

"Did they ask about the dog?" she inquired.

"They haven't even realized she's gone."

"Hmmm. Let me see what's in that basket."

"I will if you stay where you are. Tomorrow's the wash, and you've got to rest up for it."

"Bring the basket over," Cook murmured.

She did, and the two of them opened it.

"Rosalind," Cinda breathed.

The possessions within had belonged to the young girl. Cinda recognized a pair of white lace gloves, a golden locket on a chain, several of her precious books, her well-worn Bible, and a sampler. The embroidery stitches were uneven, and had been taken out time and time again, to be done over. Rosalind had preferred the company of a good book. Or her dreams.

There were also several letters, and Cinda recognized one by the distinctive seal. A dragon's head was pressed into the wax, the design from a ring William always wore on his right hand. He'd bought the piece of jewelry in the Orient, and sealed all his letters with the distinctive crest.

She picked up the letter, realizing it was the one he'd written to her, telling her to meet him that they might run away and begin their married life together. Cook's hand stayed hers, but she shook it off and slipped the single piece of paper out of its envelope, then read its contents.

She'd thought Nan had destroyed it.

Once finished, she carefully folded it and put it back inside the envelope, then placed the letter inside one of Rosalind's books. It had a red leather cover, and she set it on top of the others.

"I can't bring myself to dispose of her belongings," she told Cook. "It's all that's left of her."

Cook remained silent, her hand on the basket, as they both remembered Rosalind's affection-starved existence.

"They don't even care. She wanted more room for her *gowns*."

"We'll put it in the pantry," Cook said finally, "far in back with your mother's herbals. It's the least we can do in her memory, and they'll never even know it's there."

The mysterious Aurora was all the aristocracy could talk about. Gossip flew through the various households, all to do with the glorious woman who had arrived at the masquerade.

She'd been adorned with mere flowers in her hair and a priceless wit, and been swept off her feet by a pirate king.

William bore the brunt of his friend's teasing, as by now most of them knew he'd been the pirate who'd escorted this mystery woman up the stairs to the private rooms above. And they wanted to know what sort of dalliance he'd had with her. They were all present at the club tonight, playing their usual game of Hazard. The wager was once again low, and Charles Hailey was not happy about it.

The attention Cinda had engendered by attending the masquerade disturbed William; he didn't want her associated with him in any way. He'd not only determined to ensure she was not in any danger, but to make the men around him believe she meant nothing to him at all.

The one advantage he had was that no one knew of her, for Cinda Townshend had vanished from the London aristocracy years ago, after her mother died. No one would've believed him if he'd told them their goddess was a mere serving girl, down on her knees weeding the garden or scrubbing out dirty pots.

Since receiving the note, he'd thought of nothing but how to protect her, and decided he'd do anything necessary to achieve his aim. It was literally a matter of life and death to the woman he loved. To keep Cinda from the killer, he would sacrifice all.

"Some of the women are even tinting their hair to look more like her," Ashley remarked, studying his cards without any real interest. His concern was for Charles, who was quite drunk this evening.

"Silly chits," murmured Philip as he drew another card. "As if hair color could give most women what she had. Quite a fetching little piece she must have been, eh, William?"

Normally, he would have been loath to discuss any amorous adventure, but knowing there were many within earshot and wishing it to appear as if Cinda were simply one of a great number, he replied, "She provided me with a most pleasing tumble. Quite the sporting wench."

"Did she pad out her costume?" asked another. "Or were those curves her own?"

"Her charms were genuine. She pleased me greatly, but she wasn't all that different from any other lightskirt." William yawned, then discarded a card and picked up another. "I've been celibate far too long. Such sport is essential to a man's health, thus I will be hunting the same such amusement soon."

"Then you'll be coming with us to Madam Avice's tonight?" asked Charles. His eyes were red-rimmed, and the look he shot in William's direction was not kind.

Under normal circumstances, and loving Cinda as he did, William would have never considered visiting the house of prostitution. Now, he felt his friend was angry at him, and calling his bluff. Normal modes of behavior counted for naught if Cinda came to harm. In this nightmarish world he'd been forcibly made part of, none of the older rules applied.

He couldn't possibly refuse. Not if his instincts had any substance. And not if he wanted to keep Cinda safe.

"I believe I shall."

The bastard couldn't kill every woman in London. He'd take three or four of the Madam's girls up to one of her most expensive private rooms, and dispel all notions that one woman held his heart in the palm of her hand.

Even if she did.

"When do you wish to leave?" Charles inquired.

William acted as if the entire escapade held little importance for him. "In an hour or so. Will that suit you?"

Charles glanced disinterestedly at the others seated around the table. "I'll go with you, William. I'd be curious to see how debauched you can be." He glanced at Ashley then, and smiled a thin, tight smile. "He's always appeared to be such a paragon of virtue, you know."

"Charles, don't," Ashley muttered, clearly embarrassed for his friend.

"And you'll be coming with us?" Charles inquired. There was quite a nasty edge to the man tonight, and William knew he would not let his friend off lightly.

Ashley hesitated, and William's feelings went out to him. He'd never been able to stomach deliberate cruelty.

"Your sister is quite sick, is she not?" he inquired, giving the man an out if he chose to take it. "My uncle has several physician friends who are highly skilled, should you desire a recommendation."

Ashley was grateful for the respite from the night's festivities. Everyone knew he doted on his youngest sister. She'd been frail from the hour of her birth.

•

"Would you refer me to one you trust?" he asked William.

"I'll send my man over with a note in the morning," William answered, not missing the disgusted look Charles threw him.

"There's a Gypsy at the door, Mum," Robbie said as he stomped down into the kitchen. He removed his muddy boots at the foot of the stairs.

"What does she want?" Cook asked, looking up from a large pot of mutton stew. Though Cinda had urged her to rest through the night, she didn't want to fall too far behind in her chores. She'd started the next day's dinner during the cool of the evening, when the heat from the huge fireplace was appreciated.

"She's hungry, and has three little ones with her."

Cook thought quickly. So much food went to waste in this household, what with the three women being so particular in their eating habits. She went to the cupboard and brought out a large, round loaf of bread. Hollowing it out, she left a thick bread shell, then deftly ladled in a generous amount of the hot stew. The entire concoction was slid on a wooden plate and handed to her son.

"Take it out to her. Then come back and I'll give you some milk for the children."

Robbie did as he was told. Much later, after he'd joined Cinda and Cook at the kitchen table by the fire for the evening, they heard a faint knock at the back door.

Cook glanced at her son.

"I told her she could bed her children down in the stable, but they had to be on their way by morning."

Cook considered this. "We're probably safe enough. Gypsies rarely steal from those who feed them. And Nan isn't well enough to leave the house, not that she ever goes near the stables. And those daughters won't."

The scratching came again, and Robbie went to the door.

The Gypsy was younger than any of them would have thought. Her dark hair hung in waves to her waist, and her liquid eyes were serene.

"I thank you," she said simply, handing Robbie the plate, tankard, and mug.

" 'Twas Mum that fed you," Robbie replied, indicating Cook, sitting by the fire with Cinda.

"Then let me offer my services to repay your kindness," the Gypsy said. She walked into the kitchen with bare feet. Before anyone could say a word, she sat next to Cook and took her hand.

She held it for a long moment, staring at the broad, callused palm, before looking up and around the large kitchen.

"There is evil in this house," she whispered.

"I don't need a Gypsy to tell me that," Cook replied.

"There is also . . . I feel a sadness. A spirit is present who refuses to move on."

Cook nodded her head, feeling Cinda move closer.

"'Tis true."

The Gypsy studied her hand, each line and callus. Finally, she spoke.

"Your heart is large and generous, but it is not strong. Beware those that might work you too hard."

This woman clearly had a gift.

"Go on," Cook said.

"You had a husband, and many happy years with him."

"Yes."

"Many children."

"Eleven."

"You will marry again, and soon."

"Really?" Cook's eyes lit up, and she glanced at Cinda with a grin. "Something to look forward to, if my heart doesn't stop!"

"God's blood, Mum, don't joke!"

"He's your favorite." The Gypsy girl grinned at Robbie, showing startlingly white teeth against her olive skin. "I don't need to see your palm to know that." She glanced back down at the callused hand.

"If you are moderate in all you do, and take special precautions, you will leave this household and find a man who will make your many final years happy. No children, of course."

"And bless the Lord for that!"

The Gypsy rose and was about to leave when Cook grabbed a handful of her full skirt.

"Would you look at her palm?" she asked, indicating Cinda.

"Of course."

The Gypsy woman took Cinda's hand, and she felt a funny sort of tingling begin in her fingers and spread up her arm. The girl was silent for a moment as she studied the delicate palm.

"I see someone hiding."

"Me?" Cinda asked.

"Perhaps. But someone else, behind a false front." She was quiet as she studied the palm, bending it this way and that, moving the fingers to see the various lines, bumps, and ridges.

"There is one you love. A great love. The only love for you. You met him several months ago."

Cinda could feel the hairs on the back of her scalp prickle. *How could this woman know?*

"You will fight, and lose each other."

She tried to pull her hand away. "No!"

"No, no. It is not bad. You will tear apart, and it will hurt him as much as it does you. But you will find each other again, just when things seem their worst."

Cinda glanced at Cook, who was listening intently.

"There is another who wishes to kill you."

Robbie's eyes widened, and he glanced at his mother.

"I know," Cinda breathed.

"But this man has a sickness inside him he cannot control. His emotions are involved with your lover, not you."

Cinda could feel Robbie staring at her, and she concentrated on the Gypsy girl's clear, dark eyes.

"He will steal your lover's soul, if this man you love is not careful."

Every fear she'd had for William was crystallized in that single sentence.

"Your lover betrays you as we speak, to eyes that refuse to see. But to one who sees with the heart, everything he does is for you. Your safety."

"I know," Cinda whispered.

The Gypsy was silent for almost a minute, studying her hand. Then she said, "If you avoid lost dogs and full moons, all will be well."

"Children?" Cook inquired.

"I see three girls, and he will love them as fiercely as sons. But with the fourth, he will have the boy he secretly desires. And the fifth will be a son, also."

"He'll be keeping you busy, Cinda," Robbie joked, and Cook shot him a look, then took a deep breath.

"Will she leave this house?" she asked the Gypsy.

"Yes, and she should, for evil is in the air."

Cook sighed with relief, and Cinda said, "But will she come with me?"

"If she takes care of her heart." She glanced back down at Cinda's open palm. "Your life is already closely entwined with this man's. Do not fight him, or your fate. Try to help him."

"Should I stay close to home? Hidden?"

The Gypsy studied her palm. "You cannot. I could tell you to do so, but you couldn't. It is not your nature, nor your fate. For you, the light of wisdom only comes from the fire of passion."

After the Gypsy retired to the barn, the three of them sat around the table by the fire, drinking ale and talking. As there was no possible way to keep Robbie out of it anymore, Cook told him of the man who was after William and who they believed had murdered Rosalind.

"I knew there was a reason," Robbie said. "I knew he just wouldn't leave like that."

They retired shortly thereafter, with Robbie going back out to the stable. Cinda lay awake on another pallet by the fire, listening to Cook's uneven breathing. She would not leave her friend's side when she was feeling so poorly.

The Gypsy's prophecy came back to haunt her.

Your lover betrays you as we speak, to eyes that cannot see. But to one who sees with the heart, everything he does is for you . . .

Madam Avice sat at the far end of the salon as her girls paraded in and out. Clad only in gossamer silk wrappers that they briefly opened and closed at the customer's request, their cheekbones and nipples glowed with carefully applied rouge. Lips that promised every carnal sin imaginable were lushly colored and shaped with carmine.

The Madam simply watched, never taking her eyes off the activities in the main room. She was dressed in a midnight-blue silk sacque dress, and her long, dark hair was scraped back off her face. It fell below her shoulders in a thick braid, emphasizing her exotic features and slightly slanted eyes.

Her jeweled fingers flashed in the soft candlelight as she

stroked the head of her beloved cat, Feste. It was said she'd been displeased with her last lover, and turned him into the sleek tortoiseshell cat that now claimed her lap, staring out at the world with lovely green-gold eyes.

Madam Avice supplied the aristocracy with anything of a sensual nature they desired. Anything possible between a man and a woman could transpire within the walls of her lavish mansion.

Her girls were well trained in all sexual arts, from fellatio to flagellation. They were more than willing to imitate any pose they saw portrayed in the vast library of pornographic prints Madam had framed on the walls upstairs.

The time her girls spent grooming and perfecting their strongly sexual beauty was private, again at Madam's insistence. Even the curls between their sleek thighs were groomed, trimmed, and shaped to delight any masculine eye.

The only time the girls' nudity was on display was during calculated flashes in the parlor. Silken wrappers opened and closed, offering masculine appetites tantalizing glimpses of what awaited them upstairs, should they relinquish the proper coin.

The various rooms were equipped with any and all methods of sensory enhancement, from dildoes imported from Italy to birch switches that striped delicate skin a bright, burning red. Men could request sheaths with red ribbon ties so they might enjoy a girl and not conceive a bastard child. Or catch the French disease.

Fornication, masturbation, adultery, and more, all were practiced at Madam's private house of prostitution. There wasn't a pleasure not willingly practiced, an unnatural position that wasn't enjoyed.

And William, sitting on a comfortable couch between Philip Fleming and Charles Hailey, set his mind to the task at hand. If a night of consorting with some of the most beautiful whores in London kept his secret enemy from singling Cinda out, then he would have to take part in his friends' night of debauchery.

His male friends would have laughed could they have read his mind. Surrounded by some of the most desirable prostitutes in the entire city, his thoughts still strayed to Cinda.

"She's a pretty one," Charles said sullenly as his eye caught a blonde clad in a black wrapper. She gave him a languid look, then swept the silk aside to reveal her considerable charms. Charles stared at her, but it was clear he was still in a nasty mood. The effects of the liquor he'd consumed at the club had worn off, angering him still further.

William studied both his friends as closely as he dared. While Charles was clearly in quite a fine temper, Philip was the more steady of the two. With his blond hair and gray eyes, he often seemed a rather colorless man, the type so easy to overlook. Though he'd inherited his mother's striking bone structure, he would age badly. Philip's face was already softening from his lusty enjoyment of good food and drink.

Charles was the more hotheaded of the two, and at the moment, with his gambling debts, had more to lose than any of them.

Madam Avice left her huge, thronelike chair across the room and glided toward them, her movements unhurried and graceful. Her proportions were generous, her face smooth and unblemished by the pox. She radiated both power and confidence, as she'd created her exclusive business out of years of hard work and determination.

"And what would please you gentlemen tonight?" she asked.

William, who had decided at the beginning of the night that he would take this deception as far as was necessary, spoke first. "I'd like three of your girls, and one of the large rooms on the top floor."

He'd thought of what he had to do through the last hour of their card game, and realized he couldn't risk picking just one girl. William didn't think he could bear being the cause of another violent murder, and in this case there was certainly safety in numbers.

Madam's dark eyes glittered at the prospect of making so much money. "As you wish," she whispered. She clapped her hands, and several other girls came forward.

William quite deliberately didn't pick anyone with titian hair.

"She'll do quite nicely. And that fair one in white. And that one." He sat back on the couch, feigning comfort. He'd been to this brothel often enough in his youth to know how it was all accomplished.

The women would go upstairs and ready themselves. He would pay Madam the full amount before ascending the stairs. And considering the money that would change hands this evening, he would be allowed to spend the entire night in their sensual company.

Philip selected a tiny woman with long, golden brown hair, and Charles remained quiet and sullen, nursing the second drink Madam's blackamoor had brought him.

They chatted of inconsequential things until Madam came up to them and gently touched William's shoulder.

"The girls are ready. I'll escort you upstairs."

Without hesitating, William opened the door.

The three women he'd selected were stretched out on the huge canopied bed, each completely naked. They'd pulled the bed curtains shut behind them, and quite a lovely fire burned in the marble fireplace. They'd taken great pains to create a tableau for him, and he appreciated it.

Now, as there was nothing to do but get on with it, he determined they should all have a pleasant evening.

"What pretty little seductresses you are," he said softly, walking toward the bed and sitting down on the edge. He motioned toward his boots, and one of the women, a curvaceous brunette, knelt between his legs and began to take them off.

"There's brandy in the far cabinet," offered another, a slender blonde.

"Then we should all enjoy a drink," he replied.

No matter how sensual he knew his nature to be, he would have switched all three women in front of him for the one he could not have.

The blonde poured four glasses of fine French brandy, then gave the first to William. He raised his in a toast once all three girls had their own, and smiled at each of them. They drank and then he bade one girl position the screen in front of the fire, and the other snuff out the candles. The room was plunged into darkness as their sensual pleasures began.

The man who stood at the peephole clenched his teeth in fury. He'd been observing William's room until darkness had made it all but impossible. Now, unable to see anything, he stepped back from the peephole and quietly made his way to the ground floor.

The Madam was in the empty salon, sitting in her chair,

her cat in her lap. She was rubbing its ears, and seemed to be deep in thought.

He stood silent until she saw him.

"He finished so quickly?" she asked.

He tried to school his expression into one of calm, but the anger building inside him would not allow it.

"He snuffed out the candles. There was not enough light."

"There are other rooms that can be observed—"

"No. I wanted to watch *him.*"

In all of her years as a procuress, Madam Avice had never been afraid. She'd long considered the English to be a race of people totally incomprehensible to a Frenchwoman like herself. She would never have made the money in France she made here in London, for the English kept their vices as the darkest, most secret of pleasures, while the French were much more open about such things.

She'd never been afraid of a customer. Until now.

It was something in his eyes, the intent way he had of seemingly going inside himself when he talked about William. She didn't think it was an erotic obsession, but something much worse.

She'd never seen such naked, unguarded hatred.

Then it was as if it had never occurred, for the gentleman in question seemed both angry and frustrated, but not to the point she'd thought she'd observed.

She blinked her eyes, wondering if she'd hallucinated the entire thing. But Feste was wary in her arms, her normally relaxed little body alert.

No, she'd not imagined it. She was a woman who had both made her living and survived by relying on her senses to the fullest. Now, those instincts told her to give this man what he wanted and send him on his way.

"Would you care for your money back, or another of my girls?"

"Give me my money."

She forced herself to remain calm as she counted back the notes, all the while longing to simply throw it in his face and hustle him out the door. She watched him leave, forcing herself to remain in her chair and pet her nervous cat.

Of only one thing was she certain—she wouldn't encourage his patronage of her house in future, ever again.

CHAPTER
✤ 14 ✤

Cinda hid in her mother's garden, sitting on the stone bench far to the back of the property. She waited, praying for the latest wave of nausea to pass.

She couldn't bring herself to dwell upon what it might mean.

For almost a week she'd tried to find other reasons, and desperately attempted to convince herself of them. Nan worked them too hard; she and Cook liked to talk far into the night. But Nan had always worked them hard, and she'd always stayed up late since before she could remember.

Even as a child, she remembered knowing that anything truly magical happened at night.

Now Cook was heating the water for washing, and Mary was gathering dirty clothing throughout the house. And she was sitting in the garden, having come to collect specific herbs but wanting a little time alone with her frightened thoughts.

She wasn't surprised when Cook came into the clearing, or when the woman simply sat down next to her and took her hand in her own.

"You'd best be telling him," she said quietly.

She blinked back frightened tears. It couldn't have come at a worse time, finding out she was with child. She was very early into her pregnancy, had only missed one course of her monthly cycle. Her breasts were tender, and she was overwhelmingly tired. Those changes she could have ignored,

209

but not the sickness that came as regular as each morning's sunrise.

"I can't," she whispered.

"You must think of the child you carry. She'll need her father's name."

Cinda bit her lip. When the Gypsy had told her of children, she'd known then. She and Will were to have their first daughter, and it seemed she was as headstrong as her mother, bending to no one's schedule but her own.

"And his protection," Cook said quietly, glancing toward the townhouse. Neither of them wanted to dwell upon what Nan would do if she found out about the pregnancy.

"I'll make your stepmother a sleeping tisane," Cook said, her voice firm. Cinda knew she would accept no argument from her on this particular matter. "Robbie will take you to him, and you'll tell him tonight. For we must get you out of this house, madman or no."

Cinda nodded her head. Her condition made her so tired and confused, she was relieved to have the decision taken out of her hands.

"And if—" She couldn't finish the sentence. The thought of William being displeased with her news was so terrible she couldn't give it voice.

"I have a sister to the north," Cook said. "We'll leave within the week."

Cinda nodded, and Cook gave her a swift kiss on the cheek. "On with you, now, and gather me chamomile, lemon balm, and flowers of mullein, violet, and lime. We must ensure her sound sleep. Gather a goodly amount, for I'll make her a sleeping pillow so she'll be quiet throughout the night."

Cinda left the clearing obediently, and Cook remained on the stone bench, trying to gather her thoughts. Only when she knew she was alone did she put her head in her hands and let her shoulders sag.

She sat like that for several minutes, until she felt the gentle presence. Sitting up, she smoothed her stained apron over her generous skirts, then glanced around to ensure she had complete privacy.

"Now, don't go upsetting yourself, Nora," she began, her voice a mere whisper. "It happened to you, it has happened to her, and will probably happen to the little one she carries.

Strong wills ensure complicated lives."

Get her away . . .

"My thoughts, exactly. But her young man should be told, and I believe he will do right by her."

If Nan should find out . . .

"She won't. She's not all that clever. He loves her, Nora, I've seen the way he looks at her. And she is heartsick with love over him." She took a deep breath.

"I promise you, I'll find a way for her to leave."

The brothel was quiet as William let himself out the door and started down the stairs. The house took on an entirely different character once the dawn arrived, and looked much like any other. But under cover of darkness its true nature blossomed.

Last night had been proof of that.

Madam Avice had been sitting in the salon as he passed it. In order to ensure he'd played his part to the fullest, William entered the parlor and greeted her.

"You enjoyed your night with us, then?" the Madam asked.

"Very much so. I shall be back again, when my schedule permits."

He left, and didn't see the worried look the Madam gave him as he went out the door.

"She drank it all down," Mary reported dutifully.

Cook gave Cinda a look, and she averted her eyes before Mary could see the triumph in her expression. The housemaid had no idea the carefully selected herbs would ensure her mistress slept through the entire night and most of the following morning.

Both Miranda and Helena were taking advantage of their mother's illness, and had departed earlier for a dinner party with friends. If they stayed true to their usual pattern, neither would be home before dawn.

"I'm going to catch up with the mending while they're away," Mary said. "I just need to fetch my basket."

Cook gave Cinda a look, and she spoke quickly, before Mary left the room.

"I'm not feeling well; I'm going to retire to my room early tonight."

And with any luck, I won't be back at all.

She left the warmth of the great kitchen, and headed toward the stable for both her boyish costume and the two saddled horses Robbie had waiting for them.

"She's here, sir," Henry said as he entered the library.

There was only one woman his valet could be referring to. Before William had a chance to wonder what she was up to, Cinda entered the room.

"I had to see you," she began, a bit breathless.

He took her wrist and led her to the chairs in front of the fire. She sat, and he knelt in front of her, holding her cold hands and trying to give them warmth from his own.

"Why did you take such a risk, coming here?" he asked.

"This is—not an auspicious beginning for what I must say," she replied. "I must—ask you about something."

He'd felt guilty throughout the night, and all through the day. No doubt an account of his evening at the brothel was already racing throughout London, as it was deucedly hard for any of London's aristocracy to keep a secret.

Now, the thought of Cinda having learned of what he'd done filled him with shame.

"Let me explain," he said.

"No, I wish to speak first—"

"No. For I know it has been hard for you to understand exactly why I chose the course of action I did."

Briefly, with as little detail as possible, he told her what he'd done and why.

She stared at him for a long moment, and William realized whatever errand she'd been on, it had nothing to do with his behavior last night.

Expressions played across her lovely face, clear for him to see. Confusion, then the deepest hurt, and finally an all-consuming rage.

She stood and moved away from him. He crossed the room after her, but when he touched her arm, she whirled and slapped his face as hard as she could.

He remained perfectly still as she trembled before him, totally enraged. Her physical attack hadn't made him want to retaliate in kind, but he had to try to make her understand.

He took both her upper arms firmly in his own.

"It meant nothing to me—"

"It meant something to me!"

She drew back her booted foot and kicked. Hard.

He let her go, and she rushed for the door, but he was faster and slammed it before she got there, effectively capturing her.

"Listen to me," he began.

"*No*, you will hear me, and all you'll have to do is listen this one last time. I will *never* be part of your life again, and *never* bother you to do another *blasted* thing for me except *open this bloody door and let me go!*"

He stood his ground, staring down at her. Now he could feel anger rushing to the fore.

"You're such a bloody stubborn little fool, you have no idea the danger you put yourself in."

"You're not playing with any sort of fool, who blindly believes all you tell her! Now, after what you've done, why should I even believe your story of this madman is true?"

She wanted to hurt him the way he'd hurt her, and knew her next words would cut him deeply.

"What a perfect situation you've arranged for yourself, Will, to have me wait patiently and hide myself while you consort with countless whores—"

He grabbed her arm and dragged her over to the desk while she kicked and fought like a child of the streets. Not wanting to let her go while he retrieved the killer's note, he swiftly took down her hair and wrapped the thick braid around his wrist.

Without a word, he unlocked the drawer and handed her the envelope.

She threw it back at him, and his temper finally exploded. Moving so swiftly she had no chance to stop him, he sat down in the desk chair, let go of her hair, pulled her over his knees, and gave her buttocks several smart slaps. She shrieked her dismay, then he pulled her upright and pinned her to the desk with his body. He felt anger course through him, hot and sharp, as he stared down at the top of her head.

"Look at me."

She wouldn't.

He turned her face up toward his with a hand beneath her chin.

"You will *listen* to me," he said, his voice low, his anger a palpable thing between them. "And *I* am the fool, for over-indulging you and not realizing you possess such a willful streak. I should have taken pains to curb it sooner."

He turned her toward the desk, still pinning her against it with his body, but now her hands were free. He thought for a moment she might fight him again, but she simply picked up the letter and opened it.

The rain of faded flower petals silenced her, as did the two pieces of ribbon from her hair. Slowly, hesitantly, she pulled out the letter and read the macabre verse.

He felt the anger leave her body to be replaced by fear, and all he wanted in the world was to take her into his arms. But they'd gone too far in their anger.

He stepped back from the desk and gave her a measure of freedom. Her hands went up to her hair, and she coiled the heavy braid back into place on top of her head.

"I've never lied to you, Cinda."

"No, you have not." She was silent for a moment, then whispered, "I'm sorry I slapped you."

"I apologize for what I did as well."

The silence stretched awkwardly until William said, "What was it you came to tell me?"

She looked up at him, and he was shocked by how tired she suddenly appeared.

"It was nothing. Truly. Nothing at all."

She started toward the door and he waylaid her.

"Talk to me, Cinda. Tell me what bothers you."

"Nothing of any great import. I'll see you next at the masquerade."

He reached for her arm. "You will not—"

She darted out of his reach, her hands up, warning him off against touching her again.

"But I will. For until the one who wrote that letter is caught, it would be wise if we were not together. Don't you see, Will? This way, we can both use our skills to waylay him."

"But what he might do to you—"

"Why do you refuse to look closely at what he's doing to *you*? To *us*! We'll have no peace until he's caught, and I'll have no peace inside myself unless I help bring the cruel bastard down! Now, let me go, Will."

He simply stared at her as he blocked her way.

"Don't you see?" she said quietly, and he could hear the utter weariness in her voice. "I cannot let you go into this without trying to help."

"You don't believe I'm capable of protecting you? Of seeing to your welfare?"

"Oh, you big, bloody *fool*! Of *course* you are! But no man should have to face the devil alone."

He stayed by the door, catching her glance toward it.

"Let me go, Will."

"You will not attend the masquerade."

"You'll never know."

"All of *London* will know, you stubborn girl! They talk now of Aurora, the goddess who dispenses her favors freely. Pray, madam, what do you think they'll do when you *next* choose to appear?"

"I'll cover my hair."

"*They'll* cover *you*," he retorted, his words deliberately cruel.

"I can take care of myself!"

"Can you, now? And what would you have done with that ugly monkey, had I not stopped him when I did?"

"I might have kissed him—" She stopped in midsentence as he pulled her against the length of his body.

"If I see you at the masquerade, I'll take you away and confine you myself."

A poor choice of words, he realized as she struggled to be free. He let her go, and she backed toward the door.

"Robbie escorted you?" he asked.

She nodded her head.

He moved away from the door, turning his back to her, suddenly angry all over again.

"Get yourself home."

"You're as stubborn as your mother was," Cook said, staring at her in dismay.

Cinda tilted her chin up, determined to let no one see how torn apart she felt inside.

"I'll take that as a compliment, as well."

"Then what have you decided to do, now that you've chosen not to tell him?"

"I'll think of something."

"Don't leave me out of it, Cinda. No one should have to face this sort of thing alone."

She clenched her fist against the kitchen table, remembering the harsh words she and Will had exchanged.

"I've been a poor friend to you," she said, finally looking up into the old woman's eyes. "For your loyalty to me, you've earned nothing but misery, and this is how I repay you."

"Hush. All women get a little tetched when God gives them babies."

"Is that all a woman's good for, then?"

"What do you mean?"

"Is this the extent of it, to be shut away and bring children into the world? Then why do I have dreams inside my mind that won't be silenced, and why am I not let out into the world to try to make them real?"

"He's pitting himself against a madman, Cinda."

"And you side with him!"

"I see his side, yes."

"Even after what he did at that brothel?"

"And what was he to do, miss? Answer me that! A young lad like himself, healthy, wild, handsome, and unspoken for? Why, they'd be taking him to the molly houses next!"

She stared at Cook, still upset from her fight with Will, and not at all sure how to reply.

"He did it to lead this devil *away* from you! And had you not gone to the masquerade, no one would have known of your existence!"

"You thought it a good idea!"

"I don't know what to think now." Cook stared at her, then lowered her voice to a whisper. "That man followed you up the stairs and *took your hair ribbons*, Cinda, that he might torment your William! Does that mean *nothing* to you? When he told you what he'd been forced to do, *he'd already seen the note!* Can't you find it in your heart to forgive him?"

"I can't let anyone shut me away, ever again. Not even Will."

Cook stared at her. Cinda knew the woman was remembering various punishments Nan had used on her. She'd locked her in cupboards, and in one of the small attic rooms, leaving both spaces perfectly dark. Now the thought of being confined in any manner was abhorrent to her.

"And what of the wee babe?" Cook whispered. "Are you going to raise her on your own?"

"No." She grasped the side of the table to steady herself, and lifted her chin the merest bit higher, forcing down the doubts fluttering in her stomach. "No, I'm going to catch myself a killer and then convince that stubborn man I love to distraction that we're absolutely perfect for each other."

Neither Cook nor Cinda realized how completely Kathleen would abandon them.

They stopped by to see Cinda's godmother after church as usual, and the woman was full of excitement over the newest ball gown she'd made over.

"This one will be a delight; it's the perfect shade of blue to set off your lovely hair. And did you know there's a woman they cannot stop talking about who has hair almost the exact shade as yours, so you'll be as fashionable as the next girl!"

Cinda had thought of confiding in her godmother, but instinct told her to stay silent. They finished their tea, and Kathleen asked her if she would step upstairs so she might pin part of the bodice and fit it exactly.

As soon as her godmother saw her clad only in her chemise, she knew.

"Oh, Cinda." The dismay was apparent in her troubled gaze, as she took in the overripe fullness of her breasts. And Cinda knew the woman was seeing her mother in her yet again, but in a different way. Eleanor had been passionate, young, headstrong—and blinded by love.

And according to what Cook had confided to her, Kathleen believed she had been instrumental in her own self-destruction.

"I'm sorry I put you to any trouble," Cinda said, her pride forcing her to say the words. She shrugged into her dress, then Cook began to lace her bodice.

"And William?" Kathleen asked, clearly still struggling to take in the pregnancy. "What does he think of all this?"

"He doesn't want a woman like me."

Cook gave her the most furious of pinches at that remark, and had they not been in Kathleen's presence, Cinda felt sure her friend might have boxed her ears.

"I cannot, in good faith, send you to parties to catch the eye of a decent young man in your present condition."

"Then I cannot, in good faith, attend those parties." Cinda, now completely dressed, turned toward her godmother. "We will say our good-byes and be going."

"I have a friend in Scotland," Kathleen began. "I could write and ask if you could stay there during your confinement—"

"Please, don't trouble yourself unnecessarily. We'll be leaving London shortly, and I'll write to you care of your friend and let you know how we fare."

Once outside, the two women walked in silence for almost half a mile.

"We will be leaving London shortly, eh?" Cook finally said.

"I refuse to be looked upon as a charity case!"

"That's exactly what you're going to end up as, my girl. Or worse."

She'd thought of it, even had dreams of the woman she'd seen at the marketplace with the sickly baby in her arms. Would she end up just like her, out in the cold with a small child and nowhere to call home?

"No. I'll think of something."

"Swallow your pride, my precious, and go to him."

They walked the rest of the way home in silence.

William wasn't sure what he felt toward Cinda as he sat at the table and attempted to act as if he were enjoying himself. The dinner party was infinitely boring, not one woman there showing half the spirit he so loved in Cinda.

But that same spirit had caused him to pull her over his knee and beat her. As he was not a man given to physical punishment in any form, what he'd resorted to had shocked him. It was one thing to hold one's own in masculine company, but totally another to lay a hand on a woman.

She managed to bring out every violent emotion he possessed. Since meeting her, he'd been forced to come to terms with the fact that he was merely a man, and subject to all the passions and angers that made one human. Before, he'd been able to perceive himself as being too controlled to feel such emotions.

It had been a safe self-deception, designed to keep him from feeling anything too deeply. After his parents had died, especially his mother, he hadn't wanted to feel anything for a time. He'd had passions, of course, but of a different sort. Though he might have completely joined in the game, his heart had never been involved.

Then Cinda had come into his life, and from the first moment he'd seen her, she'd changed his world completely. And he'd never been entirely sure he liked it. Right now, he was sure he didn't. What man wanted to think of himself as ruled by his emotions and not able to keep a level head when in the company of the fairer sex?

William knew other men didn't feel the same way. Slapping or beating a mistress, even a wife, wouldn't have raised any eyebrows with most of his contemporaries. But his uncle had raised him differently. He'd seen more of the world than most, and held himself accountable to a higher standard of behavior.

He didn't understand why Cinda couldn't see his side of their argument more clearly. He was a reasonable man, and usually quite willing to treat her as more partner than plaything.

But not when her life is at stake.

At such a time, every primitive instinct he possessed came into play, and all he thought of was keeping her from harm.

"Your Grace, tell me of your uncle's garden," said a very pretty woman sitting across from him. She had dark hair and green eyes, and was really quite fetching. But he'd caught her gazing at the jeweled dragon ring on his finger and the cut of his evening clothes, and knew she asked the question without any real interest.

Now, were we to talk of my fortune . . .

He sighed, and wondered what to say. He missed Cinda, deeply and completely, the emotions overwhelming him at times. And he'd realized the only thing that had kept him alive through those long dark months after Rosalind's murder were thoughts of seeing the woman he loved.

Now, that same murderer forced them apart, for he would deny his own heart before he would bring harm to her.

He thought of the way his temper had overtaken him, and knew if he could have changed one incident in his life, it would have been trying to beat some sense into her. In not wanting to hurt her, he'd done exactly that. For Cinda was a proud beauty, and now he wondered if he would ever possess her completely.

"Your Grace?"

He came back to the present with a start. The dark-haired woman was eyeing him, a petulant curve to her lips.

"My garden," he said, remembering what she'd asked.

"No," she said, acting hurt that he was not hanging on her every word. "Ashley was asking you about those horses you purchased."

He turned his attention to his friend, who looked rather uncomfortable at having given voice to the question that had caught him daydreaming.

"I've been quite pleased with them," William said, picking up his wineglass. And he wondered, as he glanced around the table filled with both friends and acquaintances, if the killer was with him in this very room.

The killer was at the table, a mere three seats away.

He stared at William, fighting to keep his true feelings under control.

Every woman at this gathering fawns over you, yet you pay no attention to any of them. It does me no good when you consort with them all and refuse to single one out.

He picked up his wineglass, then made himself laugh at a silly story one of the guests told. But at odd moments, he found himself staring at William.

I thought it was Aurora you fancied, I thought I'd found a way to hurt you, William. Why do you upset me so? Why won't you let me get closer to you in the only way I want to . . .

More wine was poured, and conversation continued amid laughter and gossip.

And he watched. And waited.

Kathleen had finished packing her trunks, and now sat on her bed wondering how all she had planned could have come to naught. She'd wanted to show her goddaughter how much she cared for her well-being, and instead found herself more distanced from the girl than ever.

She'd be leaving in the morning, heading north and out of the city she so disliked. Away from Cinda, away from her problems. She'd probably never see the girl again.

That's right, Katie. Run away.

She lowered her face into her hands. The discovery of her goddaughter's pregnancy had upset her, so much so that for an instant she'd thought she'd heard Eleanor's voice.

Run away.

She'd run before and never forgiven herself. Even though she was a woman, she'd still been more than a match for a drunken sod like Horace Townshend.

Don't be afraid. Please. Help her . . .

It was as if Eleanor were in the bedchamber with her, and Kathleen closed her eyes tightly, willing her presence to leave. A noise at the door made her start.

Julia's servant, a short, squat man, indicated the two trunks by the foot of the bed.

"This be all that's going?" he asked gruffly.

She stood up, holding on to the bed frame for support. Pushing her hair out of her eyes, she stared at the man.

"This be all?" he asked.

"No," she said quietly, then sank back down onto the bed, clenching her fingers into fists so hard they hurt.

"No, I won't be leaving just yet."

Dear William,

 I haven't written in quite some time, it is true, but only because my health is not as it should be and I have been confined to my bed. Yet I have heard of you, and your Aurora. And how I admire her, for these four bedchamber walls are the extent of my world. Yet she has taken on all of London.

 She has excited the aristocrats of London into a frenzy of curiosity. And Daniel, as well.

 He is angry with you, William. I feel his presence belowstairs each time he returns to this London townhouse. You've thwarted him once again, as is usual.

 He cannot find this woman, and now he is even unsure of your affection toward her. I pray that you will continue to lead a false trail and keep her safe from his rage. You've never trifled with the fairer sex, William. I know this. And that is why I suspect the lady still has a hold on your heart.

I promised myself that this time I would tell you all of it, would finish this particular tale. I am feeling better today, and hope to record much more.

Daniel came for me, and took me out of service to my elderly friend. She was delighted for me, delighted that my brother had done so well for himself, for he was dressed in fine clothing and even possessed a carriage.

We rode out of London, triumphant, and I was ecstatic that my brother had been able to transcend his past and do so well for himself.

Until I learned the truth.

It involved another murder. I cannot tell you more right now, William, as it is crucial that I explain how his hatred of you came into being.

We traveled to his country estate. Its lands bordered yours, and from the day I arrived I heard stories of you and your boyish exploits. You were not home at the time, as you were traveling with your uncle. But I listened to these tales, and my curiosity grew.

I saw your gardens, and knew a man who loved such beauty would have a sensitive nature, as well. A nature so foreign from that of both my father and brother.

Please understand me, William. Though I loved my brother, I was also frightened of him. I had seen, firsthand, what he was capable of. I have been frightened from the moment of my birth, and the events of my life have only reinforced those fears.

I live with the knowledge that I am a coward, and, William, it is not easy.

The day you came home to your estate, you paid us a call. I saw you from the library window. You came striding into my life with the force of a god. You were so handsome, so clever. So gentle.

I fell in love with you then, but was smart enough to hide it.

Daniel envied you from the first. To his mind, everything he'd had to work for, even kill for, had come to you with no effort. He'd had to arduously learn to play the part of gentleman, while you'd been born to it. When the two of you went riding, William, you had the better seat. You excelled at hunting and fishing. Even with the ladies.

Daniel felt he was nothing. And perhaps, inside, like me, he was.

I knew the two murders weighed heavily on his mind. Though one had been done in my defense, the other had been committed for financial gain. Daniel had thought, quite wrongly, that we needed exorbitant amounts of money to protect ourselves. And in order to escape our past, to put it behind us forever.

I remember that summer well, both of you so young and strong. Both so beautiful. I would watch you from the windows, for Daniel had put me in service within his immense estate. I was not confident enough to learn to play the part of a great lady. I thought I was content with my duties, content just to live close to my brother and in relative comfort.

But I wanted more. And I have been punished for that desire many times over. William, while you created gardens to rival that original one, I have been instrumental in making my own particular hell.

I wanted you. I wanted to see if I could let a man touch me without feeling such total revulsion. I let you kiss me on the stairs one day, then fled. For you brought up too much feeling in me, and it was frightening.

But I could not forget.

I know you will remember me when I tell you I gave you my virginity, as you did yours to me. You would not recognize my face, for I look nothing like that young, pretty girl. Please know this, William, that you gave me a moment in time I shall remember until the hour of my death.

Yet I would take it all back if I could undo the damage.

One of the servants talked to another, then another, then finally Daniel heard the gossip. He called me to his private bedchamber, enraged. I tried to deny it, but he'd seen the small bunch of wildflowers you'd left for me. Though I always knew there was too great a distance in class and breeding between us, you were kind to me, William, and I appreciated that.

But I have hurt you, and would do anything to atone for that particular sin.

Had you merely thrust yourself upon me and used me to satisfy your lust, he might not have been as angry. But he knew I loved you, William. He knew you possessed a part of my heart he could never lay claim to, and though his affection for me was never unnatural, this enraged him no end.

Thus, he began to torment you. Your favorite dog was injured during a hunt. The horse you rode went lame inexplicably. Part of your garden was overturned, the flowers pulled up by their roots. All pranks of a dangerous and vindictive nature.

But not murder.

Until Anne, and the affection he saw in your eyes when you looked at her. He saw you both at the theater one evening, and came home to our London townhouse determined to make you suffer. I tried to intervene, but perhaps made it worse. I forced myself outside my protective shell, for a brief moment. Daniel's rage pushed me back inside, for he reminded me so of our father.

He killed her. Anne. And the other girl, as well.

My hand shakes as I write these words. I tire so easily these days. My frustration grows, as there is much left to tell you.

He is close to you, William. So much closer than you suspect. He watches your every move, and is determined to bring you to ruin. He wishes you to suffer, as he has. I've known that truth since I was a girl.

I feel so utterly helpless.

And there is no way to stop him . . .

Cinda was cleaning in the drawing room the morning Nan revealed the true nature of the marriage contract.

She'd stopped dusting for the moment, and was studying the portrait of her stepsisters. Nan placed great store in having portraits painted, for she thought it elevated her family in status. Cinda, silently studying the likeness, thought the painter had considerable talent. He'd caught the most disagreeable qualities in both Helena and Miranda for all the world to see.

Her mother's portrait, commissioned when she announced her engagement, had been sold years ago. Nan had been greedy for money even when she'd married into plenty of it. And, she obviously hadn't wanted any reminders of Horace's first wife around her house.

It hurt Cinda deeply to think of her mother's portrait in a shop, being sold to a perfect stranger. Now, pregnant with her first child, she was saddened by the fact that the only memory her child would have of its maternal grandmother was the small miniature in her quarters above the stable.

She was surprised when Nan, up from her sickbed, swept into the room, a stranger behind her. The man was in his early twenties, with long, carefully curled blond hair that had been expertly powdered. His clothing was immaculate, and Cinda had no idea how he'd taken up with such as Nan. Even now, in a crumpled day dress, her dirty wig perched atop her head, she seemed his direct opposite.

"There she is," Nan announced, indicating Cinda.

Not wishing to be cuffed for impertinence, Cinda folded her arms in front of her, dust rag in hand, and looked down at the floor as modesty decreed she should. She remained perfectly still.

"Ah, yes, she'll do nicely." The tone of his voice made her skin crawl.

Perhaps Nan and her friend were not so different after all.

"Lucinda, this is Jeffrey Templeton, second Viscount Hoareton. Jeffrey, this is my stepdaughter, Lucinda Townshend."

"She's even lovelier than you said she was, Nancy."

Cinda swallowed, wondering why she should feel afraid of this man she'd never met.

"How do you do," she said quietly.

Nan turned to Jeffrey with a smile. "She's quite the little lady, is she not?"

Cinda wished she could ask them what this was about, but Nan was playing with her again. Jeffrey was more direct.

"What a pleasure to meet you and know we shall soon be related."

The marriage. She'd been so caught up in slipping in and out of her stepmother's house, she'd forgotten all about the arrangements Nan and her father had made for her future.

She pictured herself walking down the aisle at a country church, obviously pregnant, and almost laughed in both their faces. It was either see the blackest humor in the situation or cry.

"And you are my prospective bridegroom?" she asked softly. She looked up at him from beneath her lashes. Perhaps if she forced herself to charm him, Nan would take more kindly to her questions. Now she simply had to find out as much as possible concerning what these two had planned for her.

"Oh, no, my dear. My brother is the lucky one."

"And he is here?" she replied, injecting just the proper amount of feminine curiosity into her voice.

Nan and Jeffrey looked at each other and smiled.

"He's been feeling rather poorly lately," Jeffrey said smoothly. "But you'll meet him before the wedding, I'm sure."

Cinda smiled up at him, forcing her features into a false mask of sweet femininity. She decided to dare one more question.

"Might I inquire as to his name?"

"Colin," said Jeffrey. His eyes kept straying to her bodice, and Cinda resisted the urge to cover the neckline of her drab outfit with her hands. The bodices of the plain dresses she wore as servant's garb were just starting to fit too snugly; her breasts had become heavy and full because of her pregnancy. But there was nothing to be done about it, as neither she nor Cook had money to spare for clothing.

"I'll arrange for tea to be sent up," Nan said brightly. "The two of you can spend some time getting acquainted."

It was a brutal mockery of anything resembling a courtship. Had Cinda known the proper protection of both father and family, she wouldn't have been left alone with this man. Now, with nothing but a dust rag in her hands, she felt a moment of fear.

"Sit down," Jeffrey said, indicating the couch.

She hesitated.

"Come now, I shan't bite you."

As she had no real choice, she sat. He immediately joined her, sitting far more closely than was proper.

"What poor little hands, all chapped and red," he remarked.

Cinda hated being reminded of her station in life, but now that consideration seemed trivial. For everything this man presented to the world was false. This was the evil the Gypsy girl had spoken of, she was sure of it.

She kept her gaze modestly focused on her hands in her lap, and prayed Nan would return shortly.

"What a comely little wench you are. And what a fine time we shall have enjoying each other, you and I."

His words were so outrageous that for a moment she thought she'd imagined them. Then she glanced up and saw his face, the peculiar light in his eyes, and knew nothing she'd endured within this house would compare with what this man had planned for her.

She swallowed, keeping her gaze on her tightly clasped hands. "And Colin?" she whispered, wishing she had one of Cook's kitchen knives nearby.

"Look at me."

She dared not disobey him.

"He's extremely generous." Jeffrey's thin lips curved into a smile, and Cinda found herself repulsed.

He reached for her, and she shot up off the couch. But he was quicker, and backed her up against the far wall. To her horror, she felt his hand dip inside the front of her bodice, touching bare skin.

She screamed, but the sound was cut off by his mouth covering hers. His tongue plunged deep inside, and she retched at the sensation. With a violent move, she jerked her head aside, only to have him grab her hair with clawlike fingers and twist her around till she thought her head might snap off her neck.

He kissed her again, and when his tongue invaded her mouth, she acted without thinking and bit down as hard as she could.

He pushed her away from him, and she fell against a footstool. Jeffrey stood over her, breathing heavily, his elegant hair in disarray, an angry light in his blue eyes.

Nan chose that moment to enter the room, carrying a tray full of refreshments. She'd obviously not wanted Mary to see what was transpiring and report back to Cook.

"The bitch *bit* me!" Jeffrey said in an accusing tone.

Nan carefully set the tray down, and when she faced Cinda, her expression revealed the enormity of her hatred.

"I told you she would need disciplining. But then, you're just the man to take on such a challenge, aren't you, Jeffrey?"

Cinda remained perfectly still in the corner by the footstool. She'd already judged how far it was to the door. Two people stood in the way. She'd never make it, but she would certainly fight as hard as she could.

"I shall enjoy taming her," Jeffrey said. Cinda didn't meet his gaze as she thought quickly, desperately, of what she had to do.

If she made a sound, Cook would send Robbie to her aid. If he should hear, he'd come of his own accord. And Cinda had no doubt Jeffrey would either severely injure him or claim assault and have no qualms about killing Robbie.

In a fight to the death, a nobleman's word against a servant's would always win out.

As Jeffrey moved toward her, she thought of how foolish she'd been not to ask William for his protection. In a last desperate attempt, she leapt to her feet and tried to dart around him.

The first savage slap caught her on the cheek, and she tasted blood. Still struggling to escape, her hands instinctively raised to shield her face, Jeffrey's second assault caught her in the stomach, causing her to double over in anguish and sink to the drawing-room floor.

She slipped into unconsciousness as he started to kick her.

CHAPTER
❧ 15 ❧

Nan and Jeffrey left soon after the vicious beating was finished, leaving Cinda unconscious on the floor of the drawing room where Mary found her. The girl screamed at the sight, and Victor came rushing in to see what had upset her. Swiftly assessing the situation, the Frenchman carefully picked Cinda up in his arms and bore her limp body toward the relative safety of the kitchen.

Cook, having heard Mary's scream, had been halfway to the drawing room when she saw Victor striding toward her, Cinda in his arms. She turned white when she saw the girl, her lip split and puffy, her shabby gown torn down the front, the ugly bruises just starting to turn a purplish hue.

"What has she done to my girl?" she whispered as Victor laid Cinda on one of the pallets next to the fire. Cook, realizing now was not the time to give in to the demands of her emotions, swiftly instructed Mary to bring her warm water, clean rags, and her basket filled with herbal ointments and salves.

Steeling herself against the overwhelming urge she had to break down and cry, the woman set to work.

She felt as if a part of her had died.

It was dark outside when Cinda finally came back to full consciousness. She recognized Cook's face illuminated by the firelight. The woman was sitting by her side, Robbie next to her. Cinda couldn't do much more than open her eyes, she felt so very tired and bruised. She tried to smile, but the slight motion pulled on her split lip. Cook laid a comforting hand on her arm.

"Don't move, my darling girl. Just lie quietly, now. Just rest."

Barely moving her lips, she soundlessly mouthed a single word.

Baby.

"She's fine, as strong as her mother and twice as stubborn."

She couldn't help smiling at that, then winced as tender skin pulled and stung. She felt Cook gently smoothing her hair off her forehead as she drifted back into a dark, dreamless sleep.

She had a strong constitution, and within a week was up and about. But a new resolve had been born within her soul, and she knew no one would ever beat her as mercilessly and with as much pleasure as Jeffrey Templeton had.

More of the same was in store for her should she marry into that family, and her hatred of her stepmother grew. She'd always known Nan was cruel, but now she realized the woman lacked any human feelings.

Cinda felt more imprisoned than she ever had. Nan watched their activities relentlessly, never letting her leave the house. Cook rarely did anyway, but now Robbie was also included in this new regime of watchfulness.

Thus Cinda and Cook talked in low voices by the fire, plotting a way to get a message to William.

Mary told them, three days after the beating, that she'd been informed part of her job now included watching the two of them. Spying. Her voice quivered as she admitted as much, then said she could never do anything to bring harm to either of them.

"Not after—not after I saw what she did to you," the girl finished. She was frightened of Nan, and clearly as trapped as they were. Cinda admired her courage and told her so.

"I'll get you out of this hellish place," she whispered, keeping an eye on the door. "And Victor, too."

Thus Mary became their spy, reporting each evening what she'd overheard upstairs.

"She means to push the wedding day forward," she told them this evening. "She was telling the daughters of a dinner she had with that Mister Templeton, and how they'd discussed the matter in some detail."

"And when might this be?" Cook asked.

"The Friday after next. They plan to come in and drug her," she said, indicating Cinda, "and take her to the country."

Mary was loyal, and quite clever, and had discovered even more.

"The man she is to marry—"

"Colin," Cinda said quietly, her eye on the door.

"He is not in his right mind. That Templeton man, his brother, keeps him locked away, instead of in an asylum."

Cook and Cinda were silenced by this.

"He plans to use you—to get you with child, and have that child declared the legal heir—"

"—and thus have access to his brother's fortune," Cook finished.

"Yes."

"I'll go to William tonight," Cinda whispered. The minute the words were out of her mouth, she recognized their futility. If her absence were either suspected or confirmed, Nan would take out her fury on those who remained. Mary, Robbie, or Victor might survive a beating such as she'd been given, but Cook would surely die.

No, she had to find a way to see William in secret, while Nan and her daughters were out. She would beg him for his protection, in order that her child might have a chance of surviving and Cook might as well.

"Don't not go to him because of me," the older woman said.

How easily she's always known what I think, Cinda marveled. "I can't leave you here, you know that."

"Listen, my girl. If it's between your safety and mine, I've lived a good, long life."

"No."

"Listen to me, Cinda. It's what your mother would have wanted me to do, and it's what I will do should I have to. If everything comes tumbling down around our ears the way I suspect it might, go to William and seek his protection."

"I won't leave you."

"You will if I tell you to."

The two women stared at each other, locked in verbal battle.

"It would do no good just yet," Mary whispered. "She's hired two men. Big brutes. They're posted as guards by the gates. You wouldn't get far."

Cook took a deep breath, and exhaled it slowly.

"If you choose a time to leave, it must be forever," Mary whispered, nervously eyeing the door.

"Cinda, if that monster comes back and tries to beat you again, you will escape," Cook said quietly. "William can send for us later."

You won't live long enough to see it happen, Cinda thought grimly. She shook off her frightened thoughts; she had no time for doubts. Pushing her fears down deep inside her, Cinda turned her attention back to the two women in the kitchen.

"There has to be a way. We'll find it." She took Cook's cold hand in her own and squeezed it gently.

"We'll find it."

Late that same night, the drawing room was suddenly suffused with an unearthly glow. And even a person who claimed they gave no credence to spirits that walked the night during the witching hour would have had to take back their words.

Rage shimmered in the air as a furious wind came out of nowhere to sweep through the room, moving curtains and scattering ashes from the hearth. Restless. Seeking.

Out in the hallway, the woman's spirit swept up the stairway to the bedrooms above, passing through the first locked door and looking down at the stepsisters, asleep in their beds.

Giving them barely a glance, Nora moved out of the room and toward Nan. Her locked door proved no barrier either; she simply slipped through it.

The woman was asleep, her mouth open, her thin hair matted. Her filthy wig was perched on one of the chairs by her bed, and Nora considered setting the thing on fire. With all the pomatum the woman used to dress it, the foul thing would go up like a torch.

But not before Nora placed it on Nan's head.

She stifled the urge, knowing it would not help her daughter. She had to find a way for Cinda to leave the house, find William, and obtain the protection she needed. Flitting about the room, she stopped when she saw the envelopes on the dressing table.

Careful not to make the slightest sound, she opened each one and studied their contents. When she came to the third, she silently laughed in delight.

Inside were six tickets to a masquerade, and Nora had known the family giving this particular party. They were wealthy, respected, and loved to have fun. William would surely be invited.

She lifted two tickets out of the envelope, then placed all Nan's correspondence back on the dressing table, carefully, in the order she'd found it.

Nan had recently started drinking heavily, so she wouldn't remember the absence of two tickets as long as there were enough invitations to ensure she and her loathsome daughters could attend. Nora sensed Nan wasn't as confident in her plans as she tried to appear to others.

Now, before she left this monstrous woman's bedroom, she decided to leave a personal message. Concentrating, she slowly opened the window, then slipped outside, tickets in hand. She would have simply melted through the wall, but the invitations to the masquerade would have presented a problem.

Setting the tickets down on the stone bench far back in the garden, she flitted in and out among the flowers, finding the ones she sought. Nan was well aware that bloodred roses had been her favorites, and they were in full bloom this evening. She picked a large bouquet, then added several lilies, representing her daughter.

Bouquet in hand, she floated back up to the third-story window, slipped inside Nan's bedroom, and placed the flowers all around her on top of the coverlet. Then she carefully locked the window, shimmered through it, and swept back down into the garden to retrieve the precious invitations, instruments of her daughter's final escape.

Cook felt the tickling sensation by her nose and scrunched up her face.

"Oh, Georgie, do just leave me alone," she whispered, referring to her dead husband.

The tickling continued until she finally opened her eyes. And once awake, she knew her friend was near.

"Nora? What are you up to?"

Two tickets floated by her face, and she plucked them out of the air and studied them.

"It's tomorrow night!" She considered the feasibility of the plan. "You're sure she's going to attend?"

Yes. The family that gives this party is quite influential.

"The daughters?"

Plenty of rich men will be there. What do you think?

"She has guards at the gate, Nora."

Leave them to me. Just tell me what time to distract them. For I will not leave her side until she is out of this house.

Cook felt her eyes sting with unshed tears.

"The beating . . . I can never forgive myself—"

No. Not your fault. I wasn't here, either. But I'll make her pay.

"What have you been up to?"

My roses . . . all over the bed. The bedroom door was locked tightly, so she'll know . . .

"Mmmm. I like that. You always did have quite a theatrical touch."

Guard her . . .

"I meant what I said to her, Nora. With my life." Cook could feel the presence fading.

"Does it hurt you, to appear like this?"

Can only do so much . . . then must rest . . .

"Then rest now, for there's much work to be done before tomorrow night."

Cinda woke before first dawn to see Cook sitting by the fire, plying her needle furiously. She sat up on her pallet and stretched, gingerly moving muscles that were still sore.

"Go back to sleep," Cook admonished her.

"What are you up to?"

"Go back to sleep," Cook whispered again, "for you have a long night ahead of you."

"Tell me."

"I obtained two tickets to the masquerade tonight."

"How?"

Cook smiled, never taking her eyes away from the swiftly moving needle. "Magic was in the air last night, my girl."

"What are you making?"

Draped across Cook's generous lap was the most beautiful cloth of silver Cinda had ever seen. The material had yet to take form into something recognizable, and Cinda sat up farther, pulling her knees up beneath her chin.

"Your costume, child."

"Where did you—did you steal—"

"God provides us with what we need. The Gypsy girl left this with Robbie. A present for the kindness we showed her and her children." Cook squinted at the material in the dim light from the fire. "I've changed my mind about your masquerade. Now, stand and let me pin this, for I've got to finish it soon if it's to get done."

"And what, pray tell, am I supposed to be?" Cinda asked as Cook draped the material around her and started pinning it in place. Her voice was warm with amusement. How she loved this old woman.

"We needed something simple, and Aurora certainly worked."

"Rather too well."

"The silver color made my mind up for me, as did the simplicity of the costume. You, my precious, are to go to the ball as Diana, goddess of the moon. And the hunt."

Nan woke to the sensation of something tickling her face. Slowly she opened her eyes, then sat up abruptly as she took in the dozens of red roses scattered over her bed.

Eleanor!

The flowers seemed monstrously alive as their soft, fragrant petals stroked her skin, but Nan barely felt them as she struggled out from beneath their weight, screaming.

William gazed down at the costume laid out on his bed, and wished Cinda were accompanying him tonight. For this masquerade was different, certainly not as risqué as Madam Avice's revelries had been. Tonight's masked ball was to be given in the mansion of one of the most respected and beloved couples of the aristocracy, the Duke of Cranfield and his lovely Duchess.

Had he and Cinda married by now, they would be preparing for this event together, joking, laughing, and probably spending the greater part of the afternoon in bed before rising to don their costumes and venture out into the night.

The party began at seven, and would last far into the early morning hours. And Cinda was probably home, sitting by the fire, feeling as trapped as a sparrow in a cage.

Were it not for the fact that he felt he knew who the killer was, William would have found the entire situation unendurable.

Charles Hailey was making no effort to disguise his strong hatred, telling anyone who would listen how much he despised William. The man had gone through most of his entire personal fortune, but luckily had not been given access to the rest of the family money. Still, in simply losing his own share, he would be firmly disgraced.

William was sure he could confront him publicly tonight, and bring him to justice. If all else failed, he'd simply call the man out, and risk all to put an end to his brutal destruction. For such a man was a threat to society, roaming the streets of London. Acting like a god with supreme control over people's lives. And their deaths.

If he was lucky, the nightmare would end tonight.

Once assured of Cinda's safety, he would then simply take his carriage over to her stepmother's house and spirit her away once and for all. They would marry as soon as possible, and start their life together.

He knew her moods, what roused her anger. She was so like him, a lightning-quick temper that flashed as fiercely as a summer storm and then finished. Neither of them held grudges, so he was sure she had simply seen the wisdom of his position and was quietly waiting at home for him to bring this frightening chapter of their life to a close.

He heard Henry enter the bedroom, the spaniel pup at his heels. He'd named her Undine, after a poor water sprite in mythology who had been lost and frightened, but the little dog was lost no longer. She followed her master wherever he went, with most obvious canine adoration.

"Quite an appropriate costume, sir, for one who loves the garden as much as you do."

He was dressing as the Green Man for tonight's festivities, a magical creature endowed with fantastic ritualistic abilities over both crops and human beings. To that end, his mask, which completely covered the upper half of his face, had been fashioned to support the illusion of foliage bursting from his ears and near his mouth. A thick covering of stylized leaves and branches crowned his head, and his clothing was a rich green and graced with more of the earth's vegetation.

"I'm looking forward to tonight, Henry." And William was surprised to find he meant it.

"Wouldn't you like to go to the ball, Cinda?" Miranda's voice was malicious, and Cinda kept her attention on dressing her stepsister's lackluster curls.

"Cinda at a ball? What a peculiar thought!" Helena threw back her head and crowed with peals of laughter. "And what would she wear?" she gasped, wiping tears of laughter from her eyes. "The ashes from the fire?"

"Manure from the stable!"

"Flour from the larder!"

"A piece of moldy bread for her fan!"

"Kernels of corn for pearls!"

"Barefoot of course—and a crown of coal for her head!"

Both women fell into perfect fits of amusement, but Cinda ignored them. Words could no longer hurt her. Her stepsisters could no longer hurt her. As long as Jeffrey Templeton was not within sight, she refused to be afraid.

Within the hour, Nan and her daughters left, and her true work began.

Cook fit the costume to her swiftly, sewing parts of it into place. The silver material left one of her shoulders bare, then fell in folds to her feet, adorned with her mother's jeweled slippers. Rosalind's white lace gloves covered the roughness of her hands. Cinda's hair was left loose and flowing, as much because of time restrictions as for effect.

They didn't dare steal a piece of jewelry for Diana's crown, thus Mary had woven a circlet of white rosebuds, which Cinda wore on her head.

She'd kept both her slippers and the white mask, the slippers because they were a legacy from her mother, the mask because she'd wanted a remembrance of her first masquerade. Now, she donned the intricate piece of white silk and beading, which Cook had further embroidered with silver thread, the one item the older woman had stolen.

Cook was just finishing the last of the hem when Robbie came down the stairs.

"She's chained the carriage to the wall; we'll have to ride the horses instead."

Cinda nodded her head and took off the circlet of roses. She stepped down from the kitchen table, ignoring Cook's cry of dismay at Robbie's news.

"Don't worry," she said, grasping the woman's hand and stilling its nervous movement. "Robbie's been teaching me in his spare time. I'll be safe."

"We'd best be off, then," Robbie said. "Mum, what are we to do about the guards?"

"Just wait, Rob, just wait." She glanced around the kitchen, and felt the spirit growing stronger.

All right, Nora, let's see what you can do.

"Did ye see that?" asked the first guard, leaning negligently against the gate.

"Wot?"

"That—over there." He stood up. "Who goes there?"

The wind picked up suddenly, with an eerie, wailing sound, like that of a woman sobbing.

"I ain't never heard wind like that," said the one.

"Calm yerself," replied the other. But he was alert now, whereas before he'd been lazily picking his teeth.

"Ow!" yelped the one.

"Hey!" said the other as he jumped. "What's wrong with ye?"

"Something pinched me bum!"

"Go on, you're daft! Owww!"

Then both men were ducking and weaving as something invisible firmly boxed their ears and pinched their buttocks.

"Get off me!" wailed one.

"It's evil spirits!" shrieked the other.

And both men, bobbing and fighting against their invisible opponent, raced off into the fog.

A sharp whistle came from the bushes by the gate.

"That's Mum," Robbie whispered. "All's clear."

Cinda was already in the saddle, her flowing skirt tucked about her legs, an old cape around her shoulders, and a pair of Robbie's gloves covering her fingers. Rosalind's lace gloves were in the cloak pocket, as was the crown of rosebuds. She'd put both on when she reached the masquerade.

She let the mare have her head, and the horse trotted out into the courtyard. Robbie vaulted up into the saddle and followed her.

They'd already agreed he should wait outside and watch the horses. Once Cinda came back outside with William, they could all return to Nan's together.

Now, as Victor opened the gate and Mary stood watch at the front of the townhouse, Cinda reined in her mount and looked down at the woman who had made all this possible.

"Godspeed," Cook said softly.

"Hide far back in the garden if she returns early. I'll find you there."

"Be careful." She handed her the two invitations.

"We just need the one, Mum. I'm going to wait outside and watch the horses."

"Have a care, Rob."

"I will."

Then Cinda worked the reins, guiding her horse out toward the street. Robbie had told her what direction they were to take, and now she nudged her mount with slippered heel and gave the feisty mare her head.

• She sprang into a canter, and Cinda heard Robbie clucking to the other mare as she did the same.

The evening air rushed up against her face; her hair streamed down her back. After long days of confinement, Cinda was eager to embrace the night and be gone.

She slapped the reins against the mare's rump, and the horse surged forward, hooves striking sparks against cobblestones. And Cinda felt that long-denied wildness surging upward, filling her heart and mind. Unable to contain it, she gave a wild whoop of pleasure as she bent herself close over the mare's neck and galloped into the night.

Victor closed and locked the gate before he and Mary retired inside, but Cook decided to take a stroll in the garden.

Oh, what a night it's been, she thought as she came to rest upon the stone bench.

Oh, what a night it's to be, a breathless voice answered her.

"Nora?" she whispered.

Did you enjoy their yelping?

"Oh, Nora," Cook said, then started to laugh. "They looked like little boys with fleas in their breeches!"

I thought you'd find it amusing. Wasn't she beautiful?

"The fairest of all."

Now, one more thing for me?

"Anything."

Pray, look who gives the party . . .

The moonlight was bright enough that Cook could just make out the words on the other invitation.

"Nora, you know I'm not very good at reading."

The Duke and Duchess of Cranfield.

What Nora said left Cook speechless.

If she's to have a child, she'll have to know. You'll have to tell her.

"I'd thought about that."

Somehow, with all that's happened, I think she'll understand. And forgive me.

"She will, Nora. I'll make sure of it."

The ballroom was dazzling, packed with costumed guests talking and laughing, squeaking and grunting. Cinda dismounted a short distance from the door in the shade of a great oak, then doffed her cloak and gloves and gave them to Robbie. Swiftly fastening her crown on her head and disguising her servant's hands with the lace gloves, she took her invitation and started for the main door.

The Duke of Cranfield and his lovely Duchess welcomed each of their guests personally, so Cinda was introduced to the couple shortly after she entered the grand mansion. They were dressed as French royalty, with elaborate costumes embroidered in golden thread and huge white wigs on their heads.

If Cinda searched for one word to describe the couple, she would have said goodness, for that quality seemed to radiate from the quietly happy couple.

"How kind of you to join us this evening," the Duchess of Cranfield murmured. In her thirties, with russet hair and brilliant blue eyes, her smile was genuine as she welcomed Cinda to her home.

"How kind of you to invite me, Your Grace," she replied.

"Do I know you?" the Duke asked. He seemed a good decade older than his wife, and his hair was almost completely silver. Cinda smiled up at him.

"Do you know me?" she replied, suddenly feeling playful. "No, but you don't, I am sure you don't."

The older man's gray eyes twinkled in delight. "Yes, but I do—" He stopped midsentence. "Are you not—Aurora?"

"Arthur!" the Duchess admonished her husband gently. "Don't make reference to that dreadful party!" Then she lowered her voice and whispered, "Of course we were there, but there's no need for everyone to know. And I wouldn't allow this one"—she poked her husband gently in the ribs—"to venture upstairs."

"Are you Aurora?" the Duke asked again, and Cinda caught the seriousness of his tone.

She lowered her voice, not even questioning the instinct that told her she could trust this man. "Yes. I see you know me, after all."

"Save me a dance, my dear. Your secret is safe with me. And my wife and I are immensely flattered you chose to come as the goddess whose name she shares."

That had been a happy coincidence.

"I believe your pirate king is here tonight," the Duchess murmured. "Look for a man dressed in green."

"Thank you," Cinda answered, relief flooding through her as she realized Will had decided to attend tonight's revelry.

Now, within minutes, she would have her answer.

He saw her the instant she entered the ballroom, as did many others.

William couldn't believe she had the audacity to attend yet another masquerade, after what had transpired between them the last time they'd been together. Yet there she was, smiling up at the Duke of Cranfield and chatting with him as if she'd known him all her life.

Her appearance at this masquerade threw all of his carefully thought out plans into the fire.

Now he wouldn't have a chance to put his attention to unmasking Charles Hailey, for utmost in his mind was both the thought and desire to protect her.

*　　*　　*

Another, costumed as a priest, saw the Goddess Diana enter the ballroom. The cowled man quickly glanced to the Green Man to measure his reaction.

She moves him in a way no other woman does, of that I am certain.

His hunch was confirmed when he saw William start to make his way through the dense crowd to her side.

"What game is this?" he muttered as he took her arm and started to guide her to the side of the great ballroom.

"Will, we must talk—"

"Madam, I have the best of intentions when I think of you, but you have a tendency to infuriate—"

"I carry your child," she whispered.

That effectively silenced him.

He was silent so long she thought she'd displeased him.

"I came tonight to ask for your protection," she whispered. "I will go now, as I see—"

"Stay still," he said, his voice low and rough with emotion. "Remember, I cannot act as I wish I could, for I don't know who might be watching."

"Are you pleased?" she whispered, glancing around the room as she spoke. Their backs were to a wall, and no one was about.

"Yes." The one word, the way it was expressed, told her everything she had to know. Her heart leapt within her breast as she realized he already loved the consequence of their passionate union.

"Don't smile. Act as if I am nothing to you," he said quietly. "I'm going to shake you, act frustrated, then walk away. We'll meet at the door in an hour. Stay within the light, do not venture into any of the hallways or into the garden. Will you obey me this time?"

"Yes."

"Good. Turn toward me now and say something horrible."

"You're the most infuriatingly stubborn man I've ever met!"

"Madam, the same could be said of you!"

He shook her then, and she jerked herself out of his grasp. He was about to move away when she noticed he was staring at her bare shoulder. There, almost completely faded, was the last of one of the bruises she'd sustained from Jeffrey's beating.

She felt his anger leap to the fore, and the expression in his eyes would have scared a dead man.

"Who did this to you?" he said. She saw he was so infuriated he no longer cared who watched them.

"It matters not," she whispered. "Will, let me go as planned."

But his fingers already encircled her wrist, pulling her up against him. "I will have his name."

"Jeffrey Templeton, the second Viscount Hoareton. Now, *let me go!*"

He did, and she melted into the crowd, hoping against hope that no one had noticed their second exchange.

But someone had.

How fascinating, William, the way you and your lovely lady dance around each other. The passion between you leaps so high others cannot help but notice.

It matters not if she cares for you, for all that concerns me are the emotions she stirs within your heart. And you vex me sorely, Green Man, as I wait patiently for you to pick yet another I might harm.

I've waited long enough, William. It is decided.

She will be the one.

The dancing began, and the Duke of Cranfield came to claim the dance she'd promised him.

"Your Green Man is nowhere to be found," he said as they executed the intricate steps of the dance. She was nowhere near as skilled as he, but he'd offered to teach her.

Strangely enough, she felt safe in the older man's arms.

"He is not at all pleased with me, Your Grace."

"Had I not a wife and seven children, I would be quite pleased with a fetching little goddess like you." From another man, the words would have made her feel degraded. But spoken by the Duke, with his gentle sincerity, they made her feel admired and appreciated.

"Thank you, Your Grace."

"Surely even a goddess is above mere royalty in station, and French royalty at that. Diana, goddess of the moon, I would consider it an honor if you called me Arthur."

She laughed up at him, happy for just an instant, and was immediately aware of the change in his face.

"I *do* know you, I'm sure of it. From somewhere. Might you give me your card that I might see you again?"

She hesitated.

"I assure you, I mean nothing disrespectful in asking for it."

She couldn't answer, for how could she tell him who she really was? Perhaps later, with William's protection, she might visit this man and come to know him and his wife.

If they still wished to know her, once they realized who she was.

The musicians continued playing as they danced, Cinda having faltered for only an instant.

Arthur stopped suddenly, and tightened his grip on her hand.

"Eleanor," he whispered.

Her eyes widened at the mention of her dead mother's name and filled with tears. For just an instant, she wondered what her life would have been like had her mother married a man like the gentle Duke.

"Eleanor," he said again, sounding more sure.

"No," she choked out, then twisted out of his grasp and ran from the dancers, darting this way and that, away from the brightly lit ballroom and down a long hallway until she found herself in a shadowed corner beside a large window. She slipped behind the heavy velvet drapes and wept silently for her mother, for people she might have known and different choices she might have made.

Afterward, when the tears stopped and her breathing steadied, Cinda almost lifted her mask to wipe her eyes when she was suddenly aware of another's presence.

Turning, she saw a priest.

Nan was in a foul mood, made even more so by the appearance of that Diana woman. With her voluptuous form and fiery hair, no man would have eyes for either of her daughters. Thus, another night had come to naught.

Helena was busy stuffing herself at the refreshments table, while Miranda was totally immersed in a game of faro with a group of women.

Neither activity would ensure them a husband.

She'd stared at the girl with the titian hair while she'd danced with Lord Cranfield, and something about the way she moved had caught her attention. That, and those sparkling shoes . . .

Where had she seen them before?

Jeffrey came up behind her, two glasses of wine in his hands.

"I cannot *wait* for Colin's wedding day," he said as he handed her a glass.

She hadn't trusted him before, and the way he had gone absolutely wild while beating Cinda made her even more leery of the man. But not enough to call off their bargain.

"I wish to leave," Nan said, knowing her daughters would find no man while that bitch goddess claimed all the attention. "Would you see that the carriage is brought 'round?"

Jeffrey took a sip of wine as he watched her, an amused look on his face.

"As you wish."

"A lovers' quarrel?" the priest asked kindly.

She left her mask on, but it felt hot and uncomfortable after her tears.

She nodded her head, having no desire to explain her problems to a stranger. She couldn't see his face, his cowl covered it completely.

"He doesn't love you, then?"

An odd question, and far too intimate even for a masquerade. Did he mean Lord Cranfield?

"No, he doesn't. Besides, he is a married man."

"Not that old man," the priest replied. "The Green Man."

The Green Man.

Silence stretched between them, and she was suddenly afraid.

"Do I know you?" she asked the priest, wishing they were not quite so alone in the long hallway.

"No, but I know you. And I know you are the one he loves."

She saw the flash of the dagger's blade he held in his hand, concealed in the generous sleeves of his robes.

The same dagger, she realized, he'd murdered Rosalind with.

* * *

William couldn't find her anywhere in the ballroom.

"Lost her, did you?" said the Duke of Cranfield, coming up behind him and putting an arm around his shoulders. "She seemed upset about something."

"Did you see where she went?"

"Down one of these halls, I suspect."

There were several of them; the Cranfield mansion was quite huge. He didn't want to think of what might happen to her while he looked.

Why hadn't she stayed in the light?

And where was Charles?

"He doesn't love me. You seek another."

"Don't play me for a fool." Now he was angry; she felt just a hint of the violent emotions that fueled this man's quest.

"Come away, now," he said, motioning with the dagger.

She knew, with sudden clarity, that if he managed to make her go to an even more secluded space, she would never survive the night.

He was standing slightly nearer the window than she was, obviously not wanting to be seen. An idea came to her, as she remembered cleaning countless drapes in Nan's house. These looked quite heavy, but she knew they could come down in a flash with the right encouragement.

He saw the direction of her gaze, and smiled.

"Don't. You'll regret it."

Salvation came in so simple a form that Cinda considered it a miracle.

"Reginald, *don't*," said a pretty, dark-haired dairy maid, running unsteadily ahead of an obviously drunken cardinal. The cardinal's red-rimmed eyes lit with pleasure as he spied the priest.

"I say, my son, help me capture this pretty one so that we might enjoy her together!"

Cinda started to move back toward the ballroom, confident this man was not foolish enough to murder her in front of two witnesses. For despite his brutality, she sensed a curious weakness.

He swayed toward her, the knife gleaming as she tried to distance herself from him. She felt his fingers tangle in her hair as he swiftly stole the single curl. She wrenched away, but he grasped her hand, pressing her against him for the merest instant, trying to retain a hold on her.

His loverlike touch was terrifying, and promised her swift demise. Within minutes, the other masquers, both quite drunk, would have passed them by. Were she to act, she would have to do so quickly.

She slipped from his grasp, leaving him holding one of Rosalind's lace gloves. The coarseness of her hands was the least of her worries, now.

Then she was running down the hallway as fast as her feet would carry her, praying she was fleeing in the right direction.

His deep laughter rang in her ears as she ran, along with the words he called out.

"We'll meet again . . ."

She didn't stop her wild flight once she reached the ballroom, simply rushed across the huge expanse of marble floor, then up the steps and out the door into the night.

He saw her as she cut a frenzied path through the crowd. Everyone did. And William sensed her panic, and gave chase.

She had a head start on him, as he'd been all the way across the ballroom floor when she'd gained the steps. Now, outside, he ran to his horse and vaulted up into the saddle.

"That way!" Robbie called, indicating the direction she'd fled. He was hampered by having to untie the second horse, which was dancing nervously over the cobbled drive.

"Go home, Robbie. I'll find her."

William had raised the chestnut stallion he now rode from a colt. The horse loved to race and needed no encouragement. All William had to do was gently squeeze the great beast with his knees, and the animal lunged into a ground-eating gallop.

She heard the sound of horses' hooves behind her and, convinced it was the killer, increased her speed. The delicate jeweled slippers were no protection against the slippery cobbles, and she fell, tearing the silvery material at the knee. Still, she got up and continued to run, as her life depended on it.

The great beast was almost upon her, then she felt masculine arms lifting her as she struggled. She screamed her terror out into the thick fog, and started to sob in nervous reaction as she realized it was William who held her, William whose horse she was on.

She buried her face in his shoulder, her body trembling violently.

He slowed the horse to a walk, then took her into his arms and held her tightly.

"I saw him," she gasped out. "I saw him. The priest." Even as she said the words, she knew finding the man was hopeless. There had been several in priest's garb at the masquerade, and she wasn't sure she would be able to pick him out.

His fingers shook as he slipped them through her hair, touched the side of her cheek, held her against him as if to convince himself nothing had happened to her.

"I'm taking you home with me."

He held her easily in his arms as he eased the chestnut stallion into a slow, rolling canter. They rode in silence until Cinda looked up at him.

"I can't."

"Madam, you must."

"Cook. I can't leave her."

"We'll take her with us."

"On horseback?"

"I'll send a carriage."

"No, I cannot leave her alone in that house, not even an instant longer." She smoothed her tangled hair out of her eyes and looked back up at him over her shoulder. "If something should happen to her, I couldn't go on."

How well he knew that feeling.

"Your stepmother isn't home?"

"She never returns till much later."

"Then I'll ride home and return with a carriage. Pack your things."

"Can you come in the morning?"

"And why is that?"

"She . . . she hasn't been well. I can't bear to disturb her rest."

He knew when he was beaten.

"What time, madam?"

"Seven. Come 'round the back way, into the kitchen from the garden."

"As you wish."

He only gave in to her request because he knew the killer didn't know who she was or where she lived. And even Nan didn't arrange for her servants to be beaten as they slept.

But there would be nothing preventing him from taking her out of her stepmother's house come morning.

He saw her home safely. Robbie was waiting for her, and he unlocked the massive gates before she slipped inside.

"Tomorrow," William called to her.

"Tomorrow," she answered.

Once inside the property, Robbie whispered, "She came home early tonight, but nothing's amiss. Mum covered for you, said you'd been scrubbing the hearth and would be much too dirty to assist the likes a' them."

"She must have been terrified!"

"Nah, Mum's a steady one, she is."

She slipped off her costume in her room above the stable, then quickly dressed in her servant's garb and returned to the kitchen. Cook was sitting by the fire, mending stockings, her back rigid with fear.

"She came home suddenly!" the woman whispered as soon as she saw Cinda. "I don't know why, 'tis most unusual for her."

"She didn't believe anything was amiss?"

"Not to my knowledge. Here, put some soot on your face, I told her you were cleaning out the hearth."

"A chore you'll never have to do again." Swiftly, Cinda told her dear friend that William would be coming for them in the morning.

"I'd like to see the look on her face," Cook mused, "when breakfast doesn't arrive as usual and she marches down here and sees her servants have flown!" Her brow wrinkled with concern. "Will he take Mary and Victor?"

"All of us. Now sleep, you've been up far too late. I'll pack for us both."

"I could dance on the rooftops for the rest of the night, knowing we're finally going to leave this place!"

*   *   *

Nan lay quietly in her bedchamber, but she couldn't sleep. Every time she closed her eyes, she had visions of that damned girl, clad in silver, with her reddish-gold hair swirling unbound down her back.

And those shoes . . .

They bothered her, those jeweled slippers. Some memory, buried deeply in her brain, seemed to be trying to come out. Given time, she'd remember, but she was impatient and wanted to know *now* . . .

She wondered if it was worth leaving her warm bed and ringing Mary to bring her a cup of tea. Whatever it was she was trying to remember, it bothered her and wouldn't let her sleep.

Might as well have the tea.

As she got out of bed, she stumbled against something and cursed loudly. Lighting a candle, she peered down at a basket on the floor by her bed. Helena again, cleaning out closets in the hopes that they'd soon be filled with more ball gowns and day dresses. Well, what a surprise her daughters would have when they realized there wasn't any more money for either of them.

She tried to push the basket out of her way with her foot, but it wouldn't budge.

Curious now, she bent over the parcel and opened the lid. As usual, Helena had simply jammed things inside of it, willy-nilly, with absolutely no care or organization.

She lifted out a jeweled comb, and it twinkled merrily in the candlelight. The ornament was actually quite pretty. Mayhap she could take it to a pawnshop.

Nan laid it on the bed and began to explore further. She'd unearthed most of the basket's contents before she sat back and took a deep breath. It had been rather fun, actually, like a treasure hunt. She'd take the whole lot to the pawnshop and trade it in for money she could use at her next card party.

Tangled toward the bottom was a dark green knitted shawl and a golden locket. The chain was knotted beyond repair, but Nan picked up the piece of jewelry and sprang the tiny catch.

Eleanor.

How she'd hated the woman. This tiny portrait had been painted when she was a child, and Nan took in the exquisite lace dress, the satin sash, and the tiny, embroidered slippers.

Slippers . . .

Her memory suddenly cleared, and she saw Eleanor dancing at a party, all the men eager to talk with her or make her laugh. While she had always stood to the side, in the beautiful woman's extensive shadow.

Eleanor laughing, laughing at her while she danced at the party, her tiny feet sparkling in her jeweled slippers.

Jeweled slippers . . .

"It cannot be," she whispered out loud in the quiet room. "It *cannot* be!"

But she knew it for the truth, and had known the moment she'd seen Eleanor in her memory. For the woman's daughter possessed that same grace and charm, and had used it tonight as she laughed up at Arthur Ramsey, the Duke of Cranfield.

The same way Eleanor had always laughed at her.

The same way Cinda laughs at you now . . .

The basket could have been filled with ashes for all the notice Nan gave it. Picking up her candle, she headed out her bedroom door and toward her sleeping daughters.

Eleanor fought the restraints of spirit with all her heart, but she couldn't get through. She felt like a moth beating wildly at a light beyond a pane of glass. In vain, she tried to wake Cook and warn her, conjure up a chill breeze, flicker a candle flame. Make her presence known.

Nothing. She'd used all her spiritual strength frightening the guards. Now she watched, unable to protect her beloved daughter and frantic with fear, as Nan and her daughters started toward the stable.

The sun was just rising when Cinda finished packing Cook's possessions.

How lovely it would be to sleep in William's arms tonight. And how much she needed to be with him. She would stay by his side, he would capture this madman, and nothing would harm either them or their child, ever again.

Still fully dressed, she was just stretching out on her pallet when she heard footsteps at the back door. Probably Robbie, coming to assist them in taking their bags outside.

Cinda sat up in astonishment as Nan and her daughters came down the steps. Her stepmother was furious, clad only in her nightgown and wrapper. She hadn't even bothered to put on her wig, and her scraggly hair stuck up all over her scalp, giving her a wild appearance.

Helena and Miranda followed, and when Cinda saw what they carried, her heart lodged in her throat. They'd searched her bedchamber, for Helena had her silver gown, while Miranda carried the circlet of roses as well as the white mask with its silver embroidery.

And both jeweled slippers.

CHAPTER

❧ 16 ❧

Cinda moved in front of Cook instinctively, even as she shook the older woman's shoulder to warn her of impending danger. Cook came awake in an instant, and Cinda heard her sharp intake of breath as she saw what the stepsisters had in their hands. It was damning evidence, there was no possible means of escaping this confrontation.

During the scant seconds they all stood still, facing off, Cinda quickly took stock. Here was the confrontation with Nan she'd been expecting, and she vowed to finish it this time, once and for all. If the woman so much as laid a finger on Cook, she'd do far worse than that.

Jeffrey Templeton wasn't in sight, so the odds were more evenly matched. She was a much nastier fighter than either Helena or Miranda, who were basically cowards.

Nan was her only true adversary.

"We're going to play a little game," Nan said, as she walked farther into the kitchen. "I'll ask each of you simpletons a question, you give me the proper answer. For each incorrect reply, I'll decide the proper punishment."

"No," Cinda said, and though she hadn't raised her voice, it sounded loud in the quiet kitchen.

Nan raised her plucked brows in amazement at her audacity. "Has attending a few masquerades caused you to forget who you truly are?" she hissed.

"You're the one who's forgotten, Nan," Cinda said, deliberately baiting the woman by using her familiar Christian name instead of the usual subservient form of address. "And I *know* what you are."

"Diana the Huntress," Nan said softly as she came toward their pallets. Cook motioned Cinda behind her, but she stepped in front of the older woman, giving her a gentle nudge back. At the same time, Cinda picked up the wooden peel that was leaning against the stone wall.

"Do you plan to stop me with that?" Nan questioned her, sounding amused.

"I plan to kill you with it, should you beat me again."

The woman hesitated, and already Cinda could see her daughters backing off. Nan wasn't as brave when she didn't have a bully like Jeffrey backing her up.

Cinda backed Cook around the corner, around the other side of the long oaken table that faced the fire. She was slowly maneuvering them that they might reach the door and escape into the garden. Surely they could hold Nan off from that vantage point until William arrived?

But Nan realized her intent, and acted quickly.

"Get the old crone," she snarled at her daughters, indicating Cook. The older woman's face flushed a mottled red. She'd known nothing but kindness from Cinda's mother, and had never become immune to Nan's coarse, rude behavior.

The situation changed with lightning speed. Helena and Miranda were terrified of their mother. Cook, clad only in her nightdress, must have seemed an easy target. They moved in on the woman, and Cinda turned toward them, trying to keep an eye on Nan.

"She can't fight all three of us, you little fools!" Nan screamed, her rage overflowing. "Get her!"

They attacked.

Cook tried to dart away, but Helena grabbed her by the hair. Cinda turned and brought the large wooden spade down on top of Helena's head with a satisfying crack. She staggered, then fell. Miranda backed up, cowed for the moment, and Cinda turned her attention back to Nan.

Her stepmother was almost atop her, and Cinda dropped her weapon and darted out of her reach. Then she grabbed the back of Nan's silk dressing gown and wrenched her around so she slammed heavily against the wall.

"Run!" she cried to Cook, who was struggling to get out from beneath Miranda's pummeling fists. Furious, Cinda leapt on top of the younger woman and they rolled across the kitchen floor, kicking, scratching, clawing each other. A worktable in their path overturned. Crockery and glass jars fell and shattered on the floor.

Cinda knew she had the advantage, as Miranda's heavy bulk impeded her. Years of chores and a relentless work load had toughened her body, and now she swiftly caught Miranda's hair in her hands and knocked her head against the flagstone floor.

The woman fell limply away, unconscious.

"Run!" she begged Cook, but the woman had fallen heavily to the stone floor, her face a bright florid red. She gasped for breath and Cinda realized her friend couldn't get enough air into her lungs.

Grabbing a broken piece of glass with a razor-sharp edge, she turned toward her stepmother. But Nan's expression was oddly triumphant, and Cinda's glance flew toward Jeffrey Templeton, leaning negligently in the doorway to the parlor.

Cinda kept the lethal shard of glass clutched tightly in her fingers. Her arm trembled as she glanced from Jeffrey to Nan, then back again.

"Run," wheezed Cook, still struggling for breath. "Leave . . . me."

Nan, a gleam in her eye, started toward the older woman. Cinda darted in front of her friend, but Nan simply smiled.

"Such loyalty. Touching, isn't it, Jeffrey?"

Cinda whirled on the woman. "Get *away* from her, bitch, or I'll cut your face so it's scarred worse than any pox mark!"

That enraged Nan, and she reached out toward Cinda, her fingers spread apart like talons. Cinda jumped back, then held up the glass shard.

"Keep your distance," she warned, all the time praying either Robbie or Victor would hear the commotion and come running.

"Put it down." This was from Jeffrey.

She turned toward him, still keeping an eye on Nan.

"I said, put it *down*. This is getting bloody boring, Nancy." He put his hand in his waistband and extracted a deadly looking little pistol.

"Put that down or I'll put a bullet through the old woman's head."

They tied her to a chair in front of the fire.

Cinda kept twisting her head to try to get a look at Cook. She prayed her friend was simply lying still, trying to regain her strength. She couldn't imagine the alternative.

"A lovely dress, was it not?" Nan said. She held up the silver gown, then tossed it into the fire. The flames licked and burned, greedily consuming the shimmering cloth, and Cinda remembered the time and care Cook had put into making it for her. Had it been only yesterday morning?

Both of her daughters had come around, and Nan had cuffed them cruelly for their incompetence.

"Had Jeffrey not come along when he did, the bitch might have escaped!" She approached Cinda's chair, a small shard of broken glass in her hand. "And now I think I'll mark that pretty little face of yours."

"No," Jeffrey said quietly. "It was my intervention that saved your ill-conceived plan, thus she belongs to me." His pale reptilian eyes gleamed with pleasure. "Thus I will make the decisions henceforth."

Nan stood quietly, and Cinda could sense her displeasure. Jeffrey continued, his voice soft, totally at odds with what he was contemplating.

"I wish to take her to my house in the country directly. Oh, don't worry, Nancy, I'll make sure you receive your money. But first, I'd like the use of one of your bedrooms."

Nan's eyes lit with malicious glee as she glanced at Cinda. "Of course. Never let it be said I wasn't grateful for what you did for me, Jeffrey."

The man smiled, and Cinda recoiled inside.

"I'd like to get her breeding as soon as possible."

"What about all this?" Miranda asked, holding up the circlet of rosebuds, the mask, and the slippers.

Nan glanced at Cinda. She took one of the jeweled shoes from her daughter and looked down at it, tapping the delicate heel against her hand.

"They belonged to your mother, did they not?"

Cinda remained silent.

A slow, triumphant smile spread over her stepmother's plain features.

"Burn them."

Cinda sat rigidly in the chair, holding her body perfectly still. The loss she felt was monumental, but she wouldn't give this woman the pleasure of seeing it. Jeffrey was busy, selectively loosening her bonds to the chair, then using the same strips of dirty rags to secure her hands together, then her feet.

"She's certainly a little wildcat," he said to no one in particular, "but then I rather like it rough."

He bent down and slung her over his shoulder, and the last view Cinda had of the kitchen was of Cook lying perfectly still on the cold stone floor, while Nan and her daughters laughed around the brightly blazing fire.

She turned her head just enough to see the clock in the hallway as he carried her up the stairs.

A quarter past the hour of six. Will wouldn't arrive for another forty-five minutes. And in Jeffrey's cruel hands, those minutes would surely make her wish for death a thousand times.

As they reached the top floor, she saw Nan and her daughters stream into the drawing room, shouting for Mary to come down from her attic room and fix them some breakfast.

Then Jeffrey carried her into one of the guest bedrooms and locked the door behind them.

Robbie entered the kitchen within minutes after Nan had left. He'd been at the far end of the garden, clearing brush. As he clattered down the stairs, he spotted his mother. Rushing to her side, he knelt down, then touched the ugly purple bruise on the side of her face.

"Mum?" His voice rose in panic. *"Mum!"*

Cook's eyes remained closed as she spoke. "Get . . . William . . ." She struggled to take another breath. "That monster . . . has her . . . upstairs."

He hesitated, looking down at his mother, afraid for her. She took another agonized breath.

"Please . . ."

*   *   *

William was supervising the harnessing of several horses to one of his uncle's largest carriages when he saw Robbie gallop into the stableyard. The lad hadn't bothered to saddle the horse he rode, his shirt was half in, half out of his breeches, and he was barefoot.

"Cinda!" he shouted, his eyes wild, his Adam's apple working furiously as he slid off the bridled gelding before the horse even came to a full stop.

"He's got her, that bastard who beat her. At Nan's."

Without a word, William took the reins, swung up on the gelding's back, and rode out of the stableyard like the devil was after him.

"Very pretty," Jeffrey said softly.

Cinda swallowed against the crude gag he'd devised, trying not to show fear or revulsion. He'd slowly and deliberately cut away most of her dress piece by piece while she was still tied on the bed. Now, clad in only her chemise and petticoat, she knew what would happen in this bedroom would be far worse than any beating she'd ever endured.

He positioned the knife at the top of the chemise, then slit the worn fabric so it fell away from her body, leaving her totally naked to the waist.

"Lovely," he said, though his eyes remained cold, a direct counterpoint to the false warmth in his voice.

His hand caressed her breast and she closed her eyes. She felt no shame, only fear, and her body felt cold.

"Look at me," he whispered.

She couldn't.

"*Look* at me," he said, more firmly this time, then he slapped her.

The gag barely cushioned the blow. Cinda wanted to leave her body and desperately thought of other things. She wondered about such people. Nan needed Jeffrey, and Jeffrey had to take his pleasure with a woman bound and gagged.

"Now the petticoat," he said softly, and she thought she might be sick as his fingers reached for the fastening.

Both of them started when they heard first a crash, then a scream, then the sound of booted feet coming up the staircase.

Jeffrey's reptilian eyes darted around the room, but before

he could do anything, they both heard the sound of a masculine boot kicking the locked door. On the second kick, it broke open, and William entered the bedroom.

Cinda knew, from the look in his eyes, that Jeffrey was a dead man.

William didn't even give him a chance to say a word, simply caught his jaw in a punishing blow. Jeffrey staggered back, and William caught him again, this time breaking his aristocratic nose. The third punch caught Jeffrey in the stomach, and he doubled over. William punched him again on the side of the head, causing him to go crashing to his knees.

"Stop! Please!" His voice was high-pitched and terrified, but William showed him no quarter, and Cinda watched wordlessly as the man's face was systematically beaten to a bloody pulp.

Then William started in on the rest of him. Jeffrey was clearly no match for his furious opponent as he held his hands up against his body, sobbing and pleading. William gave him one last blow to the head, and the man crumpled and fell to the bedroom floor, unconscious.

Then he came to her and gently eased the gag from her mouth, his eyes dark with fear. He took his shirt off and slipped it around her, buttoning it with shaking, bloody fingers. Once she was somewhat dressed, he caught her up in his arms and carried her from the room, down the stairs toward the kitchen.

The house was deserted, Nan and her daughters obviously having thought better of being around William while he was in such a rage.

He carried her to the kitchen, and she saw that Robbie and Mary had helped Cook into her wrapper and sat her in a chair by the fire, while Victor prepared her a cup of tea. She still looked poorly, but her breathing was better, and Cinda practically fell out of William's arms in her haste to get to her side.

She couldn't speak, simply dropped to her knees in front of the woman, took her hand, and kissed it. Cook, her eyes swimming with tears, awkwardly patted the top of her head. Her hand stilled when she saw the blood on the linen shirt.

"It's Will's," Cinda whispered.

"Did that man hurt you?"

"No." She smiled as she remembered the fast and vicious fight. "Not as much as Will hurt him."

Several men who had to be William's servants were already carrying their belongings out to the carriage. Mary and Victor stood, awkwardly apart, by the pantry door. They watched the determined procession, and Cinda could see the fear in their eyes.

"May Victor and Mary come with us?" she asked Will.

"If they wish."

The two servants packed their meager belongings with great haste, and soon the carriage was completely loaded.

"Now," said William, kneeling down next to Cook's chair. "We can leave directly, or if you'd rather rest here, I can send my men back and have them bring another carriage in a while."

Cook shook her head, then slowly stood. "I'm getting out of here right now, if I have to crawl out of this house on my hands and knees."

Robbie sighed. "Don't go all melodramatic on me, Mum. Have a care, and take my arm."

They all laughed at that, then slowly made their way out of the darkened kitchen and up the stairs into the early morning sunlight.

They were all in the carriage, with Robbie and William on horseback, when Cinda cried out, "My shoes!"

"Where are they?" William asked.

"She burned them," Cinda said, and as the events of the morning finally overtook her, she began to cry.

"They belonged to her mother," Cook explained. "Nan threw them in the fire."

"I'll go back and see if I can salvage anything," William said quietly.

"I'll come with you," Robbie volunteered.

"Go directly home," William ordered his driver. He dismounted, then peered inside the carriage window.

"Victor, Mary, I trust you'll do all you can to make these two comfortable once they arrive. Take great care with both of them, as they have sustained an immense shock."

Once the carriage had departed, he and Robbie returned to the quiet kitchen.

"You're sure we have everything, Robbie? For I don't wish to return to this place."

"Cinda packed it all up last night, so she told me."

"Give it another check, to be sure."

He approached the fire, all the while his anger still close to the surface. When he'd supervised the packing of Cinda's room above the stable, it had seemed impossible to him that Nan and her daughters could have destroyed what little the girl possessed. The china doll had been smashed, and he would have to take Cinda's miniature of her mother to a portraiturist to be repaired.

Seeing her cry for a simple pair of paste-jewel slippers, the only possession she had left from her mother, had quietly enraged him all over again. Had Nan been standing in the room, he wasn't sure he could have restrained himself from grabbing the woman and horsewhipping her.

He knelt by the hearth. The fire had died down, though several coals still burned brightly. Taking a wooden spoon from the table, he poked its handle into the ashes, looking for some trace of the shoes.

What he found astonished him.

It took both William and Robbie several hours to complete-ly put out the fire, wait for it to cool, dig out the hearth, and sift through all the ashes. They left the kitchen in a filthy disarray, and it pleased William to think of Nan coming back to such disorder with no capable servants to help her.

Exhausted, the two men finally headed home.

William found Cinda upstairs in a guest room, sitting by Cook's bedside. The woman was asleep, her grizzled old tomcat curled up at the foot of her bed. She was looking much better, though her breathing was still slightly labored.

Though he'd only stopped to wipe the soot off his hands and face, he didn't think Cinda would mind seeing him in such a state. He had crucial news for her, and didn't believe it could wait.

Ignoring his disheveled state, she came away from the bed-side and embraced him. He held her against him for a long moment, content in the knowledge that he'd finally brought her home.

"I'm sorry," she said, as he pulled another chair up beside Cook's bedside.

"About?"

"The shoes. I'm sure there was nothing left of them after all."

"No, there was." He leaned forward and took both her hands in his. "Your mother was a clever woman, and knew your father's nature quite well. Tell me what your godmother said to you when she gave you the shoes, for Robbie informed me that's how you came to possess them."

"Something about . . . for my wedding day. They were to be worn on my wedding day, on the day . . . the day I left my father's house."

He smiled.

"What is it? Tell me!"

"The shoes, my darling, are gone. The jewels are not."

"But . . . I don't understand, they were merely paste."

"Real jewels, diamonds and rubies and sapphires, will endure the most brutal of fires."

It took time for the import of his words to sink in, and he could tell she still didn't quite grasp the magnitude of it all.

"Your mother concealed a fortune with those shoes, and did it quite cleverly, right out in the open. She must have affixed them to the slippers herself, then rubbed them with wax to dull their fine luster. She passed them off as paste."

He watched as her hand slowly came up and covered her mouth.

"You're a wealthy woman, Cinda, in your own right."

She couldn't speak, merely shook her head.

"I wanted you to know this before I asked you to marry me, for now you have the necessary funds to do . . . anything you want." He paused, remembering their last argument in the library. "To even be free of me, should you wish it so."

She reached up and touched his hair, smoothed it back from the side of his face. He felt the emotion in the simple gesture, and his heart picked up speed.

"You're still a stubborn fool, Will. All I've ever wanted in the world was you."

"I've caused you a great deal of trouble."

"And haven't I given it back to you, in full?"

He laughed then, self-conscious, and stared at his hands, feeling suddenly awkward. As clumsy as a boy.

"That you have."

"You have no idea, do you?"

"Of what?"

"How much I love you." Now she bridged the distance between their two chairs and sat on his lap, ignoring the ashes dusting his clothing. Lifting her head so her lips brushed his ear, she whispered, "There's never been anybody like you, Will."

He was so overwhelmed with relief, he felt tears sting his eyes. Blinking rapidly, he whispered, "I love you, Cinda. You mean everything to me." He fumbled with his waistcoat pocket, then drew out a ring. The golden circle caught the afternoon sunlight, and the three perfect bloodred rubies flashed fire.

"It belonged to my mother." He hesitated. "I've been wanting to give it to you for the longest time."

He slid it on her finger, then kissed her hand.

"A perfect fit," he whispered, wonder in his voice.

"It always was," she whispered back, then turned toward him, wrapped her arms around his neck, and kissed him, letting him feel all the emotion she could summon up.

He was kissing her back when Mary cleared her throat gently. They broke apart, and Will didn't have the heart to reprimand the maid, she looked so very nervous.

"I've come to watch Cook, Cinda. I thought you might want some rest."

"Thank you, Mary." She glanced up at Will, and he felt nothing but pleasure as he looked down at her happy face. "But I think I'd like a bath first."

Then she gave him a cheeky look. He grinned, and had a feeling he knew how they were going to spend the remainder of the day.

"Go on, Mary, and get some rest yourself," Cook said, not five minutes after William and Cinda left.

"Oh, I couldn't—"

"There's nothing wrong with me a nice long nap won't cure."

"If you're sure—"

"I am."

Once the girl left the room, Thomas yawned, then stretched and sauntered slowly up toward the head of the bed. Cook smiled as she felt him curl up against her hair.

"Thank you, Lord, for seeing she accepted his proposal with a minimum of fuss. I was so afraid her pride would get in the way."

That said, she turned her face toward Thomas, and scratched the huge cat behind his ragged ears.

"She'll marry him, he'll capture that madman, and we can all settle down and enjoy a good night's sleep, eh, Thomas?"

The cat merely blinked.

They were married soon after.

The wedding party was small, just Cinda, Will, Henry, Cook, and Robbie. The ceremony took place in the morning.

Spring rain came down heavily, sunlight was obscured, but Cinda couldn't be bothered with such inconsequentials. For all her attention was given over to the man she'd chosen to spend her life with.

As she listened to the familiar words she'd heard countless times before, she thought they'd never sounded more beautiful.

Into this holy union, William and Lucinda now come to be joined . . .

Her wedding dress was heavy cream silk, trimmed with French lace and pearls. Both his jacket and breeches were black, but his linen shirt had ruffles at both neck and wrist, and his waistcoat was heavily embroidered with gold thread. He'd never looked more handsome.

She looked up at Will, her heart in her eyes, and gave herself over to him completely as the minister said the familiar words.

Lucinda, will you have this man to be your husband, to live together in the covenant of marriage? Will you love him, comfort him, honor and keep him, as long as you both shall live?

She declared her consent.

I will.

The minister spoke to William, and he declared his consent as well.

There was a peaceful continuity to the words of the ceremony, and Cinda was surprised to find herself so very calm on her wedding day. She wanted to be with William forever, and had been deeply honored he'd asked her to be his bride.

Look mercifully upon this man and this woman who come to you to seek your blessing, and assist them with your grace . . .

All too soon William faced her, grasped her hand in his, and took her to wife.

In the Name of God, I, William Christian Alard Stedman, take you, Lucinda Kathleen Marie Townshend, to be my wife, to have and to hold from this day forward, for better for worse, for richer for poorer, in sickness and in health, to love and to cherish, until we are parted by death. This is my solemn vow.

Then she took his hand and held his steadfast gaze, showing him how much she loved him by saying her vows after his in a soft, clear voice.

The minister held up the ring and blessed it, then William slipped it onto its resting place on the third finger of her left hand.

Lucinda, I give you this ring as a symbol of my vow, and with all that I am, and all that I have, I honor you.

She couldn't stop smiling up at him as the minister finished the ceremony. Cook was crying softly before the final prayer was over. Even Henry's eyes were suspiciously moist.

By the power of your Holy Spirit, defend them from every enemy and lead them into peace . . .

None saw the cloaked man who stood alone far back in the large church, watching the private ceremony. His gaze was fastened intently on William, and the way he was looking down at his new bride. And the man smiled as he thought of the words both bride and groom had spoken.

Until we are parted by death . . .

CHAPTER
❧ 17 ❧

Marriage to William was rather unnerving.

Cinda soon found she had no experience in living in the world her husband so confidently inhabited. Thus, she proceeded slowly, watching and learning. More than anything, she didn't want William to regret their marriage, or for her to be an embarrassment to him.

She knew he loved her as deeply as she loved him, and did not set much store by London society. She also knew that for all practical intents and purposes there was an enormous distance between them in both class and experience.

It didn't matter that her mother had come from an aristocratic family. Cinda had no idea what one did at a fancy dinner or dress ball. She'd only been to two masquerades, and found her costumes comforting to hide behind.

Today she'd chosen to spend some time in the garden. The work was soothing and relaxed her. She'd gravitated toward the herb beds, and found herself missing the garden she'd tended so lovingly while in service to her stepmother.

Nan had not fared well. She'd escaped from London one step ahead of Horace's creditors, and the house and all its furnishings were now in their hands. Cinda had heard rumors she'd fled north.

Horace had not been as lucky, and was spending his time in a workhouse. Miranda had made a hasty marriage to a skinny, pimply faced young man who had a modest family income, while Helena had managed to find shelter with a female friend.

Cinda's family home and all it contained had gone to pay their immense debts. Now, except for the jewels her mother had saved from Horace's greed, there was nothing left.

She regretted her lack of family more than any amount of coin. Thinking about the child she would bear during the coming winter, she wished she had more to give her offspring in the way of blood relations and a sense of the past.

Her godmother had sent her a letter on hearing of her marriage to William. And Cinda had answered in kind, hoping to form a tenuous connection. After all, Kathleen was all the family she had.

Cinda sat quietly in the herb garden, lost in thought, and didn't hear William approach.

"That bed was tended to just yesterday," he remarked.

She glanced up. He'd come back from an early morning ride in the park, and was dressed accordingly. Jocasta was at his side, as he'd taken her for a run. Juno, heavily pregnant, stayed closer to home.

"I quite see." She stood up and walked to his side, then raised up on tiptoe and kissed his cheek.

"We received an invitation to have dinner with the Duke and Duchess of Cranfield," he said, smiling down at her.

This was something she had known would happen, and she'd dreaded the thought. It wasn't that she didn't like the older couple, for she found them both gracious and generous. But sometimes William's world was overwhelming.

"How kind of them. When is it?"

"Early next week. A small affair, just the four of us, and several of their younger children."

Cinda could think of no other couple she would feel more comfortable with. Perhaps she wouldn't make too big a fool of herself.

"Then we should accept," she said.

"You'll write them a note?"

"Of course." She realized here was another duty she would be expected to perform, but this one was not too threatening.

As aristocratic as Nan had aspired to be, her household had been run in a rather slipshod manner. She'd been far too stingy to hire on as many servants as was needed, so Cinda still had no idea what duties went with which post. Nan had not set the best example.

"And what will you do today?" he asked.

"First the note to the Duke and his family, and then I shall— find a way to entertain myself." She saw the concerned look in his dark blue eyes and added, "Close to home."

"Would you like to come riding with me one morning?"

"Very much." *I should like to get out of this house.*

He was still frightened for her, but had told her his suspicions. If William's instincts were correct, he was very close to confronting the killer. Charles Hailey was in the final stages of his self-destruction, and William had told her he planned to confront him within the week.

"Are you happy here, Cinda?" he asked gently.

"I'm happy with you," she said quietly. "And hope I always shall be."

Her answer seemed to satisfy him.

"I can't help you, my precious," Cook said, running her fingers agitatedly through her shortly cropped curls. "I've never been in one of those dining rooms in my life. Oh, I could tell you what courses would probably be served, but you know that as well as I."

"What am I going to do?"

"I don't know. Mayhap you could watch the lady of the house, and imitate each of her movements."

They were sitting at the large wooden table in a corner of the vast kitchen. Cinda got up and restlessly paced the length of the long room, turning as she reached the immense fireplace and heading back toward their table.

"I shall hate being so tentative and careful all the time! What if Arthur or Diana misinterprets my actions, and thinks I am not enjoying myself?"

"Madam, perhaps I might be of assistance."

Cinda whirled toward the sound of that calm voice, her full skirts rustling. Henry stood in the kitchen doorway, a silver tea service in his arms. She knew he'd been upstairs in the library taking refreshment to William as he worked on various financial matters. The black and white spaniel stood alertly at Henry's side, content to follow her master wherever he went in the huge house.

Cinda felt a furious blush work its way up her throat and into her cheeks. It shamed her that she knew so little. Her pride had prevented her from simply confessing all to William and asking him to guide her through this awkward transition.

Henry entered the kitchen, set down the tray, then turned and faced her once again.

"Madam, I am at your service."

Cinda lowered her hands and glanced at Cook. Her friend shrugged her shoulders and gave her a look that seemed to say, *Swallow your pride, my girl, here's your chance.*

Cinda brought her attention back to the valet, then slowly nodded her head.

"Madam, in what way do you need my assistance? What is it you are unsure of?"

She swallowed, then forced the words out.

"I have no idea how to eat at table. A formal table."

"I see." Henry considered the matter very seriously.

"After my mother died . . . Oh, I know enough to eat bread and cheese, and how to push my food around a wooden plate with a piece of bread, but I have absolutely *no* idea how to behave at a party!"

She glanced away from him, her humiliation complete.

Henry's voice was quiet, calm, and blessedly nonjudgmental. "Madam, would you care to begin your education tonight?"

"Yes. And please, don't call me Madam, it makes me feel a thousand years old!"

She caught the merest suggestion of a smile on the older man's face before it returned to its normally serene expression.

"Well then," he said, smiling at both of them. "Let's begin, shall we?"

William finished the last account and set down his quill. He stretched, then got to his feet and walked down the long hallway to their bedroom. Fully expecting to find Cinda within waiting for him, he stopped short as he stepped into the empty room. The fire was burning brightly, and the bed linens had been turned down. All was in readiness for a delightful evening with his wife, except Cinda wasn't present.

Deciding to find her, he began his search.

She spent a great deal of time in the kitchen with Cook. He didn't chastise her for this, as he understood it gave her comfort. William would have let her spend the rest of her life toasting her toes in front of the kitchen fire, as long as she lived with him and loved him.

But the kitchen was empty as well.

This isn't like her at all.

Was she hiding from him? He couldn't imagine where. Then he caught the briefest flicker of candlelight from the formal dining room, and approached. He was about to call out and announce his presence when he heard Henry's voice, calm and firm.

"All right, you've just been served your soup."

William, fully in the shadows, could see inside the huge room. Cinda was sitting at the table, with Cook and Henry at either side. Undine the spaniel lay at her feet.

Tentatively, with Henry's encouragement, Cinda picked up a silver spoon and mimed eating soup.

"Splendid. Quite so."

And William, hiding in the shadows, felt his throat close with emotion at the look of relieved gratitude his young wife gave his valet.

Of course. The dinner party.

He felt all kinds of a fool for not anticipating her needs.

"Can we go through it once again?" Cinda asked.

"We can go through whatever you would like, as many times as you would like. Master William shouldn't be done with his books for another three quarters of an hour."

William smiled. He'd raced through his accounts as fast as he'd dared, and all because he'd wanted to be with his wife. But he wouldn't reveal his presence, for he knew it would embarrass Cinda horribly.

She didn't want to shame him, that was perfectly clear.

As the instruction began, he slipped away and quietly retired upstairs.

She came to their bedroom within the hour.

He was lying in bed beneath the covers, reading by candlelight. He glanced up as she entered the room and smiled.

"You finished early!" she said.

"A little. And how was your evening with Cook?"

"Excellent."

He set his book down on the bed and watched her as she flitted about the room, first behind the screen to undress and don a lace-trimmed nightgown, then back out to give both Juno and Jocasta a pat on the head before she slid into bed beside him.

"Don't let me interrupt your reading."

"You're quite a tempting distraction." He hadn't retrieved his book and now shifted so he could look down at her. Her smile was infectious, and he found himself catching her mood.

"Madam, you seem happy."

"I am."

"Might I know the cause?"

Playfully, she pulled at the thick lock of dark hair that fell over his forehead. "No, you may not."

"Ah, a woman of mystery."

"Exactly so."

He kissed her, then looked down at her once again.

"Is there anything you wish to ask me?"

She considered this with a slight frown.

"Not at present."

"Anything at all I can help you with?"

"No. I penned a suitable reply to our dinner invitation, then Cook and I went over my wardrobe to select a gown for the evening. But I might ask you to approve my choice."

"I would he honored." He kissed her again, more deeply this time, then slid his hand beneath her nightgown and cupped her bare bottom. As their bodies shifted beneath the covers the leatherbound book slid to the floor.

"Will, your book—"

"—can wait," he whispered against her lips. Taking her hand, he guided it to his obvious arousal and closed her fingers around the heavy shaft. "This, however, cannot."

The dinner party was a smashing success.

Though the buttered crabs, *beef tremblonque*, and gooseberry cream were all superb, William found he couldn't keep his eyes off his bride. She'd selected a green silk gown that matched her eyes, and wore the pearl necklace and earrings he'd presented her with on their wedding day. The gown's bodice was cut daringly low, and her breasts were perfection, filling the brilliant green bodice and almost overflowing its bounds.

Her hair had been dressed in a most cunning style, swept up on top of her head, then curled becomingly so strands brushed her bare shoulders. Though the food and drink was of the finest sort and the conversation witty and most pleasing, he could think of nothing but getting her home and tumbling her into bed.

Arthur Ramsey seemed to read his mind. The older man and his lovely wife were clearly enchanted by the sight of two newlyweds who could barely take their eyes off each other.

Henry had advised Cinda well. By simply being herself and resisting the urge to put on any insecure airs, she shone brighter than any precious jewel.

Afterward, instead of separating the sexes as was usual, Arthur surprised them both by suggesting they join him in his library.

"I have something for your charming wife, William. A wedding present, as it were."

He didn't know what to expect, and certainly hadn't anticipated the precious gift the older gentleman chose to give his bride.

"I saw it in a shop shortly after she died, and couldn't bear the thought of it hanging in a stranger's home," Arthur said awkwardly as he indicated the portrait that hung over the fireplace in his library.

As Cinda began to tremble, William slipped his arm around his wife to steady her.

"She was your mother, was she not?" Arthur asked gently, and Cinda nodded her head. William could see the tears slipping down her cheeks as she gazed up at the three-quarter portrait of a young girl with titian hair and dark green eyes that glowed with a vibrant inner life.

"It was painted—after she announced her engagement to my father."

Arthur hesitated. "I'm not at all sure how to tell you this, my dear."

William gave his wife a handkerchief, then took her other hand.

"Go on," he said to Arthur.

"I have a strong suspicion your mother was already with child when this particular portrait was painted." He cleared his throat nervously. "My twin, Andrew, was in love with your mother. They carried on a very passionate love affair for several months, and he desperately wanted to marry Eleanor." He smiled ruefully. "Most of us did, to be quite honest."

"What happened?" Cinda whispered. William could hear the emotion in her throat. His heart ached for her, but he suspected Arthur was telling the truth. For Cinda had never seemed the issue of Horace Townshend, a rather coarse, insensitive man.

"Andrew died in a hunting accident." Lord Cranfield stopped for a moment, regaining his composure. "Your mother was wild with grief. I tried to speak with her afterward, but she hid herself away. The next thing I knew, she was engaged to Horace."

"Because of me," Cinda whispered.

Arthur nodded his head. "I would not presume to tell you this, had I not suspected who you were after the masquerade. And tonight I had ample opportunity to observe you during dinner. Cinda, I believe you are my brother's child. For though you look so like your mother, there are mannerisms you possess that were his alone."

The older man smiled down at her, very gently. "And the grapes are her final proof."

"Whatever do you mean?" William asked. Concerned for his wife, he walked Cinda over to the chair behind Arthur's desk and sat her down. She kept staring at the portrait, and he worried about her emotional state.

"See that cluster of grapes? Held that way, by a woman's womb, they are a powerful symbol of fertility. I'm sure Horace was far too ignorant to be aware of what she was about, but Eleanor was well aware of the message she was sending."

"Why didn't she come to you?" Cinda whispered.

"Your grandfather was against the match from the start. I don't remember the reason. I do remember that my brother met with your mother secretly. They had a most unusual courtship."

William met Cinda's gaze. How alike both mother and daughter were.

"Then . . . you are my uncle."

Arthur nodded his silvery head. "I believe so. And Diana is your aunt. We have seven children that are your cousins, should you want to claim them as such—"

"Oh, yes," Cinda whispered, and William put his hand on her shoulder. She covered it with her own, and he felt how cold her fingers were.

"Now I shall leave the two of you alone. Diana planned to serve cake and tea later, but should you want to excuse yourselves earlier, both of us will certainly understand."

William looked at his wife, leaving the decision in her hands. She smiled at him gratefully, then glanced back up at Arthur.

"I would . . . we would love to join you. But could I have a moment alone with my husband?"

"Certainly." And with that, the elderly Duke left the library.

William remained silent, waiting for his wife to speak. And he wondered at all the memories she had to be reliving within the confines of her mind.

"All of my life, I've longed for a family," she finally whispered. "I felt it most strongly when I first found out I was with child."

He waited, knowing there was more.

"Cook was my family. And Robbie. Then you. And no three people mean more to me. You know that, don't you?"

He nodded his head.

"But I so wanted—a strong father. Not the weak fool I had. And aunts and uncles. Cousins."

"I know." He wanted her to realize he did understand, and would not begrudge her any feelings on the matter.

She was silent for a time, still gazing at the portrait.

"Will, do you think it's true?"

He caught the fear in her voice, and the longing. She wanted it to be true, of that he was certain.

And he'd been thinking, the entire time he'd been sitting silently by her side, there was one person he was quite sure would know the truth. And would never try to hurt Cinda by denying it.

"I think we should ask Cook."

They returned home and found both Cook and Henry in their bedroom, assisting Juno in delivering her pups.

"I heard her whining as I passed in the hallway," Cook said from her position at the mastiff's side. Juno was lying at the foot of William's bed, close to the fire. Five puppies had been born, all different colors, but it was obvious the dog was still in labor.

"I came to check the fire, and found her here with poor Juno," Henry said, continuing the story. "Between the two of us, we helped her as best we could."

William swiftly shrugged out of his evening jacket and knelt down on the carpeted floor, then cradled the mastiff's massive head in his hands.

"Thank you, both of you, for not leaving her alone."

"Oh, I couldn't, poor thing, not at her time." Cook stroked the dog's head gently.

The four of them stayed that way, gathered around poor Juno until her lengthy labor was finished and she was the proud mother of seven healthy pups. After making sure they were all comfortable and each pup had nursed its fill, William asked Henry to bring them up a pot of strong tea and buttered bread, along with some roast beef for the exhausted Juno.

Cook was about to leave and assist Henry, but William summoned her back. He glanced at Cinda.

"I need to ask you some questions," she said to her friend.

William saw the sudden knowledge in the old woman's eyes, and knew the truth before Cinda even voiced her thoughts.

"Is Horace Townshend my father?"

"No."

"Was the Duke of Cranfield's twin brother—"

"Yes." Cook leaned forward and grasped both of Cinda's hands, and William smiled at the sudden burst of joy that lit his wife's brilliant green eyes. "I have no sister to the north. Had we left your mother's house, I would have taken you to your uncle and hoped he'd believe me."

"Did she love Andrew?"

"With all her heart."

"And he?"

"The same. She was planning on running away with him, but then he had his accident and I feared for her life." Cook's voice was hushed as she quickly relived her memories. "She loved you, Cinda, you gave her a reason to live. Any joy she had in her last years was because of you."

"Did . . . does my godmother know?"

"No. I assisted at your birth, and your mother swore me to secrecy. We both lied and said you were a bit early." Cook smiled, remembering. "But I would have told you before the babe was born. I was trying to find the right time."

"Would you come to their home for dinner one evening? They would so like to meet you—"

Cook pulled her hands away from Cinda's and looked at her with such amazement that William almost laughed aloud.

"And what would I be doing, miss, mixing with the Quality?"

"But Henry could teach you—" Cinda stopped abruptly.

William smiled as she glanced up at him, and feigned ignorance.

"Henry could teach you what?" he asked gently.

She flushed. "Oh, Will—"

"Tell me." He didn't want secrets between them, ever again.

He caught the sheen of embarrassed tears in her eyes as she approached him.

"There is so little of your world I'm truly comfortable with. I feel more at home on the floor helping Juno deliver her pups than in some grand salon pretending to be an aristocratic lady."

William took her hand in his and kissed it. "You did wonderfully tonight." He turned toward Cook. "She was the most glorious part of the entire evening."

Cook's expression was smug. "I know my girl, and I'm sure it's true. She was Quality even when she was scrubbing out the hearth."

"Well, of course *you* would say that!" Cinda retaliated, frustration still in her voice. "Will, I just didn't want you to be ashamed of me."

He knew what that admission had cost her, and gathered her into the protective embrace of his arms.

"Never, my darling. You've never given me cause."

He watched as she bit her lip and her brilliant eyes were once again flooded with tears.

"All I do is cry—"

"And isn't that a pregnant woman's way?" Cook asked indignantly.

Henry had just come back into the bedroom, and this particular pronouncement made him come to a complete stop.

"Are my ears deceiving me, sir, or did I just hear Cook tell you that—"

"We're going to have a child, Henry. After the New Year. So you'll have another generation of Stedmans to help civilize, after all."

"With my help, of course," Cook added quickly.

"Why, this is *wonderful*, sir," Henry said, and William watched in absolute amazement as his usually calm and unflappable valet fell completely to pieces.

"Splendid, just splendid. Spot on, if I do say so myself." With happy tears in his bright blue eyes, he grabbed William's shoulders and gave him a quick kiss on each cheek.

"*Excellent* work, my boy, your father would certainly be proud! And a *baby!* Why, you've no *idea* how a little one is going to liven things up around here. I've got so much to do, I'm sure Cook will help me get the nursery in spit-spot shape for the child."

William simply watched, his mouth open in astonishment. This was not the cool, composed man who had been his valet over the years.

"Now, I've got to go to the cellar and bring up a fine bottle of brandy," Henry muttered as he walked unsteadily toward the bedroom door. It was as if he'd sustained a great shock to his system. "Brandy, that's just the thing, for we must certainly celebrate such a momentous occasion with all the splendor it deserves—"

The three of them were speechless as Henry left the room, and they listened to his happy muttering as he made his way down the long hallway.

"The man's gone completely daft," Cook observed. "If this is the way he acts and she's only with child, he'll never survive the birth."

William couldn't contain his mirth. He hugged Cinda to him as he burst out laughing, his shoulders shaking.

"My God, what an evening!"

"I have an uncle," Cinda whispered, wonder in her voice.

"And I've got seven puppies," William said, then began laughing all over again.

"And an aunt and cousins," Cinda said, and she started to laugh as well. "A family!"

He kissed her then, swiftly, and his smile was brilliant with happiness. "And a baby!"

"Oh, Will, a *baby* . . ."

"What did you give her to drink at that dinner?" Cook asked, her voice concerned. "Is she foxed?"

William found he couldn't stop smiling.

"Daft, you're daft, the whole lot of you," Cook said, then walked over and gave Juno a quick pat before she started out of the bedroom.

"I'm going to go see to that man of yours; he's probably out on the roof looking for his brandy." She hustled out of the bedroom, her skirts flying.

William didn't even notice her departure, for he was far too busy kissing his bride.

CHAPTER
⋙ 18 ⋘

The second threatening note arrived within the week, and this time the envelope contained a lock of Cinda's hair.

William made a habit of opening his correspondence when she wasn't near. He didn't want his wife to worry excessively. He still wanted to protect her from this evil, and as long as she stayed within the confines of his townhouse and within reach of the mastiffs, he was convinced she was safe.

When the thick lock of red-gold hair slipped out of the envelope and fell on the polished surface of the desk in front of him, he closed his eyes and took a deep, steadying breath. He wished he could simply toss the entire missive into the brightly burning fire. But he couldn't. Each note, no matter how horrifying, might contain a clue. Might offer them new hope.

With a steady hand, he opened the envelope further and slid out the note. The handwriting was immediately recognizable.

You've married a goddess so beautifully fair,
Thus here is a piece of her glorious hair,
You may wed her and bed her, this lady so fine,
But make no mistake, William, soon she'll be mine.

He slid the envelope into the desk drawer, locked it, then sat back in his chair and tried to formulate a plan.

Charles Hailey had been ill of late, a result of too many long nights gambling at various clubs and far too much drinking. As he'd been home in his bed, William had not had a chance to confront him with his suspicions.

However, last night he'd appeared at one of the clubs again, and William had seen him. He'd looked terribly haggard, as if he were truly tired of living. William had thought the threats would stop, now that Charles seemed to be faltering on the brink of his own mortality. The note changed everything.

He considered the possibility he was totally wrong in his suspicions about Charles. Perhaps the killer was a man he hardly knew, not one in his close circle of friends. He'd stopped suspecting Ashley a long time ago. They had become better friends, sharing several early morning rides.

One story in particular had convinced William that Ashley had nothing at all to do with the brutal murders. He'd told him of the first time his father had taken him along on a hunt, when he was six years of age.

Afterward, once the stag had been killed, his father had insisted he dip his hands into the animal's carcass and cover them with blood as a sort of baptism into the world of the hunt.

Ashley had refused, shaming his father further by rushing into the bushes and vomiting up his breakfast. He was quite open about the fact that he and his father did not see eye to eye on any number of things. In his own quiet way, and though he kept his share of secrets, Ashley was his own man.

William, after hearing the story, had been convinced this man could not have been responsible for two murders.

That left Charles and Philip. Charles was still the most likely suspect, while Philip, despite the handsome looks he'd been handed from his mother's side of the family, was in every other way a completely nondescript man. Bloodless. He didn't seem to have enough passion in his character to enable him to kill someone in a fit of frenzy.

William stared at the small portrait of his mother that had been painted when she was a girl. He liked to look upon it every few days. Now, it hung on one of the library walls.

He'd lost his belief in the goodness of the world the same night he'd lost his mother. She'd given him so much before she died, but he'd barely had the strength to continue after losing his parents. He hadn't even been able to say good-bye, as his father had thought her sickroom no place for a child.

Now, all William knew was that he could not lose Cinda as well. And they could not go on living this way, waiting for this madman to make his next move. Charles was out and about and frequenting various clubs. There was no reason why he couldn't find him, confront him, and bring this entire nightmare to an end.

The man riding in the carriage was at the end of his temper. He clenched a fine lace glove in his fist and stared blindly out the window.

How did you trick me, William? You feigned interest in no woman, then married within weeks. And where did you find her, when no one claims to know where she came from?

He came out of his thoughts as his carriage pulled up in front of a shop. Not waiting for his footman to assist him, he simply leapt out of the carriage and walked into the store.

"Do you remember selling this particular glove?" He set the lacy confection on the counter before the glovemaker. He studied it and the man felt his impatience rising. He'd been to several shops before this one, and no one had laid claim to the fine workmanship. The search was tiring him; he was impatient to know more about this woman William had married.

"I do."

"Would you happen to have a record of the lady it was made for? I would like to see it returned to its rightful owner."

"That's quite thoughtful of you, sir." This was from the glovemaker's wife, who had come out from the back of the shop. Her husband was searching through a small box in which he seemed to have devised a record-keeping system of sorts.

"Ah, here we are. It was made for a Mistress Nancy Townshend, for her youngest daughter, Rosalind."

He barely had time to compose himself, the shock was so great.

"Do you know her?" the wife asked, with interest.

He nodded his head, then snatched the glove back and strode out of the small shop. He didn't stop until he was safely in his carriage and racing toward home.

I killed her, I know I saw her breathe her last.

How could that girl have been wearing her glove?

His mind was a maze of confusion as the carriage turned a corner, and a thought struck him as he saw a familiar dwelling.

Without stopping to think, he pounded on the ceiling of the carriage with his walking stick, and the driver slowed the horses.

"I should like to walk a bit. Wait for me here."

"As you wish, sir."

The Townshend townhouse was only a few doors down, and he slipped past the high gate and into the walled garden. All of London knew of Horace and Nan's prodigious debts, so perhaps Nan had sold her youngest daughter's clothing. Mayhap that was the manner in which William's bride had come into possession of the glove.

Several workers were laboring in the garden, striving to keep it in some sort of order. The man approached them, hoping one of the group was intelligent or talkative.

Preferably both.

"Who lives here?" he called out.

They were only too glad to take a break from their work. One man, older than the other two, wiped his sleeve on his sweaty forehead, then took a few deep breaths before he answered.

"No one. The house was taken by creditors to cover part of the owner's debts."

"And the woman that lived here?" he said, trying to lead their conversation.

"Gone. No one can find her. Both her daughters got out as well. One married, I think."

"Could either of them have worn this glove?" he asked, bringing it forward for their mutual inspection.

"Nah. Both big as sows, and just about as sweet-tempered." One of the other men sniggered, then covered his mouth with a dirty hand.

"Perhaps it belonged to the other," the older man suggested.

"The other?"

"The stepdaughter. The one who married that wealthy bugger, and fooled them all. Quite a story, that was."

"And what was her name?"

"Lucy something. Lucy—"

"Lucinda?" offered the man, remembering the name he'd heard used at the church.

"That's the one. Made her live up above the stable, they did."

"Truly."

"But she was a little beauty. He met her quite some time ago, so my missus heard it. Kept the entire thing secret from the mistress of the house. Can't blame him, heard she had a temper like a witch."

"Did she?" The man tucked the lace glove into the pocket of his jacket, then backed away. "I'll leave you to your work. It's quite a handsome garden."

He walked slowly away from the work site as if he didn't have a care in the world. But all the time the rage within him grew, as he finally realized what had happened on that London night so long ago.

He'd killed the wrong woman.

Damn you, William. What a deceitful heart you have, trying to outfox me. For it only enrages me more.

It didn't take him long to find the small room above the stable that had once belonged to the woman William had wed. After a careful search, he found that which he sought.

In one of the corners, behind the remains of a straw mattress that had been torn apart and its contents scattered, was the matching glove.

"Lucinda Townshend," he whispered as he thought of the bride that had seemingly materialized out of thin air. "No, Lucinda Stedman, Duchess of Grenville."

He stood in the room for a time, thinking of all William would suffer when he was alone again. When he knew he was responsible for his young wife's painful death.

"Don't give them names," Will muttered as he opened one eye. He was lying in bed, as he and Cinda had just completed a delightful afternoon tryst in the privacy of their bedroom.

"I wasn't—"

"You'll want to keep them all if you do."

His wife was on the floor, clad in her wrapper, playing with the mastiff pups while Juno looked on. Her brood was plump and lively, their smooth coats ranging in color from silver fawn to dark fawn brindle to black.

"Not all of them. Mayhap one."

He sighed, then smiled. "Let me guess."

"It's just that he's so little—"

"And twice the mischief-maker of the others." One of the pups had been born the runt, a tiny brindle bundle of energy. Though he'd gotten off to a slow start, he was rapidly making up for it, yapping twice as much as any of the others and definitely making his presence known.

"No one will want him," Cinda murmured, picking up the small scrap of a dog and pressing him against her cheek.

He could deny her nothing, and knew when he was defeated. Sighing once again, he turned over in their great bed and pulled the covers up to his shoulders.

"Hermes," he whispered.

"What?"

"You should name him Hermes, for, madam, he has most certainly been like the god who withholds the gift of sleep."

She laughed, and he caught sight of her nuzzling the pup before she put him back with his brothers and sisters and joined him in bed.

"Thank you," she whispered, sliding against him, and the feel of her warm, smooth skin against his own was most comforting.

The little pup whimpered, and William began to laugh.

"His howl is his lyre," he whispered, kissing the side of her neck.

"How did you know I wanted to keep him?"

"How could I not?" He kissed her again. "Now sleep, before he has another chance to wake us."

"You'll be careful," she said as she watched him dress.

"Madam, I will."

"Don't give him the opportunity to call you out, for a man like that would most certainly follow no rules but his own."

"I'll be cautious."

She jumped up agitatedly from the bed and brushed a speck of lint from his jacket. "I can't bear to think of you in any sort of danger."

He couldn't share his feelings with her, that the thought of anything happening to her would make life unendurable. All he knew was that it was time for the nightmare to come to an end. He wanted his life back in full, for now he had everything to live for.

"How have you been feeling?" he asked.

"Not well in the mornings, but the rest of the day goes much better."

"Is there anything Cook can give you?"

"She says the sickness portends a strong babe, and that I must be very careful of what I take."

"A wise woman." He buttoned his waistcoat, then reached for his jacket.

"You will be careful?" she whispered, and he could hear the fear in her voice.

He turned and knelt down at her feet, taking her hands in his own.

"You have my word. And how could I not, when I have so much to come home to?"

The club was crowded when he walked in, and the excitement was centered around one of the tables in the far back. If his instincts were operating at their fullest, he suspected he'd find Charles Hailey at that table.

Within minutes, his suspicions were confirmed.

The young man was flushed with frustration. He'd already shed his richly embroidered waistcoat and a diamond stickpin and put both up for collateral. William had a sinking feeling tonight would see the final squandering of his vast personal fortune.

He joined the eager watching group. Philip stood off to the side, his expression unreadable. Ashley was there as well, but the look in his eyes was one of greatest concern.

"William, how kind of you to join us," Charles said, his speech only slightly slurred. He acted as if he were holding court, and William sensed he knew his time was running out. Tonight he would play king of the hill, for tomorrow would come all too soon.

His eyes were red-rimmed, and his hands shook slightly as he picked up yet another card. It was obvious he'd had quite a lot to drink.

William said nothing, keeping his eye on the disheveled man. Charles, usually an impeccable dresser, seemed almost slovenly tonight. His hair was roughly pulled back in a queue and tied with a black ribbon, and his linen shirt was torn and stained. Without his waistcoat on, one could see how much weight the man had lost. There was a wildness in his eyes, and William knew he would have to act carefully.

"Will you try your luck tonight?" Charles asked him, and it was clearly an outright challenge.

"I've come to talk to you of other things."

"Ah, William. Such a gentleman." The red-rimmed eyes narrowed. "You have no idea how deeply I despise you."

"I think I have some appreciation for the depth of your feelings."

"Do you? However could you understand how it feels to sit in my chair?"

It was time to throw down the gauntlet.

William leaned over the table, both his hands braced on its surface. All cardplaying ceased, as the gentlemen in competition shielded their hands from his gaze or turned discreetly away. The tension in the room was palpable.

"Hear this. Say or do anything you wish toward me. But include my wife in your sickness or harm her in any way, and I'll follow you to the ends of the earth and slit your throat myself."

He gambled on watching Charles's reaction, and now that bet paid off in full. The man flushed a dark, angry red, his skin mottled with rage.

"How dare you presume to speak to me in such a manner!"

"Be warned," William said softly. "I know what you've done, and no one can save you from the consequences of your actions."

"I don't wish to be saved, William. By you or anyone else."

"I wasn't offering."

He threw down his cards. "Your wife! How she even figures in this is beyond my comprehension. Why would I want anything to do with a woman more common than any I could have at Madam Avice's—"

He never finished the sentence, for William overturned the table and pinned him up against the wall. Looking down into Charles's terrified face, it was all he could do to quell the killing rage that sang throughout his blood.

She sat in the kitchen with Cook, and waited for the hours to pass. Cinda had no idea how long this was to take; she only knew she would not feel safe until William was home and this night was over.

Both women jumped when they heard a noise in the large pantry.

"Can't be rats. Thomas takes care of those." Cook dusted off her flour-coated hands on her apron. She still helped with the baking now and then, and the woman who normally ran the household's kitchen had admitted she'd never tasted pies or cakes like Cook's.

"I'll see what's the matter."

When Cook came back out of the pantry, she was all smiles. "You must see this."

Undine, her speckled muzzle covered with flour, had been attempting to climb to the top of the storage space, where Cook had placed several fine meat pies to save for Sunday supper. Now, the little dog simply looked guilty.

"I've told Henry he spoils her. Well, my girl, I'll take those pies and put them in a meat safe before I'll let you eat 'em."

Cinda laughed, then both women set to work putting the storage area to rights. Cook kept the two herbals on the shelves, as well as several other possessions, and now Cinda noticed one of her baskets had been overturned.

Rosalind's.

She bent to return the basket's contents to their proper place, and picked up one of the girl's precious books that had fallen open.

But it wasn't a book at all.

The handwriting was childish, filled with exaggerated loops and curlicues. It took Cinda a moment to realize she was staring at the dead girl's diary.

"Cinda?" Cook must have seen the expression on her face, for her voice was concerned.

"Leave this," she said softly. "Come with me."

She went back to their chairs by the fire, all thoughts of the pantry forgotten. The leatherbound book had fallen open toward the end, and a sentence had caught her eye.

Rosalind, afraid, had not wanted to go out that night.

Her voice a whisper as she read, Cinda and Cook slowly learned the innermost thoughts of the young girl. The journal had fallen open a mere eight pages from its end, and by the time Cinda finished reading and set it down, both women knew the role Nan had played that tragic night.

"She was a monster," Cinda whispered, staring into the flames. "Poor Roz never had a chance."

Cook shook her head. "She couldn't stand up to her, that I knew." She glanced at Cinda. "How do you feel?"

The guilt was gone. She hadn't even realized what a weight it had been upon her soul until its absence. Now, knowing Nan's greed had been the driving force behind Rosalind's decision that night, Cinda shook her head and clutched the leatherbound journal tightly in her hands.

"It had nothing to do with Will and me."

"Of course not, lovey. It never did."

William let Charles go, and the man slid slowly down the wall, clutching his throat and looking up at him as if he were the madman in question.

"Leave her alone," he whispered. "I won't have you hurting my wife."

"You talk nonsense," Charles hissed.

"Do you deny sending me those notes?"

The confusion in his eyes seemed genuine, but William was well aware of what a man was capable of feigning when honor was at stake.

"I know nothing about any notes."

William swallowed against the emotion building inside him. "And do you also deny your hatred of me?"

"No, that much is real."

"Leave me be, for I have no quarrel with you."

In front of his eyes, Charles started to crumble.

"Why did you take it to my father, Will? Why did you attempt to bring him into it?"

"Out of concern for you—"

"Concern?" His voice was anguished. "But he never wanted me. He wanted *you*. The *perfect* man and, in his eyes, the *perfect son*."

"Don't torture yourself with such matters." As close as he was to Charles at this moment, and seeing his extreme pain, William knew the man desperately needed help. If James Hailey couldn't see to his son's needs, then he would take the matter into his own hands.

For this man, his all-powerful enemy, was not a cold-blooded killer. He was driven by demons far more painful.

"I'll take you home," he said quietly, for Charles's ears alone.

"I am—no longer welcome there," he whispered, forcing the words out.

William could not comprehend such rigid cruelty on James Hailey's part. A movement behind him caught his attention, and he sensed Ashley's quiet, steady presence.

"You may come home with me, Charles," Ashley said. "I know my family will welcome you."

William nodded his head as he backed away from the trembling man. He no longer had an appetite for this particular blood sport. He never had. Only the most desperate circumstances had brought him to this moment in the first place.

He was halfway across the room when Charles's voice stopped him.

"Don't you walk away from me!"

Something in the man's expression warned him to move very carefully. Turning slowly, all his senses alert, he saw that Charles had somehow acquired a pistol, and was leveling it directly at his heart.

He didn't say a word, simply looked at the man.

For Charles had reached his end, and William knew he didn't have to fear for his life. He glanced at Ashley, standing to the side, and realized his friend shared his thoughts.

"Don't . . . walk away. I won't . . . have it anymore."

"Charles," William began, trying to keep his voice calm.

The gun wavered in his hand, and William took a tentative step toward him. The entire club was silent, as what was transpiring between the two men was far more entertaining than a simple hand of cards.

"Don't. Stay where you are." Charles's red-rimmed eyes filled as he tried to steady his hand.

"Put it down."

Charles hesitated for a moment, then looked wildly around the room.

"Look at me, Charles," he said quickly. "Not at them."

"I'm ruined, Will." His voice trembled with shame.

"No. No, you're not. Charles, I want you to give me the pistol."

He wavered, and William pressed his point.

"Give it to me. I don't want anyone else to get hurt."

It was painful to look upon the man; he had the expression of a desperate, hunted animal. His attention wavered, something flickered in his eyes, and for an instant William almost had him.

He knew the exact moment when he lost.

Charles swallowed, and closed his eyes briefly.

"Here's something more you can tell my father, Will."

And before anyone could stop him, Charles Hailey put the barrel of the pistol to his temple and fired.

CHAPTER
❧ 19 ❧

He remained alive for almost two days.

Blind and barely breathing, Charles was carried from the club by Ashley. Both he and William took him home, and found that Charles had truly not exaggerated.

He was no longer welcome, they would not accept him.

Thus, Ashley took his friend home, while Philip roused his minister out of a comfortable slumber and accompanied the man to the Blessington estate to give Charles his last chance at redemption.

Ashley kept his vigil at his friend's bedside, offering solace until he died.

"Will?"

Cinda's voice was tentative as she entered the library. Her husband had gone directly to the darkened room upon arriving home, and had spoken to no one. Even Henry, upon entering the room and inquiring if there was anything he could do, had been coldly and politely asked to leave.

The room was in shadows. The fire had burned low hours ago, the air within was cool. As her eyes adjusted to the dim light, she made out the tall form of her husband. He was standing in front of one of the tall windows and staring out into the night.

"Will?"

"Please leave me."

His voice was calm, utterly devoid of emotion. And it scared her more than if he'd turned and shouted in anger.

For an instant she didn't know what to do, then instinct took over and asserted itself. She couldn't leave him alone, of that she was sure. She'd seen his blackest moods before, and they hadn't scared her.

"What happened?"

No answer.

"Please tell me, Will."

He still didn't face her, but she saw him take a deep breath. It caused his shoulders to tremble. It was a fine tremor, and she wouldn't have noticed it if she hadn't been concentrating on him so intently.

She couldn't ask again, she could only hope he would want to confide in her. He'd been an independent man, sometimes a lonely one. Now she wondered if marriage had enacted any sort of change in him, and if he would decide to trust her.

"You might wish to leave this house."

Of all that he could have said, those words surprised her most.

"Will?" Now she was frightened.

"I'll understand if you wish to leave."

"What are you talking about?"

"Charles Hailey tried to commit suicide tonight—"

She covered her mouth with her hand, but still a sound of shocked disbelief managed to escape.

"—and he is not expected to survive the night."

"He's *alive*?"

"The bullet shattered his temple and left him blind. I fetched a surgeon, but we were told there was nothing to be done."

"Where—"

"Ashley Blessington took him in when his family would not."

"The poor man."

Silence stretched between them for several minutes and she fought to bridge it.

"Why would I wish to leave you?" she whispered. Her voice sounded loud in the quiet room.

"Because I have a peculiar habit. Wherever I go and whatever I do, people seem to die."

"What happened?"

"It's not important."

"It is. Tell me, Will."

Briefly, he told her.

"It wasn't your fault."

"It wasn't? Then whose, pray tell, was it?"

"Don't." She whirled away from him and went over to the large desk. Taking up a candle, she swiftly lit it from the dying coals of the fire, then placed it back on the desk. Soft light bathed the large room.

"Don't claim fault for something that had nothing to do with you." He didn't answer. "You told me Charles Hailey was on his own destructive path; there was nothing you could have done that would have stopped him."

"Oh, no, madam, I simply led him to the precipice and pushed him down the side!"

"What he did, and what his father did to him, have nothing whatever to do with you—"

"I would think, madam, that you might not want to be married to a man about whom it will be said—"

"I don't give a damn what people choose to say. Or what they're ignorant enough to listen to."

He didn't answer.

"Do you truly believe I care for anything and anyone above you? Can you think so little of me?"

"Madam, I—"

"You still don't see me for what I am, do you, Will?" Angrily, Cinda picked up her skirts and headed toward the door of the library. When she reached it, she turned and faced her husband. Only her complete rage prevented her from letting him see her heart was breaking.

"It's all I've ever wanted from you, more than clothes or jewels or *things*. I thought I knew you, Will, and that you knew me. I fought to help you with whatever you attempted, even at risk of losing you. And now I am to lose you *this* way?" She took a deep breath, and it hurt to draw air into her lungs.

He still remained silent, and that hurt even more.

"I believed marriage was a meeting of minds as well as hearts." Her voice was trembling badly now, as were her hands.

"And I wanted—I wanted—" She glanced wildly around the

dimly lit room. "Oh, it doesn't even matter anymore."

She left him standing in darkness.

There was one who exulted in Charles's untimely death.

He sat in the privacy of his townhouse now, his jacket off, his waistcoat comfortably unbuttoned, his expression one of the utmost contentment. And while he sipped at his glass of claret, he toyed with one of the fine lace gloves on the table in front of him.

She will leave him, of that I am certain.

It was all so easy now. Charles had made sure of that. Why, he didn't even have to kill the girl. For after he was done carefully spreading the most vicious rumors concerning William Stedman, not a single woman in London would want to share his life or his bed.

And you'll be alone and desolate then, William, won't you? Just as I planned. Just as it was always supposed to be . . .

The rumors and gossip began with astonishing swiftness, and were of such a cruel, hateful nature even members of the aristocracy were stunned.

But they listened. And nodded their heads. And even found the time to embellish what was said.

His mistress was found murdered in her townhouse. Her throat slit. And all because William found her with another man . . .

Well, didn't I tell you he killed that other woman in a fit of rage when his intended refused to elope with him? All his money kept it quiet. Paid off the family, you know.

Isn't he forcing that same girl to stay married to him now? Blackmail. Some sort of family secret, I believe.

And, my dear, didn't you know he and that poor Charles always had the greatest animosity between them . . .

While spring gave way to summer, the rumors spread like a cancerous growth. And though Cinda refused to leave, she and William began to lead increasingly separate lives.

Dearest William,

Time grows short. I fear neither of us has much left.

All is explained, except the identity my brother took, and how he managed to steal it from another.

He never explained it to me, how he acquired so much wealth. He only said he'd made an agreement to play a part, and as long as this part was played to perfection, we might have a measure of comfort and protection in our lives.

I knew from the start that he lied.

One night he was drunk, and afraid. I was with him, attempting to calm him, when the truth came out.

He'd been working at sea the years I spent in service to my elderly mistress. He'd thought of saving a vast sum of money in order to come back and provide for both of us. But try as he might, he couldn't save enough coin fast enough.

He'd despaired of ever seeing me again.

Then two people boarded the ship he worked, and his life changed once again.

Little Philip Fleming and his mother were running away to the Colonies. His mother was the most beautiful woman, an actress who had bewitched Philip's father. After his birth, she'd loved him deeply but still wanted to keep her career on the stage. Her husband disagreed, and they'd fought bitterly over the years. Finally, she left him, taking the child he adored.

Daniel was fascinated by them both. As he and Philip were the only two young boys on board, they shared something of a friendship. What was more, the resemblance between the two was uncanny. Daniel even arranged his hair so he might more resemble the young aristocrat.

I must relate this part of the story quickly, for the murder of a child is most distressing to me. A storm blew up, the ship was torn apart. Daniel and Philip were adrift at sea, with only a small piece of the ship to cling to. They held on through several days and nights, until early one morning they saw a ship in the distance.

Both had thought they were to die, and now the prospect that they might be rescued became reality.

That ship did not see them, but that night Daniel held young Philip's head beneath the dark water and drowned him. The boy was weak, and put up no struggle.

Daniel had confiscated his family ring, and now made sure his clothes were in rags. Unrecognizable. As he'd spent many a day on the ship talking with Philip about his life back in England, now my brother put his clever mind to remembering what he could.

He decided to become Philip.

A ship picked him up, and he feigned loss of memory. The ring ensured he was brought back to England, where his father was frantic with grief. He never suspected that the boy they brought back to him was not his own. I've often wondered if he wanted to believe what he saw, for I surely know what the mind is capable of.

The elder Fleming was never the same after the death of his beloved mistress. He found comfort in this new Philip, and Daniel was kind to him. But whether the emotion was genuine or expedient, I could not truthfully say.

Thus, by careful observation, my brother learned to be a gentleman. And came for me, then fetched me back to his country estate.

When I learned of what he'd done, I knew my brother had no chance of redemption. There was an emptiness in him where conscience should have resided. I have long ago stopped fearing the dark, for I know it is everywhere, perhaps inside everyone.

The last of my hope for him died during that long night as he drunkenly confessed what he'd done. I prayed for his soul, and that we would be allowed, through God's mercy, to live out our lives in the quiet countryside.

It was not to be. You came home, William, and fate set events in motion.

Philip Fleming is your enemy. Not Charles Hailey. You think your opponent dead, but even as I write this account he is making plans to ensure your bride's demise . . .

She didn't know how to reach him anymore.

Oh, she knew what he was doing. He didn't want her to have to be a part of it, any more than he'd wanted her to be a part of it when he'd been tracking their murderer.

But in neither case had he counted on her possessing more than her fair share of stubbornness.

She refused to leave.

She refused to stop talking to him.

And, most important of all, she refused to give up hope.

"How can they talk about him that way!" Mary whispered to Cook as she prepared Cinda's breakfast tray. Cook was baking, and though all her concentration seemed to be on the various pies, cakes, breads, and buns she was preparing, her heart ached for her young mistress.

"He's the best employer I've ever had," Mary continued, her tone scathing against those who would contradict her. "I don't believe a word of it!"

"See that you don't," Cook said softly as she watched the oven. Though she fully intended to do something about this, she hadn't quite figured out what. In the meantime, it would do no good to let the bread burn.

"She'll be up before I get to her room," Mary said sadly, making a few last adjustments to the breakfast tray. "Mussing the bed, so's it looks like he slept with her."

"Keep quiet about that, miss. The good people of London don't need to know everything!"

"Of course!" Mary's wide blue eyes were filled with hurt, and Cook patted her arm gently. They were alone in the kitchen, as she'd started the baking and Mary had come down early as well.

Once Mary left on her way upstairs, Cook sat down at the large table by the fire, her chin in her hand. She'd never come up against anything like this before. It seemed the whole city was taking delight in William's bad luck.

And the sad thing was, she didn't believe he'd had anything at all to do with the poor boy's suicide.

She had few close friends, and trusted no one other than Robbie, Cinda, or William. And as both of the latter were in no mood to help, and her son had relatively little power, she was stumped.

The Duke and Duchess of Cranfield.

The thought slipped into her mind so effortlessly that she sensed Nora's presence immediately.

"And why should they help?" she whispered into thin air.

That note he wrote you, thanking you for taking care of our girl. He said whatever you might need in future . . .

Hope began to bloom within Cook's heart as she remembered the exquisitely written letter that the footman had delivered to her room. Cinda had read her the parts she couldn't quite comprehend.

"But surely they know—"

No, they do not. For almost everyone knows Arthur and Diana would never condone such ugly lies, and would certainly not want to hear them.

"And they are powerful as well."

Tell them . . .

Nora's presence faded away as another of the maids stumbled into the kitchen, trying to rub the sleep out of her eyes.

"There's a love," Cook said softly to the young girl. "Would you watch the baking and take it out when it looks done?"

The girl nodded, still braiding her brown hair down her back, her slender fingers nimble.

"I won't be gone long."

Burned bread or not, some things couldn't wait.

"You have a visitor, Your Grace, by the name of Cinda's cook," the servant informed the Duke of Cranfield. He put down the book he'd been reading and glanced toward the doorway of the drawing room.

"Now, this is a pleasure!" He stood as he saw Cinda's friend. At her side was a young man he assumed was her son.

"I'm sorry to come so early, Your Grace, and unannounced—"

"Nonsense!" Arthur interrupted the woman, then escorted her to a chair in front of a briskly burning fire. The mornings were cool, and he so loved to sit by the fire.

"Will you have tea or coffee? And as I still have no idea what your Christian name is, my dear, would you enlighten me? I didn't mean to be rude in addressing my letter to the cook."

"Sir, my name's not important—"

"Jane," said her son quietly. "Her name's Jane."

"Jane it is." Arthur poured her a cup of tea, then handed it to her. He noticed the woman's broad hands were shaking, and set the cup down on a table.

"Jane, you have no reason to be frightened of me."

To his amazement, the woman burst into tears and proceeded to tell him the most remarkable story.

When she finished, and after he'd handed her his handkerchief to mop up her tears, his decision had been made.

"I'll accompany you both back home, and see if I can talk to William."

"If you would," she hiccuped, and his heart went out to her. Reaching over, he covered her hand with his own.

"You have a visitor, Your Grace," Henry said quietly.

William spent most of his days in the library, certain Cinda would not bother him. She still insisted on taking meals with him, and keeping up some sort of pretense of a conversation. Though it was tearing his heart out to ignore her, he acted with the knowledge that what he'd decided was best for her.

He'd brought nothing but pain into her life.

"Send him away—"

"Hello, William." Arthur swept into the library, doffing his hat and coat and seating himself in one of the chairs in front of the fire.

It was clear the older man wasn't going to be dislodged.

William studied him for a moment, then resigned himself to the gentleman's company.

"Henry, if you would be so kind as to bring us some refreshment?"

"As you wish, sir." The valet's tone was rather cold. William had been amazed at his servant's siding with Cinda. Henry told him, by every look, word, and deed, what a dreadful mistake he thought he was making.

Once they were alone, Arthur came directly to the point in his usual roundabout way.

"We haven't seen much of you and your new bride."

"We've been rather busy."

"You lie rather badly, William."

He couldn't find the words to answer the older man. Finally, he decided to trust what was in his heart.

"She shouldn't have to face any of this."

"That's quite true. Neither should you. But I'd say you should be thankful you made a fine marriage, as such a union can offer much in the way of consolation. And comfort."

"I don't want her to be a part of it any longer."

"And have you consulted her about any of this?"

"She is aware of my feelings, yes."

"But she doesn't agree with you, I take it?"

Both men were silent as Henry returned and placed a silver tea tray on the table next to them. They waited until he left the library to resume their conversation.

"I had a most extraordinary talk with Jane this morning."

"Jane?"

"Your bride's cook."

"I see."

"My boy, why didn't you come to me as soon as this madman began threatening you?"

And William knew, looking into the kindly gray eyes, that he'd been defeated.

"I didn't— I couldn't drag you and Diana into such a sordid mess."

"But we love you, dear boy. And have since you came into the world."

He glanced at his mother's portrait on the far wall, and the older man didn't miss the gesture.

"Are you afraid of losing her?"

How like Arthur, to cut to the heart of the matter. He couldn't meet his friend's eyes; he simply stared into the fire and willed himself not to feel.

"You are. But tell me this. If you end up sending her away, how is that any different?"

Once he had his feelings totally under control, William faced the kindly Duke.

"It's better for her."

"It's killing her, William."

He closed his eyes then, and covered them with his hand. And felt Arthur's touch on his shoulder, firm and comforting.

"It was a terrible thing what happened to James Hailey's son, but it had nothing whatever to do with you."

William shook his head.

"You didn't put the gun to his head. If truth be told, Charles died a long time ago."

William didn't answer. Couldn't.

"Jane told me what people are saying. She was the only one with the courage to come forward and do so. She's still protecting Cinda, and I deeply appreciate what she did."

"I'm not angry with her," he whispered.

"More with yourself?"

William nodded his head.

"Don't be. You'll come to see, in time, that the only people who matter are the ones who already believe in you."

"How can she still love me?"

"How can she not?" The older man lowered his voice. "They say you're ashamed of her."

This opened his eyes, and he glared at the older man as he began to laugh delightedly.

"Oh, so that's how it is! They can say all they want about you, but touch a hair on her head—"

"That's how it is. That's why she should leave."

"That's why she cannot." Arthur gracefully rose to his feet and extended a large hand. "Come on, my boy. Join me for a ride in the park. The air will do you a tremendous amount of good, and I daresay those mastiffs could use the exercise."

William stared at the older man's hand, and knew it for the lifeline it was. He grasped it, and allowed the Duke of Cranfield to pull him to his feet. The older man embraced him quickly, then stepped back and smiled down at him.

And outside the library door, his ear pressed as close as he dared, Henry smiled.

Cinda was still asleep that morning when William came to their bedroom. He sat down on the side of the bed and woke her with a kiss.

She eyed him warily.

"Can you forgive me for being a fool?" he asked.

Her eyes filled with tears before she could attempt to control the rush of emotion. She'd never been able to, around him.

"Oh, I think so."

He lay down next to her, outside the covers, and she went into his arms. He smelled of fresh air, leather, and horses, and she kissed the side of his neck, then his cheek.

"You went out?"

"With Arthur."

"Oh."

"You have quite a few champions within this house, madam."

"And what does that mean?"

"Your cook—Jane—went to see Arthur this morning and convinced him to talk to me."

"I see." Now she couldn't stop smiling. How like Cook, to defend her to the end.

"And Henry has been a bear."

She laughed.

"I'd forgotten how much I missed that sound."

"Then I don't have to leave?"

The sudden vulnerability in his eyes started fresh tears in her own. She'd known he hadn't meant it, yet she hadn't been able to conquer the distance between them.

"No." He paused. "Would you have gone?"

"Never."

Their marriage started anew, and Cinda looked back upon it as one of their happiest times. They went riding together, and to the theater with Arthur and Diana. And within a fortnight, Diana decided she would give a party to celebrate their wedding.

"For you really didn't have one. It was such a small wedding."

They were in the Ramseys' large library, sitting together after dinner.

"If you think it wise—" Cinda began.

"I do. You must be introduced to society properly, and since you have no mother or father to do it for you, Arthur and I would be more than happy to take charge."

Cinda liked the feeling of leaving preparations in Diana's capable hands.

"Could you . . . could I invite my godmother?"

Diana wrinkled her nose prettily. "I thought she lived farther north."

"She's still in London."

"Then we must invite her. Now, about your ball gown—"

Cinda found herself swept along in this feminine conversation, but she only had eyes for her husband. He seemed less worried of late, as he laughed with Arthur by the fire.

He'd come back to her bed the night after the Duke's visit, and she couldn't have wished for a more tender or ardent lover. He was always careful of their baby, and she'd found the love she had for her husband deepening even further.

Life was very good indeed.

He'd spotted them at the theater together, and what he'd seen had enraged him. For William's bride wasn't about to leave him.

Why do you continually defy me, William? Why do you take such delight in thwarting my designs?

And now, with the Duke and Duchess of Cranfield's invitation in his hands, he stared into the fire and made his plans.

Cinda entered the ballroom with her husband and created an absolute sensation.

Few of the aristocracy had been given a chance to see them together since the gossip had started, as their appearances in town had been sporadic. A morning in the park, an evening at the theater. Now, as they were the guests of honor, everyone could gaze to their heart's content.

They were announced as they proceeded into the immense ballroom, its wide expanse packed tightly with people. A collective murmur went up as Arthur Ramsey informed everyone present that Cinda was his niece, for the Duke and Duchess of Cranfield had the power to negate even the most vicious rumors. And they were using that power to its fullest extent tonight.

The excited noise from the crowd died down, then Diana smiled at everyone present as her husband asked William and Cinda to begin the dancing.

Cinda glanced to the side of the ballroom and spotted Cook, looking a trifle uncomfortable in another new dress. Robbie was by her side. Grinning, she reached up and tugged gently at her earlobe, careful not to catch her diamond earring.

She caught sight of her godmother, standing alone at the edge of the crush of people, and touched her husband's shoulder.

"Would you wait for me, darling?"

She deftly maneuvered herself through the crowd of onlookers until she was at her godmother's side.

"You look lovely," Cinda whispered, then kissed the older woman's cheek. She saw the fear leave Kathleen's eyes, to be replaced by a happiness almost painful to look upon.

"Thank you." Kathleen was clearly flustered as Cinda led

her over to Arthur and Diana and explained their relationship. Arthur immediately took the woman beneath his jovial wing, and Cinda could see her godmother visibly relaxing.

Then, returning to her husband's side and taking his hand, she allowed him to lead her out onto the dance floor.

Her introduction to society had begun.

Bess stood just outside the window. The man who owned her had insisted she accompany him, and had been in such a mood she hadn't dared refuse. Now, hidden among the bushes and gazing in the window at the glittering throng of people, she recognized the girl from the market who had given her child a chance.

Bess knew her master wished to harm this girl. Murder her, in fact. She glanced across the huge ballroom to where the Duke and Duchess of Cranfield stood, talking to several of their guests. Diana Ramsey was well known among the poor, for the work she did. Many a time Bess and her little family had been on the receiving end of that lady's goodness.

If I could get to her, tell her, warn them . . .

Determination fired her blood, and she started around the huge mansion, then up the steps. If no one was watching her, perhaps she might be able to catch the woman's ear.

"Hey, now! What's the meaning of this!"

The man guarding the door was a no-nonsense, burly-looking fellow.

"Please, if I might speak to the lady of the house—"

"The likes of you? Come around to the kitchen tomorrow morning and she'll find you some food, but don't be bothering her now."

"But I must—" She stopped in midsentence as she saw her master come out of the Cranfield mansion, an enraged expression on his handsome features.

She darted around the side of the great house, but he was quicker. He caught her up against him in the darkness, then slapped her sharply across the face.

"What're you doing, sneakin' 'round like some bloody thief?"

She couldn't tell him the truth, but she could act like the simpleton he thought she was.

"I was hungry! So much food in there, they wouldn't miss a little—"

He slapped her again, and she tasted blood in her mouth. Dragging her behind him, he started toward his carriage. She glanced back at the brightly lit mansion and wondered how she was ever to warn any of them.

Or why she should even care.

"It was a wonderful evening, wasn't it?" Cinda asked her husband as she watched him get ready for bed.

"I thought it went rather well." He blew out the bedside candle, then climbed into bed beside her.

She snuggled happily against him. "After tonight, nothing more can hurt us, unless we let it."

"You're a most determined woman."

"If I have my way, we shall be together forever."

He laughed softly. "Hardly forever."

"For a long time, then."

"Yes." He smiled into the darkness. "Arthur and Diana put an end to all those rumors quite effectively, did they not?"

"I admire them so. From the first moment I met them, I sensed such goodness of spirit. To find myself related to them was a gift beyond compare."

He kissed her forehead. "You find yourself worried you might embarrass me, but it was your family that prevented me from succumbing to ruin."

"Surely the rumors would have faded in time."

"Not without doing irreparable damage."

"But you did not let them."

"Not without help from both Jane and Arthur."

"But you made the final decision."

"You will never stop believing the best of me, will you?"

"Never."

He kissed her then, as they lay tightly entwined beneath the covers.

"Will?"

"Yes, dear heart?"

"I'm so glad it's finally over."

Bess slipped the last piece of her threadbare clothing off, letting it pool at her feet. She stood in front of the fireplace in her master's bedroom. He hadn't bothered taking her back to the room in St. Giles, but she was confident her son Ned was taking care of his baby sister.

Now, she had to keep her wits about her in order to thwart her master's evil mood. She swallowed against the fear in her throat. Her instincts told her she was in for a rough night that had nothing to do with what normally went on between a man and a woman. Even a man and his whore. She'd given a lot more thought lately to simply taking her two children and disappearing. For he no longer had much use for her, and her instincts also told her that could only mean one thing.

He'd watched her take off her clothing. She could sense his gaze upon her, even though she kept her own on the thick oriental carpet against her bare feet.

"Lie down."

She complied. His speech was slurred; she knew he'd drunk quite a lot once his carriage had taken them home. Now she could only hope he wouldn't beat her too badly. If she managed to get back to her babies, she'd leave him.

He pushed her legs apart, then knelt between them. She wanted to keep her eyes closed, but she knew from painful experience he would slap her face until she opened them. He liked to know she was fully aware.

But this time was different.

"I want you to play dead," he said softly, and his tone of voice frightened her far more than any of his beatings ever had.

She wasn't sure she understood what he wanted of her. Bess licked her dry lips, then swallowed against the sudden fear that closed her throat.

"Play . . . dead?"

"Play dead, bitch!" he snarled, grasping her unbound hair in his fist and pulling until tears came to her eyes.

She nodded her head, then went perfectly still. It was one of the hardest things she'd ever done, forcing herself not to respond with revulsion as he brutally explored her body.

His elegant, aristocratic fingers encircled her throat. She felt his rigid arousal against her bare skin and knew he was thinking of the girl.

When his hands squeezed between her legs and his fingers roughly invaded her, Bess gasped involuntarily. Her eyes flew open, but she barely had time to see the fist that smashed into the side of her face.

"Play *dead*, you bitch!" he whispered as he continued to brutally fondle her.

Blessedly, unconsciousness came to claim her.

CHAPTER

❧ 20 ❧

"Madam, have a care!"

William started forward, intent on protecting Cinda from herself. She was in the midst of the garden, reaching upwards toward the roof of a small folly, a miniature Greek temple where grapevines twined overhead. The object of her desire, a particularly plump bunch of purple grapes, was barely in reach as she balanced precariously on a wooden chair.

He was thwarted in his task as both Juno and Jocasta appeared. The mastiffs shadowed Cinda wherever she went, and now Jocasta thrust her massive frame between William and his wife.

At the same instant, Cinda plucked the grapes from the vine, then jumped down from her precarious perch.

"You, too?" William asked the dog, and was rewarded by a quick swipe from the mastiff's tongue. He laughed as he fondled the dog's ears, then turned his attention to the woman he loved.

"You've bewitched everyone in my household."

"That isn't true." She came to his side, offering him some of the dark purple grapes. "I merely had a taste for some fruit."

"I would have fetched it for you."

"Will, I'm with child, not bedridden." She smiled up at him, and he sensed her indulgence.

"Then take pity on your poor old husband and sit with him awhile."

"Old?" She laughed, then followed him down the garden path to a marble bench set back among several Scotch pines. Both Juno and Jocasta padded after them, and settled themselves in the shade for a nap.

"And where is the untrainable one?" William asked, glancing around for a sight of Cinda's pup.

In answer, she put two fingers to her mouth and whistled sharply. A crackling sound came from the underbrush, then a gangly, three-month-old mastiff puppy came bounding out. Hermes still possessed the same cheerful personality he'd had as a baby, but now the brindle mastiff had become a menace to both himself and the household, knocking things over and making a complete nuisance of himself.

But Cinda loved him, and that spared him almost everyone's wrath.

The puppy almost knocked them over in his haste to be petted. Cinda gave him a grape, which he promptly swallowed without so much as tasting it. The look of utter canine adoration on his face was so comical William was hard-pressed not to laugh.

"He will outgrow such behavior," she said confidently.

He eyed her until she laughed, then offered him another grape.

He took it, popped it into his mouth, then kissed her.

"And what are your plans for today?" he asked.

"I thought I might take a walk with the dogs. Then Cook and I are going to work in the herb garden a while, and then—"

"Madam, have a care you don't tire yourself."

She tweaked his nose.

"I shall. And you?"

"I have something for you."

"Oh, Will."

He heard the gentle reproof in her voice. In the past few weeks, since the Ramsey's lavish ball, life had been good. He'd showered her with gifts of all kinds, but he had a feeling this particular possession might mean more to her than all the jewels in the world.

Before she could say anything more, he handed her a piece of paper.

She read the title slowly, and he watched as comprehension

flooded her features. She raised her face to his, and the stark joy in her green eyes caused his heart to catch.

"Oh, Will! *Thank* you!"

"I thought you might like it—" He caught his breath as she flung herself at him, her arms around his neck, the deed to her mother's house fluttering in the summer breeze.

He accompanied her on her walk as they discussed what to do with the property.

"The garden has been tended to, and is almost exactly as you left it." He'd known how much her mother's garden had meant to her. The small plot of land had a sentimental value to him as well, for it was there they'd first met.

"Will, would you mind terribly—what I mean is—"

"Tell me what you wish."

"I should like my godmother to live there." She rushed on. "I know she has been quite outspoken in her feelings toward you—"

"It's your property, darling, to do with as you wish. And I should not be offended at all, for haven't we proven her wrong?"

They were almost back to the house, the dogs behind them, when Cinda stopped.

"Will." Her voice was hushed.

"Are you—is something wrong?"

"No." She took his hand and placed it over her stomach. "There. Did you feel it?"

He shook his head.

"Wait. There!"

Still he felt nothing.

"What is it?"

"I felt her—I felt her move!"

He looked down at her upturned face, and it was as if joy illuminated her from within. They stood very still together, his hand on her stomach, her hand over his.

"Could you feel it?"

He shook his head, regretful that he hadn't, but loving the happiness suffusing her features.

"Her?" he asked, arching an eyebrow. The feelings he had were so deeply emotional, he attempted to mask them with humor.

"Will you be disappointed if I give you a daughter?" Now

her green eyes were concerned, and he wanted to take away any care she might have. He didn't want anything to worry her. Each day, in every way, he merely wanted to see to her happiness.

"Not at all." He caught her hand as they started back toward the townhouse. "Girls are much more fun than boys, what with tea parties and dances and such."

"You'd let them go out on the town and socialize?"

"I'll lock them up till they have gray hair!" He laughed, and hugged her against his side. "Darling, I shall love any daughter you choose to give me as dearly as a son, and cherish our children each and every day."

"Thank you, Will."

He couldn't resist teasing her. "And after all, madam, when have you ever obeyed me?"

John Stedman arrived back in London later in the week, and Cinda found her days full with the demands of her household. It seemed that William's uncle was only to be back for a fortnight, then he would be leaving for Paris.

He congratulated them on their marriage, and at dinner that evening proposed yet another party.

"I'd like to celebrate William's wedding, and properly welcome Cinda into the family." He grinned at her, down the length of the large dining-room table. Arthur and Diana had been invited to dinner, and it was a lively affair.

John and Arthur rarely ran out of things to discuss, and Diana was not at all shy in making her opinions known. William had obviously grown up in an atmosphere in which he'd been both expected and encouraged to speak his mind, which he did with an intellectual relish.

Cinda had been intimidated at first, but followed Diana's excellent lead. Now, having navigated many such dinners, she joined in with abandon.

"A party! What fun!" Diana smiled up at her husband. "Arthur and I shall help you in any way we can."

"But perhaps something a little out of the ordinary," John mused, picking up his wineglass and taking a sip.

"Not too unusual," William said.

John laughed. "He's right to be worried. No, Will, nothing too strange for the aristocracy. Perhaps a dinner party combined with a masquerade. If I delay my departure for Paris, that will give all of us plenty of time to plan our various costumes."

"Then invitations should go out this week," Diana mused. "I could certainly help with those."

"How she loves to plan," Arthur said, gazing down at his wife with adoration in his eyes.

"I shall leave the preparations in the ladies' capable hands," John announced. "And I shall occupy myself with getting the garden ready. As it is quite mild in the evenings, we can hold part of the gathering outside."

Plans were discussed, various guests were mentioned and added to a swiftly growing list. Costumes were suggested amid hoots of laughter, and another celebration was under way.

Cinda decided to keep her costume a surprise. She'd decided on a Persian *peri*, or angel. The costume consisted of loose pants, a voluminous blouse, and a jeweled vest. Her hair would be worn up on top of her head, and the most cunning slippers would adorn her feet.

William tried to persuade her to tell him, but she wanted to surprise him. Also, as being married had brought out a strong streak of overprotectiveness in him, she didn't want him to decide her costume was too risqué.

The townhouse was cleaned from top to bottom, and copious amounts of foodstuffs were purchased. The kitchen became a beehive of activity in preparation for the big day.

The guest list was made up, and invitations sent to one and all. As news of this particular party leaked out, an invitation became one of the aristocracy's most highly coveted items.

It was to be a most festive affair, and everyone happily went about their work to ensure it would be a celebration no one would soon forget.

All but one.

"Take your sister and hide in the cupboard, there's a love." Bess handed the baby to Ned as she glanced toward the door. She'd heard his booted feet on the bottom flight of stairs, and knew she didn't have much time.

She'd meant to run away, but Ned had been sick. She'd wanted to wait until he was better able to travel and endure the life that would await them. Now she wondered if she'd been wise to delay.

The footsteps sounded louder.

"Don't make a sound, Neddie," she whispered, kissing the top of her son's head. "No matter what happens, don't let him know you're here."

"Yes, Mum." The boy's eyes were huge with fear. His face looked haunted; he seemed a wizened old man in a boy's slender frame.

Smoothing his curly hair back from his forehead, Bess made her decision. Nothing the three of them found on the street could possibly be worse than what he put them through. Now she had only this one day to endure, and they would be free of him forever.

Both children had barely been shut in the cupboard when he entered the room. Immediately upon sensing his presence, she knew he'd been drinking. Whatever he'd been about, he was in a deadly mood, with rage ready to break through at a moment's provocation.

He sat down at the table. The attic room, tightly shuttered even during the day, was dimly lit with the stub of one candle. She'd tried to make it last as long as possible, but knew better than to expect him to sit and eat his meals in the dark.

Nervous, she swiftly prepared his afternoon meal. Setting it down in front of him, she rushed to get his tankard and fill it with ale.

He didn't touch his food immediately after she set it in front of him, and that should have been her clue.

His arm swept the table clear, sending the wooden plate and tankard to the floor. Grabbing her arm, he pulled her up against the table and pinned her with his strong, muscled body.

Before, when he'd beat her, she'd managed to send Ned outside with his sister. They'd seen the aftermath, the bruises and cuts, but never the actual attack. Now she could only pray her son would remember her words and choose to obey them.

"You've been no help to me," he muttered, then forced her farther down on the table. The wooden edge was cutting into the backs of her legs, and he hoisted her up on top of its surface, then down on her back.

"You and those brats," he whispered, glancing around the

room. Bess kept her gaze carefully away from the cupboard where her children were hiding.

"Where are the little bastards?" he asked.

"I sent them away, so we might have some . . . time alone," she whispered.

He nodded his head.

She readied herself for the feel of his fists, but the punishing blows never came.

"It's time we said good-bye, Bess," he whispered, then smiled a smile that made her stomach turn over.

Too late, too late, too late . . .

Her own fear had finished her. As if in a trance, unable to move, she watched as he pulled a wickedly sharp dagger out of his boot and held it in front of her face.

She'd never thought she would beg him for anything, but Bess found she didn't want to die.

"Please," she whispered. "I'll leave, you'll never see me again—"

"Oh, no," he whispered, his grin lighting his entire face. "You see, I have to get in some practice slitting throats. For tonight's party. And as I'm mightily tired of your plain little face—well, this serves two purposes."

She screamed then, as the knife came down with killing force, then screamed again as she saw the cupboard door explode open and Ned launch himself at her attacker's broad back.

"It looks lovely," Diana said to Cinda as she surveyed the garden. "Like an enchanted forest."

Guests would be arriving within the hour. William had already locked the mastiffs away, as they wouldn't be comfortable with so many strangers in their home. William was upstairs dressing, as were Cook and Robbie. Arthur and Diana had brought their costumes over this morning.

All was in readiness for tonight's revelry.

"I cannot thank you enough," Cinda said.

"It wasn't any bother." Diana took both Cinda's hands in hers. "Arthur and I weren't blessed with a daughter, so I find we are doubly blessed in that we found you."

"You are so kind."

The elder duchess sighed. "And you are so strong. I admire

your spirit, Cinda. You're good for William, as he is for you. Your marriage should be celebrated for all the joy it will bring you both. That is my fondest wish for you."

Cinda impulsively hugged her aunt, a woman who had become as close as a mother in such a short space of time.

"Now, run along upstairs and make yourself beautiful," Diana whispered, tears glittering in her eyes. "For tonight is your night."

Guests began to arrive soon after, and Cinda searched the garden until she found her godmother. She and Julia had just arrived, and Cinda marveled at the change in Kathleen. For she no longer looked afraid, and seemed to be enjoying herself.

As she explained about the townhouse, and what William had done for her, Kathleen fought back her tears.

"I was so wrong, Cinda, believing the worst in him. And now, after what Arthur and Diana have told me about Eleanor, I . . . I was so very blind."

"No," Cinda said, her arm around her relative. "Please don't blame yourself. I think Mother would be happy, knowing you were living in the house she always loved."

Kathleen dried her eyes and nodded her head.

"You have no idea how I'm looking forward to the birth of my great-grand-niece."

Cinda smiled at her godmother, and knew all traces of bitterness had left her. Only happiness remained, a happiness so complete it filled her to overflowing.

"I want you there. I want you with us, always."

William was shocked at how much his wife's costume astounded him. And aroused him.

Had he been given a chance to approve it, he most certainly would not have done so. For the harem-style pants John assured him were perfectly proper in the Far East were positively indecent here in London.

Still, she looked splendid. And how they'd both laughed when each had realized their costumes complemented each other. William had chosen to be a sultan, thus they were perfectly matched.

The crush of guests spilled out of the drawing room and into the garden. John had strung the surrounding trees with

Chinese lanterns, and the glowing lights gave the greenery an otherworldly glow.

William watched as his wife flitted from guest to guest, ensuring that each person was comfortable and having a fine time. And he couldn't believe she was the same girl who had expressed trepidation about being one of the Quality.

As with everything else she attempted, Cinda would triumph.

He'd come dressed as the Minotaur, a sort of personal joke. And he'd spotted his victim immediately, for she shone brighter than any other woman at the masquerade.

He'd even gone so far as to kiss her hand when they'd been introduced, enjoying the way William's eyes had narrowed in consternation.

Now, it was only a matter of time before he managed to get her alone . . .

The party went on into the late hours of the evening, toward early morning. Though dinner had been served hours ago, food was still artfully arrayed on long tables set up outside, so guests might eat whatever and whenever they wished.

Henry, assisting one and all, made the mistake of trying to go back and quiet Hermes. The pup had been howling at his first taste of being shut away, and though Henry had attempted to shush him through the door, his actions had done absolutely no good. Opening the door a mere crack, he'd been bowled over by the exuberant puppy, who had escaped and headed toward the excitement.

He raced after him, just in time to see him jump up on Cinda and try to swipe at her face with his large tongue. She laughed, then grasped his paws and held him gently until he began to quiet.

"It's all right, Henry," she called out. "I've got him."

And Hermes, drunk with his own cleverness and freedom, began to caper about the garden.

Most of the guests had left, including Kathleen and Julia. The crowd was thinning out. And as each person said good night and thanked William and Cinda for their hospitality, the party started to draw to a close.

The unmasking had occurred at midnight, and now, close

to three in the morning, it was only a matter of time before the evening was over.

Henry gave the mastiff pup a warning look, but the dog merely barked delightedly, then raced off toward the far end of the garden.

The last few guests were having coffee in the library when Cinda heard Hermes' pitiful howls. She started to laugh.

"Poor thing, he's lost. I'll go get him."

"I'll go with you," William began, but one of John's physician friends waylaid him with a question.

Smiling at her husband's perturbed expression, Cinda slipped out of the library and headed toward the garden.

The night air was cool and fresh against her face, the pants of her costume a welcome change from the voluminous skirts she usually wore.

"Hermes?" she called, to be answered by a pitiable series of yips.

"Oh, you big baby! Come here!" She clapped her hands, but the mournful noises continued. The sounds of muted conversation and laughter became fainter as she walked to the back of William's vast garden.

Toward the maze.

She still didn't like it, and only entered it when her husband accompanied her. Thus, it was to her utter dismay that she saw Hermes sitting partway inside the entrance to the vast series of intricately designed hedges.

"I'm not going in after you," she called. "Come on, puppy. Come, come." She clapped her hands.

Hermes, thinking this a delightful new game, turned and raced farther into the maze.

"No!" Now the pup's antics had ceased to be amusing. Though the moonlight was bright, and a full moon hung high in the cloudless sky, Cinda found her patience wearing thin.

"Hermes, come! This instant!"

The pup responded to her tone of voice, and started to trot toward her. She entered the mouth of the maze, then caught him, gently grasping one of his ears with her fingers.

"Oh, what a little pest you can be," she murmured, petting him as he quivered at the attention and licked her fingers. Will was right, she spoiled him terribly. But he was usually so lovable, she couldn't stay mad at him.

Turning, she saw the man standing at the entrance to the maze.

Cook was nodding off in a chair by the fire, a combination of too much sherry and not enough sleep of late. She'd found that she loved planning elaborate entertainments as much as Lady Cranfield did, and both of them had truly outdone themselves tonight.

Something brushed her cheek, and she swatted it away.

"Rob, stop your mischief . . ."

She felt it again, and she opened her eyes. In front of her, floating in midair, was Cinda's glittering mask. A confection of golden silk and glittering beads, it had seemed as airy as thistledown when she and Cinda had seen it in the shop window.

Now, in Nora's mischievous hands, it was literally weightless.

She grabbed it, then glanced around the vast drawing room.

"And what nonsense is—"

The garden, in the maze. He's got her—

"Who?" And now she felt Nora's fear; the room fairly vibrated with it.

Madman. Must go to her. Get William . . .

Cook struggled to her feet just as Henry came in the door carrying a silver tray laden with empty glasses.

"He's got her!"

"Who?"

"That monster! In the maze—"

"What on earth?" Diana entered the room and rushed to the side of her friend. "Jane, whatever is the matter?"

"William! Master William!" She was panting in her exertions by the time she reached him and grabbed one of his billowing sleeves. "The maze, he's got her in the maze!"

He didn't even stop to question her. To her everlasting relief, he simply believed her. Turning to his uncle, he shouted out a terse command as he raced toward the French doors.

"Let the dogs loose. Then follow me."

"Do I—know you?" she asked. She remembered the Minotaur from the party, but at the moment couldn't place the man with the particular costume. He smiled, and she could see the whiteness of his teeth clearly in the bright moonlight. Hermes growled, which was quite unusual for the good-natured pup. Cinda, feeling suddenly afraid, backed farther into the maze.

"Why didn't you leave him?"

She couldn't stop staring at his masked head. This man did not think in any rational way.

"Why didn't you leave him?" he asked again.

She swallowed.

"You're a foolish girl, forcing me to kill you." He laughed then, and she saw the dagger in his hand.

Her mind felt as if it were caving in upon itself. The same irrational panic she'd felt at the other masquerade threatened to overtake her, only this time Cinda knew there would be no one to come to her rescue. Not this time, not this late, not this far back in the garden.

By the time she was missed, he would have murdered her.

"Go on," he whispered, his eyes gleaming through the openings of the mask.

She couldn't believe what she was hearing, let alone make her limbs move.

"Go *on*," he said again, louder this time, and she finally understood his intent.

He wanted to hunt her.

The high walls of the hedge gleamed darkly in the moonlight. And she wondered if the instant she turned her back on him, he'd simply stab her to death.

"I liked it when the others were afraid," he whispered.

Frightened tears came to her eyes and she blinked them away.

"We discussed the maze this evening, you and I."

So they had. And she had admitted her fear of it, never dreaming such an innocent confession would be used against her.

"I'll even give you a bit of a start," he whispered.

Her legs were shaking so she could barely stand. Hermes whined and pressed against her side.

"I'll kill you anyway, whether you move or not."

She never knew why, but those words broke her out of her cocoon of fear. Turning, she darted into the maze, hearing his amused laughter. She ran, turning this way and that, then blindly rushed into a dead end.

He was still laughing.

Hermes was at her heels, but the mastiff was no longer playing. He simply stayed close to her side, looking up at her as if to ask for direction.

Already, she'd lost.

"Are you ready for me, Lucinda?"

She couldn't bear the sound of her name on his lips. Turning, she ran back the way she'd come, then took another turn and was again surrounded by the dark hedges. Panting, she stopped.

It was no use, for he'd find her eventually. She'd run to another dead end, he'd corner her, and it would be over. She thought of William, and all they would lose should this madman succeed.

She bit her lip against the sob that threatened to erupt. It took all the courage she possessed not to simply cover her face with her hands, give up, and surrender to her fears.

Hermes whined, and she petted his head. Then stopped.

The soft, glowing light beckoned to her, pulsating with life, illuminating the maze farther in. She started toward it with a purely instinctual reaction.

Follow me . . .

Now she knew fear had driven her quite mad, for she heard her mother's voice.

The light shone a bit brighter, then disappeared around the corner of the hedge.

Follow . . .

With nothing but faith to guide her, Cinda grabbed Hermes' ear and started to run toward the light.

He raced through the garden toward the far back of the grounds and the vast maze. Both Juno and Jocasta caught up with him and stayed at his heels, their forelegs reaching far in front of them as their ground-eating gait covered the distance. They were silent hunters, with powerful necks and chests. Neither gave themselves away by so much as a whimper.

As he reached the entrance of the maze he'd played in since he was a child, William felt any sense of restraint or civilized behavior fall away from him. It was time this particular hunter was run to ground.

He would finish it.

The hunter was close behind her, she could sense it. Still, she ran toward the light until it spilled out into the center and she saw the small pagoda outlined in the distance. Breaking into a dead run, Hermes at her heels, she made her decision quickly.

She'd attempt to climb up on the roof, and from there, wait it out. Perhaps the killer would get lost in the intricate passages of the maze. Within the hour, after the last guest had departed, William would let the dogs out. The mastiffs would surely find the intruder on the grounds.

If Hermes would remain quiet, all would be well.

She reached the pagoda and, careful to stay in the darkness of the trees that surrounded the one side, began to climb. Hermes waited below among the bushes, his tail beating frantically.

"Stay!" she hissed, and for once the pup seemed to obey.

She felt no sensation in her hands, even when she looked down and noticed one of her fingers was cut and bleeding. Cinda felt a curious detachment from her body, almost as if she were no longer inside it.

In a skirt, she would have been helpless. But the pants allowed her more freedom, and she scrabbled up the side of the structure and onto the slightly slanted roof. Years of work had made her body strong, and she panted only slightly as she kept an eye on the direction she'd come.

Mayhap he was lost.

She sat down slowly, balancing carefully, then flattened herself against the roof. Now, all she could do was wait.

Within minutes, she saw her adversary enter the clearing. Taking off the bull's head mask, he set it on the grass, then began to scan the clearing.

Hiding up on the roof, Cinda waited. And prayed.

He was almost to the pagoda when Hermes attacked.

Will heard the sound of the pup's furious fighting, and it spurred him toward the clearing. That, and Cinda's scream.

His legs pumped furiously; the air that filled his chest burned his lungs. All he could think of was getting to her in time to protect her.

The knife blade flashed in the moonlight, Hermes yelped, and Cinda watched as the pup was flung aside to lie in a crumpled heap on the ground.

Her adversary had heard her, now he'd seen her. She watched as he began the short climb up onto the roof, the dagger in his mouth. And she waited until he had just hoisted himself up on the roof before she ran to the other side and jumped.

The ground rose up to meet her, and her ankle made painful contact with it, twisting sharply. She clawed her way to her feet, but her lower leg burned with agonizing pain. Turning her head, she saw the monster who hunted her jump gracefully to the ground and start toward her, the knife blade glinting in the moonlight.

He was almost upon her when one of the mastiffs burst into the clearing. Jocasta leapt in front of Cinda, and as she fell and tried to struggle to her feet, she screamed as the knife came down upon the large dog, again and again.

The mastiff's attack was so swift Cinda barely saw what happened next. Jocasta was on top of the murderer now, and had managed to capture his arm in her massive jaws. The knife dropped and the man screamed as the dog crushed the bones of his hand beneath her teeth.

Juno joined her littermate, and the two dogs would have killed the man had not William called them off. Jocasta staggered away, then slowly collapsed on the ground, while Juno licked the side of her face.

William hauled the killer to his feet, then stared at him incredulously. And Cinda remembered his name.

Philip Fleming clawed at her husband, his rage beyond control. Cinda watched as William slammed his fist into the man's face, then his stomach, then his side. But he was fighting a madman whose hatred gave him incredible strength. Both men rolled across the moonlit lawn, locked in the deadliest of embraces.

Cinda watched the fight as she tried to stand. Balanced heavily on her uninjured leg, she scanned the clearing, looking for the knife.

She saw it, just as the two men rolled toward her. Swiftly kneeling, she reached for it, then grasped it. And felt it wrenched sharply out of her hand.

Their enemy had it.

She tried to roll away from him, but her billowing pants leg had caught beneath the murderer's elbow. Will grasped Philip's wrist as he attempted to aim a killing blow toward her. She felt the sharp blade slice into her side as Juno thrust herself in front of the flailing knife hand.

The dog took the next wound, and the next, but such rage fueled William's actions that he wrestled the knife from his adversary and held it for only an instant before slashing it cleanly across the wild man's throat.

He gave a gurgling, choked cry, then blood sprayed out from the side of his neck, darkly soaking the front of William's shirt. Cinda watched as he held the struggling man down, completely dispassionate, and watched him die.

Her arms were around Juno's massive neck as she tried to stand. Once on her feet, she felt a throbbing pain at her side and a sticky, burning wetness. When she touched her ribs, her hands came away wet with blood.

The scene in front of her began to blur. She thought she saw William step away from his enemy, then fling the dagger through the air and deep into the small copse of trees that had been planted in the clearing. Then he was turning toward her, and she was trying to talk to him. But no sound would come out of her mouth.

She reached toward him with one hand as the other clutched at Juno's collar. Cinda tried to steady herself, tried to walk toward him.

Then the roaring in her head grew louder, her vision dimmed, and she slid slowly to the ground.

He was carrying her out of the maze when John met him, Henry at his side with a torch. William's uncle assessed the situation at a glance and took complete charge.

As two of his friends who had still been at the party were physicians, John put them to work. One followed William and Cinda back to the house, while the other remained with John inside the maze and attended to the dogs as Henry held the torch.

Juno was the only mastiff well enough to accompany William back to the house.

Once inside the mater bedroom, all was silent as the physician set to work on Cinda. Both men slid off her vest, then the physician swiftly cut away the costume from her side.

"It's a clean wound," he muttered as he began to dress it.

"And the child she carries?" William whispered.

"Luckily, the stab wound didn't affect the baby. Unless, of course . . ." He let his words trail off as he continued ministering to the jagged wound.

William glanced up and saw Cook hovering in the doorway. He had a fleeting memory of how he'd stood in the same doorway, watching someone he loved in so much pain and being unable to comfort them.

"Come," he said softly, motioning for her to step inside.

She rushed to Cinda's bedside. When she saw the wound, she didn't make a sound, simply listened as the physician talked to William, the tears running silently down her weathered face.

"It's not as shallow as I first believed," the physician said quietly, never taking his attention from the task at hand.

William sat by the bed the entire time, holding Cinda's hand, his gaze intent on her still face.

"The dog protected her, eh?" John's physician friend smiled grimly. "Well, you have her to thank that your wife is still alive. But as for the shock she's sustained tonight—"

"What are you saying?" Will interrupted him.

"She's a delicate thing." He'd finished wrapping the wound, and now pulled the covers up around Cinda's still body.

"All we can do now is wait and pray. And see if she'll fight to live."

CHAPTER
❧ 21 ❧

Darling, come back to me . . .

She'd left her body on the bed, and while looking down on the four people below had heard something about a wound and a baby. And William, looking so very sad, sat by the bed and held a woman's hand.

But she was no longer there.

Another light called to her. Another voice.

Darling, come back to me . . .

The light was stronger now, surrounding her, and she looked toward its center.

The pain had been tremendous; she'd fought to live with every instinct she possessed. Then she'd lost sight, feeling, and movement, and finally could hear nothing around her. Then there was no more pain, only a peaceful silence.

Silence. Then she felt more alive than ever before.

She'd cast off her body, and filtered sensation through spirit, with more intensity than she'd ever felt in her life.

She didn't want to feel the pain. Yet that pain in her side had been as nothing compared to seeing William kill a man.

A mortal sin. And all because of her.

She'd tried to comfort him, but he hadn't heard her. And it was only when she'd touched him and her fingers went right through his arm that she realized what was beginning to happen.

There had been darkness, and the sound of wind. Then she'd seen light, and instinctively moved toward it once again.

Her mother, a meadow filled with the most glorious wildflowers, and light all around her as she walked.

I'm here . . .

She couldn't use her voice, but felt as if she were speaking within her mind.

Darling, come back to me . . .

I want to . . .

She moved closer toward her mother, tried to reach for her hand. But Eleanor kept walking, her back turned, and Cinda couldn't reach her.

Wait!

Her mother turned, then looked at her with so much love she felt it throughout her entire spirit.

Come back . . .

The voice was fainter now, and Cinda wondered at that.

Did you call me? She couldn't take her eyes off her mother.

Eleanor shook her head, and Cinda could feel the sadness behind the gesture.

Then . . . why am I here?

Her mother's green eyes, so like her own, were filled with emotion. Sadness. Compassion. And so much love.

One last time . . . had to say good-bye . . .

Don't leave me! Cinda felt as if she'd cried out, but no sound came out of her mouth. Nothing she could hear. Yet she knew her mother understood.

I'll never leave you . . . you know that . . .

The light started to fade, and Cinda panicked.

Was it you? In the maze?

Her mother nodded her head.

I couldn't let you go . . . yet now I must . . .

She reached for her mother, and it seemed she was farther away.

Talk to me, she implored, suddenly frightened.

Look . . . her mother answered.

And she saw it all, the deceptions and arguments, the masquerades and plots, the anger and vengeance and passion and fear that had driven them all. It was as if snippets of memories flashed across her mind.

But most of all, she saw Will.

And whether battling her or loving her, making her laugh or kissing her tenderly, she knew with stunning clarity she couldn't leave him.

Not yet.

We have a baby, she told her mother.

Then Eleanor smiled, and nodded her head.

You were always such a wise little girl . . .

She was crying now, but tears seemed such an inadequate release when your entire body could weep.

You must go back . . .

Cinda couldn't look away from her mother, even though her image was growing fainter.

I know. I want to.

She could hear her heartbeat again, and the sound shocked her.

Remember me . . . me . . . me . . .

Her mother's words merged with her heartbeat; she felt the wind against her skin as it seemed to tighten and re-form around her. Darkness surrounded her, and then she was in the bedroom once again.

A single candle burned by the bed, and she saw a man. He was holding a woman's hand, and kneeling by the bed. He seemed so alone and her heart went out to him as she realized it was William.

This time, she was determined to touch him.

She knew she'd succeeded when pain bloomed sharply against her side, and she stiffened her body against it as she slowly came back to life.

He couldn't give up, even though the physician had not given him much in the way of hope. He remained by her side, with Cook at the other. And it seemed to William that as long as he touched her, she wouldn't leave him.

"Darling," he whispered, touching her brow, smoothing the fiery hair away from the face that had captivated him so long ago. "Darling, come back to me."

He felt it the same instant Cook did, the faint tremor that shook her body.

"Cinda? Darling?" He tightened his hold on her hand as she slowly opened her eyes and looked up into his face.

"Dear God," muttered the physician. "This is most unusual."

William barely heard him, he was so intently focused on the woman he loved.

"Cinda? Can you hear me?"

She nodded her head, ever so slightly.

"The baby is well," he whispered.

Slowly, so slowly, she mouthed the words. He had to put his ear to her lips to hear them.

"I know." She moistened her lips. "Pup?"

"I don't know. John and another physician are back in the maze, attending to Jocasta and Hermes. Juno came back with us; she wasn't hurt as badly."

"He tried," she whispered.

"I know he did," William said, thinking of the valiant fight Hermes had put up, giving Cinda valuable time.

She turned her head toward Cook.

"Don't, my precious. Save your strength."

"I saw her."

"Sleep, lovey."

"I saw her. In the maze. She guided me through to the end."

Cook merely patted her hand and nodded her head.

"Then I saw her again . . . afterward. She said she came back to tell me . . . good-bye."

Cook's hand stilled, and sudden understanding filled her red-rimmed eyes.

"You were all there," Cinda began, but Will silenced her with a kiss on her forehead.

"Sleep, darling, you've got to rest."

"But you *were*."

He nodded his head. "I believe you. Just rest, I want you to close your eyes."

She clutched his hand tightly as she obeyed his request. He remained by her side for the rest of the night.

Cook walked out the French doors and onto the huge terrace in time to see the last of the sunrise. She sat down in one of the chairs and gazed out over the garden.

"We did it, Nora," she said quietly.

There was no answer this time.

"Oh, I know you're not there. And I know you meant that good-bye for both of us. But if it comforts me to talk to you one last time, then where's the harm?"

She sat quietly, watching the sunlight spill into the garden and light everything for yet another day.

"It's a funny thing," she said, rubbing her hands against the cold morning. "I always thought I'd go first. Prayed for it. It's too painful by far, Nora, being left behind."

No answer. She didn't sense another presence, but kept talking.

"Oh, it's not so bad if you've got someone. She's got him now, and he's always wanted her." She sighed deeply. "I suppose I'll feel less alone when the children come."

"Jane?"

The voice startled her out of her seat; she'd become used to not hearing an answer.

"Jane?" Henry came out on the terrace, a silver tea tray on his arms. "I finished preparing breakfast for John and his friends. When I saw you outside, I thought you might want to join me for a cup of tea."

"That's kind of you, sir."

He poured her a cup, then passed her a plate of muffins.

"Who were you talking to?"

She choked on her food, but quickly recovered.

"No one. No one was there."

He smiled then, and she realized for the first time that Henry really had quite striking features. He was a rather nice fellow, actually, and she found she couldn't lie to him.

"I was—talking to an old friend."

He nodded his head. "My brother passed on over ten years ago and I still talk to him."

Cook broke off another piece of muffin and knew she'd found a friend. "Ah, but the question is, does he answer?"

"Sometimes."

She smiled then, and topped off his tea.

The following morning, Arthur called on the household and inquired of William what he planned to do with Philip Fleming's body. John's friend who had attended to the mastiffs had also carried the body back to the house, where two of the servants had prepared it for burial.

Cinda was sleeping peacefully, so William took some time away from his wife to attend to this pressing problem.

"I can't very well go over there and tell the family that Philip is dead, and he was quite mad."

"Do you have any other ideas?" Arthur asked.

"I thought perhaps I'd say a footpad ventured into the garden, and there was a fight. Philip got in the way and was killed."

"Splendid. I shall go with you, if you wish."

"I'd like that."

John had elected to remain with the mastiffs. Juno was already up and about, while Jocasta would take several months to recover. Hermes was the real tragedy of the evening, as the young pup was still not out of danger.

William hadn't had the heart to tell Cinda.

They reached Philip's townhouse later that same morning, and several of William's servants carried the body inside.

The house was impeccably kept, yet it seemed cold to William. The servants were confused as to who was in command. William realized Philip had led a largely solitary life, as his father spent his days at their country house.

One servant indicated he should follow her upstairs. After a quick word with Arthur to let him know where he was going, William accompanied the older servant up the stairs.

She unlocked a bedroom on the third floor, and William stepped inside. It had not been thoroughly cleaned in years, and the painfully thin woman huddled beneath a dusty coverlet was quite ill. But what struck him most was her immobility of expression, the lack of animation in her eyes, the stillness of her mouth.

Assessing the situation in a heartbeat, William called to his servants and had them bring the woman downstairs to the warmth of the fire. Once she was propped up in a comfortable chair and a clean blanket wrapped around her, William haltingly told her the story he'd created.

She stopped him before he'd said more than three sentences.

"I knew what he was, William."

That she knew who he was surprised him.

She summoned her servant, and requested that the old woman bring her some papers. When the woman returned, she gave him a satchel containing a considerable amount of written material.

"This is for you," she said quietly. "It cannot make up for what my brother did to you or your bride, but it might help explain the demons that drove him."

He was curiously touched by what she'd done for him, and it must have shown in his expression for she attempted a smile.

"You'll remember me, in time."

"Will you be able to care for yourself?" he asked her.

She nodded her head, the expression in her eyes still curiously absent. "Certainly better than when I was locked within that room." Summoning up what emotion she seemed capable of, she reached out and weakly grasped his hand.

"William?" she whispered. "Thank you for bringing him home."

Arthur rode home soon afterward, as he was worried about his wife. The events of the previous evening had upset her terribly, and he was anxious to offer comfort.

He found her up and about, her russet hair swept into a makeshift knot on top of her head, her bright blue eyes alive with compassion.

"The poor child, Arthur! He'd been sitting out in the bushes all night, waiting for one of us to come home. And when I did, well, Roger was quite insistent I have nothing to do with them but I couldn't leave a baby out in the cold, and so hungry—"

"My dear, whatever are you talking about?"

"His mother. Some brute tried to slit her throat, but she managed to escape. He beat the boy quite badly, but the little fellow hit him over the head with a bucket and managed to knock him out, enabling them to escape—"

"Where is this woman?"

"In the sickroom off the kitchen. I sent for our physician and he's already examined her. He's assured me she will recover in time. But in the meantime, oh, Arthur, the poor children!"

He sighed as he put his arm around her and brought her close to his heart.

"Yes, mother, you may add several new chicks to your brood."

William read the letters straight through by the fire that same evening, all the time keeping an eye on Cinda. Their contents astonished him, and in a most peculiar way comforted him.

For evil one could understand was infinitely less threatening.

The handwriting was instantly recognizable as that which had graced both notes, and he wondered at a brother who could make his sister write such horrible things.

You'll remember me, in time . . .

He did remember the thin, frightfully ill woman. Emma. She'd been a shy but pretty housemaid, and he'd cared for her. Now he stared at the letters in his hands and wondered at how such an innocent and impulsive action from his boyhood could have set such utter hatred into motion.

Two murders, a monster of a man, and an innocent boy. Then two more, his mistress Anne and poor young Rosalind.

Philip Fleming. No, not Philip. *Daniel.* Daniel had hated him, hated him with a mind warped by illness, hated him with a passion that knew no bounds.

Hated him enough to try and kill Cinda.

It's over now. That's all that matters.

How little he'd known the man who had called himself Philip Fleming.

How little you knew Cinda . . .

He thought of what their lives would have been like, had their original elopement succeeded, and realized he'd hardly known the full strength and mettle of the woman he'd fallen in love with. And thinking of her, and all they'd been through, brought an impulsive and heartfelt prayer to his lips as he sat in his chair by the fire, clutching the letters in his hands.

He didn't inform Cinda of their contents straightaway, but locked them in his desk. He would share them with her when she was stronger.

Almost two weeks had passed since that horrible night. He'd rarely had her to himself, as masses of visitors came and went at all hours. Just yesterday, her godmother had arrived, laden with choice morsels all designed to tempt Cinda's appetite.

Most of the time, he simply watched her sleep while he prayed, thanking God profusely for allowing her to live.

The nightmares had stopped, for his dream was alive.

Today, she was sitting up in bed when he knocked on the bedroom door.

"Are you feeling up to a visitor?" he asked as he walked into the room.

"I always have time for you." She plumped the pillows next to hers and indicated he should join her in bed. He took off his boots and climbed in beside her, remaining outside the covers.

"I'm getting so bloody bored of bed rest!"

He laughed, delighted to hear her complaining. "Madam, I know your health is improving when you start to feel confined!"

"What did you do this morning?" she asked, and he could tell she was desperate for news outside of her bedchamber.

He told her of his morning ride, of the work he had planned for the garden, and of the various flowers coming into bloom.

"It sounds so lovely."

"In another week, I'll carry you outside and you can see for yourself."

They talked of inconsequential things, but he saved the best for last.

"Would you like one last visitor?"

"Who?" Her curiosity was piqued, he could tell.

"Just a moment." He slipped out into the hall and across the way to another bedroom. Signaling to Henry, he gathered his guest together and headed back toward their bedroom.

She was sitting up in bed when he entered, Hermes in his arms. The puppy was still bandaged and rather weak, but just that morning they'd received word he would survive no worse for wear.

She hadn't dared ask about him, and he knew she'd thought her beloved pet was dead. Now, as the mastiff puppy saw the person he adored most in the world, his tail began to beat against William.

She burst into tears as he laid the dog on the bed in front of her, and Hermes attended to those tears with his large pink tongue. The puppy's massive body fairly quivered with joy, and Cinda, her arms around his neck, looked up at William with an expression that tore at his heart.

"He really is quite splendid, don't you think?"

The thought made him laugh, but as he watched her hug the ungainly animal, the emotion shifted. He found himself close to childish tears as he thought of all that might have been taken from him.

His reaction shamed him, a violent aftershock to all that had occurred. Until this moment, he hadn't let himself contemplate such a lonely life. He couldn't have lived without her, he knew that now. He'd deliberately pushed his fears away, and now, in this peaceful aftermath, they assaulted him full force.

She was studying him as she petted Hermes, and he turned his face away from her, not wanting her to see such blatant weakness in him.

"You've been strong for far too long, Will."

He shook his head, and raked his long hair back from his face with his fingers. His eyes burned, but he refused to let the tears fall.

"You protected me against all odds."

She touched his shoulder but he still couldn't look at her. He had to compose himself, he had to be strong.

"You're also a man who possesses deep feelings."

He couldn't answer, his throat was so tight.

"All of which, combined, make me love you all the more."

He looked at her then, as if seeing her for the first time. She was sitting up in their bed, her hair long and unbound down her back. Clad in only a white nightgown, she'd never looked more like an angel to him.

He reached out and pulled her down beside him, gently, because of her condition. Hermes gave a great sigh of contentment and settled himself at their feet.

"Madam, must you always insist on seeing the best in me and be determined to find it?" he whispered.

"Always," she replied.

She felt exactly right in his arms; her presence gave him great comfort. Tucking his chin against the top of her head and breathing in her scent, he blinked furiously against the tears still threatening to spill.

And he realized, at that moment, that she'd given him the best parts of himself, and through her intense love let him see a world he'd thought quite dark through new eyes. Her coming into his life, believing in him, loving him so fiercely and completely, had changed him forever.

He would never be as lonely again, for her presence filled the most secret parts of his soul. His arms tightened around her as he wondered if she would ever know how much he loved her. And owed her.

But it was the sweetest of debts, and one he would willingly spend the rest of his life repaying.

"You'll keep looking, then?" he whispered, still not quite able to meet that knowing gaze. He felt her smile against his neck.

"Always."

EPILOGUE

And they lived happily ever after . . .

"Mama, put this one on!"

"No, this one!"

Cinda laughed as her two small daughters surrounded her while she sat at her dressing table. Her hair had been dressed, and she sat in her chemise, petticoats, and stockings, putting the final touches on her face makeup.

The argument in question concerned the suitability of a particular face patch. Six-year-old Elizabeth Jane wished her to wear the star, while four-year-old Rosalind Kathleen liked the crescent moon.

She glanced up as William entered their bedroom, buttoning his waistcoat.

"Papa, the star!"

"No, the moon!"

"The stars, the moon, and the sun," he teased, sweeping Rosalind up into his arms and giving Elizabeth's long dark hair an affectionate ruffling. "Anything you wish for, my darlings."

"I'll wear both," Cinda decided, and she watched in the mirror as William discovered what the argument had been about. He laughed, setting Rosalind down on their large bed.

"You must be good tonight," he admonished his two children. "Don't tire Cook out."

"Of course, Papa."

"We'll be good, Papa."

Cinda couldn't disguise her smile as she watched both her daughters with their father. Elizabeth was her little romantic, while Rosalind had the makings of a hellion.

William had told her the truth that afternoon in the garden when he'd assured her he would love any daughters she gave him as much as any son.

Luckily, less than a year ago, she'd finally presented him with one. Christopher John, Kit to his family, was presently in the nursery with Cook.

She was carefully placing the first beauty mark by the corner of her mouth when Cook entered the bedroom, five-month-old Kit cradled against her ample bosom. Eleanor Frances, the eldest of the four Stedman children, was at her side, chattering away.

"Mama, see what Cook gave me!"

Cinda held out her hand for her daughter's offering, then looked down at the hazelnut in her palm.

"Do you know what it is?" Eleanor asked, her pretty face flushed with excitement. She'd been named for both their mothers, and held that special place only firstborn children have in their parents' hearts.

"A tiny carriage," Cinda said. "The fairy folk ride around in them."

Eleanor turned to Cook, who tugged on her braid.

"Didn't I tell you she would know, lovey?"

"Have you ever seen one?" Eleanor asked her mother.

"A fairy or a carriage?" William said as he came up behind them, teasing his eldest. Both Elizabeth and Rosalind were crowded around the dressing table again, waiting for their mother's answer.

"A fairy! Did you see one?"

Cinda carefully set the nut down on her dressing table and thought of the picture her mother had sketched for her, that long-ago day in the garden.

"A few. They come out at dawn and dusk, and play among the flowers. They like to steal foxgloves."

She glanced up at Cook. "And ragwort seeds their tiny steeds," she whispered to the older woman, then turned back to her mirror and the second black patch.

"You're not putting them both on, are you?" Cook asked,

her opinion of this particular folly evident in the tone of her voice.

"Why not?" William took Kit carefully out of Cook's arms. "He's getting fat," he remarked to no one in particular.

"He's a baby," Cook said. "He's supposed to be fat."

"Well, my little man, off you go to another night in the nursery." William kissed his son, then handed him to his mother. She kissed him as well, then gave him back to Cook.

"Come along, girls," she called, and three faces turned toward her with varying degrees of frustration etched upon their countenances.

"But we want to see!" wailed Rosalind.

"I'll put my dress on now," Cinda said, jumping up from her dressing table and heading toward the bed, where a ball gown of spun-golden satin and lace was spread out.

"You spoil them," Cook admonished her.

"I know."

"Just like the dog," William muttered, and was rewarded by a low woof. Hermes, who had never quite attained an appearance of elegance, peeked out from beneath the bed.

"I'll call Mary," Cinda began.

"Madam, I can still lace a lady's gown faster than any maid," William informed her.

Cinda turned toward Cook, a totally unrepentant look on her face. "He's right."

"Go on, then," Cook said, her expression mock-stern, and the girls giggled as they watched their father lace up their mother.

When she was finally dressed, with gloves, slippers, and fan, and mask in hand, Cinda twirled around in front of her children, causing the golden skirts to swirl out around her like a bell.

"Mama!"

"You look so pretty!"

"Isn't she pretty, Papa?"

"Indeed she is," William replied. "Now, off to bed, or you won't have time for a story."

"What are you again, Papa?" Rosalind asked.

"The last time I checked the looking glass, I was your papa," he teased.

"No, what are you this time?"

Cinda could barely hide her smile. She'd found, over the years, that she loved having children and was rather good at it. And William had proved to be an excellent father. In truth, he spent more time with his children than out in society. Many a morning, she came across him with his daughters, happily digging in the garden.

"Hades."

"And Mama?" she piped up.

Eleanor sighed, and gave her sibling a look perfected by eldest sisters the world over. "Mama is Persephone, and Papa kidnapped her and took her to the underworld. But then she talked and talked and begged and begged and he let her go back home, and that's why we have spring. Right, Papa?"

Cinda admired her husband's perfectly straight face.

"Yes, that's correct," he said.

"So she took him out of the darkness," Elizabeth said dreamily, and Cinda caught Will's eye and shook her head. Their middle daughter was too romantic by far.

"Yes, she did," he replied, giving her a wink. "Now, off you go to bed—"

"—and a story!" Rosalind insisted.

"Yes, a story," Cook agreed. "Now kiss your parents goodbye, and off they go!"

Sitting in the carriage across from her husband, Cinda couldn't resist the urge to tease him.

"So she talked and talked and begged and begged?"

He leaned across the distance that separated them and kissed her soundly.

"And look where it got her."

She smiled at him, almost bursting with her secret.

"You've been looking a trifle pale of late, darling," he said. "Have you been feeling poorly?"

"Oh, just a little sick in the mornings."

It took him mere seconds to divine her meaning.

"Another?"

She nodded her head.

"You're sure?"

Again, she nodded, and felt the smile on her face widen even farther.

He kissed her, and when they finally sat up again, he'd

shifted so he was sitting next to her.

"Boy or girl? For you seem to have the most remarkable ability to predict whether we have sons or daughters."

She thought back to the young Gypsy girl who'd sat at a kitchen table in front of a fire so long ago and given her the hope she'd so desperately needed.

"A son."

He placed a finger beneath her chin and raised her gaze to his.

"Why, Cinda, what is this I hear? Another son?" His delighted smile grew broader. "Can it be possible that you've finally decided to bend to my will and do what I believe is best?"

She brushed his lips with hers, then drew back slightly, prolonging his torment. Before his lips claimed hers, she whispered a single word.

"Never."

"Quiet, my girls, or we'll wake the baby."

Kit was fast asleep in his crib, while Cook, Eleanor, Elizabeth, and Rosalind were gathered on comfortable chairs by the fire. Hermes was stretched out on his favorite worn rug in front of the flames, while Thomas the cat claimed the back of Cook's chair.

"I believe it's Rosalind's turn," Cook began.

"Oh, she always wants the same story!" Eleanor fumed. "Can't she pick something different?"

"You know the rules," Cook said calmly. "Whatever she wants."

"Pick something with pirates, Rozzie," Elizabeth urged. "And a princess."

Rosalind pretended to consider all this, while Cook almost laughed out loud. The littlest girl's choice never varied from night to night, and they all knew it.

Henry entered the nursery, a tray with warm milk and buttered bread in hand.

"Have I missed the story hour, darling?" he asked, setting the tray down on a table by the fire.

"You're just in time," Cook replied, and as she looked at her husband she marveled at how he seemed to grow more handsome and distinguished each year.

Henry settled himself in another chair, while Cook let Rosalind climb into her lap.

"Have you decided?"

"Yes!" she said, looking defiantly at Eleanor. The older girl groaned, while Elizabeth laughed.

"I want the story about Mama and Papa."

"All right, my precious girl." Cook leaned back in the large chair as Henry began to pass around the bedtime tea.

"I'm going to tell you a story," she began, "about your beautiful, courageous mother and your determined, dashing father, and how they met one summer's night in a moonlit garden, once upon a time . . ."

Come take a walk down Harmony's Main Street in 1874, and meet a different resident of this colorful Kansas town each month.

A TOWN CALLED
❧ HARMONY ❧

__KEEPING FAITH by Kathleen Kane
   0-7865-0016-6/$4.99   *(coming in July)*
From the boardinghouse to the schoolhouse, love grows in the heart of Harmony. And for pretty, young schoolteacher Faith Lind, a lesson in love is about to begin.

__TAKING CHANCES by Rebecca Hagan Lee
   0-7865-0022-2/$4.99   *(coming in August)*
All of Harmony is buzzing when they hear the blacksmith, Jake Sutherland, is smitten. And no one is more surprised than Jake himself, who doesn't know the first thing about courting a woman.

__CHASING RAINBOWS by Linda Shertzer
   0-7865-0041-7/$4.99   *(coming in September)*
Fashionable, Boston-educated Samantha Evans is the outspoken columnist for her father's newspaper. But her biggest story yet may be her own exclusive–with a most unlikely man.

If you enjoyed this book, take advantage of this special offer. Subscribe now and get a

FREE
Historical
Romance

No Obligation (a $4.50 value)

Each month the editors of True Value select the four *very best* novels from America's leading publishers of romantic fiction. Preview them in your home *Free* for 10 days. With the first four books you receive, we'll send you a FREE book as our introductory gift. No Obligation!

If for any reason you decide not to keep them, just return them and owe nothing. If you like them as much as we think you will, you'll pay just $4.00 each and save at *least* $.50 each off the cover price. (Your savings are *guaranteed* to be at least $2.00 each month.) There is NO postage and handling – or other hidden charges. There are no minimum number of books to buy and you may cancel at any time.

Send in the Coupon Below

To get your FREE historical romance fill out the coupon below and mail it today. As soon as we receive it we'll send you your FREE Book along with your first month's selections.